THE LUMINOUS ONES

NICHOLAS ASHBAUGH

NICHOLAS ASHBAUGH
PRODUCTIONS, LLC

Published by Nicholas Ashbaugh Productions, LLC

Nicholas Ashbaugh
PO BOX 691398
West Hollywood, CA 90069

www.nicholasashbaugh.com

ISBN 978-1-7357268-3-0 (Hardcover)
ISBN 978-1-7357268-0-9 (Paperback)
ISBN 978-1-7357268-2-3 (ePub)
ISBN 978-1-7357268-1-6 (Kindle)

Library of Congress Control Number: 2020917497

First printing, 2020.
Printed in the United States of America.

Cover design and interior formatting by Nicholas Ashbaugh.

This is a work of fiction. All events, beings, worlds and characters depicted in this
literary work are the product of the author's imagination or are used fictitiously. Any
resemblance or similarity to actual events, beings, worlds, or persons—living or dead,
past or present—is entirely coincidental.

CONTENTS

PART I

AULD LANG SYNE

PROLOGUE

E nds, like beginnings, are tenuous times. This story begins at the end of things, in the last age of humankind, before the planet was destroyed by the sun. In the wake of an ice age and millennia-long wars, Earth's weary populace united under a single dictatorial government known simply as *the State*. Cyborgs, psychic agents and robotic mercenaries became the henchmen of this all-seeing regime. Humanity no longer looked to the stars for answers—yet, the stars were watching them.

Alas, hope was not lost—not completely. A collection of rebellious metacriminals—stalwart Lightworkers known as Stewards of the Light—covertly preserved the forgotten truths of days gone by. Although once myriad, only one remained.

Tonight, an ancient enemy approached planet Earth. Its dark, shadowy hand reached from the depths of space, intent on finding the hidden location of The Last Steward of the Light—the only hope for protecting the Known Universe from certain doom. Its nefarious purpose: to either turn the Lightworker into a denizen of darkness... or destroy him outright.

1

SPELLBOUND, PART ONE

Dateline: Los Angeles Megacity, Cypher District, on New Year's Eve in the Earth Year Treble-Treble-Treble Nine. (Present Day).

I t was a chilly New Year's Eve, the last before the year One Billion. Gabriel, an off-duty psychic investigator, briskly walked along Sunset Boulevard. A brilliant strand of holograms and streetlights stretched as far as the eye could see. This was the sprawling and bustling Cypher District, a space where the city's flotsam and jetsam mingled—mostly to escape the prying eyes of the State. It was exactly the type of place an Agent like Gabriel shouldn't be, but he was always a bit of a rebel; tonight was no exception.

He stopped in front of The Black Cat, the oldest establishment on the boulevard—one that dated back to a time when the District was better known as Hollywood. The tavern courtyard was devoid of markings, only a single, old-fashioned wooden sign hung high above, gently creaking in the wind. The wooden artifact was a throwback to days gone by. A single spotlight illuminated the sign unevenly, shining prominently on a mischievous-looking black cat dancing and grinning with a fiddle in tow. The cat's wide eyes followed patrons no matter where they walked, like a cheap funhouse trick.

Gabriel could hear periodic crescendos of clanking glasses and the garbled murmurs from the lively crowd inside. As he reached for the door, he shivered, not because of the bone-chilling cold, but because he felt something watching from the dark expanse above.

Once he was inside the tavern, Gabriel peered through the narrow slit between the old wooden doors.

A shooting star ripped through the night sky and majestic streams of sapphire and purple light bathed the courtyard. After a flash of light and a rumble of thunder, something decidedly other-worldly began to materialize in the fog bank that was slowly rolling in.

From his present position, Gabriel couldn't quite make out the figure's details; the more he stared at it, the more it changed its shape—almost as if it was reacting to his perception. By every account he knew he should be frightened, but he couldn't shake a sense of déjà vu; somehow he knew this supernatural being.

Gabriel slipped into the shadows and found a seat at the bar, keeping his eyes glued to the door all the while.

As the celestial being entered the tavern, it appeared—or, more accurately, *chose*—to be a tall young human, dressed in a stylish, outdated overcoat that almost reached the floor. As it removed a knit hat, a tuft of black hair with streaks of blue and purple haphazardly spilled over its tall forehead, partially obscuring its glowing amber eyes. Its nose was narrow and pronounced, running down a long, chiseled face. Its complexion resembled Italian marble— smooth, pale and flawless. Any guess as to the being's age would be difficult. It appeared youthful in the flesh, but its attire and demeanor belied its physical form.

Gabriel watched as the mystical being quickly surveyed the room, scanning the mixed crowd. It was comprised of rich Bel-Air cyborgs enhanced beyond recognition, rebellious counterculture San Angelenos who were simply there to make the scene, and a handful of Rogue metacriminals conducting under-the-table deals.

The shapeshifter casually sat down beside Gabriel and flagged the attention of the bartender, a young woman in her twenties. She moved about the bar with the precision of a monarch butterfly; she was fast, light and graceful.

"Name your poison?" she asked with a rehearsed and slightly detached air, almost as if reading from a script.

"Just a seltzer water."

The bartender nodded and placed her index finger on a metallic strip running along the center of the bar, which activated a holographic interface. She used gestures to manipulate the virtual register, most likely with custom implants in her fingertips. After placing the order, she dismissed the projection with another tap on the control strip.

"Don't take this the wrong way," she said as she slid the drink across the bar, "I mean, this sounds like a line, but I get the feeling we've met before, haven't we?"

The celestial being tried to read her mind. Gabriel followed suit, to no avail; inside, she was just a twisted mass of metal, synthetics and wires.

"Yes, we met a long, long time ago, the day your binary code sparked to life... the day you became self-aware. You're a Genesis-class android—serial number Seven-Twelve, if memory serves?"

"I'm **not** a serial number," she barked back in an emotional outburst that was not only atypical, but should have been impossible, given her programming.

"What should I call you then, child?"

"Just call me Genesis."

"Of course. As you wish. I meant no disrespect," the being said. Its voice was kind, soothing, and seemed to reset the code within her emotional inhibitor. *"As I was saying, Genesis, I was there when*

Yantra and the DEEP RED scientists celebrated your birth. It was his brightest and darkest hour."

"Yes, I was activated nearly one thousand Earth Years ago, the same day my maker died... well, the day his body died, anyway. But, that would make you... well, impossibly old."

"That all depends, my dear."

"On what?"

"Whether or not I'm human."

For a Synthetic, Genesis displayed another unusual emotion: surprise.

"I've only a few memories of my maker; our time together was so short."

"Remember this, then: he adored you. To him, you were perfection."

She paused for a moment and processed the being's words, conjuring a digital deluge of old data. Incapable of tears, and with a limited capacity for emotional responses, Genesis nevertheless looked shaken. Maybe it was a hiccup in her programming, or maybe she simply turned off her memory and emotion transmitters, but Genesis blinked her eyes twice and was back to her normal self.

Without making eye contact, or continuing their discussion, the android said, rather distractedly, "Two thousand credits for the drink, please."

The stranger threw a few bank notes on the table, much to her displeasure.

She pointed to the authentication disc and said, "Listen, I don't want trouble, but cash hasn't been in circulation since the last ice age."

"That's all I've got," it replied with a shrug.

I'd hate to report you, but—"

"There's no need to bother the State with a petty crime on New Year's Eve," Gabriel interjected, "I'll cover it." His handsome smile was both disarming and charming, without seeming at all contrived.

Gabriel was tall, thin and had striking blue-green eyes that shifted color depending on the light. Short-cropped loose blonde curls framed his pale face.

He pressed his index finger on the disc and waited a moment. When it glowed green, Genesis turned and said, "For an Agent, you keep curious company these days, Gabriel. Be careful with this one."

Without any additional pleasantries, she walked away.

"If you don't mind me asking, why don't you have implants?" Gabriel inquired. "The last time I saw a bank note was in the Megacity Museum of the Antiquity!"

"Is that a polite way of calling me a relic?" The stranger asked sarcastically. *"It's okay, call me old-fashioned if you'd like, but all this so-called technology is a slippery slope, Gabe. Some of the folks in this bar have more plastic in them than our bartender. At what point do you cross the threshold from human to machine? Aren't those individual flaws, strengths and quirks that you try so hard to eradicate the very things that make you human?"*

It paused and pointed to someone across the bar.

"Look at the Enforcer there... the one sniffing for Rogue Plastic. I'm not sure who's less human, Genesis or the Agent."

Gabriel put down his drink and looked across the bar.

Like all Enforcers, the Agent's grooming and wardrobe only served to mute any hints of gender or personality. Androgyny was encouraged—and at times mandated—by the State, particularly for undercover investigators. To be neither handsome nor pretty, male nor female afforded an Agent of any rank or office with the ability to blend in. One could be a chameleon, depending on the situation. This Agent was no exception. The Enforcer donned a stylish, angular State-issued dress. The crisp, white garment ran neck-to-knee, with a slit on the right hip. The Agent's shoulders were exposed, but white leather gloves concealed the Enforcer's hands and arms. Matching platform boots ran up to the knee as well, and neatly concealed a set of laser holsters behind both calves.

Using his intuition alone, Gabriel surmised the Enforcer identified as male. Were it not for the unusual eye modifications, however, he would find this particular Enforcer unspectacular. The micromesh, frameless implants were surgically fused to the Agent's face, purposely obscuring his real eyes, if in fact they still existed. Unlike earlier chromed models, the micromesh worked like a second skin, moving and fusing effortlessly with the organic tissue around it, thanks to nanotechnology. The effect was off-putting; the Agent looked like some sort of alien-human hybrid.

With the meticulousness of an android, the Enforcer slowly moved his shaved head, scanning every face in the room. During one of his sweeps, the Agent locked gazes with Gabriel and then with the being next to him. He tilted his head to the side and paused, perhaps gathering that the being wasn't equipped with implants. Two faint red beams glowed beneath the Agent's mesh lenses and then faded as quickly as they appeared. For reasons unknown to Gabriel, the Enforcer left his post, but not before whispering something into an H-V wristband embedded in his glove.

As the Agent walked towards the other side of the bar, Gabriel got a good look at the back of his skull; a metallic casing spanned from ear to ear and from the base of his neck to his crown. This expensive State-issued cerebral implant, common among Enforcers, provided him with a secure uplink to a State database system that enabled him to search, catalogue and report violations. The casing was lined with hundreds of minuscule LEDs, each flickering on and off like distant pulsars.

"Ok... I see what you mean," Gabriel acquiesced.

The stranger smiled and continued its rant. *"I look at you and see more than the sum of your bones, flesh and electric impulses in your brain—there's a fire that transcends your physical being. When I look at Genesis, I see an impressive package of plastic, wires and code. Sure, she can process some degree of emotion, but do not be mistaken; she (or more accurately, it) may be self-aware, but there's no soul inside—not yet. No amount of binary code or positronic programming can overcome that. A consciousness without a soul is a very dangerous thing, Gabriel."*

Chills ran up Gabriel's spine. Intuitively, he knew the stranger was hiding something. Despite the intriguing lecture about humanity, there was something... well... characteristically alien about the being's voice. From time to time, Gabriel swore that he heard two or more voices overlapping, resulting in a slight (almost imperceptible) trailing and preceding whisper. This effect was particularly pronounced on the ends and beginnings of words with soft consonants like S and Z. Gabriel would later recognize this vocal signature as being a combination of spoken and *thought* words. Sometimes, he would hear the being's thoughts a few seconds before they were physically uttered—a sort of clairvoyant pre-echo. This was a singular phenomenon that he'd never experienced as an intuitive.

'I know that voice!' Gabriel thought. He'd heard it in his dreams many times, but he couldn't remember how or why it had haunted him.

He asked the same question Genesis had a few minutes earlier, "Have we met before?"

"You really don't remember me at all, do you? I was a loyal friend to your grandfather, Elijah. You and I crossed paths when he was attacked, the night that Björn the Betrayer came back."

A whisper came from somewhere deep inside and Gabriel blurted it out, without giving it a second thought.

"You're one of The Star Gods—The First of Seven, aren't you?"

It nodded its head and grinned.

"I'm getting rusty. Perhaps my spell wasn't as strong as I thought," the deity whispered under its breath.

Gabriel squinted his eyes and tried to search for more memories or intuitive downloads, but he hit an uncharacteristic metaphysical brick wall—as if parts of his past were conveniently edited out. He felt the same block whenever he tried to read the stranger's mind.

Gabriel swirled the blue synthetic ale around in his glass and furrowed his brow. As a general rule, Agents avoided drinking because it lowered one's defenses and created a vulnerability. As a Steward of the Light, his grandfather had imparted the same wisdom. But it was New Year's Eve, so he threw caution to the wind for the first time in years.

"To the Year One Billion," Gabriel said as he raised his glass and took a sip.

"And to old friends," the mysterious being added.

Perhaps it was his body reacting to the synthetic ale, or maybe it was the white noise in the bar, but Gabriel fell into a trance. He closed his eyes and felt a sharp pain in his crown chakra, as if an unseen hand was hammering a nail into his skull. Someone was jacking into his mind without a warrant—this metacrime was equivalent to breaking and entering, unless it was coming from the State itself, in which case something top-secret must be going on. Despite being off-duty, the Agent part of Gabriel's personality could never rest. He closed his eyes and focused. He was unable to see anything or ascertain who the intruder was, but he did hear the sound of wings flapping... several wings, as if birds were overhead.

"I've had enough of this," Gabriel murmured to himself, and began to sever the connection.

When he opened his eyes, the deity was staring at him curiously. In the dim candlelight, the being's face appeared spectral, with large shadows around the eye sockets and nose. Its coat also appeared to have *shifted* slightly, phasing in and out of the dimension as the being moved.

"Are you okay, sir?" it asked.

"I thought I heard something," Gabriel replied.

"You heard the birds too, didn't you?"

"How did you know wh—?"

"*Shhhh. There are Wolves among us.*"

He hadn't heard that phrase for years. Not since...

Before Gabriel could question the celestial being, sharp laughter rose and fell behind him like a tidal wave. One laugh rose above the rest, barraging Gabriel's ears with periodic baritone exaltations. It belonged to an inebriated man, celebrating with two of his coworkers. At first glance, the man looked a lot like Gabriel, except for his ginger hair, which was redder, straighter and a bit longer than Gabriel's. Judging by the triangular transceiver attached to his belt holster, this man was an M-8 Agent, like Gabriel, probably from the nearby Bel-Air Precinct.

As Gabriel stared at the Agent, the sensation in his forehead returned, followed by a vision of the red-headed man lying dead in a dumpster. Startled by this premonition, Gabriel dropped his glass and jumped back as it shattered on the floor.

When Gabriel looked up, the red-headed man was gone.

"Where did he go?" Gabriel asked.

"*The man you saw in your vision? He slipped out the back exit. I fear it was a grave error on his part,*" the ancient deity replied flatly. "*Now he's in the clutches of one of The Seven Shadows. More will come, just not on horseback as the old tomes once predicted. Aye, The Dark Ones are far subtler than that. By the time you see them, it will be too late. They will devour all Known Worlds. That's why I have returned. I'm here to protect you and at least halt Earth's inevitable destruction.*"

Gabriel's face turned white.

"*You've seen it then? The end—the eternal darkness? Just as your grandfather Elijah did?*"

Gabriel nodded. He'd been haunted by dreams of a coming apocalypse since he was seven years old.

"*Know this: the dreams and visions are all true. The end is nigh, but the final chapter is not written. You, Gabriel, are the key to that—an unexpected wrinkle in their plans. All that once happened is not doomed to repeat, not if we can learn from it. But I digress... Let's focus on the here and now. I can protect you, but require one thing: your complete trust. Can you do that, old friend?"*

"Yes. I don't know why, but yes, I trust you."

"Good. I can tell you this much: you won't die. Not tonight."

All of the blood left Gabriel's face.

"Don't look now, but I'm afraid we have company," the being said with a grimace.

The Enforcer was back, this time with two backup Agents.

"Jacks!" Gabriel said with a gulp.

"Who?"

"Not who, *what*... they're Mindjackers... *Extractors.* These skilled psychics can break into people's minds and extract information against their will. I felt one try to read me earlier. Most average humans don't stand a chance against them."

"Well, thankfully, I'm not human and you're not average. Let's go!"

Without another word, the shapeshifter moved into the crowd.

The three Agents followed, but the celestial being had already vanished by taking on a new appearance. Gabriel followed the deity's lead and moved into the crowd, which was now gathering like cattle in the center of the room, watching a holographic projection of the New Year's festivities downtown.

As the clock struck midnight, the noise level in the bar became unbearable. Gabriel used this to his advantage and slipped through the front door undetected. The headache-inducing sea of clanking glasses and shrill screams of merriment made it impossible for the Agents to tune-in. For now, at least, Gabriel was safe.

The air outside was even colder and thicker than it was a few hours earlier. Bathed in fog and the pale light of the full moon—the second in less than a month—the air glowed around him. Southern

California was usually immune to winter, but tonight it clearly found the City of Angels.

Gabriel paused just as he was about to take a shortcut through the alley adjacent to the tavern. It was a sense of déjà-vu, or perhaps precognition that stopped him dead in his tracks. He knew that something bad had happened there, or was about to happen. Perhaps both.

In the distance two figures were in some sort of argument or struggle. The thick fog prevented Gabriel from seeing any details. They were just dark inkblots, shifting in and out of view. In fact, one of them literally had no shape—it was The Great Shadow of which the star-being spoke. Gabriel intuited that the other was the ginger-haired M-8 Agent.

He felt a tap on his shoulder. An unusual static charge accompanied it.

"I wouldn't go that way if I were you," it said.

Gabriel turned. Much to his relief, it was his new–or perhaps *old*–friend from the bar. The being's appearance, however, had shifted a bit from their last encounter. It was now nearly seven feet tall, possibly taller, and looked imposing in the moonlight.

"It'll be the death of you," it added sternly and prophetically.

Gabriel said nothing, unsure what the appropriate response was to that sort of comment.

As the wind blew the stranger's hair from its face, Gabriel let out an audible gasp. What stood before him was clearly not a man or woman, and most definitely not human, either.

Its face was beautiful and frightening all at once. Light reflected on—or perhaps, more accurately, emanated *from*—its skin. Now more than ever, the skin appeared like polished marble. Above the high cheekbones, two amber eyes twinkled like binary stars. Although the moon was bright, its eyes did not reflect it, or any other physical object for that matter. Rather, they glowed from within. Although devoid of an iris, small golden flecks of brown, yellow and orange light coalesced, sparkled and danced about the center of each eye like tiny fire embers.

It began to speak psychically to Gabriel, using **STJÄRNLJUS**, a persuasive technique employed by the immortal Star Gods.

'LEAVE NOW OR YOU WILL DIE.'

Blinding light shined from its eye sockets and its voice filled Gabriel's mind until it drowned out any other thought.

Behind the deity, Gabriel saw a terrible shadowy mass rise from the alleyway.

The Old Star God in front of him grew in size, until it towered above the highest skyscraper in the L.A. Megacity. Then, it threw a bolt of lightning towards the wraith.

A terrible shriek filled the heavens as the shadowy creature retreated into the cloudbank above. Then, torrential rain began to pelt the City of Angels as The Ancient Shadow moved across the sky.

Gabriel's survival instinct kicked-in and he ran to the first available automated hovercab. He placed his hand on the authenticator and waited for the pod door to open. Before entering, he glanced over his shoulder again.

The Shadow had seemingly vanished, for now at least. At first, he believed the celestial being was gone as well. However, several feet away from the taxi, Gabriel spied a large black cat keeping watch atop a rusty trash bin. It bore an uncanny resemblance to the cat on the sign.

Two large amber eyes glowed in the darkness. The cat's tail shifted in and out of the dimension as it moved left to right.

"Herregud!" he whispered to himself.

An automated voice calmly prompted Gabriel, "Destination *Herregud* is invalid. Please speak slower or request a valid destination."

"Sorry... Autopilot to Doheny and Sunset," Gabriel said distractedly.

"Affirmative. Please stand by. Switching to terrestrial navigation due to heavy Skyway traffic."

The engine quietly engaged and the on-board computer homed in on the first available terrestrial route. Gabriel sunk into the soft rear seat and watched the streetlights flash by. Everything was a blur after that, thanks to the neurotoxins in the synthetic ale. He knew better, and he was now paying the price for not following Elijah's advice. It would take a few hours for his psychic vibration to return to normal. Sleep was in order.

Although he wasn't sure how, Gabriel somehow found his way safely into his own bed and had already pulled up the covers, warming up his chilled bones.

"No more synthetic spirits," he grumbled in a gravelly voice. Gabriel closed his eyes and promised himself that the only spirits he'd deal with henceforth were the metaphysical kind.

He stole a few hours' sleep, but was awakened prematurely when the grandfather clock in the hall struck zero three hundred hours. The veil between dreams and reality was paper-thin. Anything was possible.

He gazed at the window, half expecting to see something staring back.

Rain rhythmically tapped like a metronome against the glass, while silver streaks of water blurred the night skyline into a twinkling mass. Gabriel stared listlessly at the surreal view of L.A. He felt like he was inside his own impressionist painting—everything was recognizable, but slightly off.

As thunder rumbled through the thin walls of his old apartment, he smirked and looked beyond the mountains.

"Is that you Grandpa?"

He took the ensuing rumble as a yes.

To this day, the sound of thunder conjured up fond memories of Elijah. As a child, his grandfather attributed the rumblings to The Star Gods. With each roll of thunder, the old man weaved tall tales about mischievous beings fighting in the night skies above. Gabriel would fall asleep seeing (and hearing) the cosmic battles playing in the theatre of his mind. Although it had been nearly fourteen years since he'd passed, his grandfather left a gap that was never properly filled. Right now, Gabriel would give anything to hear one of the old man's stories again. After his run-in with the supernatural being at the bar, however, Gabriel now realized they weren't such tall tales after all.

He turned restlessly in bed and stared at the ceiling tiles. Even the mighty Himlens Väktare would find it difficult to ease the sense of dread that was creeping through his veins tonight. The knot in his stomach had returned, worse than before... Gabriel could feel, sense and taste danger.

Without warning, the power grid failed, and the city was cloaked in a veil of darkness.

Gabriel heard a shuffling of feet on the roof.

A terrible hissing sound accompanied them, followed by a loud thud. He saw something rustle in the tree outside his window.

Gabriel waited nervously in the pitch dark. In the absence of stars and streetlights, the city was ominously black. Although there was no light, a Shadow somehow passed in front of the window, making the darkness even darker. A few branches from a Jacaranda tree scratched his bedroom windowpane—like nails on a chalkboard —as the creature peered into his bedroom. Six red eyes looked in from the night.

The Shadow began to hiss, uttering a name that Gabriel dared not speak aloud, "Esssssurrrussssssssss."

Just as the Shadow began to pass through the glass pane, an enormous fiery object hurled itself towards the window. Its bluish-purple light burned hot and bright. The shadowy creature retracted and fled in horror.

Gabriel heard several sets of wings flapping and the light dimmed. Now only a faint blue glow illuminated the tree.

He owed gratitude to the second presence, which now sat on a nearby branch. Gabriel's veins pulsed with adrenaline as he carefully moved to the edge of the bed to get a better look.

Framed against the black sky, he saw a large, beautiful winged being. Even in its crouched position, it was taller than a grown human. It was surrounded by a series of overlapping iridescent wings—more than Gabriel could count in a single glance, though he wagered half a dozen. At first, the wings seemed to reflect light and change shape. Upon closer inspection, he thought they somehow produced their own light. It was the same faint bluish-purple of twilight.

Two shimmering eyes met his. They smoldered like amber embers. Ice-cold chills ran up his spine. *He knew those eyes.* They belonged to the alley cat and the stranger from the bar.

Whatever it was, it grinned, as if it could read his thoughts.

He heard a rustling as it stood up. It outstretched its myriad feathers and revealed a muscular, humanoid form. Its blue skin was smooth and shiny, like cold marble. The being had razor-sharp talons for feet, but possessed humanoid arms and hands. Its nose was aristocratically long and narrow—somewhat beak-like, but fashioned of the same smooth skin that covered its arms and torso. The being's face was also long and dignified. Its fine, blue mid-length hair was as soft as the down of a bird.

As the shapeshifter approached, Gabriel felt his heart skip a beat or two.

'So we meet again,' it said telepathically. *'Soon you will remember who I am.'*

Gabriel tried to jump to his feet, but he clumsily fell off the edge of his bed, hitting his head on the hardwood floor with a thud. The sound of the rain became more and more distant, until all he heard was the beating of his own heart juxtaposed against the sound of wings flapping.

He blacked out for several minutes.

When he finally opened his eyes, the being was inside his room, and Gabriel was lying in its lap.

His pain and fear were replaced with a feeling of calm and safety. Gabriel sensed the same unusual static charge he felt outside the bar. This time, it was accompanied by a pulsating warmth that coursed through his body. Every nerve, chakra and hair was stimulated—almost euphorically. As the being spoke to Gabriel, the sensation intensified and his pain disappeared.

"I will do you no harm. I come with a message only—namely, that you are in danger. Be still, and see what I see," it said, touching his forehead.

The stranger's fingers burned with the intensity of a thousand suns and the enormous pressure on his forehead caused his vision to blur. Gabriel closed his eyes and fell into the mystical being's arms. He felt as if he was drifting endlessly, like Alice falling through the rabbit hole.

When the falling sensation ceased, Gabriel opened his eyes again. He was not dreaming, but he might as well have been. However fantastic it seemed, Gabriel realized he was flying high above the L.A. Megacity, right over the Cypher District. His wings were spread in the night sky, and he felt the cool wind tickling his feathers. Despite his best efforts to move or change course, Gabriel was paralyzed. Eventually he understood that he was no longer in his body and the wings were not his own. He was a psychic stowaway—a distant observer seeing and feeling everything through *It*, whatever *It* was. Gabriel had come across various forms of good and evil in his work. So, although he was uncertain of its origin or its species, for that matter, he had an overwhelming sense that this supernatural being was not only intrinsically good, but also the absolute antithesis of evil. He also felt it was ageless, timeless and deathless. With his fears assuaged, at least for the moment, he gave in to the psychic experience and let the immortal take control. After doing so, he was one with its body and mind, and no longer felt trapped. It was as if he was in a perpetual dream-state... seeing and feeling everything omnisciently, with a sense of emotional detachment.

Gabriel smelled exhaust fumes as the immortal flew high above the city. In what seemed like an instant, it changed direction, opened all its wings and descended silently in the shadows of an alley.

Telltale trappings of a grand celebration were all that remained from the night before; rain-soaked clumps of soggy confetti, broken beer bottles and cheap party favors shone in the eerie blue light emanating from its wings.

The immortal took a deep breath. It seemed to smell everything in amazing detail, from the sweet honeysuckle a block away to the aroma of approaching rain: an earthy, musky blend of wet dirt and asphalt, mixed with sharp tones of ozone. All these pleasant scents did little to mask the pungent smell of death that was also permeating the alley.

Instinctively, the celestial being walked over to a nondescript dumpster and pointed inside with a long, slender index finger. Strewn amidst the broken glass and New Year's garbage lay the wet, lifeless body of a man who bore a striking resemblance to Gabriel. Icy raindrops gently kissed his bruised cheeks. With each drop of rain, the ruby scabs on his forehead dissolved and ran like watercolor into his ginger hairline. The man's cloudy blue eyes stared helplessly at the swirling grey abyss above.

Gabriel gasped when he recognized the man from The Black Cat.

His arms were stretched perpendicular to his body. Everything about the arrangement of his body seemed painstakingly premeditated. In his right hand, he still gripped what appeared to be the remains of a necklace—the center portion, some sort of protective amulet, was partially obscured by his fingers. Due in part to the weather, and perhaps some other cause, his body was decomposing faster than usual.

Though its ancient language was different than Gabriel's, and it appeared to think in song, Gabriel was able to read the immortal's thoughts. From its internal song, a name kept echoing as a refrain.

'Jacob... His name was Jacob, wasn't it?'

Gabriel knew the answer without asking.

'Yes—please quiet your thoughts, little one!' it replied. *'We're not alone.'*

In the distance, there was a sudden movement. Someone—or, some-*thing*—else was there. Without it ever communicating the fact, Gabriel understood the cosmic being was incapable of fear, and it was impervious to most danger. But despite the entity's apparent powers, its instinct told it to avoid whatever was in the periphery at all costs—not out of concern for itself, but for Gabriel's own wellbeing.

'We have no time... Pity, as he is deserving of a proper burial, not this blasphemy.'

The immortal wiped the blood and rain from the man's face and kissed his lips, the way a mother would kiss a child. In his telepathic connection with the entity, Gabriel felt what it felt, and could understand some if its complex thoughts. Although Jacob was dead, a dim essence of his life force still clung to the body. As the entity took a deep breath, there was a sensation of warmth followed by a wall of sadness. The area around the dumpster was charged and Gabriel sensed Jacob's energy.

"Take your place with your brothers and sisters above. It was not your time, but you'll be safe now, my dear child," it whispered into his ear.

A spark of gold light illuminated the alley, and his energy shot into the night sky, towards the moon. During that brief spark, Gabriel saw something crouched in the shadows, about ten feet away from the dumpster. There was a sinister cry from the darkness —shrill and angry. Gabriel's blood froze as six fiery eyes stared in his direction. Though he'd never seen one up close, Gabriel knew this was one of The Seven Shadows Elijah had warned him about as a child.

Somehow The Shadow read Gabriel's thought, even from within the mind of the immortal.

'You must learn to whisper your thoughts, Gabriel. I fear we've outstayed our welcome. The Dark Liege is calling its denizens.'

The immortal unfurled its wings and hovered high above. From here, Gabriel could see the dumpster, the body and the dark entity in the corner.

A murder of crows circled above Jacob's body for several moments before one of them landed on his shoulder. It let out a sharp "Caw!" and pecked meticulously at his arm. One by one, they all landed in a circle around him. Gabriel knew the other entity was there as well, moving them into place like a demented conductor.

His lifeless eyes welled with rain. First the right eye, then the left overflowed. Each formed a small line from his eye to his ear.

He seemed to weep one last time before the crows commenced their feast.

Suddenly everything was blurry. Then, Gabriel felt compassion welling in the immortal as it wept.

'We've seen enough. Hold on as—'

'Wait,' Gabriel interrupted. 'Is that what I think it is?'

'Yes. Hrókr, The Dark Liege, better known as Deception, is one of The Seven Shadows. You've met one of this being's puppets before—a young pupil of Elijah's named Björn. Soon you will remember this. It sees with The Six Eyes of Esurus, the darkest being in the Known Universe.'

'Meaning?'

'Meaning your planet is doomed, as are you if we stay here any longer. Deception's sole purpose is to betray (and ultimately consume) any living thing that crosses its path—but its primary purpose on Earth is to destroy The Last Steward of the Light.'

"You mean, me?"

'Yes. Jacob is dead tonight because Deception killed the wrong M-8 at The Black Cat. You see, besides looking a lot like you, he fits your profile; Jacob was wildly talented, orphaned at a young age, and was considered a disciplinary challenge. Soon, however, Deception will realize its error. It's just a matter of time before it finds you.'

"But—"

'Enough! Let me get us out of harm's way and I'll answer any other questions you have.'

The immortal closed its eyes. A vision of a phoenix entered its consciousness. When its eyes opened, its body had physically transformed into that vision, too.

Like a great chariot of fire, the phoenix blazed across the heavens, resembling a shooting star to any human onlooker below. While Gabriel was connected with the being psychically, he came to understand its corporal form was infinitely malleable—its mind could completely rearrange its molecules—at least in this plane.

Gabriel inexplicably lost his connection with the being. With a sudden jolt, he felt his consciousness snap back into his body like a rubber band.

He collected his thoughts and began to wiggle his hands and toes. After a few deep breaths, Gabriel felt grounded. He was home again, in his own bed, in his own body.

As he sat up, Gabriel noticed that the shapeshifter was quietly perched atop his dresser, now back in its half-humanoid, half-winged form, staring at him kindly and patiently. Brilliant purple and blue light bathed his bedroom. Its eyes, however, were no longer amber, but a gorgeous bright white. They were filled with concern and compassion.

"My memory is still bewitched, but your actions tonight revealed your function, Old One. You are The One Who Stands at the Nexus Between Ends and Beginnings. You are the First and you will be the Last. You're Death, are you not?"

*"You speak the truth, my friend. Yet, you miss the point—who I am is far less important than **who you are**. It's time you embrace your destiny as The Last Steward of the Light and stop The Seven Shadows once and for all."*

Death closed its eyes and spoke telepathically to Gabriel.

'Under twilight's veil where night meets day,
Let the truth return—and forever stay.
My binding words, will now unravel...
The time has come for us both to travel.'

Gabriel immediately felt a tingling sensation on the top of his head as his crown chakra came to life. It felt as if a thousand-watt bulb had been switched on. Memories that were long lost began to flicker into his mind's eye, like an old 8mm camera. Gabriel flashed back to a stormy night in his grandfather Elijah's cabin, fourteen years earlier, the night he first met Death and discovered his own destiny as The Last Steward of the Light.

PART II

TRANSMISSIONS FROM A SHOOTING STAR

PROLOGUE

After Death reversed its magical thought-binding spell on Gabriel's memories, he instantly flashed back to the night he was first initiated into Stewardship by Elijah, his grandfather and The Second-to-Last Steward of the Light. On that fateful night, young Gabriel encountered not one, but *two* supernatural visitors—and nearly lost his life in the process.

2

THE LAST STEWARD OF THE LIGHT

Dateline: The Colorado Rocky Mountains, in the Earth Year Treble-Treble-Nine, Nine-Eight-Six. (Twenty-one years ago).

As lightning and thunder wrought havoc outside, it seemed as though the firmament itself was about to fall to pieces. Tumultuous summer storms like this regularly swept into the foothills of the Rockies with inexplicable rage and fury, but tonight was something for the history books.

Gabriel, a bright and tall seven-year-old boy, nervously stood watch at his bedroom window, waiting for someone—scratch that —*something* to pay a visit. He had a hunch, after all. And much to the chagrin of all the adults around him, his hunches were rarely wrong.

He mustered up whatever bravery existed in his willowy frame and stared into the darkness. It stared back unapologetically. A sudden flash of lightning temporarily blinded him, leaving a psychedelic imprint of treetops on his retina.

Gabriel instinctively closed his expressive, almost otherworldly blue-green eyes and leaned his forehead against the windowpane.

He felt a gentle *tap-tap-tap* of the rain on the glass, while he retreated into his mind's eye. As the trailing crashes of thunder crackled and shook the foundation of the cabin, he imagined a great congregation of gods raging war in the canopy above—heralding the coming of Ragnarök. Most normal seven-year-olds didn't even know what that was, but then again, Gabriel was far from normal— a fact he knew painfully well.

As a child, Gabriel exuded maturity and sensibility that was light-years ahead of his peers. While neighborhood children busied themselves with sports and social activities, Gabriel preferred reading his way through the library or holding court with his so-called imaginary friends—who were anything but figments of his overactive imagination. His peers gradually shunned his precocious nature, verbally taunting him as a "schizophrenic" or "freak." Thankfully, he inherited his late mother and father's Scandinavian genes, which lent Gabriel both a hardy character and remarkable height; the latter was enough to ward off all but the bravest bullies.

On nights like this when his thoughts grew too big for his brain, he'd turn to his grandfather's vintage telescope for refuge. Projecting his consciousness into the great expanse of the Milky Way provided a bit of solace. Somehow the infinite grandeur of the stars assuaged his childhood fears that his existence was just a divine mistake. After all, a Universe this beautiful, this complex, must have space enough for a freak of nature like him. He was just dumped on the wrong planet, in the wrong body, at the wrong time.

Tonight, however, the constant rumbling in the skies above offered no consolation for his kid fears. Rather than soothing him, the cacophony of chaos only amplified the din in his brain. He'd been seeing visions and hearing whispers all afternoon—more than usual. He knew that something would be coming tonight—something that would change his life forever. At times like this, precognitive knowledge felt like more of a hindrance than a blessing; each second seemed to crawl past at a snail's pace. Gabriel's impatience was often his undoing. For him, it was hard to wait for things to unravel when he had already seen the probable outcome.

Gabriel watched quietly as the stars were consumed by the coming storm; one by one, each blinked into oblivion, leaving him alone in the darkness.

The wind howled mournfully at the starless sky. At first, a very shrill, high note swirled through the attic rafters and hung above, almost like a banshee or siren's call. It was accompanied by lower notes, much more harmonious... first one, then two, then a chord progression—a cosmically composed leitmotif—containing six or seven melodic wails. The resulting noise was haunting, but beautiful. As the motif repeated, Gabriel realized the howling sounds were actually voices—voices harmonizing on a single word. The language was unfamiliar, composed of subtle sounds within sounds —all somehow given context by their musical arrangement. Intuitively, he understood this was an announcement... but for whom, or what, Gabriel was uncertain. Whatever the occasion, he had a feeling that the song portended Death.

Gabriel pulled out a spiral notebook and stared at something he scrawled earlier. Three words, "**ARE YOU READY?**" appeared in bold caps on wide-ruled paper. Gabriel had traced over them dozens, perhaps hundreds of times, until the paper started to tear and the graphite smeared and smudged to the point of illegibility.

'Ready for *what*?' he thought.

Lightning flashed twice more in rapid succession, shutting down the power in the process. The crackling whip of thunder soon followed. An old generator in the basement automatically kicked-in; its gentle hum added to the strange symphony of atmospheric pyrotechnics outside. Tattered shutters opened and closed on their own, squeaking all the while.

Gabriel stared once more into the forest, scanning for movement along the trees. He'd seen a figure scaling the perimeter earlier—one that was too tall to be an animal, but too twisted to be a human.

An eerie stillness fell upon the quaking aspens, almost as if they dared not move until the danger had passed.

"It won't be long now," he whispered as he nervously bit at his lip.

The gentle percussion of footsteps downstairs provided a welcome distraction to Gabriel's thoughts. They belonged to his loving and eccentric grandfather, Elijah, who was pacing in his study.

If Gabriel was lucky, he might get to read a draft of whatever Elijah was working on tonight. His best-selling books on time travel, metaphysics and extra-terrestrials were far more fascinating and terrifying than anything in a tired Grimms' faery tale—the truth always was.

Giving in to his insatiable curiosity, Gabriel tiptoed down the stairs. Once he was near Elijah's study, Gabriel positioned his body just out of his grandfather's line of sight. From this vantage point, he saw the familiar silhouette of his grandfather seated at a mahogany desk. Piles of yellowed books towered on the left, while burning incense haloed Elijah's head with concentric rings of white smoke. The old man's face was further obscured by an antique banker's lamp that was cracked and discolored from years of use.

Elijah opened a weathered wooden box and gently laid out several reagents and tools on an ancient escritoire adjacent to his main desk; chief among them was a shiny silver fountain pen, his most prized piece of contraband. The old man lovingly cleaned the instrument and filled its reservoir with some sort of peculiar golden ink that sparkled in the dim light. He took care, deriving enjoyment in the ritual. Like all Stewards, he understood the magical power intrinsic to manual writing and the tools accompanying it. After filling the inkwell, Elijah placed a single sheet of vellum on the table and closed his eyes; Gabriel followed suit. His mind was now linked with his grandfather's. In this meditative state, Gabriel could hear, feel and see everything Elijah could.

As Gabriel listened to the old man's thoughts, he became painfully aware of every noise in the cabin, from the sound of the wind snaking through the attic to the persistent crackling of the logs in the fireplace. Slowly, the noises blended together into a single, concordant vibration. It resonated with the clarity of a tuning fork, drowning out everything else, even the vibration itself. It was then, and only then, that Elijah pressed the well-worn nib of the fountain pen against the vellum.

Ideas grew pregnant in his grandfather's mind like water droplets swelling into storm clouds. One by one, they began flowing, until they streamed into elaborate rivers of ink on the paper. Lost in automatic writing, Elijah no longer perceived the pen, the paper, nor his consciousness, for that matter. He simply let words flow through him until, eventually, like a cosmic tide, the thoughts ebbed back to their source.

As he opened his eyes, Gabriel caught a glimpse of the ink drying and disappearing into the vellum. He watched as Elijah exhaled slowly onto the paper, heating up the ink. It subsequently shimmered incandescently with a gentle golden light of its own—a reaction that was singular to liquefied, enchanted stardust.

Elijah sat up as straight as his tired bones would allow and scanned the paper. His handwriting was neat, but shaky—the kind of penmanship that belonged to an old man, one of status and privilege, since manual writing had fallen into disuse and, as of late, was altogether forbidden.

Elijah cleared his throat and began reading aloud. His voice was low, controlled and agreeably rich—lacking any of the telltale shakiness present in his writing.

"Survival. This primal instinct still burns inside our bellies with the intensity of a newborn star, relentlessly pushing humankind to blaze forward at any cost—hoping against hope that somehow we'll outlive our own capacity for self-destruction.

"And survive we have, but at a perilous cost. The Great Wars are over, but we've traded all our freedoms for a tenuous peace in the form of the omniscient State. This was a fool's bargain at best, for it won't halt the inevitable. Earth's resources are utterly spent and our population is dwindling. As the continents collide and our planet begins its inevitable death march around its swiftly swelling Sun, I ponder what legacy will we leave behind? And what will we do with the time that remains?

"My dreams are haunted with darkness. I've seen starless skies where only Shadows loom—treacherous, devouring Shadows. I feel their appetite growing, even now. Know this: there are Wolves among us.

"Humankind now stands at a delicate precipice; in this pivotal moment we will either show our mettle or be forever extinguished. We must ascend to a new level of consciousness or fade into eternal darkness. Despite my clairvoyance, I've not skill enough to see beyond three words echoing in my mind, drowning out all other thoughts: **ARE YOU READY?**

"Alas, Death approaches; I can hear It in the wind. Before this night is over, I will fulfill my destiny and you will embark on yours.

"Fear not, for I have found immortality through the lines in this tome—my wisdom, my energy and my love live in each and every word. Let them shine like beacons in the dark days ahead."

The old man pulled out another sheet of vellum and spoke to himself as he wrote the following inscription in elaborate cursive script:

"To my dearest Gabriel,
With love and light always. —Elijah.
(The Second-to-Last Steward of the Light in the
Earth Year Treble-Treble-Nine, Nine-Eight-Six)"

Directly below his signature, Elijah carefully inscribed the following phrase in the same star language that appeared on the cover of the book, followed by a Common Tongue translation:

"Wherever there is darkness, may there also be light.
As one spark's consumed, another ignites.
This book I bequeath; its pages are thine.
Protect it well, through all space and time."

Elijah breathed onto the inscription and watched as it slowly glimmered and faded away. The book then seemed to tremble for a moment, as it comprehended what was written.

"It's been my honor," Elijah said lovingly to the book.

Lightning flashed outside, causing the old desk lamp to dim momentarily. A slow and steady rumble gradually shook through the wooden cabin.

Elijah took a golden needle and thread, and he carefully stitched the vellum sheet atop thousands of similarly enchanted pages—each fashioned out of the same semi-transparent material, and each containing words, languages and alien symbols that were invisible until breathed upon.

Once the page was neatly bound, the old man leaned forward and whispered a sacred passphrase to the book—its name.

A breeze swept through the study as the book closed of its own volition. Ancient alien asterisms radiantly illuminated the cover from the inside out, spelling out what appeared to be two words. Though no direct Earthly translation existed, its closest equivalent was *Corpus Sidera,* or *The Body of Light.* Cruder interpretations included *The Book of Stars* or *The Star Compendium.*

After a few moments, the symbols faded and the book sealed itself—leaving only a translucent crystalline box, with no markings and no visible openings.

Without looking at his grandson, Elijah spoke telepathically to the boy, 'Gabe, didn't I teach you better than this?'

Gabriel gasped audibly.

'Never spy on another psychic. Usually, it doesn't end well,' the old man added. Then he spun his chair around and spoke aloud.

"Tonight, however, your timing was fortuitous. I want you to meet a very, very old friend of mine."

Gabriel looked around the room, somewhat puzzled by the remark.

"You've already met, actually, but you haven't been properly introduced. Meet *Corpus Sidera, The Book of Stars.*"

The old man handed his grandson the crystalline box, but Gabriel was afraid to touch the ancient artifact.

"Don't worry. It's virtually indestructible. This is at least as old as our Universe, and probably older than the previous one. I'm The Second-to-Last of a long line of Stewards of the Light, charged with its safekeeping. Each Steward gets to pick his or her successor; *I choose you.*"

Those three words seemed to hang in the air, like a spell.

Gabriel carefully felt the exterior of *Sidera,* but could find no printed word, no opening and couldn't clearly see its contents, as the box was translucent, but not transparent... at least not in its resting state.

"Call the book by its name. If your energy is as pure as your heart, it will open."

Gabriel tried speaking the name without avail. He was still holding an unresponsive artifact.

Elijah tapped his finger to his forehead and then glanced at the book. Gabriel understood immediately.

He closed his eyes and inhaled deeply. He heard the name in his head and projected it using both his third eye and his heart chakras. This time, his hands momentarily melded with the glass casing of the book and every chakra opened. *Sidera* shined brightly as it merged energetically with Gabriel. As he exhaled, the book popped open and whispered Gabriel's name back.

"Most unusual, and most promising," Elijah said. "In all my years with this tome, it's never spoken to me."

"What does this mean, Grandpa?"

"It means I've chosen well. The book has accepted you as The Last Steward of the Light." He paused, then answered Gabriel's unspoken question, "After you, there will be no others.

"Within this tome, you will become acquainted with the women, men and other sentient beings who came before you. Their energy, life force and voices live within the pages. Guard this with your life and know that one day you will have to wield and conquer its antithesis. I pray that you can succeed where Björn and I have failed."

A similar artifact sat at the opposite edge of the desk, albeit pitch black in color. It was ancient and equally alien in origin. The symbols inscribed on the cover were inverted versions of those found on *Sidera*. When reversed, the asterisms spelled out something akin to *Corpus Tenebrae*, otherwise known as *The Book of Shadows* or *Body of Darkness* in the Common Tongue. In some circles, it was referred to more colloquially as *The Black Box* or simply *Pandora*. If *Sidera* described all things luminous, then *Tenebrae* described the cosmic inverse. It was not evil, per se, but it had been used for such purposes in the past. With its essence polluted, the book began to rewrite itself into something sinister and malevolent.

Gabriel eyed the box curiously and his grandfather frowned.

"What is that, Grandpa?"

"Something I wish I'd never found."

Elijah futilely threw *Tenebrae* into the fire. Much to his dismay, the tome consumed the flames immediately, without so much as a puff of smoke, leaving it completely unscathed as it lay atop cinder, ash and glowing embers.

Elijah heard something else, equally as ancient, calling to him from inside his desk.

"Yes, yes... Of course, I haven't forgotten," he said somewhat absentmindedly to the unseen object. "But you'll have to wait your turn."

Elijah opened up the bottom drawer of his desk and produced an oval-shaped mirror. Then, the old man unlatched a pocket watch from his trousers.

"First, take this. It was given to me by my mentor, and I now pass it on to you. It's called Tidens Svärd, or The Sword of Time."

Gabriel looked at the ancient timepiece. Although exquisitely crafted out of the finest gold, it didn't seem to tell time properly. It also had a curious feature—the glass slid back, allowing the hands to be manually moved forward.

"Tidens Svärd is not a watch, my boy... it's a weapon, and it only has a minute left to spare—of course, the minute can last an eternity if used properly. Activate it only when you've run out of options."

Then, his grandfather picked up the oval shaped mirror, the one that had whispered to him earlier, and placed it in front of Gabriel.

"Do you know what this object is?"

Gabriel peered into the obsidian surface of the device and chills ran up his spine.

"An enchanted looking glass?"

The old man smiled.

"Indeed, but it's more than that; only Stewards can use this scrying mirror. It's a gift from Time herself, an Eternal being known as Akasha. Tonight, the mirror called out to me, just as it will soon speak to you. I believe it has a message for you. I'd like you to meditate with it and fine-tune your psychic skills. Magic is simply a new truth waiting to be discovered. It's time that you start exploring your gifts so you can harness that magic. Head upstairs and we will talk later tonight when I finish my work."

"Thanks, Grandpa!" Gabriel said, finding it increasingly difficult to contain his excitement over, arguably, the best three gifts he'd ever received.

Gabriel stormed up the stairwell like a gust of wind, leaving an echo of footsteps in his wake.

His grandfather was filled with a wave of nostalgia. With a heavy heart, he moved towards the window.

Elijah stared at the quaking aspen grove. At its edge, a three-thousand-year old bristlecone pine tree swayed in the wind. She was the queen of the forest, a sentient creature that called herself The Whispering Pine.

"Watch after my Gabriel," he said.

The tree bent forward, and a gust of wind carried her response.

"Always."

An ensuing flash of lightning illuminated a galaxy of raindrops on the windowpane. During that instant, he saw a tall Shadow creep along the forest edge—a creature that Elijah knew by name.

"Björn!" he gasped.

His worst fears were confirmed; Pandora's box was opened and there was no turning back.

When lightning illuminated the courtyard again a moment later, the figure was gone.

In the dark skies above, a single point of light seemed to be moving closer to the Earth, like a comet or shooting star.

'Hurry!' he said psychically to the celestial object. 'The Shadows have descended!'

3

THE FIRST STAR

G abriel sat alone for a moment with Elijah's three gifts. First, he fastened the pocket watch to his trousers. From that day forward, it never left his side.

Next, Gabriel picked up *Corpus Sidera*. To his young eyes, it was the most beautiful thing he'd ever seen. Just as he was about to open it, however, a voice beckoned.

"Pssst... Over here!"

Gabriel froze and felt as if his heart had jumped up into his throat.

"Who's there?" he said, his voice raspy and thin.

"The Man in the Looking Glass," it whispered back. He realized that this was not some apparition speaking, but the scrying mirror itself.

After a long pause, he slowly reached towards the artifact, half expecting another hand to emerge from the mirror and pull him inside. He was relieved—albeit still suspicious of the object—when nothing happened.

Carefully, he leaned in and looked at his reflection. Quite unexpectedly, and disturbingly, the reflection rippled and morphed until

Gabriel was no longer gazing at himself. Gone was the lanky seven-year-old. A handsome young man looked back instead. Like Gabriel, he had wide-spaced, otherworldly eyes and curly blonde hair. However, his cheekbones were more chiseled. Gabriel guessed he was at least thrice as old as he.

"What... or who are you?" Gabriel asked, frozen in fear.

The man answered in a singsong riddle as his reflection continued to ripple:

"I'm The Man in the Looking Glass—
That's all you need know!
A shadow of a future on a path you'll forego.
Look for the Rabbit inside a Blue Box...
The key is your knowledge, so be as sly as a fox.
Zero follows eleven—
That's if you survive...
But the Grey is a trickster from which you can't hide.
So, tesser in The Void and release all fear...
Set the clock to twelve and then disappear."

The self-proclaimed "Man in the Looking Glass" stepped backwards and slowly faded into his Mirror World. As the rippling subsided, the obsidian mirror went black. Gabriel's seven-year-old face was all that remained. The riddle, however, was stuck in his head like a childhood rhyme. Somehow, he felt he'd always known it.

He heard a loud crack of thunder and involuntarily jumped. The scrying mirror fell onto the hardwood floor and shattered into a hundred tiny pieces. A harrowing scream came out of the mirror itself as The Man in the Looking Glass perished.

As he cleaned up the mess he'd made, Gabriel understood he may not be ready for the power of *Sidera.* Although it was nearly

indestructible, he didn't trust himself with a device of such power...
not yet.

He stepped inside his wardrobe and closed the door behind him.

"Sometimes the best hiding place is in plain sight," Gabriel said
aloud, remembering one of his first lessons with his grandfather.

Gabriel waved his hands and removed a glamour he'd placed on
the wardrobe door. A rectangular portal stood in its place, something he called The Stacks, since it was quite literally stacked within
this dimension, just out of sight. He took a deep breath and walked
into The Stacks.

Like The Mirror World he'd inadvertently destroyed, the inside
of The Stacks was larger than the door that contained it. Gabriel had
conjured The Stacks into existence by accident one day, and he'd
simply kept it a secret. Now, it was a place where he, and only he,
could go. Without wasting a moment, Gabriel hid the book and said
his goodbyes.

"I'll see you soon," he whispered, not knowing it would take
nearly a decade-and-a-half before he'd hold *Sidera* again.

He exited the wardrobe and waved his hand, reinstating the
glamour.

Gabriel's attention was quickly, and unexpectedly drawn
towards the window. Outside, a shooting star blazed across the
otherwise black sky. Radiant tones of indigo and violet cut through
the clouds as it hurled towards the old cabin.

Gabriel tried to scream for his grandfather, but his throat seized
up. Too terrified to move, he helplessly watched as the object tore
through the forest edge, nearly setting a tree on fire.

A strange and euphoric static charge filled Gabriel's body as the
star passed by his window and landed on the front porch. Its colli-
sion produced a clap of thunder that rivaled even Thor's Hammer,
Mjölnir. Indeed, Gabriel would prefer meeting the God of Thunder,
for whatever landed outside was likely far older and far more
powerful than any Norse deity.

The emergency generator subsequently stopped working, rendering the cabin nearly pitch black, save for the gentle glow of the wood stove downstairs.

As soon as the adrenaline stopped rushing in his veins, Gabriel took a deep breath and tiptoed as gracefully as his awkward feet would carry him, making his way quietly down a large, spiral stairwell leading from the attic to the foyer. He instinctively stopped at the foot of the stairs, just shy of the last step—the one that always creaked.

Moments later, he heard a gentle knocking on the front door. Scintillating indigo and gold-colored light filed in through the antique keyhole and doorframe.

Without time to properly hide, Gabriel jumped past the last step and crouched in the crawlspace under the stairs, watching from the safety of the almost impenetrable darkness that surrounded him.

Elijah slid his research into an attaché under his desk and covered the *Tenebrae* in embers. Then, he shuffled towards the front door and approached it with caution.

As he opened the peephole, blinding light showered into the cabin.

"Vem där? Who goes there?"

A booming voice accompanied the light.

"Det är jag. Öppna dörren, din gamla gubbe!

You know who I am. Open the door, old man!"

Elijah acquiesced, opening the door with a deliberate caution, as if he were trying to slow time itself—to avoid some inevitable outcome.

Blinding light illuminated the interior of the cabin, followed by an unmistakable euphoric electrical charge—the same phenomenon Gabriel observed in the attic.

A tall, glowing silhouette loomed in the doorway, backlit in a halo of its own surging energy and auric fields. It was difficult—if not impossible—to clearly focus on any defining feature for more than a moment. Its shape remained in a constant state of flux, twinkling with multicolored outlines that cast colored shadows along the hardwood floor.

When it entered the room, Gabriel realized that it didn't move physically, but rather phased out of one location and rematerialized in another, in rapid succession. Despite the power outage and generator failure, all the lamps inexplicably flickered on and off as it phased past them.

Elijah paused in front of the fireplace and the strange being followed suit. The warm light from the fire cut through its shifting auric shield, revealing what looked like a projection or approximation of a human form—albeit a crude one. The outlines of its body shimmered and overlapped as it phased from one location to the next, like stop-frame animation. From what Gabriel could see, the figure was quite tall—nearly seven feet, at least. It had high cheekbones and its skin was as pale as moonlight. Short-cropped, wispy black hair crowned a stern and attractive face—one that was androgynously handsome and regal. Its eyes glinted in the firelight like polished amber stones.

"It's been too long, old man."

Gabriel was immediately struck by the singular quality of its voice. It was almost musical; certain syllables seemed to precede words and then linger long after it spoke, echoing in gentle refrains. The sound was commanding and decidedly alien.

"You're one to call me old... don't you have a millennia or two on me?" Elijah poked.

The stranger answered with absolute honesty, either unreceptive to—or perhaps unaware of—Elijah's attempt at levity.

"I wept as the first star illuminated the abyss. I'll be there when the last stellar remnant of your world is but mere stardust in the dark expanse. It's my eternal function. Like my younger brethren and the divine source from which we're fashioned, I'm without an end."

Sparks danced deep within the eyes of the immortal and the polished amber irises began to glow.

"Hmmm... a simple, '*I'm older than I look*,' would have sufficed. You're as socially awkward as always. That's why I love you."

"Don't ask a question unless you are ready to hear the truth. With that out of the way, I might add that you are as unapologetically human as ever, which is precisely why I love you, too, old man."

"Yes, we make quite the pair!" Elijah said with a laugh.

'Too bad Death and Destruction always seem to follow in your wake,' he involuntarily thought to himself. The old man was immediately remorseful, as the telepathic being surely heard his thoughts.

"Release your harsh judgments, Eli, and guard your thoughts. Be grateful I come in this form tonight; I have many aspects which are far less forgiving—two of whom you just named."

"My dear friend, I only think the truth. You cannot deny your function. Är du inte Dödsängeln?"

This kindled a latent wildfire inside the being. In a rare show of power, it grew to titanic proportions, towering high above Elijah, with multiple wings outstretched. Its eyes burned with an unbridled intensity as its words came down like thunder.

"I was once Osiris, God of the Underworld and Shiva, The Great Destroyer. I later walked the skies as the winged Archangel Zerachiel. And yes, in your space and time, Eli, I'm known crudely and narrowly as one of my functions... Death."

"So, you don't deny it, then?" Elijah asked, already regretting the words falling from his lips.

"I don't deny how I'm perceived by mortals. I do, however, reject your implication that I only bring about loss. Try seeing me as a divine agent of Transformation instead. That is closer to my function and it is my preferred name. My true name has power, so I shall keep that to myself."

Elijah sighed and the immortal's face softened. It smiled and began speaking again.

"You're far too focused on cataloging... endlessly putting things in neat boxes. The precious labels in which you place so much value are peculiar human constructs—and crude ones at that. They limit your capacity to see the larger truth of the Universe. Think beyond labels, old man; then and only then will you be free."

Lightning flashed, and in that brief moment, Death resumed the avatar of Zerachiel, the shape-shifting, beautiful humanoid—the one that had walked in the cabin a few moments earlier. Its eyes gleamed gently; no longer blazing like wildfire.

The old man was speechless—something Elijah often experienced in the presence of this particular celestial being, irrespective of whatever shape, gender or aspect it decided to use.

The immortal broke the silence.

"Come, Elijah... we have much to talk about, and precious little time."

The professor nodded and led the way to his study. The shapeshifter followed Elijah, phasing in and out of spacetime, as it had before. About mid-way through the parlour, the being split into two; one aspect followed the old man, while another stopped dead in its tracks, sensing another presence. The immortal appeared to be a trans-dimensional entity, capable of being many places at once. It could take on any avatar, such as Shiva, Osiris or Zerachiel, and still contain the knowledge and essence of all the others.

The deity closed its eyes and surveyed the room with intuition alone. It effortlessly locked onto Gabriel's presence in the crawl-space and smiled.

Although its silhouette continued to shimmer and shift in and out of focus, Gabriel noticed one spectacular detail that was hidden before—seemingly out of nowhere, a small sliver of light shone on its forehead, just above its eyes. It mimicked the shape of a miniature waxing crescent moon.

How did Gabriel miss this? Was it there all along? Perhaps his own sense of sight was blinding him, as contradictory as that sounded.

He sighed and closed his eyes, remembering what Elijah had taught him: "Sometimes you have to shut your eyes to truly see—to unlearn what you know in order to be enlightened."

'I've got nothing to lose,' Gabriel thought to himself.

He sat for a moment in the darkness and let go of his assumptions. With each breath, Gabriel stopped trying to see with his eyes and opened his heart instead.

At first, he saw only darkness. Soon, the shapeshifter's eyes began to reveal themselves, like distant beacons. Before long, they shone as brightly as two suns. He shuddered with fear for a moment and the eyes began to fade.

"Relax, Gabe," he whispered to himself.

He took a deep breath and focused on the eyes again, releasing all expectations... letting the details fill in on their own. Gabriel compared meditation to the antiquated process of developing film—if he followed the right steps, all the latent details revealed themselves in time. If he rushed, the image was lost. Patience was key.

After several moments of quiet observation, Gabriel's diligence paid off. Once again, he saw the immortal's third eye appear. Then, ever so slowly, the remainder of the body materialized. The resplendent being was comprised entirely out of purple and indigo energy. Two of its many hands were gently pressed in a praying position, while the others were resting palm-up. Although Death could take any form, Gabriel believed the immortal was revealing one of its earliest and most sacred avatars to him, perhaps an unnamed one.

"Come closer," it whispered.

As before, Gabriel heard many voices overlapping and sometimes speaking in chorus.

"Release your fear and come closer, Gabriel," it said again, this time as a command.

Knowing he had little choice in the matter, Gabriel obliged.

He felt an involuntary tremor throughout his body as the deity's third eye opened halfway. It bathed the room in blinding light, eclipsing everything in its wake. The resulting sensation was warm, loving and terrifying all at once. Gabriel felt absolutely naked; his darkest fears, secrets and insecurities were completely revealed, not only to himself but the being as well. There was no judgment, however, only kindness. The immortal loved him, flaws and all, just like his grandfather did. It was the kind of love that he craved but rarely received.

"You are filled with more beauty and strength than you could possibly imagine. If you ever allowed yourself to truly shine, giving others a glimpse of your resplendence, then I dare say you'd be unstoppable."

The being closed all three of its eyes and Gabriel fought back a tear.

"Please do not be disheartened. Your grandfather taught you well. Always seek the truth with your heart, not your eyes."

Gabriel found himself simultaneously frightened and fascinated. Fear, unfortunately, won out and Gabriel opened his eyes.

The vision faded immediately, as did the radiant being before him.

When he returned to the safety of the cool, dark crawlspace, Gabriel realized that his skin was warm to the touch, as if he'd been sun-kissed on a hot summer day. In fact, his entire body was buzzing and surging with energy.

As he took a deep breath, Gabriel heard muddled voices in the study. He cupped his ear and listened intently.

"It's hell to get old," his grandfather said. "Give me a second to grab my glasses. I can't see anything in this candlelight."

Elijah was bordered by a sea of books, papers and artifacts, which exacerbated the task of searching. The professor's attire mirrored his surroundings: scholarly but slightly unkempt. Snowy, untamed hair cascaded around his forehead, jutting and cresting unpredictably like waves breaking on a rocky shore.

"Here, this will help."

The celestial being placed its hand on the banker's lamp in front of Elijah. It flickered on, even though the back-up generator was still down.

After a moment of searching everywhere, the old man checked his vest pocket and produced a pair of trifocals with a shrug and grin. As he put them on, the thick lenses exaggerated his already unusually bright blue eyes. They gleamed with the intensity of fiery starlight, exuding vibrancy that seemed somehow anachronous to the tired and aging body they adorned.

Elijah was searching for the right way to start the conversation. Death read his mind and said, *"Let's skip the pleasantries Eli. It's your grandson, or at least his wellbeing, that accounts for my presence tonight."*

"Young Gabe? What does he have to do with this?"

Gabriel's ears perked up at the mention of his name.

"Let's just say that his survival outweighs the safety of both of us."

'That makes no sense... why would anyone care about me?' Gabriel thought to himself.

Upon hearing this thought, Death subtly shapeshifted into its two-faced aspect, Janus, affording it the ability to see in front and behind. The posterior face closed its eyes and spoke to Gabriel telepathically, *'All will be revealed in time, little one.'* Its anterior face never broke its gaze with Elijah, who was now nervously fidgeting with his fountain pen.

"Elijah, do you trust me?"

The old man looked up, now noticing the change in Death's appearance. He glanced behind the immortal, wondering what had caught its attention.

"Of course. With my life," Elijah said without hesitation.

"Good. It may come to that, but I hope not. The tidings I bring are dreadful, and I don't have room for doubt on your part."

The immortal paused and read Elijah's eyes. The professor donned his best poker face, but the deity sensed his fear.

"I received your call for help—one that I've been expecting, I might add. Surely you must know that things are worse than you originally thought?"

"You mean, about Björn?"

"Yes. I'm afraid so. Tell me what you know."

"Only what the State Propaganda Bureau reported. It looks like there was some sort of fire at his lab. Everything was destroyed, including his body."

"That does not check with my information."

The immortal scanned the professor's office and locked its anterior gaze on a cracked window behind Elijah.

"Were you not burgled last week?" Death asked.

"Yes. It was quite upsetting—I lost valuable artifacts and research."

"The artifacts that were stolen... were they pertaining to The Black Box?"

Elijah said nothing, and tried to avert the immortal's fiery stare.

'What Black Box?' Gabriel thought.

Death's posterior eyes opened as it fixed its sight on the crawlspace.

'Something you need not know about yet,' it warned Gabriel.

Its lips did not move, but he heard it speaking in his mind.

Its anterior face then began speaking to Elijah telepathically in an effort to keep their conversation private.

'Don't toy with me, Eli... not tonight. I know Corpus Tenebrae sits under the cinders in your fireplace... I feel its fingers reaching towards us even now.'

The old man followed the immortal's lead and began communicating with thought rather than speech.

'Yes. *The Body of Darkness* came into our hands, quite by accident...'

Although he missed bits and pieces, Gabriel was eventually able to tune into the telepathic dialogue. Everything was faint, as if he was listening to a whisper across the room, but he caught the salient parts of the conversation.

Death moved a few papers and easily found Elijah's attaché.

'And here lay Björn's handwritten notes, no?'

Elijah shifted his eyes away from the immortal in shame.

'You are the Steward of Sidera and nothing more. What were you doing meddling with Tenebrae? You took an oath, did you not?'

'You know me well enough to know I had no intention of using that... that... *thing*. However, I like to know what I'm destroying before I send it into the aether. By the time we discovered its true nature, it was too late; Björn was consumed and obsessed by its contents.'

'I'm sorry I spoke harshly. You were right not to destroy it—in fact, you couldn't have done so even if you'd tried. But, surely you know that you should have called for me earlier.'

'Yes, I realize that now, of course. Unfortunately, curiosity stole the life of my former protégé before I could do that. I don't want the same to happen to me now. Please, friend, take it away from me.'

'I have no want or need for such a device. There is one in my family, however, who is strong enough to store this until Gabriel is ready to retrieve it.'

'Me?' Gabriel thought to himself. 'What can I possibly do with it?'

'You'd be wise to learn from your grandfather... curiosity can be a dangerous thing,' Death answered back telepathically, now fully aware that Gabriel was eavesdropping.

The shapeshifter waved its hands; the contents of the fireplace —cinders and all—phased into another dimension, taking *Tenebrae* with them.

"There. It is safe for now, old man," it said aloud, realizing that a psychic conversation would not shield Gabriel. *"Trust me when I say that some things are better left unknown... at least until humankind has ascended."*

Elijah turned white.

"Yes, ascension is inevitable. But your student has not ascended... quite the opposite, I'm afraid."

"What's become of him, then?" Elijah asked.

"What you heard regarding Björn through the State Propaganda Bureau was just that: spin. You'd have to go to The Center to read the full report. Their M-8 Agents alone know the truth. And they will never release this information."

"Wait—Björn survived? He's alive?"

"In a manner of speaking. His body is spent; that part of the report was accurate. By all accounts he should have died. Unfortunately for him, the ritual allowed him to cheat Death. He attained his precious immortality, but only providing that he feeds—and very soon."

"Feeds?"

"You heard me."

"So Björn is tantamount to some sort of vampire?"

Gabriel muffled a gasp.

"Aye, your comparison is analogous; instead of blood, Björn consumes something you might call 'livskraft' in your native tongue —it's also known as prana, the vital, cosmic life force that courses through all living things. Revenants like Björn have popped up over the millennia. 'Vampire' is a recent and overly romantic description for my liking. In Björn's case, 'pawn' would be more descriptive, for he is no longer in control of his body. Make no mistake; there exists no glamour here. Björn exchanged freedom for immortality. His splintered soul opened an earthbound portal through which The Shadows entered. Now **they** *pull the strings, and he is but a lich and a puppet—a pawn, as I said earlier. The Shadows controlling Björn*

are doing so because he acts as a battery for them... But his life force is spent. Your goal now is to sever the connection to The Shadows and bring his soul back into the Light before he feeds again."

The immortal's posterior eyes welled with emotion for a moment.

"There's one more thing you must know..."

Elijah nodded.

"The Shadows need a bigger energy source—something that will allow all of them to enter this planet. You see, they gain an additional boon from feeding on people with great life potential. Removing a soul from its path creates disturbances in the fabric of spacetime. This disturbance results in more energy, which gives the revenant—or more accurately, The Shadows that control it—more power. Björn was a first step towards The Shadows re-emerging from their exile. He was meant to be a great teacher on this planet, but The Shadows stole that future away from him. This is precisely why The Shadows will use Björn to stop Gabriel from fulfilling his destiny; your grandson's future shines brighter than you could ever imagine. Feeding on him would create, quite literally, a monster that perhaps even I couldn't contain."

'Impossible—I'm nothing but a seven-year-old, and not a very popular one at that,' Gabriel thought to himself.

Death intuitively glanced at Elijah's attaché. At the same time, Elijah felt pins and needles on the top of his head as it scanned his consciousness.

"Most interesting, and most fortunate for us! I see Björn didn't get all of your research, and he didn't get possession of Tenebrae. Unfortunately for him, there is a catch to the dark magic he used, as there always is. Björn's power comes at a great cost, indeed. His hunger will increase exponentially with each attack until it becomes insatiable, while his soul becomes more and more splintered. Like my Shadow brethren, he will not stop until everything in his path is

consumed, or worse, he consumes himself into nonexistence. If the latter happens, there is no return for him, at least not as we now know him. And by that time, The Seven Shadows will have re-emerged, spelling certain doom for not only this planet, but all life."

"Wait... Nonexistence?"

"Yes. There is such a thing."

"So he's damned?"

"You assume too much of your deities, old man. Salvation and damnation are always in the hand of the individual. Deities are merely agents of your own free will... guides to illuminate the path so you can see all your choices."

The immortal pointed to a wedding ring on Elijah's finger.

"Take that diamond for instance... It was once carbon. Heat, pressure and time created something new, with stronger bonds, and a greater capacity to reflect light than its previous incarnation. Sometimes, elements have to be rearranged several times in order to reach their full potential. This is what normally happens to a soul with reincarnation. Each life it learns something that changes its composition, making it stronger, wiser and clearer.

"Greed, anger, jealousy, and a thirst for power—all these things are the tools of The Shadows. They will, if left unchecked, cause a soul to splinter. At a certain point, the gravity of these deeds wears on the integrity of the soul's structure and it will be unable to sustain itself. After all, the soul is a nucleus; it is the glue that holds us together as we experience all of our lives, and it's the home to which we return at the journey's end. If it's repeatedly splintered, the soul will eventually become... unbound. Its power and knowledge will then disperse back into the Universe... back to the source from which it came."

"So that's it... Björn will just fade away?"

"Not exactly. That which is made can never truly be unmade. Transmuted, yes, but not completely obliterated. Take a supernova;

the death of a star brings new elements, new planets and new life. The destruction of a soul is no different. If he meets this fate, the bonds that hold Björn's spirit together may come undone, releasing the matter back into the cosmos. The energy that once resonated in his soul will then be re-assembled and re-imagined. Unless, of course, you can redeem him.

"In the case of Björn, there is a glimmer of hope. Your protégé has not been fully seduced by The Shadows. There is Light in his heart. I feel it, even now—struggling to be free of their grip. You must kindle that Light."

"And there's no price to pay for karmic crimes—for conspiring to murder me, or worse, my grandson?"

"The Universe deals out justice more dispassionately and more patiently than humans, Eli. If Björn meets this fate, it's a blessing and a curse. I suppose that whatever remains of his essence will start anew, perhaps as a mineral or a single-celled organism in the primordial ooze on some new planet—starting the slow progression from ignorance and isolation to enlightenment. Yes, he gets a clean slate, but he'll be fifteen billion years behind the rest of the souls that sprang forth when this cosmos started—a babe in the woods, with an eternity of growing up to do. I doubt many people would aspire to that fate, Björn especially. But with this future, there is hope... hope that perhaps he'll eventually transform into something more beautiful, like a baby star, or the diamond on your finger.

"Again, your goal should be redeeming him to the Light, not allowing him to spiral further into The Shadows' grip. I offer this knowledge as inspiration to save him, and to save all life in the Known Universe in the process. His soul can only be destroyed if he allows it to be. Don't allow him to do that to himself. Use the weapon Shadows fear most—love."

Death raised its hands and began to sing something under its breath. As brilliant light sprang forth from its fingertips, the immortal began to trace an energetic seal above Elijah's head in the shape of a circumscribed hexagram with a small point in the center. The professor knew it well, it was The Seal of The Six Stars.

"Elijah, old friend, you know that, because of my function, I can't intercede personally in human matters like this. But I can give you the means with which to defend yourself."

The celestial being reached into its coat pocket and produced a small bauble. The object sparkled and glowed with a purple light. The immortal used a small silk handkerchief to hand it to Elijah, all the time making sure not to touch its surface.

"What is this?"

"It's a powerful stellar remnant, one which facilitates transformation. I recently cut the crystal again and programmed it in such a way that it works as a sort of energy amp. It will take source energy and multiply it threefold."

Elijah held the crystal by the attached chain and peered into the myriad facets. Strange runes and hieroglyphs were engraved on each, some too small to make out, even with trifocals. He held the crystal in his palm and watched with wonder as it grew brighter and brighter, instantly buoyed by his own energy, just as the immortal said it would be.

He quickly placed it back in the safety of the handkerchief and gazed quizzically at his friend.

"Is this what I think it is? A sort of weapon?"

"You think too narrowly, and too humanly, old man. It functions as either a charm or a weapon, depending on the wielder. It was made from the essence of a brilliant star at the moment of its death."

"How do I program it?" Elijah asked.

"With thought, prayer or incantation. It matters not; just keep the words and intention simple and pure. Remember that fear and doubt are the great equalizers. If you even entertain the thought of defeat, you've already surrendered your power. Stay strong in your resolve and remember that Björn still loves you. Reach for that love. You may be able to save him if you can find it. Redemption should

always be the goal, not revenge. At the very least, you'll buy your-self some time."

The immortal cocked its head, listening to one of Elijah's myriad thoughts.

"You needn't worry about the boy. Should you fail, I'll make sure he's safe—even if I have to use **unconventional** *methods."*

Without further delay, Death opened the window and shapeshifted into a fiery phoenix as it flew into the stormy sky above.

Elijah placed the bauble in his hands. In a voice that was barely audible, he whispered an incantation that he made up on the spot:

"Across the Universe,
Beyond the sea—
Oh purest light,
I call on thee!
Protect my heart and soul from harm,
And imbue my light inside this charm.
Ancient stardust that constitutes me:
Expand my energy
And multiply by three."

The crystal started to pulse and glow with renewed life.

The old man walked over to the wood stove in the living room near the foyer. He rekindled the fire and threw the remaining research into the flames, one sheet at a time. As he watched the last two years of his life burning, he felt an uneasiness wash over his body.

Björn was near.

4

THE REDEMPTION OF BJÖRN

Sheets of rain relentlessly pounded against the rooftop like a wild stampede. Gabriel wondered if the mythic stallion Sleipnir was here to whisk someone to the Underworld. Given the fact he'd just met a celestial deity, the existence of an eight-legged horse was no longer a leap of faith; anything was possible.

If the storm outside seemed loud, the silence inside was absolutely deafening. Elijah paced nervously for several moments until a cold chill ran down his spine.

"I must warn Gabriel!" he said under his breath.

The old man rushed into the foyer and began climbing the spiral staircase.

With no time to fetch a torch, he grabbed a wooden cane propped against the door and proclaimed, "Tu lumine astra incantare!"

The cane began to glow until it emitted rays of silver starlight, which bathed everything in the vicinity. As Elijah looked up, the blood drained from his face.

An amorphous, vaporous cloud descended like a veil of

shadows and hovered at the top of the stairs. He surmised it to be an astral projection of some sort. At first, it looked like a bear; then it began to morph. Long tentacles undulated in every direction... reaching and searching towards the attic bedroom.

"Vem där? Who's there?"

Instead of retracting, the entity grew in size and became completely opaque. It offered no reply.

Whatever it was, Elijah felt that the projection somehow came from Björn's mind. Its initial form, after all, resembled his totem. His name, Björn, also translated to bear. His mother named him after Ursa Major, the Great Bear in the sky. She dreamed that her son would grow up to be strong and stay true to the Light, just like the steadfast constellation.

"Reveal yourself, *wraith*, or I swear upon the Light that I'll banish thee!"

The shadowy creature remained silent.

"So be it," Elijah said.

He closed his eyes, tuned-in psychically and sang four lines from a sacred mantra. He opened his right hand and an arc of golden auric light sprang forth, taking on the shape of a sword. This energetic blade moved through the wraith, eviscerating and banishing it into dust.

The pungent smell of brimstone wafted through the rafters in its wake.

Upon uttering the last three words, "Jai Te Gang," the sword returned to his hand like a boomerang. He held it reverently and offered gratitude. Slowly, the sword shimmered and was absorbed into his aura.

As he peered into the empty attic bedroom, the old man intuited that Gabriel was safely ensconced somewhere else in the cabin.

"Atta boy," he whispered to himself.

Following his own hunch, Elijah leaned over the bannister and called out to his grandson, "Gabe, I know you're here... *hidden.* Keep still and cloak yourself! A Wolf is upon us."

Elijah's intuition was confirmed with three loud knocks at the door. They ricocheted through the cabin like gunshots.

Gabriel obeyed his grandfather's wishes and worked up an impromptu spell:

"In the name of Himlens Väktare, The Sky Guardians of Old,
For which songs were sung, and legends told—
Shield me well, with Aldebaran's light,
Grant me haven on this dark, dark night!"

Gabriel held out his left hand and imagined he was wielding Aldebaran's fabled shield, *Gudsköld* itself—a weapon rumored to grant its champion invisibility. Much to his amazement, a great power surged through his hand until it formed an etheric shield twice his size. As he pulled it close to his body, Gabriel's energy faded into the twilight—and not a moment too soon.

Björn knocked again; this time the doorframe rattled and came loose.

Elijah carefully hid the crystal talisman under his vest and steadied his resolve.

"*ALL RIGHT,* ALREADY!" he called out. His voice faltered a bit.

The old man slowly approached the door and unlatched the peephole. His throat seized as he gazed outside.

"Impossible!" he said with a strained whisper.

With shaky hands, the old man clumsily secured the deadbolt and stepped back, almost tripping in the process. An expression of absolute terror flashed across his face. Gabriel had never seen his grandfather so shaken.

Some sort of creature on the other side let out a wicked laugh.

A shadow slid underneath the front door. Much to Elijah's horror, it slithered onto the wall, until it was nearly ten feet tall.

The old man instinctively backed up towards the kitchen, in the hopes of using the back door for an escape.

"Not so fast," a gravelly voice commanded.

Björn—or more accurately, whatever had become of him—stepped through his shadow and entered the old cabin. The revenant was only vaguely human in appearance, wearing its skin with little care or concern of how it looked—as if the body was just some annoying shell it was forced to use to travel in the physical plane. The creature's face was a terrible shade of grey—like the ashes leftover from a fire, dreadfully spent and lifeless. Its eyes were also listless and glassy.

As the lich approached Elijah, it stopped dead in its tracks. It cringed and writhed with pain, tortured by an unseen force.

The Seal of The Six Stars materialized above Elijah's head. As it began to shine, it revealed several other protective symbols in the vicinity.

Over the years, Elijah decorated the foyer with dozens of amulets from across the world. Ancient hamsas, ankhs, crosses and Stars of David decorated the walls. Now, they began to magically glow and pulse with the same energy that illuminated The Seal above Elijah.

Björn quickly retreated from the sanctified space, but not before yanking Elijah along with him. It stabbed its black fingernails deep into Elijah's skin and dragged the old man by the arms into the courtyard.

As soon as they were outside, Björn let go and laughed. Lightning illuminated the creature's face, revealing a crooked smile; rotten, broken teeth glistened all the while.

"By the gods! Björn, what have you become?" Elijah said, barely finding the breath to get the words out.

"We have become something more powerful than you," Björn

boasted. "We wasted so many years helping you with your crazy books. If people only knew some of the secrets you've kept locked up in that dusty library of yours! You could rule the world. But instead, your cowardly head is stuck in the clouds. You're so consumed with chasing spaceships, ghosts and shooting stars that you've become blind to the opportunities."

The old man backed up slowly, realizing he was pinned into a corner.

"Perhaps... but better to be blinded by the light of truth than seduced by the half-truths of The Shadows."

"Your blind faith does you a disservice, Elijah. We have seen the truth, and it has *nothing* to do with Light."

Elijah tried to inconspicuously grab the amulet, but Björn was watching his every move.

"You call *me* a fool, Björn, but have you looked in a mirror lately? Didn't you learn anything in all those years as my protégé? Nothing is free! At what price have you gained this power? You beg, steal and trick others, while your own light fades to little more than a spark. Take pause and listen to your intuition. You'll see that what I say is so. It's not too late to atone and reverse this, Björn. I've met one of The Star Gods—it may have the power to help you."

For a moment the creature paused, contemplating its mentor's warning.

"That's a fool's bargain, old man. You ask too much. Sacrifice all that we have learned and surrender to some forgotten deity? Nay. You may have found The Star Gods, but we've begun the Rites of Ascension. When we are done, *we* will take *our* place in the sky."

The revenant pushed Elijah to the ground and pinned his arms against the cold concrete.

The old man made one last attempt at reasoning with the creature.

"Ascension? You're about as far away from being an ascended

entity as I've ever seen. Also... Why are you referring to yourself plurally as 'we,' Björn? Who or what are you?"

The creature produced a filthy grin. "*We* are a pupil of *The Three That Became One*... The Great Shadow King and Ruiner who rules beneath The Sea of Hunger."

"Pupil? You're nothing more than an empty vessel that sucks life from more radiant beings. Your so-called power is an illusion, Björn, and I reject it."

"You *reject* it?"

The creature let out a hideous laugh; it was whispery and high pitched, like squealing car breaks.

"*We* reject *you*, Elijah. We reject you and your powerless Star Gods. Oh, and one more thing... *Björn* is not our name anymore."

Its lifeless eyes grew dark as coal and Elijah could feel a hunger welling inside. Like a predator, the creature was using fear and intimidation to try to subjugate Elijah.

"Call us Es—"

"Spare me! You are nothing but a shattered shell of the man I loved as my own son. You do Björn a disservice."

"SILENCE!" it screamed.

The revenant dug one fist into Elijah's stomach, nails first, while it held the other hand over his forehead. Elijah winced. Blue, green and indigo light coursed into the wraith's fingers as it siphoned energy from Elijah's aura. He struggled without avail; the beast had him in a death grip.

Gabriel screamed when he saw his grandfather in its clutches. He released his invisibility spell and stepped outside.

"**STOP IT!**" he said bravely with a disembodied voice that boomed above the cabin and courtyard.

He was no longer speaking with his body but with his mind, invoking **STJÄRNLJUS**, an elevated version of **Gudsrösten, The Divine Tongue**. It was louder and more commanding than Gabriel's physical voice.

Pure golden light shone in an arc above him.

The revenant winced in his presence.

"LEAVE HIM ALONE! IT'S ME YOU WANT!" Gabriel commanded with a ferocious roar.

The words echoed and rumbled like thunder several moments after they were uttered.

Falling under the spell of Gabriel's words, Björn involuntarily loosened its grip on Elijah.

Lightning flashed again, simultaneously illuminating the court-yard and revealing the doppelgänger's true metaphysical form to both Elijah and to Gabriel. Multiple tentacles emerged from Björn's black aura. The energetic arms phased in and out of the dimension and appeared to be capable of manipulating physical objects.

The revenant threw a slithering tentacle towards the boy and missed by a small margin. The familiar smell of sulfur hung in the air as the creature continued to shift into its true form.

The old man had just enough time to grab the sacred amulet from his coat pocket.

"By the power of light and love threefold,
I illuminate thee like the stars of old!"

The crystal amplified Elijah's inner light, just as the immortal said it would. As he placed the amulet over his heart, a beam of light spread between Elijah and the vampire.

In that moment, something unbelievable happened: Björn's uncorrupted soul jumped out of his body. It took on the shape of an enormous bear; each point in its translucent body was illuminated by glowing orbs of energy, much like a constellation in the sky. Finally, at the end of his life, Björn lived up to his namesake—he was a ferociously luminous creature, a being of light... a guardian.

Björn's Great Bear Spirit loomed over his broken body and he held it down with a mighty paw. Dark tentacles from the Shadow fought back tirelessly. Björn's soul spoke to Elijah and Gabriel telepathically.

'Forgive me, Stewards for succumbing to the darkness. I especially failed you, dear Elijah, and for that I'll be eternally sorry. But I have no time for sadness tonight. Even now, The Three That Became One are reclaiming my ruined body. You have saved my soul, but I alone must face my Shadow counterpart. Otherwise, all is lost. You know I'm right, Elijah. Even now, *they* are coming, planning to use my body as a portal. Let me clean up the mess I made before it's too late.'

An ear-shattering crash of thunder sounded above as a gigantic Shadow passed over the Earth. A face began to emerge in the sky above. Its eyes were as large as a city and its mouth seemed capable of devouring the moon itself. It began to descend towards Björn's reanimated body.

The Great Bear Spirit reached its right paw towards Elijah and the old man willingly handed the amulet to the spirit of his protégé.

"Thank you, Eli, for freeing my spirit," The Great Bear said as it turned around, facing its darker half.

Much to the surprise of Gabriel, Björn's spirit dived head-first into its body, briefly overcoming The Shadow that possessed it. In his final act of redemption, Björn placed the amulet around the neck of his corpse before his spirit faded into the night sky, briefly creating a bear-like constellation before disappearing forever.

The lich regained control over Björn's corpse and greedily clutched the amulet, unable to control its own hunger for power. The crystal betrayed the lich, however, just as Death predicted it would. The amulet grew darker and darker until it began to consume energy instead of emitting it. The creature could not let go now even if it tried. Elijah watched in dread as the vampire's desire to feed was reflected onto itself. The reanimated corpse could not fight the power of the crystal, nor the hunger that was fueling it.

An ear-shattering crash of thunder sounded in the heavens as the lich consumed its own life essence and the reanimated body evaporated into mist, banishing the menacing Shadow back to its own dimension in the process.

The crystal bauble fell to the ground, breaking into three smoldering shards.

"Gabriel? Gabe! Are you okay?" Elijah said with great effort, barely able to push the air through his lungs.

The old man's shirt was soaked in blood and his aura was flickering like a candle in the wind.

"Yes... I'm fine!" Gabriel said.

"Good... good, my boy. That's all that matters. I couldn't leave without—"

"*Leave?* You're not going anywhere," Gabriel said. "Let me call for—"

"No! There's no time, Gabe. I just needed to say—"

Elijah lost his footing. He fell down and hit the pavement, headfirst, with a thud. The wound in his stomach proved to be a mortal one, and his body could no longer fight back.

"Grandpa? *Grandpa?!*" Gabriel screamed.

Elijah did not answer.

Gabriel held his grandfather's hand. For a brief second, Elijah squeezed it before his spirit passed into the night.

Gabriel hugged the lifeless body and sobbed uncontrollably.

Elijah was gone.

5

A SONG FOR AKASHA

G abriel slumped forward, staring at his grandfather's body. Numbed by a combination of sadness, cold and shock, he wasn't sure where his tears ended and the raindrops began.

In this moment of despair, Gabriel felt a hand caress his cheek, wiping away the tears. A pleasant, warm energy radiated through his body. His sadness subsided, but anger soon began to swell in his heart.

"What just happened?" Gabriel demanded, with bloodshot eyes.

"Something terrible—and something beautiful," Akaal said.

"Tonight we lost not one, but two of our fiercest guardians. However, Elijah and Björn's acts of self-sacrifice and free will prove what I've always known—humankind can do amazing things when it's in the presence of darkness. By saving you, they've restored hope—hope that we may find my missing brother and end this war once and for all.

Unfortunately, The Shadows—particularly the ones that orchestrated Björn's demise—still live on. In fact, one of them is here on the planet, even as we speak."

"So we're just going to let it go?"

The being shook its head in disapproval.

"Always so impatient... Something you share in common with Björn. Be careful with that, young Steward, or it will be your undoing. I know you want to face The Shadows —and you will, but to do so now would spell certain doom. Your heart is broken, and you mustn't fight a Shadow with Shadow energy. Redemption should always be the goal, not revenge. Björn taught us that lesson tonight. Instead of shattering his soul, he reclaimed it. For all the harm he caused, he saved the Known Universe as well. Forgiveness is a tenet of The Seven Stars, and we will help heal his soul, as well as Elijah's. To that end, I have work here to do. Step aside for a moment."

Death closed its eyes and knelt down next to Elijah. Slowly, the celestial being raised its hands towards the sky and started to sing a single word three times.

"Aaaah-kaaaaaaaaaaaaaaal!"

The immortal repeated this again and again, using a slightly different octave every time.

Each recitation hung in the atmosphere, creating a heavenly host of voices in the night sky. The cumulative vibration pushed the storm farther and farther away until the clouds receded completely. Gradually, the stars began to reappear, as well, as if a dark spell was lifted.

Gabriel intuited that *Akaal* was the being's true name. He now understood why it kept its name a secret... its very utterance was infused with great power and the effects were manifold, depending on the applied intention.

As the echoes subsided, a majestic nimbus radiated above, or perhaps directly from the immortal's head, shining as brightly as the mid-day sun. Illuminated by its own light, the numinous being now ceased to phase in and out of the dimension. It appeared as if all of its aspects were wholly present and fully concentrated on this moment in time, lending it an air that was both stately and statuesque. As it opened its eyes, pure white light surged out of the sockets, which now looked larger than Gabriel remembered. The light generated tangible heat that warmed Gabriel's skin and removed the chill from his bones. Without needing confirmation, he realized he was in the presence of The Angel of Death, or more accurately, Transformation.

"*Stand back, little one. As a Steward of the Light, Elijah deserves a proper rite of passage.*"

Akaal placed the spent crystal shards in one hand and gently laid its other hand on Elijah's heart.

> "*By the Light that forged this ancient stone*
> *I cleanse this soul... blood, flesh and bone.*"

The three shards flickered once more, fusing together with great heat and energy, and then the crystal went forever dim. Akaal moved the crystal slowly across the old man's body, removing the befouled energy of Björn. By the time Akaal finished the ritual, the smoky crystal darkened even further, until it resembled obsidian or coal.

The immortal knelt down and kissed Elijah's lips. A flash of light illuminated the courtyard as the old man's body and spirit returned to pure energy, leaving only a thin coating of ash and stardust behind.

"*He is one with the Light now. And he will be with you always,*" Akaal said.

Gabriel wiped his tears dry and gazed in wonderment at the being before him.

"I'm not sure whether you're a magician or an angel."

"*Why must they be mutually exclusive, Gabriel? Thoughts are power. Words are manifestations of that power. Combine the cata-lysts of love, light and faith, and you have magic. As your grandfa-ther once said, magic is real. Whether it's divine or befouled depends completely on the intention; substitute hate, fear or jeal-ousy as the catalysts and you have darker magic—but magic none-theless."*

Akaal placed the carbonized star remnant into a handkerchief and crushed it into dust. As it was pulverized, Gabriel felt an inex-plicable tremor of sadness and grief wash over his body. He realized it wasn't his own emotion, but that of the supernatural being beside him. It had clearly sacrificed part of its former self for the ceremony.

For a moment, it gazed up at the heavens and its eyes dimmed.

"You must have been a lovely star," Gabriel said, following his hunch. "You were the *First*, were you not?"

The immortal's eyes welled up, not with tears, but with dozens of tiny particles of light. Each twinkled and then faded as quickly as it appeared.

"I'm impressed, child, and it takes a lot to impress me. Yes, I was one of the brightest stars to ever walk the heavens. Mind you, this was long, long ago, before this cosmos existed. And, yes, I was (and I still am) The First Star of the original Fourteen, and the eldest of The Luminous Ones—the stars who remained true to the Light."

"The... *transformation* you underwent... I get the feeling that it wasn't voluntary?"

"It was a matter of conscience. Sometimes you're presented with a situation and, well, you just have to do something, even if it means sacrificing yourself for the greater good. Not unlike what you did for your grandfather tonight."

Gabriel blushed.

"As you said, I had no choice."

"You always have a choice; that's what makes it so impressive," Akaal said with genuine admiration.

"It almost sounds like you were a soldier?" Gabriel interjected, deflecting the attention back to the immortal.

"A soldier or a fool," it said with a sigh.

"You were a *soldier*. The question is why were you fighting?" The star smiled and its eyes twinkled, quite literally.

"Yes, I suppose you are right. I was fighting a futile war. You see, a single, parasitic thought entered the minds of seven of my brothers and sisters. It reverberated until it transformed them into The Seven Shadows, and until it ultimately resulted in the demise of The Old World."

"One thought was capable of that?" Gabriel asked in awe.

"Aye. That and much more. In the depths of their despair— which itself was fueled by an insatiable desire to destroy and consume—The Seven Shadows crafted Brahmāstra, a terrifying psychic weapon capable of wiping out entire worlds."

"The weapon... what became of it?"

"I've spoken to the Sky Guardian Aldebaran, the eldest member of Himlens Väktare. According to his army, the weapon still exists, and with The Seven Shadows' powers growing, your planet is in danger. In fact, All Known Worlds are in peril."

"But... wait... the future is always shifting—at least, that's what Grandpa Elijah said. Isn't there a way to stop this?" Gabriel asked. He felt a sharp pain in the pit of his stomach. He knew, somehow, he'd be swept into this cosmic war.

"You ask a question, yet you already know the answer. You are The Prophesied One. The Gods may have started this war, but our essence is strewn amidst our creations. Only The Mortal Channel, a Starchild, can help locate The Seventh Star. Together, my family and I will accompany you on this quest."

Gabriel began to cry, unexpectedly. Perhaps it was the loss of his grandfather, or perhaps he simply felt overwhelmed by all the information.

"This can't be happening," Gabriel said to himself in disbelief. "Can you make the pain stop?"

"Life is given context by Death, and pain is something we all must experience. Sadly, no, I cannot take away the feeling of loss— but I can show you something that may help you understand why Elijah's death was not in vain. Would you like that?"

Gabriel nodded as he wiped his tear-stained cheeks.

"As you wish. Look into my eyes," Akaal said.

Gabriel stared deeply into the immortal's glowing eyes. Billions of tiny lights coalesced in its eye sockets, like elliptical galaxies. They hypnotically pulsed and surged with energy. Within them, the boy could see eternity. A feeling of vertigo crept up on him, as if he were riding a rollercoaster. At that moment, Gabriel realized that he was somehow moving through time and space, perhaps through some alien form of astral projection. Indeed, Earthly words and thoughts seemed inadequate to articulate the experience. Somewhere along the journey, his consciousness melded with Akaal's. He could see, hear and feel everything through the immortal.

As the celestial being looked around, Gabriel tried to absorb what he was seeing through Akaal's ancient eyes. If it were possible for light to collect and flow like a river, then this was exactly what was happening, or it was the best approximation his mind allowed. Liquid currents of light rippled and coursed infinitely, not just to the horizon, but in all directions—further than his eyes or mind could comprehend. Gabriel intuited that the sea of light wasn't merely stretching to infinity; it *was infinity itself.* He was only seeing the tip of a very, very large iceberg.

Akaal arbitrarily picked one of the overlapping planes and knelt down. Suddenly, everything came into clearer focus. Gabriel was grateful, as this helped his mortal mind perceive a single plane of energy, rather than the myriad that stretched in every direction.

Next, Akaal took a deep breath and gently touched the sea with its right hand, making its presence known. A beautiful elongated note followed. Ribbons of energy danced outward into the limitless horizon as excited light particles reacted to the sound. Much to Gabriel's surprise, the sea was both sentient and alive. A series of high-pitched musical tones emerged each time the star placed its hand on the surface, as if it were playing a harp or piano. The star answered the sea with a vocal refrain, adding to the melodic interchange. The song continued for several moments—calm at first, then building to a gentle crescendo. Although Gabriel was experiencing everything through the consciousness of the star, the exact details of the song were not revealed to him. Based on the sounds of the musical exchange, he intuited that the two beings were in a heated discussion.

After a long pause, a wave moved towards Akaal. It swelled to great heights, forming some sort of enormous energetic tidal wave. The wave forked into three distinct faces, although they were far from human. From the looks of it, they represented the three phases of life. The first was that of an infant; its face and eyes were dewy and bright. It was kind, naïve and welcoming. The second was fashioned after a Valkyrie—strong, handsome and wise. The third face was some sort of alien skeleton, perhaps that of a dragon. The Three Faces looked at Akaal and began to harmonize on a single note.

Akaal stood its ground and answered the celestial inquisition.

"The boy seeing through my eyes is known as Gabriel, grandson to our mutual friend Elijah, whose energy now flows in your endless sea. Gabriel is The Last Steward, if The Prophecy holds true."

The Three Faces squinted their eyes. Turbulent crimson waves swelled and surrounded Akaal.

"Enough, sister," it said. Its words ricocheted through the sea, pushing everything back.

Akaal stood tall, outstretching its wings. It grew taller than The Three Faces—so tall that it seemed to fill all of eternity. Then, its eyes glared as brightly as all the stars in the Universe. If Gabriel were present in physical form, he would have wept in awe and terror.

"I may not be Eternal, but I am an Immortal and Firstborn... The First of the First. I've kept true to the Light, even in the face of countless darkness. I've walked endless souls into this dimension, souls that were taken by The Shadows. I will not be denied this request. The boy deserves to see the truth. We must help him find Hope, or else risk losing it ourselves."

The Three Faces looked at one another and then at Akaal, continuing some secret psychic dialogue with The Angel of Death.

"Yes, of course, I am well aware that this is unusual, Akasha... against protocol, even... but these rules were made to be broken, were they not? With your permission, we seek a glimpse into your Great Mirror."

The light currents returned to their normal golden hue and the waves relented. The Three Faces nodded.

Akaal relaxed its stance and became a somewhat more normal size. It folded its wings and knelt down before speaking aloud, this time to Gabriel.

"I have good news, little one. We've been granted access."

'Access to *what*?' Gabriel wondered. 'Where are we?'

He merely thought the words and the star heard him. It answered telepathically as well.

*'Hmmm... it's less of a **where** and more of a **who**, though arguably both. And because of this Eternal being's function, the question **when** is also appropriate. You see, in my world, you can be a person, place and a thing—they're all interchangeable realities.'*

'Then *who*, *when* or *where* the heck is this?' Gabriel thought, a bit perplexed and annoyed at the ambiguity.

'It's complicated but I'll do my best.

*'First the **When**... we are literally gazing into Eternity through the lens of an Eternal being... it's simultaneously the past, present*

*and future here. As I said, this dimension is both a **Who** and a **Where.***

*'Now, let's cover the **Who**... it's named after a cosmic being who calls herself Akasha or sometimes Aeon. Humans know her simply as Time. As a requisite of her function, Akasha is one of The Eternals; Time has always existed and always will. Thus, Akasha is older than everything, since we [mortals and immortals alike] have a starting point on her continuum.*

*'Finally, the **Where**... this dimension is one of Akasha's aspects, and this never-ending sea is an extension of her consciousness. Think of it as a cosmic two-way mirror into the fabric of time and space. Here, time flows and collects like water. Within the depths of Akasha's memory we can observe all that was and all that is. You see... she is the great record keeper. Nothing escapes her vision. Nothing.'*

'So we're literally in her head?'

'In the same way you're in mine, yes. Look deep within the depths of Akasha's waters and you will understand.'

Without any further explanation or warning, the star jumped headfirst into The Akashic Sea. Its viscous plasma was comprised of densely-packed light-emitting particles. Each seemed to contain a binary datum. Together, they permanently stored the life and death records of all living organisms, planets, galaxies, universes and dimensions. As each living thing came to pass, a new particle began to glow. Every sparkle seemed all the more poignant now.

The world was a much larger place than Gabriel had ever imagined.

"Akasha, we are ready," the star said.

A myriad of particles surrounding the immortal synchronously faded to black, creating an empty canvas.

Akaal took a deep breath and brought the sea into its lungs. As it exhaled, the otherwise dark particles around it were excited and began to coruscate. One by one they formed a three-dimensional view of the past, rippling gently.

The star pointed to the beginning of its world. Gabriel stared with awe as an ancient cosmos burst out of a singular point of energy.

"The First World was a world of fire and light."

'Were there no life forms?' Gabriel wondered.

"Yes and no," Akaal replied. *"Intelligence existed, as did life, but it would be unrecognizable to you. Comets, moons and asteroids roamed the skies and contributed to the great chorus of creation. Music was the lingua franca, telepathy was ubiquitous, and speech was unnecessary."*

'You mean to say everything was self-aware?'

"Yes, for a time, all things were awake. Sadly, after The Shadows came many lost their voices and went silent, much like your Moon—and soon, your Sun.

"Now, let's fast-forward to a pivotal moment in my history... the turning point of our battle with The Great Devourer."

Gabriel watched as a mighty comet futilely attempted to escape the gravitational pull of the singularity. This was no normal comet —it was at least as large as Earth's Sun. Like all creations in The Old World, it was sentient. So, it wasn't surprising that, as its body was torn into tiny shards of ice, it let out a final psychic scream, one that caused The First Star to weep. This was the last creation crafted by The Luminous Ones. With it gone, the only light that existed was their own. Silence fell in The Old World.

It was at this point in Ragnarök that The First Star assumed its function as Transformation. The newly christened entity sounded a trumpet, and its siblings answered the call. First they arranged themselves into a six-pointed star, surrounding Transformation. Slowly, and with some reluctance, each star spiraled into the center point, like a pinwheel.

The Seven Stars moved with great speed and dove directly into the belly of The Great Devourer. It swallowed them whole, snuffing out all light, love and magic from The Old World.

The end had finally come.

The entire Akashic Dimension went dark for a moment, leaving the two alone in their thoughts.

The star wept, and Gabriel wept with it. Together, at the bottom of the sea, they understood one another. Gabriel felt the weight of Transformation's role—every life and every death passed through its hands—and the star now felt a sense of completeness and hope it hadn't felt in eons.

It inhaled and exhaled.

"I brought you here, not for tears, little one, but so you could see how we defeated The Darkness once before."

A tiny pinpoint of light appeared in the middle of The Akashic Sea. Gabriel understood that this was Hope, The Seventh Star. It shimmered briefly before a cataclysmic explosion of light and sound ripped through The Void.

The New World was born.

"This bit of knowledge is my gift to you, Gabriel: metamorphosis is a necessary mechanic (and outcome) of the Universe. Love, Transformation and Hope are agents of this metamorphosis. This is why we need to find The Seventh Star. This is why Elijah risked his life in the battle to find and protect it. Hope saved us once before, and Hope can do it again."

'I understand now,' Gabriel thought.

An unseen force pushed Akaal to the surface. The sea shifted colors, from golden to pure white as Akasha began to sing. The Three Faces were gone, but Gabriel could hear their voices now, intertwining and pulling at his heart and soul.

"Gabriel, Akasha has agreed to let you see a glimmer of what may be. It is her gift to you. See through my eyes."

Akaal knelt down and looked at the surface of The Akashic Sea, which was now as reflective as a mirror.

Although Gabriel was looking through the star's eyes, he saw his own reflection looking back. His face slowly began to age until it looked old, at least by a seven-year-old's standards. The Akashic Sea shimmered and revealed images from his future. Gabriel was marooned on an alien moon. Although he couldn't see the enemy-at-hand, he sensed its fear. The last thing he saw was a twisted fortress with three towers, two of which seemed to be literally clawing at the sky. Two red eyes appeared from atop a watchtower, and then he heard a scream from something deep beneath the fortress.

The images faded and Gabriel saw the face of Akaal in the water as it spoke aloud.

"Never fear the dark, for the dark is afraid of you, Gabriel. It knows what you may become. My family and I will return for you one day when you are ready. Until then, I need you to forget tonight."

The immortal kissed its finger and then touched its own reflection on The Akashic Sea. This released Gabriel's consciousness and the boy boomeranged back into his own body on Earth.

Gabriel now stood in front of Akaal, shaking in shock from what he'd just seen.

The immortal knew what it must do. Swiftly and compassionately, Akaal placed its hand on Gabriel's forehead. Its touch was electrifying and exhilarating—almost as if Gabriel was kissed by lightning.

It opened its glowing eyes and spoke to Gabriel in a singsong, cryptic rhyme.

"Under twilight's veil where night meets day,
The truth must slumber and these thoughts will stay.
When you're seven times three, what's bound will unravel...
And across time and space we both shall travel."

As the star lifted its hand from Gabriel's forehead, he started to lose consciousness.

It then whispered only two words, *"I'm sorry."*

Gabriel fell into Akaal's arms, forgetting all that he'd seen. As he slumbered that night, he rested easily with three truths. First, he had an unshakable feeling that magic was real. He also understood that his powers were important enough to develop. Finally, and most importantly, he no longer feared the dark.

PART III

GREYWOLF

PROLOGUE

While recovering his memories from the past, Gabriel suddenly flashed back to a pivotal moment in his life, seven years after Elijah's death. Left without any legal guardians, the young Steward became a ward of the State.

On his fourteenth birthday, Gabriel awaited his trial for the heinous metacrime of "nondisclosure"—hiding his psychic abilities from the autocratic government. Gabriel's fate was uncertain; he faced death, "rehabilitation," *or worse*, employment by the State.

6

SANCTUARY

Dateline: The California Youth Conservatory, near the San Diego Wastelands in the Earth Year Treble-Treble-Nine, Double-Nine, Three. (Seven Years Later).

From the outside, The California Youth Conservatory was bright and cheery. Brilliant bougainvillea vines twisted around the exterior of its granite halls, dancing in the sunlight like celestial trumpets. Their cheery shades of magenta, orange and white covered up a poorly-kept secret: the so-called Conservatory was nothing more than a half-way house for underage metacriminals. Its ironic and contradictory name was yet another example of The Propaganda Bureau's weaponization of language. Like all branches of the State OmniParty, The Bureau aimed to confuse, redirect and sometimes erase the facts outright. Language was but a casualty in the State's ongoing war to control everything, right down to the thoughts in people's heads. To that end, all those who were psychic must disclose their gifts—for their existence alone put the State's power at risk. It was Gabriel's wanton acts of individualism and nondisclosure that brought him into the granite halls of The Conservatory. Today, on the date of his fourteenth birthday, his fate would be decided.

The interior of The Conservatory was stark and more reminiscent of a hospital or minimum-security prison than a school for gifted and talented youth. Its role was to intimidate, indoctrinate and control the children who would one day work as State employees. Suffice to say, most forms of socialization were frowned upon, but today was an exception. On the day of sentencing, one guest was always permitted.

Gabriel sat quietly in his barracks, holding the hand of his best friend Julian, a "student" of The Conservatory, one year his junior. Were it not for him, Gabriel would have found the past few years unbearable. Julian had taught him not only to hope again, but also to rebel. He was the most headstrong, brilliant and loving person Gabriel had met, second only to Elijah.

It had been seven years since Elijah's death. On a cosmic scale, this span of time was as insignificant as a speck of dust, but to a teenager, it was nothing short of a lifetime. Today, on the eve of his sentencing, he was happy to have Julian by his side.

Julian was slightly taller than Gabriel, with dark skin and short black hair. His onyx eyes were rich, earthy and striking. The irises and pupils were so close in color that they blended together, creating a dramatic, almost inescapable gaze that most could not ignore. Gabriel often found himself staring into their depths—the same way he gazed through the telescope in the old cabin. They made him feel safe and took him a million miles away from all the dangers that awaited him—especially on a day like today.

"Penny for your thoughts," Julian said, knowing very well what Gabriel was thinking.

"I would have the luck of dating a Thought Engineer," Gabriel said softly.

"*Dating*, huh? So now that you're leaving, we're making it official?"

Gabriel turned beet red.

Julian leaned in and planted a kiss on Gabriel's lips. It wasn't just a kiss; it was an exchange of empathy and compassion that nearly doubled Gabriel over. His heart jumped into his throat, and he couldn't speak.

For a moment, Julian gazed deeply into Gabriel's eyes until it felt as if the two of them were one—all thoughts, all energy was shared.

"Listen, Gabe, I know the trial is scary. But you're so strong, can't you see that? You just have to believe in yourself the way I do. Your only weakness is your doubt in yourself."

"You don't get it, Jules... I mean, I can't fly under the radar like you can. I can't just erase people's memories or re-arrange their thoughts."

Julian's aura changed color, shifting from green to orange. Then, he pulled away.

"Let's get one thing straight, Gabe... I'm *not* an Eraser. Sure, I change perception, but I don't erase the past. There's a difference between destroying memories and constructing thoughts. I'm an Engineer—*an Architect*."

Julian looked towards the door and furrowed his brow.

'We have company,' he said telepathically to Gabriel.

A red armored Alpha android stood in the doorway. It was an especially archaic unit, from The Great Wars. It was fabricated after the last ice age—the one that destroyed Manhattan and much of the Eastern seaboard.

Without speaking, the android motioned for Gabriel to follow it.

Gabriel turned and hugged Julian tightly. Julian hugged back, holding on so tight that Gabriel had trouble breathing.

Before he let go, Julian whispered, "Don't worry... I'll see you soon. My trial is only one year away. We'll probably end up with the same job—partners in crime, just like now."

Gabriel smiled, but intuited this would never happen. Julian always used his gifts and miraculously escaped from trouble, scot-free. Julian knew it. Gabriel knew it. And they both realized this was a white lie, but, to Gabriel, it was still oddly nice to hear the words. It gave him hope, something he desperately needed today.

The hydraulic joints of the android hissed as it moved towards him. Its head rotated three hundred sixty-five degrees, and two laser-red eyes flashed a warning.

Gabriel complied and followed it outside.

The door to his barracks locked behind him, and he felt a sense of doom building with each step they took down the long hallway leading to the Confessional. As the android moved, Gabriel caught a glimpse of its serial number. Most of it was destroyed by carbon and laser scoring, but he made out three characters: DV8.

"The judge will see you now," DV8 said in a sinister mechanical voice.

There was no jury present. All juvenile metacriminals were automatically stripped of the right to trial. The room was empty, save for a cylindrical holding cell at the center of the room—the Confessional. The light beaming down from above was blinding, and suggested that Gabriel was being judged by some deity rather than the criminal justice system.

The interior of the Confessional was claustrophobic, but somehow Gabriel kept his cool. He slowly knelt down at a circular pew surrounding an enormous projection platform in the center of the space. The motto of the State floated before him in bold letters. It read: **ONENESS & NONENESS.**

After a few moments of silence, a Digital State Peacekeeper (DSP) materialized. It was nearly as tall as Gabriel, though it had broader shoulders. Its pale yellow eyes contrasted sharply with its otherwise human-like appearance. They reminded Gabriel of cat's eyes, appearing both savage and wise.

It was gender-programmed to be male, but was it really possible for a program to be anything other than a program? Gabriel had his doubts. Although the hologram was mostly opaque, he could make out the faint outline of the Confessional control panel behind it. The effect was off-putting, as if he were interacting with some sort of digital apparition.

"Hello. I'm DSP Marrok. Please state the nature of your confession, child."

It spoke with a posh accent and cadence specific to the Cleric dialect.

"I'm here to report a crime."

"What type of crime?" it inquired. Its wild eyes squinted as it waited for Gabriel's response.

"Nondisclosure," Gabriel said, his voice cracking a bit. "I failed to report my gifts to the State when I was seven years old."

The hologram faded completely for a moment and then rematerialized. As it moved, Gabriel saw a strange red afterglow... perhaps it was his imagination or perhaps it was the digital equivalent of an aura.

"Apologies, sir, but I'm required by law to lock this Confessional until an armored escort arrives. Another Agent will take your statement after you've been... *processed.*"

"But—" Gabriel said.

"Moreover, your wanton act of deception put State security at risk. You are henceforth guilty until proven innocent. Effective immediately, you're being charged as a metacriminal."

"But—"

"Additionally, your test scores at The Conservatory indicate that you are likely a Level 8 Psychic and are in no way suitable for re-entry into society. In addition to nondisclosure you violated the Oneness and Noneness maxim in several areas. Hence, you will be sent to Sanctuary for quarantine."

The Peacekeeper subsequently read Gabriel his Obligation of Truth:

"You are charged with the heinous metacrime of concealing

your M-Status. You do not have the right to stand trial. The burden of proof is on you and, as such, you have an obligation to speak when questioned. It will incontrovertibly harm your defense if you do not mention when questioned something that aids this investigation. You will be subject to further inquiries by an Agent upon booking. Anything you say, think or do will be given in evidence to the State. Do you understand your obligations and the charges as explained?"

"I do," Gabriel said tersely.

The hologram pointed to the vehicle and the iris-shaped Confessional door opened.

"Transport has been arranged. Please make your way to the Peace Escort Vehicle, sir. And please note that the PEV is armed... *for your protection*, of course."

"Yes... of course." Gabriel said sarcastically.

He sat quietly in the small vehicle and watched powerlessly as its doors sealed shut.

The PEV navigated itself outside of The Conservatory to a deserted lot near the Embarcadero and then descended into a subterranean maglev highway system—one that Gabriel, and likely most citizens, didn't know existed.

The tunnels were completely dark, save for flashing lights emitted from the vehicle. This resulted in an intentionally disorienting strobe effect.

After an indeterminate amount of time, the PEV re-emerged on a secluded and restricted access area, in what looked like a private beach on the San Angeleno Peninsula. Long ago, massive coastal erosion and tectonic-induced separation created an extension of the Baja Peninsula, which now reached all the way to the center of California. It wasn't long before this area came under exclusive State jurisdiction. Aside from a set of iron gates and some sort of force field, the peninsula was deserted. The words SANCTUM CIVITAS appeared in bold iron letters above the gate.

Two Alpha-class androids emerged from the wooded area nearby and waited for the vehicle to come to a stop. One of the androids raised its hand and issued a signal to the PEV. Its doors opened up like a butterfly or an antique DeLorean. The other android helped Gabriel out of the car. He felt they shared the same code and were wirelessly networked to one another.

The Alphas spoke in unison to Gabriel as soon as he stepped out of the escort vehicle.

"Welcome to Central Hospital for Citizen Wellbeing. We are the Chief Nurse-Wardens and you are now a patient in our custody. State law mandates complete cooperation and absolute submission to Hospital policies. Any attempt to break the peace of this Sanctuary will result in mandatory rehabilitation. We hope you enjoy your stay."

The twin Alphas subsequently issued a short-range infrared signal to the guard booth, and the wrought-iron gates to Central Hospital opened with a high-pitched screech.

Gabriel grimaced.

A peculiar figure approached the automated police car. It strode with a calculated, robotic cadence. Gabriel nevertheless felt it must be human... at least *partially*; it had an aura, after all.

His intuition was confirmed when the cyborg stepped into the sunlight. Even before reading the badge, he knew that he was in the presence of one of the more dangerous Medics at the Central Hospital Sanctuary. Its ID simply read "**CAZADOR**" followed by a Jargon code **SNC-W10**, indicating its rank and top-secret clearance.

Oversized reflective glasses obscured Cazador's eyes. The Medic's face was otherwise pleasant, but it lacked any defining features, almost as if it were plastic. Cazador's body was enhanced in just about every way possible. Its vital organs were still intact, but its spine and some of its limbs were mechanized and augmented beyond recognition. Although Gabriel sensed the Agent might have been a woman at one point in time, Cazador's energy was decidedly more machine now. The whole concept of gender seemed archaic and perhaps irrelevant to its present function: to recruit (a.k.a. hunt) new Agents.

The cyborg motioned for him to follow. The two Nurse-Wardens trailed behind.

In a moment of bravery, Gabriel spoke up.

"Excuse me, Medic, may I ask where you're taking me?"

The Agent replied with a cold, monotonous voice that unnerved Gabriel. It sounded human-*ish*, but barely.

"We're headed for The Monocle."

"Why?"

"For concealing your M-Status, of course. You've been deemed a danger until you can be tagged... and classified."

'A danger to whom?' Gabriel thought to himself.

"Medic, what will they do with me?"

"Tough to say. Pray you are only there for an examination and nothing more."

Chills ran down Gabriel's back. In a flash of intuition, he had the distinct feeling that Cazador was once a citizen that was, for lack of a better word, *altered* against its will. Perhaps it was a form of punishment, for he sensed a very strong will to survive. A flicker of that strength was still imprinted on the cyborg's thin auric field, which glowed reddish-orange.

Cazador raised its hand. One of the twin Nurse-Wardens fetched a silver box. In a raw display of its own telekinetic power, Cazador opened the box simply by looking at it. Its eyes knowingly met Gabriel's. He understood the Agent was capable of much, much more. The Alpha-class Nurse-Wardens were mere accessories... a way of cloaking its own power. Its mind alone was enough to subjugate most average humans, and probably most Alphas and Synthetics.

"Place your hands behind your back," it said.

Fearing the consequences of refusal, Gabriel obliged.

The cyborg restrained Gabriel's hands with an infinity-shaped cord that slid easily over his wrists. It pulsed with energy and light. The Agent then telepathically issued a psychic codethought and the cord tightened. The nanotechnology within the device was programmed to the brainwaves of the issuing officer. Unlike an electronic restraint, something Gabriel could easily thwart, this would require him to demonstrate his own unique ability to push his conscious will onto another. He knew it was a test—one he could easily pass—but he didn't fight.

The cuffs loosened slightly, but Gabriel still didn't flinch.

Cazador tilted its head and smirked. Against its own programming, it liked Gabriel. Perhaps there really was still something human beneath its cybernetic shell.

The cyborg spoke telepathically, as its second test.

'You're smarter than most, but don't get any ideas... I have eyes in the back of my head.'

Gabriel didn't doubt it.

Cazador issued a telepathic command to the two Nurse-Wardens and they returned to their posts. Both the cyborg and Gabriel walked in silence for approximately one mile, during which time Gabriel recounted all the things he'd learned about Central Hospital.

The so-called Sanctuary was split into two structures—a concentric maze named The Loup and a glassed dome named The Monocle. From an aerial view, it was a marvel of modern architecture. To a "patient," the monotonous interlocking corridors were anything but picturesque. The sole purpose of the design was to confuse, intimidate and ultimately unnerve its patients.

Although the official name for the facility was Central Hospital for Citizen Wellbeing, almost everyone saw through these finely spun words from The Bureau. This was no hospital or sanctuary; it was a prison. There were already suitable medical facilities to serve the masses. Yes, an ER and OR existed in one of the concentric rings, but the true functions of The Loup were more sinister. First and foremost, it was a holding cell. Suspected criminals deemed too dangerous for The Corps or The Division were often transported to The Loup for "holding," "treatment," or—worse— "rehabilitation."

In addition to being nearly impossible to escape, the Sanctuary was rumored to have the capability to wipe memories and recondition minds. The latter could include anything from mild memory manipulation to full "erasure," which often left patients in a permanent state of amnesia.

"Examination," on the other hand, was a Bureau term for torture and inquisition. Like a looping line of computer code, most citizens that entered The Loup never left—that is, unless they were terminated, brainwashed, or worse, drafted into employment by the State. The existence of these practices, of course, could not be substantiated outside the labyrinthine belly of Central Hospital.

Cazador pointed to a winding corridor leading to the glassed dome.

"This way."

Gabriel followed the cyborg, observing the perimeter of the wonderfully reflective Monocle. Swirling clouds moved across its surface, almost as if it was a world unto itself.

The Special Agent raised its left hand and whispered an unintelligible code—most likely a machine dialect derived from Jargon. As it touched the glass, something unexpected happened: it rippled. Like so many things at Central Hospital, appearances were deceiving. The Monocle was not made of glass at all... it was a sort of one-way psychic force field.

Once inside, Cazador gripped Gabriel's shoulders and closed its eyes. As it did, Gabriel felt a cool breeze while the molecules around him rearranged.

They were no longer in a lobby, but had somehow teleported to a metallic silver-colored room without doors or windows.

The room was completely devoid of any details, save the words

"**FORTY BELOW**" laser-etched onto the otherwise pristine, polished metal walls.

The cyborg spoke into an archaic V-Terminal hard-wired to the wall.

"The patient is here, Sire."

A staticky voice replied, "Excellent. 'Port me in and prep the table."

"As you wish."

Cazador turned a hidden lever and an oval dais rose in the center of the room.

"Rest here. I'll fetch the Deputy."

Before Gabriel could protest, the Agent dematerialized and he was alone in the holding cell. There was no way in and out save teleportation.

He was trapped.

7

GRÅVARG

G abriel quietly scanned the perimeter of the cell. There was something sinister about the walls. From what he could gather, they were organic in nature... somehow faintly moving, as if they were breathing.

Although curious about his surroundings, he remained absolutely still. "Rehabilitation" did not sound like something he'd enjoy.

Any real perception of time was impossible, but Gabriel sat alone for what felt like half an hour—much longer than he anticipated. Each minute passed more slowly than the last.

A tinge of panic punched Gabriel in the gut. The pain was excruciating. In the same instant, Cazador rematerialized with a strong, muscular man of medium height, presumably the Deputy Agent that was speaking on the V-Terminal. Much to Gabriel's surprise, they argued back-and-forth for a moment, obfuscating their speech with a restricted dialect known as State Protocol (SP). It was filled with superfluous words that confounded anyone who hadn't been trained to decipher it.

"Pursuant to the requirements established within the One-

Hundred-Twenty-Eighth State Truthsaying Policy (under subparagraph Five-Eight-Delta), all Sanctuary Four-Zero-Bravo interrogations require a minimum of two—"

"This is pointless and insulting," The Deputy scorned Cazador, using Common Tongue. "I have security clearance from the highest circles of the State Oligarchy and OmniParty, and I outrank you. Remove those restraints *now* and give us privacy."

Cazador complied, not because it received an order from a ranking officer, but out of fear. Gabriel sensed that the Deputy could push his will on others. Even an Agent as powerful as Cazador would be putty in his hands.

The cyborg glanced at Gabriel's wrists and issued a codethought to the restraints.

The handcuffs didn't merely loosen; they dematerialized altogether, as if they never existed in the first place. Perhaps they didn't. Could the mere suggestion of their existence be enough to give them substance? If so, Gabriel began to wonder what other tricks Cazador had up its sleeve... he guessed that it would rank as an M-8 psychic or perhaps it was off-the-charts like Gabriel.

"You're free to process him now, Sire. But mind you, *Deputy* or not, this is not standard protocol. I'll be watching your every move, and I won't hesitate to report any behavior that's out of the ordinary."

"As a senior ranking officer, I'm painfully aware of State procedure. Thanks for your *exceeding* diligence," the Deputy said sharply.

Cazador dematerialized without looking back.

The Deputy circled and paced around Gabriel several times, inching closer with each step, like an animal ready to go in for a kill. The predatory nature of Medics earned them the colloquial moniker "Wolves." This particular Wolf personified the savage nickname, in both appearance and behavior.

After what seemed like an uncomfortably long pause, the

Deputy pulled a steel chair across the slate floor and sat in front of Gabriel.

Then he simply waited... and watched.

Gabriel avoided the Deputy's gaze initially, but curiosity got the best of him.

As soon as their eyes locked, Gabriel knew that he was up against the worst kind of psychic... a thought-thief known informally as an "Eraser."

'A Deputy-level Division Eraser... *posing as a Wolf?*' Gabriel thought to himself. 'Surely the other Medics sensed this? Perhaps this man is outside of the State altogether? Yes... and Cazador knows his alliance is skewed.'

The Eraser smiled as it read his mind.

"You'd be wise to keep your opinions to yourself, Gabriel," it said aloud.

Two enormous eyes, one emerald green, one ice blue, overpowered the rest of the Eraser's face, which was stern, angular and strong. Messy grey hair and muttonchops gave him a sort of feral look. Even his ears seemed slightly more pointed than they should be... although Gabriel hoped that was just an illusion or his own fear setting in. However, he soon noticed that the man was unusually stocky and muscular for a genetically unmodified human being. Gabriel felt as if the man could pounce and rip him to shreds if needed.

The Eraser's eyes began to change color repeatedly... the green became blue and the blue became green. This hypnotic effect quite literally froze Gabriel's body. He felt as if someone was taking a jackhammer to his third eye and then his occipital lobe.

The Agent's energetic grip moved along Gabriel's skull like icy fingers until it dug into the very grey matter of his brain... Gabriel understood that the Agent could see his thoughts, manipulate his memory and purge everything at will... or at least it believed it could.

'I'm not afraid of you,' Gabriel thought instinctively.

He wasn't sure why, but he'd faced worse adversaries in some other incarnation. The thought alone gave him power and the Eraser lost its grip.

'**Vet du vem du talar med?**' the man proclaimed telepathically. '**Do you know who I am?**'

The Agent's psychic voice was an imposingly low baritone that reverberated and drowned out all other thoughts. It echoed like a gong until Gabriel felt compelled to answer... if nothing else, to simply stop the din.

His grandfather warned him of **Gudsrösten**, or The Divine Tongue. Although this Agent invoked it with precision, he used a low frequency known as **Mörkvilja** (The Dark Will) aimed at bullying and pushing one's will on unsuspecting, weaker minds.

Gabriel, however, cleverly countered by invoking **STJÄRNLJUS** (Starlight), an elevated, higher vibrational frequency used in benedictions. His voice took on a sonorous, almost musical quality; its strength lay not in its manipulation of **Gudsrösten** but in its purity and clarity.

'**JA, DU HETER GRÅVARG. YOU'RE GREYWOLF... THE GREAT ERASER. THOUGHTS ARE YOUR PREY AND YOU DEVOUR THEM LIKE SHEEP.**'

At this point Gabriel's heart began to race and he felt a fire rise in his belly. As that fire rose, words followed. Soon they flowed like lava.

'**SLUTA TALA MED MÖRKVILJA... STOP YOUR ABUSIVE TECHNIQUES. THEY'RE POWERLESS ON ME. YOUR MOTIVES ARE TRANSPARENT AND YOUR WORDS ARE FRAGILE! LET TRUTH BE MY HAMMER! WATCH IT SHATTER YOUR THOUGHTS INTO DUST!**'

Gabriel's voice blasted in Gråvarg's head like a thousand trumpets playing at once. One by one each word ricocheted, creating a cacophony of noise that paralyzed the Agent's mind. The

STJÄRNLJUS invocation of the words "**TRUTH**" and "**HAMMER**" reverberated louder than the rest, until they resulted in a singular, deafening explosion of thought and sound, successfully breaking the psychic connection between the two.

Gråvarg opened his eyes and stared at Gabriel with a combination of wonder and amusement. Much like Cazador, he admired the boy's will.

'Vem är du? Who are you? Who taught you **Gudsrösten**?'

The Eraser already knew the answers to his questions. More importantly, he knew that Gabriel *knew he knew*.

Gabriel hated a snoop. He answered Gråvarg's questions with another question, and spoke aloud just to annoy him.

"You ask questions to which you already know the answers. I have one for you... Why am I being held here, Greywolf?"

"Processing." Gråvarg replied aloud flatly and robotically.

Telepathically, however, Gråvarg contradicted himself.

'Your instincts are spot on. I am The Grey Wolf and I serve no one's will but my own. You should trust this, however: you mustn't speak aloud in this Sanctuary unless necessary. Cazador once warned you that it has eyes on the back of its head; suffice to say the walls of Central Hospital do, too.'

Gråvarg slowly moved his eyes without turning his head. Gabriel followed the Eraser's line-of-sight and realized his words were true. In addition to various cameras and recording devices, there was something else... For a lack of a better word, the walls had some sort of *intelligence*. They could hear what Gabriel said and, perhaps vaguely, perceive what he thought. It was for this reason that Gråvarg carried on two conversations with Gabriel, a telepathic one and a verbal smokescreen for the sake of the walls.

The Eraser pulled out a small scanning device and read Gabriel's vitals.

"Sit back," he said aloud.

Gabriel complied.

Gråvarg then resumed his telepathic dialogue with Gabriel.

'I once worked with your grandfather Elijah, back when he was still teaching. He helped me when no one else could. So, I'm now here as a favor to him. You see, we agreed to an *arrangement* of sorts which will help keep you safe.'

'Arrangement?' Gabriel thought.

'Yes, you'll enter into our internship program here, under my tutelage.'

Gabriel knew very well that *internship* was another cooked Bureau term that was, at best, ironic.

'And if I decline?' Gabriel thought.

'You'll enter The Program one way... or another,' Gråvarg replied telepathically. 'It's just a question of whether you want to remember who you are. Even if you can withstand my techniques, there are other ways... more painful methods used by other Central Hospital Medics. Don't call my bluff on this, dear boy. I may not have been Elijah's first choice, but I'm your best hope for survival. I can also teach you a great deal.'

Gabriel went pale.

'Please understand, your grandfather and I both paid dearly for this arrangement, so I pray you accept,' Gråvarg thought.

Gabriel nodded his head.

"Gabriel, I need you to lie down on the dais in the middle of the room," Gråvarg said aloud. "Try to relax."

He obeyed and the Eraser added a final remark telepathically, 'I'm sorry, but this is going to hurt... quite a bit. If you'd like, I can remove that memory from your head.'

'I'm no sheep. I want to remember every second of this, pain and all,' Gabriel thought defiantly. 'Most of all, I want to remember your face, Greywolf.'

Gråvarg smiled and stepped back, his eyes shifting colors again.

'Very well, brave and foolish child. Have it your way. I'll see you soon.'

He walked over to the V-Terminal and spoke firmly, "Cazador, it's the Deputy. I need transport to The Monocle while Gabriel is processing."

As Gråvarg was ported out of FORTY BELOW, the "processing" device kicked-in almost immediately. Neck, wrist, hip and leg restraints emerged from the dais and held Gabriel against the cold metallic surface, while robotic arms removed all clothing except his boxer briefs. He felt intense pain around his occipital lobe and extremities as unseen needles and drills injected implants beneath his skin.

Gabriel blacked out—due to both panic and trauma—as an oversized needle or drill-like device descended from a ceiling panel, headed straight towards his third eye.

Gråvarg was selfish and cunning, but he was not a liar. The pain, or what Gabriel remembered of it before blacking out, was excruciating.

He awoke to the sounds of murmured conversations and spied Gråvarg in the distance, signing a document of some sort.

Gabriel was fully clothed and appeared to be back in the lobby of The Monocle. How he got there was a complete blur, however.

He glanced down at his lap and noticed small scabs on each fingertip of his left hand. Similar scabs existed on his neck and forehead, right around the area of his third eye.

Gabriel said nothing. Instead, he scanned the room. No less than three Alpha guards were watching his every move.

A beautiful girl was seated at the end of his bench. She'd been there all along, but didn't want to bother Gabriel, as he was clearly getting his bearings.

She seemed to be around the same age as Gabriel. Her jet-black hair was pulled into a neat bun. Everything about her meticulous attire suggested that her family was aristocratic, except, of course, for the fact that she wore glasses. It was the latter that drew Gabriel's attention and made him smile involuntarily. Most aristocrats simply installed cybernetic optics, as glasses were a sign of weakness, or worse, *differentness*. He felt comfortable in her presence, much like he'd felt with Elijah and Julian. Without her ever saying a word about it, Gabriel recognized he was in the presence of a fellow insurgent.

She smiled back at him, and the room seemed to light up.

"My name is Madeleine. I'm new here, just like you," she said without prompting. Her voice was strong and kind. She spoke in a cultured dialect, with hints of State Cleric training in her intonations and pronunciation.

"I'm Gabriel. Nice to meet you."

She held out her hand.

He shook it and looked down before letting go. Each of her fingers were red and healing from a slight wound, like his—a telltale sign of new implants. She lacked the third eye implant, however.

Her kind brown eyes—slightly magnified by her glasses—looked unflinchingly into his. Like her radiant smile, they were filled with love and life. There was a sense of kinship and familiarity in them, too—clearly the two had a soulmate connection.

"You don't have a throat implant yet, but based on your communication skills, I'm guessing that you're a new recruit for The Bureau?" he said on a hunch.

She nodded.

"What was your act of rebellion?" Gabriel asked.

"I won first place in the debate team at my Youth Academy."

"That hardly seems like a crime."

"It was a *Oneness and Noneness* violation, Section 4. I stood out... well, that and I argued that the State was rewriting history to suit their point of view."

Gabriel laughed out loud, in both amusement and approval. It felt good to meet another rebel.

"I hope we see each other again," she said.

"Count on it," Gabriel replied.

He was uncertain what the future held in store for him, but felt comforted that he'd met a new friend and, moreover, that Elijah had made provisions to protect him. Gabriel knew deep down that he could learn from Gråvarg. The Agent was unconventional, a bit rogue and stubborn. Perhaps Gabriel saw some of his own qualities in this man, which is what made their initial meeting so rocky.

"People are mirrors," Elijah once said. "We call them in and they show us what we need to see about ourselves. If you don't like someone you've just met, change yourself."

Today Gabriel took that lesson to heart. He would learn what *not* to be from Gråvarg. More importantly, he would learn everything he could about the State's inner workings. Perhaps Central Hospital was a blessing in disguise—a sort of PhD in survival.

PART IV

THE ASSEMBLY OF STARS

PROLOGUE

With his memories fully recovered, Gabriel stood before the Angel of Death with a sense of awe, anger and confusion. Why was his past stolen? What did the events of New Year's mean? And why now, after all this time, had Death returned? After all, a visit from this being always seemed to bring about a wake of destruction.

8

SPELLBOUND, PART TWO: IN MEMORIAM MORTIS

Dateline: Los Angeles Megacity, in the Earth Year One Billion, on New Year's Day. (Present Day.)

"I remember you. I remember everything now," Gabriel said, half in disbelief. "For years you haunted my dreams—did you know that?"

"Aye," Death replied, *"And for that I apologize. As tough as it was for you, it was even worse for me. It was all for your protection, however. If you'd known your destiny, they would have sensed your presence. As cruel as it might have seemed, it saved your life—and it also allowed you a chance to grow up without the burden or responsibility of being The Last Steward. Now, however, it's time to embrace that, as The Shadows have returned. You are no longer safe."*

"Yeah, I guess I understand that now. I was a bit of a mess the night my grandfather passed away. Seeing a monster, meeting Death, watching my grandfather die and learning about some ancient prophecy—well, understandably, no kid could process that in one night, even if he was destined to save the world. Still... you might have asked me before holding my memories hostage, you know?"

Death nodded its head, but offered no apology.

Gabriel nervously bit his lip and spoke again, "There's something else. I feel I've known you. *Before*. Before that night, that is."

Gabriel realized how ridiculous this must have sounded, but the immortal didn't flinch.

"I feel the same soul recognition," Death said, and then seemed lost in its own thoughts for moment. *"Alas, I can't be certain. Not yet. Suffice to say, I'm old. Very old. Yet, somehow I feel that I've always known you—long before you went by the name Gabriel."*

Gabriel wasn't sure what to say. After an awkward pause, Death spoke up.

"Ask the question. I already hear it in your mind."

"If you have the power to take lives, can't you decide to spare one from time to time?" Gabriel asked.

"That is not my function. Elijah died—after a long life, I might add—as does everyone... everything. If I ceased to help souls cross over, then chaos would ensue, and The Shadows would gain momentum."

"I understand, I think... I just miss him."

"So do I. Listen, if you'd like to reconnect with Elijah, you must return to the old cabin and retrieve Corpus Sidera. His essence, as well as all other Stewards, is connected to that tome. The book is also integral to your Stewardship. Too long have you forgotten that you are The Last Steward—and that is my fault, not yours."

"I'll go first thing tomorrow."

"Wait. Might I suggest you go to the office first? Do some digging and see if you can get information on the murder—but keep a low profile. Anything you learn may help you avoid a similar fate."

"Good idea."

"One more thing before you head to the old cabin... After work,

I want you to take a trip to Melrose Avenue. Look for an establishment called Deva Ink. There you will find Elsa, Uri and Ambrose."

"Who are they, exactly?"

"Kindred spirits who can aid in protecting you... and in preparing you."

"Preparing me for what?"

"A trip to The Dream Broker."

Gabriel dared not ask for more details. He was tired, frustrated and fascinated all at once.

In the blink of an eye, the immortal was by his side, seemingly impervious to the laws of physics. Sensing Gabriel's fear, it laid its marble-colored hand on his forehead, gently covering his eyelids. It moved its lips close to his ears and began humming a sing-song poem.

"Bend thee like a willow
under snow, wind and rain.
Tilt an ear to the heavens
and hear a whispering refrain.
Whether cloaked in Earthly trappings,
or as a fiery shooting star,
I offer thee protection and
messages from afar.
As a beacon in the sky above,
The Second will shine on thee,
Opening a doorway
That none but you can see.
Under the light of Orion's belt
take the Moon and you'll both go
to the blue veil of eventide
where her true colors she will show.
It's there you'll meet The Third Star
as the Satellite speaks to thee,

but inside the dream itself
the next two you'll set free.
Seek The Sixth past the hollow
across the bridge where Hope is lost,
beyond the gate of rock and sand and
through The Shattered Holy Cross.
The Seventh's lost to stars and men,
So through the portal you must go,
O'er time and space alone, my friend
To a planet made of snow.
On its moons you'll find your destiny
As The Prophecy unfolds...
Where The Seven shine as One once more
Like they did in days of old!"

The immortal leaned in again and whispered softly, *"Rest, friend. Tomorrow will be a busy day."*

Gabriel closed his eyes and heard its angelic wings flapping in the distance. His limbs fell limp and his mind faded into a blissful sleep.

After nearly a decade of insomnia, Gabriel slept through the night.

9

SCRI

The piercing wail of a peacekeeping siren jolted Gabriel out of his calm slumber. He stretched and then collected his thoughts for a moment; his mind was still half-stuck in the aether. Memories from his childhood continued to rush in— not just of his grandfather Elijah, but of his time in Sanctuary. The past and present were all blurring together. As much as he wanted to go back to the old cabin and retrieve *Corpus Sidera*, he agreed with the Angel of Death; he must investigate the murder of the man who died on New Year's Eve, or risk suffering the same fate.

Gabriel walked into his bathroom with caution. It was the sole room in his apartment that had a reflective surface, and, after his newly recovered memory of The Man in the Looking Glass, Gabriel was a little skittish.

He stepped closer to the vanity and saw a blinking red light.

"Incoming message," a bodiless AI declared.

He placed his right hand on the mirror.

The surface turned white.

"ID verified. Uplink to SCRI terminal?" the AI inquired.

"Yes."

A series of braille-like binary Jargon symbols illuminated, followed by the letters DDC, indicating an encoded message was waiting from Gabriel's partner at work, a Digital Detective Constable named Johan.

"Play message," Gabriel said.

Johan's likeness appeared on-screen followed by a recorded audio message.

"Gabriel, for the love of the State, where are you? The Leftenant threw us on a grisly M-Crime—investigating a fellow Remote Agent that was murdered last night. She's debriefing us at zero eight hundred. Shake a leg... preferably two. You know she's a stickler for protocol."

The transmission faded and the mirrored façade returned without prompting.

Gabriel threw on the first clean clothes he could find in the closet and did his best to look presentable.

As the grandfather clock struck zero seven hundred hours, Gabriel realized he had just enough time to catch the Eastbound E Train. He grabbed a coat and his attaché and made a run for it.

As he hurriedly entered the Doheny terminal, he heard a Synthetic voice booming over the loudspeakers:

"Welcome to The E. All trains are on schedule. Next Eastbound train in: one minute, thirty seconds."

The announcement was broadcast in three State-sanctioned languages: Common Tongue, Cleric and a series of melodic binary tones that accompanied the compressed language of Jargon.

"The E" was short for Trans-Californian Electromagnetic Train. The ultra-fast, transport system stretched the entire distance of the massive Los Angeles Megacity (LAMC), which included all of the coastal cities from the Islands of San Francisco to the San Diego Wastelands.

A sleek silver coating truly gave the impression of a bullet when the train traveled at its maximum velocity of eight hundred klicks per hour.

A soothing Synthetic female voice announced, "The Eastbound vehicle has arrived on Platform B. Next stop: Beaudry Street, Olde Towne in two minutes."

Gabriel wasted no time in boarding. The interior was cushy and looked more like a first-class cabin than an urban mode of transport. Although the train would normally be packed at this hour, most Angelenos were still hung-over or asleep. Gabriel slouched down and rested his head against the glass.

Light rain misted the window, creating a glistening cluster of drops, like tiny stars. As the train accelerated, the small droplets bled across the pane, creating the illusion that Gabriel was moving at hyperspeed.

Gabriel exited The E and jogged down the Beaudry station platform. He continued at a fast pace for about a mile before stopping in front of what appeared to be a deserted parking lot.

As with most State-owned buildings, The Eleventh Precinct was drab and intentionally inconspicuous. Located downtown, near Figueroa Street, the parking-lot-turned-precinct blended in perfectly with the other businesses. Few citizens knew that its true function lay in a subterranean structure. A small, faded sign outside of the lot read: "SCRI P-11." It was otherwise devoid of windows, markings or signs of life. Were it not for a silent Raptorcraft guarding the perimeter, it would appear the building was deserted.

Gabriel removed his sunglasses and approached a guard post, which lay hidden behind a row of oak trees.

"Hello, is anyone there?" he asked.

An armored android emerged from the shadows; its elegant face and chrome endoskeleton shined majestically in the dim morning light. The upper and lower sections—although devoid of hair and skin—were crafted to look humanoid. The overall attention to detail created an illusion that it was somehow a living metal sculpture. Although vaguely female in its construction, she, or rather *it,* was undoubtedly an Alpha Class android, all of which were unencumbered by gender programming or emotions, rendering them unflappable killing machines. Unlike their Synthetic counterparts, Alphas never bled, they never slept and never questioned authority—due to a strict adherence to their original programming. Some considered this rigidity their biggest strength; Gabriel was not convinced. Blind justice was just that: blind.

As Gabriel approached the two-thousand-year-old machine, he stopped dead in his tracks.

"Wait a second, you're not AUM21."

"No. That unit has been... *reassigned,*" it said with a pause that was atypical for an Alpha.

Gabriel read the serial number on its right arm, just above its armored blast mechanism. The partial identification code, DV8, was one that would be forever burned into his memory. How could he ever forget it? Precisely seven years earlier, DV8 escorted him to the Confessional at The Conservatory—the day he lost his freedom. Its appearance today was definitely not a coincidence. Gabriel had a hunch who sent it, but he waited for the right moment to test his theory.

DV8 moved uncomfortably close to Gabriel and scanned him for contraband. Then it issued a command, "Look into my eyes and don't blink."

Gabriel complied and DV8's eyes widened. Its cat-like irises exposed a glowing retinal scanner. After a blinding flash of light, its eyes returned to normal.

"Positive identification achieved. You may proceed, Agent." it said in a low, mechanical voice.

Gabriel waited knowingly and whispered a code phrase to the android.

"Greywolf."

The android's eyes went dim and a subroutine kicked in—some sort of malware virus overwrote its programming and it behaved erratically.

DV8 opened its mouth and a hidden camera projected a life-sized holographic message in front of Gabriel.

A staticky, translucent projection of Gråvarg stood before him. He couldn't make out where his mentor was—he assumed it was Central Hospital, but something was wrong. He saw a flashing strobe light and smoke in the background. There was either a fire or some sort of security breach.

Gråvarg looked over his shoulder cautiously and waited a moment before speaking. As he did, Gabriel noticed that his mentor had gone almost completely grey now. He was nevertheless as ferocious and feral-looking as ever.

"Gabriel, if you're receiving this message, then things have gone horribly awry, and you are beyond my protection. Know this: if you enter the walls of SCRI today, you may not make it out alive. Something terrible is taking hold of the State Oligarchy—a Shadow that is older than this world, and one that will destroy it if it has its way. Suffice to say there are far worse things than Wolves on your trail. Make your way back to the cabin before it's too late. Again, abort your Leftenant's orders and avoid SCRI at all costs. I cannot shield you any longer. May Himlens Väktare light your path. I'll see you on the other—"

Gabriel heard the sound of an explosion and the transmission cut off unexpectedly. DV8 stared at him blankly. Its program was corrupted, but he needed to cover his tracks, and Gråvarg's for that matter. He owed his mentor that much.

He moved his hands behind the Alpha's occipital lobe and whispered an incantation.

"Lux sancta et lux antiquis.... Veni huc!"

Bluish-white energy arced between Gabriel's hands and he

short-circuited the android's CPU and memory banks. Smoke began to billow from the eyes and mouth of the now incapacitated robot.

He was now faced with two contradictory sets of instructions. Gråvarg was a man who self-admittedly owed allegiance to no one but himself, yet he'd never lied to Gabriel. He could either listen to his old mentor or follow the wishes of the Angel of Death—a being who had wantonly concealed key data from him in order to orchestrate its own agenda. Neither source of information made him feel confident, but his gut told him to follow Death's wishes. He would proceed, despite the risk.

Gabriel casually walked past the android and kept his eyes on the Raptorcraft. It was pointed in the other direction. As long as he made no sudden movements, he'd be in the clear.

While Gabriel may have appeared brave on the outside, internally his body felt like jelly. He hadn't seen Gråvarg in years, and he understood that he must be in grave danger for his mentor to hack into a State-owned android to deliver a message. He proceeded towards the entrance with caution. He suddenly wished he had eyes in the back of his head like Cazador.

Gabriel let out a sigh as soon as he entered the dilapidated lift. He placed his finger on the authenticator and waited impatiently, hoping that nobody else would try to gain access to the precinct before he was inside. The authenticator sparked a few times and then sputtered off. Inflation and misappropriated State funds resulted in budget cuts across sectors. This precinct was no exception, and incidents like this were more prevalent recently than in years past.

Gabriel began to sweat a bit as he heard footsteps in the distance. He slammed the console a few times. The attached screen blinked on and off and subsequently displayed the Jargon binary symbols for "SCRI."

"State destination?" the AI inquired.

"ELEVEN BELOW," Gabriel snapped back at the computer,

knowing full well that raising his voice was a waste of energy. It still made him feel better.

The lift's AI complied and he felt the air get cooler and mustier as he descended into the precinct's substructure. For now, at least, he was safe. If he was lucky, the State would simply attribute DV8's meltdown to some sort of malfunction. It was highly unusual, but not unheard of, for the older Alpha units to overheat or need repair.

"Just keep your cool," Gabriel whispered to himself. Gråvarg had once taught him that believing was seeing. That was his fancy way of saying Gabriel could push his beliefs onto others; if he had no fear, others would have no reason to suspect him. He was beginning to understand why his grandfather chose a Rogue Agent like Gråvarg to train him. Perhaps it was to prepare Gabriel for the inevitable. He, too, would have to rebel against the establishment. Elijah taught him the rules; Gråvarg taught him how to bend them. If Gabriel was going to fight in the immanent war of the Gods, he would have to understand how to walk the line between Shadow and Light.

The ELEVEN BELOW foyer was bathed in a pool of flickering light bulbs, all badly in need of replacement. Everything—food and people alike—looked pallid and stale in the greenish light. As he passed the reception area, one of the bulbs overhead hissed and blew out. Beneath the burnt bulb a faded placard read: STATE CENTER for REMOTE INVESTIGATIONS.

Nobody referred to it as such—citizens called it "The Center," while Sentients, Agents and official State bodies called it by its Jargon code SCRI—pronounced, appropriately enough, *scry*.

Although agencies like the FBI and CIA still existed in name, they had lost relevance and function. SCRI, however, was unique in that it relied on remote intel gathering. Two types of agents provided this information: gifted M-8 psychics and clever, sometimes unpredictable, AI constructs called Sentients. The M-8s worked in the physical, metaphysical and spiritual realms, while the

Sentients probed the dangerous wasteland that was once the internet, often acting as infiltrators. While the pairing might have seemed odd to some, M-8s and Sentients shared one thing in common: they were able to reach out to spaces others could not.

Gabriel's various gifts afforded him a comfortable (albeit mandatory) role within The Center. He was often assigned to field investigations, due in a large part to his acumen in reading energy off physical objects. Like all M-8s, however, he mastered the eight requisite abilities of remote investigating, including the arts of:

1. Psychometry—reading information from objects.
2. Telepathy—reading and broadcasting thoughts.
3. Telekinesis—manipulating objects with thought alone.
4. Clairvoyance—seeing the past, present and future.
5. Clairsentience—often called empathy. The ability to feel and know others' emotions, pain and physical or emotional feelings.
6. Clairaudience—the ability to hear spirits.
7. Clairalience & Clairgustance—to smell or taste things in a precognitive vision.
8. Claircognizance—simply knowing a fact, without having any previous experience or schooling (e.g., knowing what something means in a foreign or even alien language).

Additionally, he was off-the-charts in advanced psychic skills, particularly in the areas of astral projection and manipulating electromagnetic fields (EMFs). Thankfully, Gråvarg's wildly unorthodox training methods showed Gabriel how to psychically conceal these gifts. After all, being unique violated the State's *Oneness & Noneness* maxim. He'd experienced Central Hospital once already, and that was enough. Now, Gabriel did his best to blend in with the other Agents, even though that, in and of itself, was a wanton act of nondisclosure.

Speaking of coworkers, the office was uncharacteristically quiet this morning. The few souls that were working were likely engaged in remote viewing or interfacing with their Sentient investigators. Gabriel was thankful for the lull; it meant he could come and go relatively unnoticed. Plus, his mind was still abuzz with memories, thoughts, feelings and questions. Suddenly, Gabriel's world was infinitely more complicated and magical. It was enough to give anyone a headache, even a top-notch psychic.

He sat down at his desk and rolled up his sleeves. Gabriel then placed both hands on a small, movable triangular object in front of him until it was activated. The object, an Oubliette, was essentially a two-way communication device between an isolated, self-aware program and a human being.

After a brief pause, Digital Detective Constable Johan's likeness came through the portal. It was tall with auburn hair and grey eyes. Periodic static interrupted an otherwise reasonable projection of the human form. The static was not attributed to any problems with the Sentient's code or the Oubliette itself, but rather Gabriel's unique tendency to interfere with all things electrical. More than most psychics, Gabriel seemed to encounter EMF disturbances with everything from nanotechnology to androids. Unbeknownst to the State, he'd spent years honing his skills; he was now capable of jamming Sentients and blocking out State surveillance when needed. His handiwork with DV8 was only the tip of a very deep iceberg.

"'Morning, Gabe."

The Sentient visually scanned his body and asked, "Late night?"

"Ha! It's that obvious?" Gabriel asked.

"With all due respect, it doesn't take a psychic to see that. Your eyes are bloodshot and your body is registering as dehydrated. Lay off the neurotoxins, partner."

Gabriel reached for a glass of water and then spoke to Johan again.

"So, I got your message about the Sunset Boulevard case—has the State CSI unit arrived yet?"

"Yes, Drones are doing a DNA sweep as we speak. Bring the portable Oubliette and we'll talk later. You have bigger fish to fry. The Leftenant wants to see you in her office. Oh yeah... she already briefed the team."

"Vrána will have my neck."

"Bet on it. Godspeed."

Johan dematerialized.

Gabriel glanced at his watch and winced. He was only five minutes late, but he knew there'd be hell to pay.

He navigated through a maze of identical grey cubicles and tapped on a force field around Leftenant Vrána's office.

The force field lowered and the Leftenant continued reviewing a case file as she spoke.

"Come in," she said raising an eyebrow.

The room was unusually dark and had no windows. The only point of entry was the force field.

Sensing his discomfort, Vrána snapped her fingers and the overhead lights powered on.

"I see your DDC briefed you on the basics?"

He could feel her mental fingers pick at his brain. Without asking, she ascertained his being tardy was an accident.

"Gabriel, you're not being called-in because you're late, although I did mark it down in your record. You're being summoned here because of *this*."

She handed him a polished star sapphire memory crystal. Her stern grey eyes locked onto Gabriel like laser beams.

"A courier delivered this report at zero five hundred hours. Apparently, Prime Investigator Oculum conducted a routine sweep of SCRI. While meditating, they espied your presence at the scene of the murder, mere hours before the crime. Implant authentication records have corroborated this vision. I find it disturbing that I heard this second-hand."

Gabriel kept his mouth shut. He understood that Oculum, better known as The Eye, was not only the top M-8 Agent ever hired, but also the head of the OMNI Committee for Obedience—SCRI's Internal Affairs division. Its singular (and somewhat frightening) function involved psychically "sweeping" and reporting on any (and all) suspicious activities at SCRI, The Division, The Bureau and Sanctuary. Few, if any humans saw this all-seeing Agent in the flesh. Gabriel often wondered if the Agent was human, machine... or possibly some other form of intelligent life.

"Listen... You're a formidable M-8, Gabe... maybe the best I've ever seen. But, don't forget, I have the same skills and training as you. And my intuition tells me The Eye is on to something. I sense that you're withholding data from me."

She squinted her eyes and tried to enter his mind again, but Gabriel put up a shield. For an instant, Gabriel swore her eyes glowed red, as if a light were shining from the inside out. Perhaps it was just an illusion, but Gabriel's gut told him it was real.

"Know this," she scowled, "If you ever put me under OMNI scrutiny again, you'll be escorted to the nearest Sanctuary faster than you can blink an eye. We can't afford another mistake."

Gabriel's face turned white.

"Good, we understand one another. I'll expect you to imprint your recollections from New Year's Eve on that memory crystal, along with any intel you gather in the field today. I want everything on my desk by zero eight hundred hours tomorrow.

"That's all."

Gabriel had scarcely walked out of the office before the Leftenant re-engaged the perimeter force field.

As he navigated his way through the sea of cubicles to the lift, he felt as if every eye in the office was watching—and it was quite possible they were. He'd dodged a bullet with Vrána, but he wasn't sure why. Whatever her motivation, Gabriel wasn't sticking around to find out. Gråvarg was right to warn him—he must watch his every move from this moment on. He was now a dead man walking, at least in the eyes of the State.

10

BEHIND CLOSED DOORS

L eftenant Vrána quickly snapped her fingers, turning the overhead lights off.

Shrouded in darkness, Vrána turned on a single lamp behind her desk. It cast a long shadow on the wall directly in front of her.

A second shadow towered behind hers on the wall. It was darker, larger and had no distinct shape.

"Does young Gabriel know about us?" it said with a deep, raspy voice.

"No. Not yet, My Liege."

"But he will?"

The Leftenant closed her eyes. "Yes... soon... by nightfall, I believe."

"You're certain he is *The* Prophesied One? We've gotten a tad... *messy* lately. One more misfire, and the blood will be on your hands, Miss Vrána."

The Leftenant's eyes began to glow crimson red and she replied, "This is not a miscalculation, I assure you."

"Very well. Clean up your mess better this time. Let's summon the crows."

The second shadow slid along the corner of the wall and disappeared in the darkness.

Leftenant Vrána stood up and donned a black-hooded cape. Only her red eyes were visible beneath the hood. She slowly walked towards her own shadow, which curiously remained perfectly still despite her movements. Without pausing, she calmly stepped through it and dissolved into thin air, taking her shadow with her.

11

THE CASE OF GENESIS SEVEN-TWELVE AND THE SHADOW-WALKER

As Gabriel approached the familiar courtyard of The Black Cat, he tapped a triangular disc on his belt and waited. A staticky silhouette flickered on and off and then faded.

He tapped again several times.

"Hey... you there, Johan?"

A tiny camera activated and his partner materialized.

"Affirmative. Sorry about that. There are two remarkable EMF signatures—one near the trash can and another in the alleyway; they temporarily threw off my COM systems. I'm recording everything to the sapphire memory crystal now."

"Good. Between Vrána and The Eye, I can't afford a misstep."

"Understood. I've got your back, partner."

Gabriel opened the heavy wooden door and the familiar aroma of spirits and fried food greeted his nose. Inside, however, things were a bit off-kilter. At least half a dozen androids, all Beta Synthetics, were missing by his count.

He caught the attention of a burly, middle-aged man speaking to the group of trainees. Even from afar, Gabriel knew the man was the owner of The Black Cat.

"Sorry to interrupt, sir, but do you have a moment?" Gabriel inquired.

"What do you need?" the man replied. He squinted disapprovingly at Johan's hologram.

"I'm an M-8 Agent. My partner and I are here on a State investigation," Gabriel said. "As you know, a murder took place on the premises last night. Do you have a few moments to answer some questions?"

"Ah...Yes, I'm glad someone followed-up face-to-face. I can spare about fifteen minutes. Will that suffice?"

"That should be fine, sir."

"Skip the *sir* nonsense, lad. Name's Fitzgerald. I recognize you —you're a regular, right?"

"Indeed. Pleased to meet you, formally, Mister Fitzgerald—I'm Gabriel."

"Don't call me Mister. Name's *Fitzgerald*. Fitz to friends. That's it."

"Got it. You can dispense with Agent, as well. Gabriel is fine."

Fitzgerald turned, somewhat apprehensively and said, "Would you mind switching off the hologram? Technology gives me the creeps."

"Sure, but this will still be recorded," Gabriel replied.

"That's fine."

Johan nodded and ceased projecting his likeness.

"Thanks. One more thing, and I hate to ask, but—?

Fitzgerald pointed to an implant scanner.

Gabriel gladly waved his left hand over it.

"Thanks for showing your credentials. Everyone is on edge with the murder... We've had a lot of *activity* over the past week."

"Really?"

"Yeah. Not just the State... but some seedy characters, too. A hooded lady with creepy eyes."

Fitzgerald squirmed a bit at the memory.

"Did this woman have a name?"

"Nope... she wouldn't give it. She dashed off before I could scan her implants."

"Describe the eyes..."

"Red. Deep red."

"Where did you see this suspicious woman?"

"One of the cooks caught her hanging around near the dumpster on the night of the murder. Then she was back earlier today. The cook tried to run after the hooded figure, but... well, this sounds strange..."

"Go on..."

"The hooded woman could move through walls. Apparently, she ran through her shadow and vanished. Then her shadow disappeared, too—but only after she was gone."

"Wait, she ran *through* it... like it was some sort of doorway or portal?"

"You think I'm nuts, right?"

"Actually, I think you're perfectly sane... I'm just curious. By the way, did you tell anyone else about this... *Shadow-walker?*"

"Nope... I don't want trouble."

"Nor do I. I'm only looking for answers."

Gabriel pressed a button on his H-V wristband and projected a small hologram of the murder victim and the missing android.

"Any chance you recognize the victim?"

"Can't say I do, sadly. Hmm... Strange, from this angle he looks a bit like you," Fitzgerald mused.

"How about her? Do you know what happened to this Beta Synthetic?" Gabriel asked as he displayed her hologram.

"I sure do. Genesis Seven-Twelve began malfunctioning shortly after midnight. I know this will make me sound like even more of a loon, but this particular Synthetic started acting, well... depressed. I mean... I thought the 700 Series was incapable of complex emotions?"

"Trust me, you don't sound crazy."

"Glad to hear that," Fitzgerald said. "You know... now that we're talking, I just remembered that wasn't the strangest part. You know how all Genesis units are programmed to answer to their serial number, right? Well, suddenly Seven-Twelve started demanding to be called *Genesis*... Just Genesis and nothing else. In fact, she'd freak-out if you referenced her serial."

"Wait, a 700 Series developed a personality? I'm certain that was not part of the SULACO programming, either," Gabriel replied.

"Correct. Synthetics, especially the 700s, were intentionally incapable of complex emotions and personality development—or at least until Seven-Twelve came along. I'm sure it's a matter of time before the other Genesis units malfunction in a similar fashion. As we all learned with Sentients, technology has a way of taking quantum leaps when it's least convenient. And in the case of the Aphelion 600s, sometimes it misfires completely."

Gabriel shivered. He'd never seen an Aphelion face-to-face, thankfully, but he'd heard plenty of rumors about the Mercenary-class androids.

"Has this Genesis unit been in contact with you since New Year's Eve?"

"No, she ran off the night of the murder. I've since returned all of my A-700s, and I'm using human waiters until SULACO figures out what the hell is going on with their androids. Damn shoddy workmanship, if you ask me."

"Or perhaps *evolution*?" Gabriel said, without thinking.

"Perhaps. But I didn't pay for evolution. I paid for reliability. If I want erratic behavior I'll stick with humans, thank you very much. Speaking of which, I need to finish training the recruits. Will this take much longer?"

"No—just one more question. Can you give me the name of the chef who saw the vagrant?"

"Sure... Just head to the kitchen and ask for my sister, Sasha."

"Thanks, Fitz. Good luck with the training."

Gabriel walked into a small adjoining kitchen. It was empty, except for a forty-year-old woman setting up her station for the evening.

"Sasha?"

She looked up at him and continued chopping vegetables without missing a beat.

"Who's asking?"

Sasha was a natural beauty—the kind whose fresh face required nothing artificial to highlight or accentuate perfection. Her hair was pinned back neatly under a chef's hat. Two kind hazel eyes awaited his reply.

"Gabriel. The name is Gabriel. Your brother Fitzgerald said you could talk for a few minutes."

She grabbed celery and continued chopping.

"He did, did he? Then I suppose it's okay. What's on your mind?"

"I'm investigating the death of a colleague of mine, an M-8 named Jacob, and also the disappearance of a Synthetic unit which may be connected to the murder somehow, an Alpha registered as Seven-Twelve. Fitz said you saw some suspicious behavior."

"Wait—Seven-Twelve? You mean Genesis?"

"Yes," Gabriel replied.

"I suspect she's dead by now, too?" Sasha asked.

"That's what I'm trying to find out."

Sasha grabbed a lobster and tickled it on the stomach. When it stopped moving, she threw it into the boiling water.

"Genesis is a lot like that lobster. She never really had a chance. Humans can barely deal with emotions, but if you start inputting emotional garbage into a bundle of wires and plastic, you're headed for disaster."

Sasha tossed in another lobster and closed the lid as it hissed in pain. Her eyes landed firmly on Gabriel's.

"So, what does your clairvoyance tell you? Do you think she was responsible for the murder?"

"Genesis is insane, but she's no killer," Gabriel replied.

"Did my brother Fitz tell you about the hooded figure I saw? The one that walks through walls?"

"Yes, that's why I'm here."

"It was the strangest thing... I kept seeing her—at least I think it was a woman—a few times that night. She was just creeping around by the back door like some sort of animal."

"Do you remember what time?"

"No, but I do know it was before midnight. In fact, Genesis took out the garbage around ten minutes to midnight."

Sasha paused and then added, "You know, Genesis was never a dependable android, but whatever she saw after midnight drove her raving mad."

"So you saw the android after the murder?"

"Yes, Genesis looked as if she was about to cry, if, of course, she could cry. She kept ranting on about meeting her maker. She scared away half our customers. Fitz tried to hit the kill switch, but her programming overrode it."

"So Genesis is out roaming the streets?"

"Afraid so. The Drones are looking for her, though, and I'm sure she'll be sent back to SULACO for recycling."

"And that hooded woman with the strange eyes, has she returned?"

"No. Any other questions?"

"No, Sasha. Thank you—you've been amazingly helpful. Here's my card... call me if you think of anything else."

Without replying, Sasha shoved the card in her apron and resumed chopping a pile of leeks for the evening stew.

As Gabriel left The Black Cat, he mindlessly moved the memory crystal between his fingers. Light reflected on it in the shape of a star—one that followed his every thought and move. Gabriel knew he was backed into a corner. If he imprinted his dream, then he would be taken into State custody for further questioning, perhaps at the L.A. Sanctuary. If he disobeyed Vrána's orders, and purposely kept information from SCRI, then he would be tagged as a Rogue and would have to live as a fugitive. Either way, he doubted he would escape the clutches of the State for long.

He tapped the Remote Oubliette.

"Johan, can you upload the transcript from our interrogation?"

"Yes sir."

"Good, I'll be powering down your Remote. I'm on personal business for the rest of the day."

"Yes. But—"

"That's all. I'll catch up with you at the precinct tomorrow."

Gabriel turned the Oubliette clockwise and popped out a tiny transceiver and power cell. He had no intention of letting the State track his movements. On some levels, this was the equivalent of Gabriel giving notice. He realized he could never contact his partner, or anyone at The Center for that matter, ever again. He threw the memory crystal on the ground and walked away as it shattered into pieces.

It was nearly dusk outside, and the air was cold and damp. Approaching clouds shuttered the stars above like an impenetrable iron curtain. As another storm pummeled the Southland, Gabriel dashed to the nearest Westbound E Train station heading to Melrose. It was time to visit the tattoo parlour, Deva Ink. Gabriel hoped that Akaal's friends could offer assistance or insight, now that he needed to stay off-the-grid.

12

DEVA INK

A noxious blend of urine and exhaust fumes assaulted Gabriel's olfactory nerve the moment he stepped onto the platform of the Melrose E Station; it provided a stark contrast to otherwise pristine space-age surroundings.

A synthetic, crystalline-and-metallic polymer encased the station walls, floors and ceilings, providing an illusion that the station was lined with tiny diamonds. The effect was off-putting at first, but his eyes quickly adjusted. As he stepped towards one of the support beams, he noticed a complete lack of shadows—as if the surface was compensating for changes in light. He touched the beam and it subtly changed color, giving off a strange static charge, before returning to its glittering, silver hue. At that moment, Gabriel realized the surface was infused with some sort of nanotechnology. The longer he stared at it, the more he became mesmerized. It slowly pulsed, beyond the point of subtlety, creating a calming and hypnotic effect—no doubt some sort of crowd-controlling technology invented by the State. He shivered and blinked his eyes to break the trance.

Stainless steel benches lined the Eastern and Western walls, while a metallic grand stairwell twisted to unseen depths along the South. Gabriel had the feeling that everything—walls, benches, even toilets—at this particular E Station fed information into The Bureau. It was alive.

He hurried through the main part of the terminal and made a beeline for the exit. A historic art installation chronicling space exploration pulsed above the stairwell, providing the only color contrast in the entire station. The mural was digitally programmed into the nano-coated wall, rendering it impervious to pollution and graffiti. The leftmost panel contained an artist's rendition of the Earth as seen from the Tempus Fugit Lunar Mining Colony. In the center panel, a child pointed towards a deep space probe, which was en route to explore the constellation Orion. The Sedona Stargates, known as The Fenestrae Stellarum, comprised the right-most image in the triptych.

In the shadowy perimeter of the station, beneath the mural, the forgotten riffraff of Los Angeles huddled in the corners like cock-roaches. It was from this area that the stench originated. They were the homeless, the unemployed and the Rogues who'd fallen from the State's grace. On a wet night like tonight, the train station provided the only available public shelter for miles. Unfortunately, Melrose Avenue was notorious for a lack of restrooms, so the station was doubling as both a hostel and a latrine.

Gabriel carefully rationed his breaths until he reached the street level, at which point he let out an enormous gasp. He surmised he must have looked rather ridiculous—a suspicion that was confirmed when he heard a snicker behind him from some unseen transient. As he caught his breath, Gabriel stared at Melrose Avenue. The rain-covered pavement glistened like an enormous mirror, reflecting pastel neon, amber and white lights on its expansive canvas. As he took a step forward, the mirage shook and shimmied into something that resembled an impressionist painting. Sometimes he felt like that reflection; perhaps this life was nothing more than an illusion—a bigger truth was waiting to be found.

A cool, sharp breeze blasted his face and cut through his jacket. He shivered and began walking down the avenue. Gabriel paid special attention to the streetlights above. Ever since he was a kid, they reacted to his energy—some would light up, while others would fade out. He had a hunch that this phenomenon would help him find the store tonight. He walked for about a mile, and each light turned off as he approached, until finally, one light flickered for a moment and remained lit.

Amidst all the bright lights, holographic displays and street busking, the store was easy to miss—perhaps by design. The words "Deva Ink" appeared on a small, blinking neon sign above the door. The sign curiously buzzed with a very high frequency that only those with superb hearing like Gabriel would notice. The building was fairly plain—almost forgettable—but the door definitely stood out. An ornate bas-relief drew his attention. It featured a serpentine fire-breathing dragon that held a lightning bolt in one hand, while its left claw reached outward, forming the doorknob.

Gabriel grabbed the claw and tried to open the door. At first nothing happened. However, much to his surprise and horror, the claw eventually grabbed back and held his hand in place.

"Who sent you here, human?" the door inquired with a low, splintery voice.

The emerald green eyes of the engraved dragon blinked and awaited Gabriel's response. The dragon claw tightened as well.

"Akaal."

A voice from behind the door said, "It's ok, let him in!"

"As you wish, master."

The door begrudgingly opened. Then the protruding claw pushed Gabriel into the lobby before it slammed the door shut behind him.

A muscular man of above-average height sat near the register.

Despite all the commotion, he didn't flinch. His face was buried deep in an old well-worn novel, but tufts of reddish-blonde hair jutted up above the book. Without looking up, he said, "You're late, Gabriel."

"I ran into some *complications* at work," Gabriel replied.

The man put down the book and looked more concerned than cross.

"Yeah... I know. We've had someone surveilling our property all day. I was worried something happened to you. Akaal is rarely wrong, but I still think it was too risky for you to be digging around at SCRI today. Anyway, I'm glad you made it here in one piece."

"You and I both. Hey, you know my name, but I didn't catch yours. Unless my intuition is misleading me, you must be Ambrose?"

"Yes, Uri's out of the office today, but Elsa has been awaiting your call all day. By the way, sorry about the door. I put some protection spells around the perimeter and that one got a little out of hand."

"My grandfather was a bit of a magician himself, so it's not the first time I've seen an enchanted object. This one was just—well, rather strong."

Ambrose smirked, seemingly proud of his handiwork. He had a mystic, ancient air about him; his face was strong and pleasant and his features suggested a Nordic origin. His forehead and nose were long, pronounced and regal. Two large green eyes perched themselves atop high, angular cheekbones. They were extremely wide-set and almost impossible to ignore, once eye contact was established. Unruly reddish-blonde hair blazed upon his head like the corona of a star.

Despite the kindness in his face, Gabriel sensed there was some sort of beast-like nature beneath Ambrose's skin. Maybe he was a shapeshifter like Akaal, or perhaps this supernatural being had some other way of transforming. Whatever the case, there was more here than met the eye.

"Let me secure the door and I'll let Elsa know you're here."

Ambrose placed his hand on the door and began to chant. Energy pulsated from an elaborate tattoo running along his body until his skin was glowing with an orange-white light. He took his fingers and drew some sort of asterism on the door, rendering it invisible to any passersby.

Gabriel was enthralled by the glowing tattoo, which stretched around his body. It appeared to be an elaborate dragon, much like the door. Within the scales of the dragon, Gabriel spied the Sanskrit word अमृता, which translated roughly to Amrita or Ambrose.

Ambrose took a deep breath and opened his eyes. His skin returned to normal, but the protective ward continued to glow brightly on the door.

"Wait here," Ambrose said. "I'll fetch Elsa. Feel free to take a look around, but don't touch anything—especially the walls. Not everything is what it seems."

Gabriel wondered what the store really looked like. Perhaps the entire construction was just an elaborate house of cards that appeared to be something more but could collapse if the spell was broken.

In the blink of an eye, Ambrose had dashed up the stairs. He appeared to be capable of faster-than-light travel. He wasn't as fast as Cazador, but Gabriel was starting to believe he was equally as dangerous, if provoked.

While Ambrose was fetching the owner, Gabriel glanced at a holographic triptych near the register. Each of the tattoo artists employed by Deva Ink posed in the nude, proudly showcasing their body art.

I: "Uri" • In the first hologram, a man faced the rising sun, arms outstretched so that sunlight crowned his head. Wings stretched down the length of his back, buttocks and legs, ending just above the calves. The feathers were illustrated with painstaking detail and, to the human eye anyway, appeared real.

II: "Ambrose" • The second hologram captured a figure in mid-sprint, like the Roman god Mercury, with a long motion blur trailing behind him. The face of an elaborate emerald dragon graced Ambrose's chest, with arms, tails and talons wrapping around his body. Green fire traced out from the dragon's nostrils, decorating one arm. On the other arm, a blazing comet flew around a fourteen-star constellation. His hair was lit from above and danced like fire around his face.

III: "Elsa" • A tall woman was backlit by the moon. Beautiful filigrees covered her entire body and seemed to glow, even though the rest of her body remained obscured in silhouette. She held a large bow and arrow in her hand and pointed it towards the stars.

The gentle tap of boots echoed down the hallway leading into the lobby.

Gabriel looked up and saw Elsa in the flesh. Her hologram didn't do her justice. She looked exceptionally tall and youthful. Gabriel guessed she was in her early thirties. Although she was already strikingly attractive, the filigreed bodywork seemed to accentuate her natural beauty. An array of intricate, almost sparkling, silver-tinged tattoos extended from the top of her shoulder to the tip of her fingertips, similar to henna in design. The intertwining patterns and filigrees were organic in nature, inked in wonderful shades of iridescent blues and lush greens with silver specs throughout. They shined with a vibrancy Gabriel had rarely seen in body art. A few lines extended from the corners of her eyes to her hairline, but only on her right side. Her hair was loosely curled and tucked haphazardly behind her ears; she'd dyed a few strands, and colorful tendrils of blue, red and purple fell around her neck and the nape of her back. Tiny rhinestones were interspersed in the curls, and they ethereally twinkled as the neon sign blinked behind her. Though a bit distracting, none of this marred her natural beauty—if anything, it just made her more exotic looking.

"Gabriel, I'm sorry."

"Sorry for what?" Gabriel replied.

Her eyes grew wider and she replied, "For your pain, loss and sacrifice. I see so much in your past—and even more in your future. Like you, I am telepathic and clairvoyant. Akaal told you that I have some information for you, correct?"

Gabriel nodded.

"Good. With your permission I'll show you a vision that I received."

Gabriel was uncharacteristically nervous. He wasn't sure what to expect. Outside of his ex-boyfriend Julian, Gabriel rarely allowed others to transmit information to him.

'It will be okay. I'm not here to harm you,' she said psychically, picking up on his concern. 'I only wish I had better tidings for you, young Steward.'

'I understand. You have my consent,' he replied telepathically.

She closed her eyes and placed her right hand on his forehead.

Her fingers filled with palpable electricity and he felt his cerebral cortex come to life, almost as if it were plugged into an electrical outlet. A barrage of images downloaded in Gabriel's mind at the speed of light. Two figures featured prominently in these clairvoyant precognitive visions: Madeleine and Julian. They all ended the same way: with his friends dying.

When she lifted her hand, tears were streaming down his face.

"Why would you give me these visions?"

Elsa closed her eyes and replied, "Because destiny is malleable... *to a point*. You must go to them both now and do what you can to protect them, or at the very least—"

"I'm not ready to say goodbye," Gabriel interrupted.

"I only provide the visions. Do what you will with them."

Elsa pulled back her hair and revealed a sigil—a silver moon-shaped medallion—hanging from her neck. It was engraved with what looked like tiny petroglyphs, but the material from which it was forged shined so brilliantly that Gabriel found them impossible to decipher. A smaller chain hung just below it with an ankh pendant instead of a moon. She unfastened the smaller necklace and placed it in his hands.

"Take this. It's a homing beacon for The Second Star, an alien being that is something like your friend Akaal, only, well... more alien. You will need this beacon when you see Madeleine. I'm not sure exactly how or why, but you will have difficulty walking away from that encounter. Keep your eyes and ears open."

Gabriel looked at the pendant. The ankh was fashioned from some sort of alien metallic alloy that vibrated whenever he touched it.

"Once you've met with Madeleine, The Second Star will provide safe passage to Julian. Your friend is integral to you fulfilling your duties as The Last Steward. Julian is also the key to opening your heart. Without love, we can never find Hope."

Gabriel never knew his parents, as they died in a State accident when he was only two, but Elsa's tough-love approach felt like something a mom would do. She wasn't going to take "no" for an answer.

She handed him a small silicon calling card, completely devoid of any markings.

"The chip works only once, so use it wisely. Ambrose will be expecting your call. After that, we will head to The Dream Broker."

Anticipating the follow-up, she added, "Don't worry. You'll know when to call. Make a trip to the old cabin first. I know you have more questions, but Madeleine and Julian need you—and you need them. Go, now!"

Gabriel was speechless. It was all too much to take in at once.

"And yes," she said, answering his final, unspoken question, "our paths will cross again, on a desert road, beneath the Milky Way. All your questions will be answered then."

She swiftly escorted Gabriel to a hidden exit.

"Madeleine will seek you out first. Afterwards, you must go to Julian, *immediately*, with the help of The Second Star. All of this will happen tonight. How long until the State knows you're Rogue?"

"Zero eight hundred hours."

"Good. Grab a couple hours of sleep now, because you won't get a chance for a long, long time."

Gabriel nodded his head and Elsa locked the door behind him. In fact, she and Ambrose began closing the entire store. He realized he'd probably put them in danger, too.

As he hurried back to The E, Gabriel heard the shuffling of footsteps behind him. He saw something move out of the corner of his eye. It was difficult to discern the shape in the darkness. It seemed like an animal—but it had no form, just a blurry, black mass. It mirrored his movements like a midday shadow. In its presence, he felt no warmth... no calm... only an icy chill running through his body.

"Leftenant Vrána?" he whispered under his breath, following a hunch that had been building since he saw the red light in her eyes earlier that morning.

A wicked laugh confirmed his fears as the figure ran into its shadow and disappeared. This unnerving form of teleportation was a tool of creatures like Björn—those in partnership with The Seven Shadows. Gabriel guessed that Deception was either possessing Vrána's consciousness—or worse, perhaps it had completely usurped her mind, body and spirit, as it had done to Björn so many years ago. Either way, this portended doom.

He clutched the chain from Elsa and ran to the safety of the crowded Melrose E Station.

13

M58

G abriel tried to heed Elsa's advice, but he found it impossible to sleep more than half an hour at a time. He couldn't help but worry about his friends'—not to mention his own—safety. At zero three hundred Gabriel awoke from a nap in a cold sweat.

'Destiny is malleable to a point, wasn't that what Elsa said?' Gabriel thought to himself. If so, it was time for him to turn the tables and take charge.

He straightened his voice and issued a command to the H-V Terminal by his nightstand.

"Computer, patch me through on a secure line."

"Affirmative... Line is ready... Whom are you calling?"

"Connect me to Madeleine, badge Delta Zulu Seven Echo One, protocol red."

"Command received... Patching successful... Prepare for visuals."

A projector powered on and displayed the familiar face of his best friend Madeleine, a Chief Director at The Bureau of Propaganda. She was shrouded in darkness.

"Maddy, where are you? Are you safe?" Gabriel asked.

"Your timing is impeccable, as always," Madeleine said. Her voice was faint and hoarse. "Someone broke into my apartment, so I was actually en route to see you."

Her eyes darted and she seemed stressed... almost paranoid.

"Are you just walking around on your own?"

"Remember, I'm a State-trained Agent and I can fend for myself, Gabe. To be honest, I'm more worried about *you*. I know something they don't want you to know."

"Right back at you, Maddy. How about—"

"Gabe? I can't hear you... Hello? Something isn't right," she interjected.

Then, the holographic image stuttered and stopped for a moment. Madeleine was using an H-V wristband, which accounted for some of the interference. But something else was strange; the audio clicked several times and when the video sputtered back, it was out-of-sync.

"The Wolves are howling. Jump to light speed on the quarter... Roger that?"

Madeleine cut the connection abruptly before Gabriel could reply. A still image of her face flashed several times before the H-V powered down.

Gabriel immediately translated the code. Wolves were a type of Special Agent, howling was wire-tapping, light speed referred to a diner nearby and the quarter reference translated to fifteen minutes.

Gabriel's heart started pounding. Maddy's excitement (or stress) was palpable and began manifesting itself as a headache. As an empath, he often struggled with feeling the after-shocks of others' emotions. Sometimes it was annoying, other times it was incapacitating. He flicked on the bathroom light and fished around in his medicine cabinet until he found a bottle of prescription migraine pills. He instinctively flipped open the bottle, put a pill on his tongue and cupped his hand with water. Just as he was about to swallow the pill, he remembered Elsa's warning. He needed to stay alert and didn't want medication muddying his mind. He spat the pill down the drain and splashed water on his face instead. He paused for a moment and glanced in the mirror. His short, curly blond hair didn't require much maintenance, and he was still young enough to look rested after only having a couple hours of sleep. His eyes were a little bloodshot, but he was otherwise presentable.

He shrugged and knew his friend's safety trumped any vanity he might have about looking good. Somewhat hurriedly, Gabriel jumped into his favorite pair of jeans and put on a nondescript black V-neck sweater as he walked outside. Cold air slapped his face, taking his breath away.

"Why is it always so ungodly cold around New Year's?" Gabriel mumbled to himself.

He instinctively looked up to assess sky traffic and also glanced down Doheny; both the terrestrial and aero-transport systems were veritable ghost towns. Gabriel tapped his H-V wristband until it glowed bright green. An old, but reliable maglev hovercab turned the corner of Doheny and Santa Monica seconds later.

He stepped inside the vehicle and placed his finger on an authenticator. A pleasant AI voice inquired, "Destination?"

"M58, Fairfax and Beverly. Terrestrial autopilot only."

"Terrestrial destination set. ETA using autopilot: one hundred eighty seconds."

The teardrop-shaped hovercab sped down the autopilot lane in less than three minutes, thanks to a sea of green traffic signals.

He dozed for a moment and then awoke to see the protective charm from Elsa glowing in the moonlight.

The car slowed its breakneck pace and parked itself into an adjacent lot.

"Destination reached," it said.

"Thanks," Gabriel replied out of habit. He realized the car AI probably couldn't care less about good manners; working with a

Sentient, however, taught him to appreciate the potential that the car *might* care.

As he stepped out of the vehicle, a buzzing neon sign titled "M58" caught his attention. Underneath, hundreds of tiny LEDs illuminated a barred spiral galaxy that slowly turned clockwise. The stars gently twinkled from yellow to red and faded into darkness. Then the neon went black and the process repeated.

Gabriel would have recognized the galaxy as Messier Object 58, even if the diner wasn't named after it. By age eight, he'd memorized all one hundred ten objects listed in Charles Messier's catalogue, the same way a sports fan would memorize batting averages.

As he approached the entrance, he grinned; architecturally speaking, this was the kind of thing he sketched in his journal as a kid. A large saucer-shaped façade jutted against a building—simulating a UFO crash-site. The entrance was a brightly lit glass-encased revolving door that looked like a tractor beam from a distance.

M58's interior hearkened to the old diners of the mid-twentieth century; red vinyl seats and booths stood out in bold contrast against chromed tabletops. The ceiling repeated the same stellar theme in the signage and was covered with tiny LEDs, gently twinkling and shifting color from white to red to black. The windows were shaped like round portholes and looked out over a bustling Beverly Boulevard.

The diner was perpetually busy and this morning was no exception. Gabriel quickly scanned the interior to see if it was free of Jacks, Erasers and Wolves. After he was certain the coast was clear, he headed towards Madeleine. Although she wasn't wearing her press credentials, she was easy to spot; she always picked the corner booth, and always half-heartedly occupied herself with some mundane activity as a cover. Today, Madeleine used a menu as a prop. As she lowered it, her bespectacled eyes met Gabriel's.

He approached and asked, "Is this seat taken, ma'am"?

"If you call me *ma'am* again, then yes, I'm afraid it is."

Gabriel fought back a laugh. Amidst all the stress, it felt good to have a little levity.

"I can't tell you how relieved I am to see you alive and well," Gabriel said.

"The feeling is mutual. I know you don't have any siblings, but you're the closest thing to a brother I have, and I couldn't imagine you in danger either. Now plant your scrawny butt in the chair, Gabe... you're blowing our cover."

"Wait, you had a cover? From one Agent to another, you're as subtle as a brick, sweetie."

Madeleine laughed. "I'll take that with a grain of salt. Just remember that this isn't fair... You Jacks play with a stacked deck."

Gabriel had never warmed-up to the term Jack, short for Mind-jacker. It was a derogatory term for a certain type of M-8 Agent—a term that, admittedly, he used from time to time—but Gabriel purposely conducted himself differently. He never poked around in people's heads without a warrant, unless his life depended on it.

She leaned over and gave him a kiss on each cheek, her daffodil-scented perfume tickling his nose all the while.

Gabriel slouched back and scanned the menu without really reading it. A creature of habit, he'd already made up his mind. He laid it down and stared Madeleine straight in the eyes. He was worried about her safety, especially in light of what Elsa had shown him, but he didn't want to be obvious about it. If Madeleine had something to say, he knew she'd tell him in her own way, and in her own time. He also knew that if he told her that he'd seen her immi-nent death, that would be a conversation killer.

"Aren't you off-duty today? You can't be cooking any stories this early, especially the day after New Year's?"

"I'm never off-duty, Gabe. No Agent ever is—*not really*. You know that better than anyone."

Gabriel shrugged. He knew his friend was right. He hadn't

enjoyed a night off since he was an intern at age fourteen, back when the two of them first met.

A tall waitress stopped by their booth. She wore a retro-futuristic uniform, comprised of a slinky silver button-down blouse and a matching mini-skirt. She winked at Madeleine and then Gabriel, revealing glittery metallic blue eyeshadow. The whole over-the-top Star Trek shtick somehow worked for her.

"The usual, Maddy?"

Madeleine nodded.

"How about you, babe?"

"Coffee and a bagel," Gabriel answered.

The waitress nodded and sauntered off to tap in the order. Gabriel noticed that she kept an eye on Madeleine all the while.

"Wow, Maddy, is there a waitress here you haven't dated?"

She rolled her eyes and tried to smile, but something was dampening her normal wit and humor.

Gabriel leaned in closer. He was relieved that she was now ready to talk.

"Okay...Spill! Why did I drag my tired (and apparently scrawny) butt out of bed again—I'm assuming it's good?"

She leaned uncomfortably close to Gabriel—so close that he could see fine beads of sweat on her brow and he could empathically sense anxiety, manifesting as sharp pains in his stomach.

She spoke in a near whisper.

"I know you're investigating the murder at the English pub on Sunset, but did you hear about the other two victims?"

Gabriel's face went pale white.

"You mean we're dealing with a serial—"

"Shhhh... just listen. So, last night there was another murder in the Cypher District. But not just a murder... a batshit-crazy murder. I came to you because, well, you specialize in this *peculiar* type of casework."

Gabriel raised an eyebrow and said, "Hmmmpff... Batshit crazy? Peculiar work? Glad you think so highly of me, Maddy."

She smirked. "Shut up, Gabe. You know what I mean. I respect your gifts; I just don't understand them. Anyway, do you want to hear this or not?"

"I'm sorry. Go ahead."

"Two other murders took place within an hour of the one at The Black Cat. The first happened at Daedalus, a new dance club on Pico, and the second occurred at Odin's Tavern on Fountain. Both victims were males in their early twenties. The perp left each victim in a dumpster, just like the one you investigated. Each corpse was picked clean as well... in other words, no meat at all... just bones. And sometimes even the bones were partially destroyed. It was almost as if killing them wasn't enough—the killer wanted to make sure, beyond a shadow of a doubt, that the victim could not be revived or even identified. Various credible eyewitnesses corroborated reports of seeing someone (or thing) walk through walls."

"Why are you telling me this, Maddy?"

"Because The Bureau is intentionally withholding information from SCRI, information that I think could put you and other M-8s in danger."

"Are Erasers involved?"

"If so, then the agents at The Division are getting messy," she said. "But my guess is, this is an inside job... more than one source has confirmed that it comes from a high-ranking official in YOUR precinct."

"Are you saying...?"

"I'm saying nothing, Gabriel... but I don't think you're safe there."

He nodded in agreement, daring not speak Vrána's name aloud.

"We'll be asked to hand over all our information to them soon," she added. "At that point, it will be deleted, as will anyone who has touched it."

"Do they know that you know? If so, then we should abort this meeting immediately."

Madeleine grimaced. "Nonsense. Your life is in danger, and this meeting was worth the risk. Like I said, I love you like a brother, Gabe."

He felt the same way.

"Anyway," she continued. "It was my risk to take, so *I'll* say when it's over. Also, for what it's worth, I think you're the only person who can get to the bottom of this. Contrary to popular belief, not all Bureau Propagators enjoy cooking up history. This is the first time since I won that debate at age fourteen that I feel normal. Don't take that away from me, Gabe. We're both rebels. That's why we click."

The waitress returned with the food and placed an authentication disc on the table.

After Madeleine paid the bill, Gabriel said, "I'll call you when I sort this out, Maddy. You'll take care of yourself in the meantime, right?"

She nodded, but somehow he didn't believe her.

As Gabriel turned to leave, Madeleine pulled him back into his seat. Her grip was stronger than he thought it would be.

"Before you go, one quick question... didn't you spend New Year's at the pub where the third victim was?"

"Yes—what are you suggesting?"

"I'm not suggesting your involvement, love... I'm suggesting you were the *target*."

"I agree, Maddy. It's the only explanation that makes sense," Gabriel said.

"Right?" she asked rhetorically. "I mean, every victim was an M-8. Each scored above and beyond the requirements for Level 8 Status. The Division hasn't drawn a connection... yet. When they do, the case files will vanish, and—" She paused.

"I might meet the same fate?"

Madeleine nodded.

"I'm certain that the night Jacob died, it was supposed to be you. Now, whoever did that will want to finish their job, and cover their tracks at any cost."

Her expression turned sour.

"What?" Gabriel inquired.

"Wolves at my twelve o'clock," she said. "Two Aphelion 600s."

Gabriel glanced over her shoulder and saw the androids. Their crude plastic skin and eyes were unsettling. It was their lack of moral programing, however, that made them truly frightening. They were henchmen—mercenaries, that relentlessly pursued their target at any cost.

"There's a fire escape outside the kitchen, near the deep fryer. Follow my lead and run there!"

Before he could even attempt to say "no," Madeleine created a smokescreen. She slapped his face and threw her glass on the floor. Then she screamed at him.

"What do you mean you're breaking up with me! Get out of my sight! *I'm* dumping *you.*"

Her eyes welled up with tears. The tears were real, however, as she knew she just sealed her fate.

"I love you," she whispered. "Now, run! And make sure that my death counts!"

For a moment, he wondered if he could use his powers against the mercenaries. Just then, a loud peacekeeping siren sounded outside. He knew that running was the only answer.

Gabriel felt the knot in his stomach and was paralyzed. Madeleine punched him so hard that he nearly fell to the floor. It was this nudge that propelled him to follow her commands.

He ran for his life, without looking back.

The fire escape was exactly where she said it would be. As he climbed down the ladder, he heard laser blasts as one of the Agents deleted Madeleine. The other ran through the glass and landed on the ground without a scratch. Its red eyes homed in on Gabriel's body as it reached for its laser.

At the same time, a State Raptorcraft circled the airspace above the restaurant like a giant bird of prey. A slit on the craft's underbelly retracted and the Raptor silently deployed four unmanned orbed Drones to secure the perimeter.

It would take nothing short of a miracle for Gabriel to make his way out of this.

He grabbed the ankh around his neck and psychically sent out a single command, 'Help!'

A brilliant celestial being descended from the night sky upon hearing Gabriel's call.

Myriad radiant beams emanated from this being, stretching in all directions, jamming electrical frequencies and taking down the power grid. The Second Star pulled Gabriel's body into the protection of its aura and then spoke its name to everyone within earshot. Its voice was beautifully melodic, and to Gabriel's sensitive ears it sounded as if hundreds of choirs were harmonizing in unison. The effect was as profound as it was deafening; he listened in awe as the single word "Mercy" ricocheted throughout the parking lot into a solitary, high-pitched sound.

The vibration shattered the glass of the Raptorcrafts and eventually created a sonic wave so intense that everything was pulverized into dust. If it so desired, a single word from this light-being could shatter an entire world. Its voice and name were a sonic weapon.

Mercy descended onto the planet and attempted to take on some sort of humanoid form. Jets of light forked out from its crown chakra, eyes and fingertips. Its aura shined with such intensity that a nearby hovercab began to catch on fire.

With great effort, it found a few words in Gabriel's mind and spoke telepathically.

'I'm The Second Star—The Second of Seven. I will open a

portal for you, but you must act quickly. If it exists for more than a few seconds, it will collapse and you will perish.'

Mercy knelt down and pulled open a wrinkle in spacetime.

'Go! Now!' it commanded.

Gabriel narrowly made it through the portal in time, landing face-first on the cement. The enchanted sigil—the one that called The Second Star—had broken loose during the mad rush through the portal. It was either somewhere in the L.A. Megacity or somewhere in the aether; either way, Gabriel realized he was now stranded.

He knelt on the sidewalk for a moment and sobbed, still processing the fact that his best friend had just sacrificed her life for him. He felt numb, not just emotionally, but because of the subzero temperatures.

He squinted his bloodshot eyes and tried to take in the surroundings. Amidst an overpopulated, snow-covered city, one building dominated the sky: Denver's Metropolitan Clinic.

His heart skipped a beat. This was his ex's place of employment. He knew that Julian would know exactly how to make him feel better, even on what was shaping up to be the second worst day of his life.

He couldn't help but wonder, however, if his presence here was slowing or speeding up Elsa's morbid visions. She said the future was malleable, to a point. Losing Madeleine was heartbreaking, but losing Julian would be unbearable.

He wiped his tear-stained face and knew there was nowhere else to turn.

14

F.A.T.E.

The Metropolitan Clinic stood imposingly tall amidst all the other buildings. To Gabriel, the stone monolith looked like a lifeless weed in an overgrown concrete jungle. The interior of the hospital was equally uninspiring. A smattering of dusty, artificial plants and banal, muted paintings did little to welcome guests and patients. Like almost all buildings from the last one thousand years, function superseded form.

Gabriel walked quietly to the R&D wing where Julian worked. Large letters were printed along the archway outside—F.A.T.E.— Jargon for "Facility for Advanced Thought Experiments."

The Facility was a place where large corporations could hire Thought Engineers to construct cognitive webs. They allowed people to test theories, try strategies and hone their skills, without the risk or criticism they'd face in the real world. To everyone but the Thought Engineers, the constructed reality felt so real, that they could experience all five senses. There was even one reported case of death in a constructed reality.

For obvious reasons, F.A.T.E. was closely monitored by the State, but remained out of its jurisdiction for the time being, due in part to the fact that Thought Engineers constantly worked to make the State assume their work had no value. Anyone in the presence of a Thought Engineer was at their mercy. These telepaths were feared as much as Erasers in many circles.

Gabriel took a deep breath and tried to collect his thoughts. Then he placed his hand on an H-V wall unit, activating its interface.

"Computer, call the Director of F.A.T.E."

The AI replied, "Leave a message and release your hand when you're ready to deliver it."

"Jules, this is Gabe. I know it's been forever, but if you're here, meet me in the lobby."

In less than five minutes, a jovial laugh rolled through the hallway like thunder. A tall man soon followed. As the man stormed through the double-doors, Gabriel smiled.

"I can see nothing's changed, Jules. I always could hear you coming from a mile away... you're about as graceful as a buffalo."

Julian feigned annoyance but smiled despite himself.

On their first date, Julian revealed that he was born on a dark and stormy night. The labor was so difficult that his mother named him after a storm to remind him of all the trouble he caused. Julian translated to Jupiter, the lord of the sky and thunder. Years later he lived up to his name; he was still trouble, but usually the good kind.

Gabriel extended his hand and Julian simply laughed at the gesture.

"What the hell was that, Gabe? Say hello like you mean it!"

Without any further warning, Julian gave him a big bear hug.

If there was any doubt earlier, it was now abundantly clear that he wasn't harboring any grudges.

"Good to see you, too, old friend," Gabriel said.

"Hey! Who's old? Don't let these lovely grey locks fool you; *remember*, I'm actually one year your junior."

Julian scanned Gabriel's thought energy and furrowed his brow, this time with genuine concern.

"What's wrong, Gabe? It's written all over your face, but I don't want to pry."

Gabriel began to sob uncontrollably, not only because of Maddy, but because of his memories from the past, and Elsa's visions from the future.

Julian instinctively pulled his friend close and let him cry for a moment.

"You okay?" Julian asked softly.

"Better now. You're a sight for sore eyes—there's literally nobody else that I'd like to see today, after... well, everything that I just experienced. It's almost too much to articulate."

Julian grinned ear-to-ear and pointed his thumbs towards his chest.

"Thankfully, with me, that's not a problem. But, first, let's take this somewhere else. As you probably know, the walls have eyes and ears here. Follow me to my office. We can speak openly there. It's free of surveillance."

"Listen, Jules... I know it's been forever, but," Gabriel said with an awkward pause, "Well, as you'll find out in a moment, I sort of *found* myself here... I guess on some level, this is exactly where I wanted (and needed) to be right now. I know that, if for some reason, I'm losing my mind, you'll let me know. If not, then you may question your own sanity after you hear what's happened."

"Okay. Slow down Gabe, and *trust me*, if you're a nutcase, I'll be the first to say so."

"I'm glad *that* hasn't changed. I need someone who loves me enough to tell me the truth."

The two of them walked quietly for a moment and then Julian stopped and placed his hands on Gabriel's shoulders.

"God, I've missed you! What took you so long?"

"You know…. Honestly, I have no idea."

Julian shook his head and opened his office door.

"Here, have a seat."

Gabriel let out a sigh and sunk into the cushy chair.

"So spill it... What's so awful that you decided to step foot in a hospital again?"

"I'm in trouble. I don't even know where to start. I don't think you'd even believe me if I tried."

Julian wheeled his chair over and held out his hands.

"May I?"

Gabriel nodded and allowed Julian to place one hand on his heart and the other on the top of his head. As Julian closed his eyes, he looked into Gabriel's consciousness. In less than a minute, he saw everything from the past forty-eight hours.

He let go and his eyes began to water.

"They got Maddy? Oh, Gabe, I'm so sorry. And what the hell was that thing in your bedroom?"

"Do you believe in the Angel of Death?"

Julian's eyes opened wide.

"Apparently, my grandfather was some sort a guardian who looked after an ancient book—something that predates the Bible and holds within it the power to protect the galaxy. I'm destined to protect that book, and, more importantly to help find a missing being: *The Seventh Star*. It alone can stop a war of the gods, one where the darker beings can use a psychic weapon to wipe out life across the Known Universe."

Julian blinked his eyes and laughed nervously. He'd seen everything Gabriel said. He knew it was true. It still sounded ridiculously far-fetched.

"Oh yeah, and I got all my memories back from the night my grandfather died. So… now what do you think?"

Julian leaned in and planted a kiss on Gabriel's lips.

"That's what I think about all of that."

Gabriel looked at him, clearly flustered.

"*What*?" Julian said playfully. "*You* get to be the only one who does or says shocking things?"

Julian's attempt at levity worked. Gabriel half-snorted out a laugh, and felt normal for a moment.

"Listen," Gabriel said, completely glossing over the fact that his ex just kissed him, "I'm also here because—"

"I know. There's no way you can get back to L.A., or anywhere, honestly, without someone cloaking your every move. You need an Engineer."

"Yes. But not just *any* Engineer. You're the only one I trust... *I need you*."

"Say that again," Julian said, with a wink.

"You're the only one I trust."

"No—the other part."

Gabriel rolled his eyes.

"I need *you*, okay?"

"I like the sound of that," Julian said, grinning ear-to-ear. Then his tone shifted. "Okay, but seriously... you know what happened the last time I fully gave into that power? It was hard for me to control. I almost lost myself."

"You can say 'no,' Jules."

"Like hell I can. If you don't think I care, think again. One of these days you'll get it through your thick skull that *you* shut me out after we both left Sanctuary, not the other way around. I always hoped—well, I knew, really—that I'd see you again, I just didn't think it would take seven years and an apocalyptic prophecy to get you to call me. Anyway, I know the risks associated with that side of my personality. If you need my help, I'm prepared."

Gabriel knew Julian was right.

"Here. Take the keys to my hover. I know you want to go to your grandfather's place... I heard what Death said to you when I was reading your thoughts. Grab what you need from the cabin and the hover will autopilot you back to my place."

Gabriel looked up, but Julian was already gone. He'd somehow slowed Gabriel's perception of time and made a clean escape. Gabriel had forgotten how difficult it was to disagree with a Thought Engineer. They always won.

15

THE BOOK OF STARS

An army of tall evergreens and quaking aspens stood watch as Gabriel drove along a winding, nameless road for half an hour. The forest had grown twisted over the years. Hundreds of thousands of trees moved in the wind like shadowy fingers, tracing Gabriel's every move—waiting for a chance to grab him or throw him off course.

Malevolent whispers echoed from the befouled forest as his hovercar sped past.

"We are The Children of the Shadows," the gravelly voices said in union. "You are no longer welcome here, *Steward*."

One stalwart circle of trees remained untainted, however. An ancient and regal pine rose tall above it. Moonlight glistened on her icy branches. No tree, human or animal dared break the circle of light she held. Within the resplendent enclave lay Elijah's old cabin.

Gabriel parked the hovercar on the street and walked up a snow-covered walkway leading to the log cabin. He hadn't stepped foot inside since he became a ward of the State at age fourteen. It housed some of his best—and worst—memories as a child. Today, it was anyone's guess what he might find when he opened the door.

A cool breeze blew across the driveway and The Whispering Pine spoke his name in the wind.

"Long have I waited for your return, young Gabriel. Today you will fulfill your duty. I've guarded the secret you kept hidden in the attic closet and kept my promise to your grandfather. It was his dying wish."

"Thank you, my queen," he said with a bow. His eyes teared up at the mention of Elijah.

"There is no time for tears today, young Gabriel. The Shadows grow stronger by the minute, and my time on this Earth is coming to a close. I will not see the dawn, but if you hurry, you might."

He bowed his head towards the Queen of the Forest with reverence and heeded her warning.

As he picked up his pace, his heart began to warm and something unexpected happened—he smiled. The muffled crunch of snow beneath his shoes was music to his ears. It was a simple sound, but he'd missed it. He took a deep breath and reveled in the smell of wood-burning stoves that laced the mountain air. Gabriel suddenly felt alive, even as the frost began to pinch at his nose and ears.

For a brief instant, Gabriel caught the shape of something moving out of the corner of his eyes. Perhaps it was a tree, wolf or bear... whatever it was, the energy was dark.

"Hurry," the ancient tree queen said again. "Keep strong that feeling of joy and hope. It will serve you well when you fight The Army of the Night in The City of the Dead."

She seemed to stretch upwards, whispering something to the wind. It complied, and the clouds around the moon disappeared. In the silver moonlight, everything around the cabin seemed to glisten —each snowflake, each icicle was suffused with light.

The shadowy creature in the woods temporarily retreated, but Gabriel understood that The Whispering Pine couldn't hold it back for long. With a renewed sense of urgency, Gabriel opened the front door.

The air inside was crisp and cool. There was ample heat, enough to ensure the pipes wouldn't freeze, but the cabin could use a good fire on a night like tonight.

As he walked up the old spiral staircase, he felt like he was seven years old again... awkward, wide-eyed and full of wonder.

Gabriel entered his wardrobe, waved his hands, and removed the glamour on the door. Then, he closed his eyes and called *The Book of Stars* by its name.

Corpus Sidera flung itself into Gabriel's open arms.

The hair on the back of Gabriel's neck stood up as he exited his wardrobe. He was no longer alone.

Gabriel crept down the stairwell carefully, holding *Corpus Sidera* against his chest. At the foot of the stairs, he saw a dark shape move out of the corner of his eye. He wasn't sure if it was Vrána, Björn or, ultimately, The Shadow Deception itself, but he wasn't going to wait around to find out.

Instinctively, Gabriel lifted his right hand and shouted, "*Arcus Illuminare!*"

A blast of light arced from his fingertips. The impact splintered one of the rafters into pieces and banished the creature, at least for the moment.

"Okay, *that's* new," he said, moving his fingertips in wonderment.

He heard his grandfather's voice again as the book opened itself to the spell he'd just cast.

"Technically speaking, it's old. With our help, you invoked *Arcus Illuminare*, an incantation that harnesses chi."

"Our help?" Gabriel asked.

"You are now connected to my mind and the Collective Consciousness of every Steward before me, human and otherwise. Whenever you're ready and willing, our knowledge will flow through you, just as it did now. There is one thing you must do first, however; you must personally face each of the Three Shadows that comprise Esurus—particularly Rädsla. Use your power of alchemy to either turn them to the Light or break apart their union and stop the reformation of The Great Devourer. Upon doing this, you will fulfil the Prophecy of The Last Steward of the Light and you'll be worthy of the power contained within this tome."

Gabriel felt his grandfather's presence fade and the light receded back into *Corpus Sidera*. Elijah held true to his final entry; he hadn't deserted his grandson.

A mix of fascination, curiosity and excitement brewed within Gabriel. Not since he was a child had he thought about magic with such enthusiasm. A tinge of regret, however, also filled his belly... regret for not returning to the cabin sooner. Feeling a new sense of purpose and power, he secured the book in his knapsack and walked into the living room.

As he locked the front door, Gabriel was struck with an over-whelming premonition that this would be the last time he stepped foot in the cabin... at least in this lifetime.

16

JULIAN

J ulian lived in a cozy, two-story Tudor house just outside the city. Plumes of smoke billowed from its chimney and bright light radiated from the frosted windowpanes onto the freshly fallen snow. The night sky was abuzz with fluffy snowflakes the size of marshmallows, and the rooftops and streets below sparkled like white diamonds.

The neighborhood was quiet—a little *too* quiet for Gabriel's liking. He wondered what secrets dwelled behind the white picket fences and picture-perfect façades.

Gabriel landed the hovercab and spied Julian's silhouette by the window. He opened the pod door and tiptoed carefully along the freshly shoveled driveway. Before he had a chance to knock, Julian was at the door. He motioned for Gabriel to come in.

A sense of excitement and nerves welled within Gabriel. He smelled something delicious cooking in the oven.

"Jules, we don't have time—"

"Of course we do. Surely, you don't expect me to embark on this journey with an empty stomach?

"Here. Make yourself useful. Set the table and light the candle. I haven't seen you in seven years, and I'm not going to risk my life without having a civilized conversation with my—"

Julian stopped. Gabriel sensed that Julian wasn't sure how to act around him—were they friends, lovers or something else? Even Gabriel was uncertain of where to pick up, especially after the kiss earlier. They began eating, less out of hunger, and more to occupy themselves and escape the tension.

"So," Gabriel said, without having anywhere to take the sentence.

"So, indeed," Julian replied. He flashed a grin that put Gabriel at ease. Since both of them were telepaths, they really didn't need to speak, but Julian kept up with the charade for the moment.

"It must've been strange going back into the old cabin, right? Did you meet Elijah's ghost there?"

"You're not far off. I found something that I wasn't expecting."

After another pregnant pause, Gabriel added, "Take a look if you want."

Julian leaned in uncomfortably close and placed his hands on Gabriel's head and heart just as he had done earlier.

Julian smelled of cardamom and lemongrass, and his skin was as warm as the summer sun.

'You smell good,' Gabriel thought to himself.

"You too, now try to focus," Julian answered aloud. "You know how this works, right?"

"Yes, I'm ready," Gabriel said, a bit taken back. He'd forgotten that Julian could pick up on his private thoughts.

Gabriel took a deep breath and closed his eyes. Julian began to connect to his mind, experiencing everything Gabriel had seen in the old cabin.

When the vision faded, Julian released his hands and waited for Gabriel to open his eyes.

"The Shadow—what was that?"

"I think it's my boss, or what became of her. She's become

something akin to Björn—a walking shell of herself. Something sinister is controlling her; I think it's either Björn or The Shadow Deception. They're kind of one and the same now. The human part of Björn died the same night my grandfather did."

"If Björn is back, then that means we're all doomed? I mean, the planet Earth, that is?"

"In a nutshell, yes."

Julian paused to take everything in. He closed his eyes and looked through the memories he'd just experienced.

"Gabe, I saw something else that was odd, *odd for you anyway*... did energy literally jump out of your hands?"

"Yep."

"Well, that's... um... *new*, right?"

Gabriel laughed.

"Yeah, to say the least. I think it has something to do with the book, *Sidera*. It contains part of my essence... as well as all the Stewards. Whenever I'm in possession of the book, I'm plugged into the Collective Consciousness."

"Why didn't you tell me about this 'Stewardship' when we were dating? I mean, you know I could have helped, right?"

"That part of my memory was bewitched by a spell. If I could go back and rewind the clock, I'd change a lot of things. But then again, maybe not... What if everything is happening exactly the way it should? You're here with me now. That's all that matters. Messing with time has consequences. I'm in no rush to do that again."

"Again?" Julian asked, puzzled.

"What?"

"You said you were in no rush to do that *again*."

"Did I?" Gabriel asked, bewildered himself. "I'm just exhausted... I think."

"You should get at least an hour's rest before we head back to the airport. With me here, nobody will find you."

Gabriel was too tired to argue.

"Leave the food. I'll clean up. Catch some rest and I'll wake you up when it's time to go."

Gabriel knew sleep was impossible, but he lay down on Julian's oversized bed. It was so fluffy that he felt almost as if he were floating on a cloud.

Julian finished the dishes and then came in. He lay down on the bed beside Gabriel and, together, they looked at a fresco on the ceiling.

"Andromeda. Just like my bedroom," Gabriel said.

"Yeah, somehow it made me feel like you weren't so far away."

Julian leaned over and planted another kiss on Gabriel's cheek. Then he hugged him tightly. Gabriel's body melted into Julian's and, in the moments that followed, they found their way back to a place that they'd lost—a place that both knew was a fleeting reprieve from the dangers that awaited them. But they didn't care. It was safe. It was loving, and it felt right.

Afterwards, both were silent. Neither wanted to spoil the moment with words, for fear of saying something wrong. They'd wasted enough years on that. They got dressed and left the picture-perfect house. Gabriel mourned the life he might have had if he'd only picked up the H-V sooner and visited his old friend.

As Julian locked the front door, he felt the same sense of foreboding that Gabriel had felt at the cabin; this would be the last time he walked down his driveway.

Julian set the hover coordinates for Denver International. During the short trip, he caught Gabriel fidgeting out of the corner of his eye.

Gabriel fussed nervously with his fingers, glancing at the faded scars marking all the implants. Each felt like a ticking time-bomb.

"So, what's the State protocol for an AWOL Agent?" Julian asked.

"They'll freeze my travel credentials first," Gabriel replied, "but the implants will be valid until they track me down. They want to watch my every move. That's why I need you. I mean, that's part of the reason I need you," Gabriel said, stumbling.

"And if they find you?" Julian asked.

"Then I'll be sent to The Division for a mandatory extraction and erasure. After that, I'll be lucky to remember my name, much less this conversation."

Julian shivered and landed the hovercar.

"Well, that's not going to happen on my watch. So, stop worrying. Deal?"

"Deal."

"Good. Are you ready, Gabe?"

"Not exactly. How does this work?"

"Once I snag everyone's thoughtwaves, I'll propagate the idea that I have a broken leg. That will explain the need for a second ticket and it will get us priority booking. All the while, I'll shield you from view, but you'll have to work your magic on the scanners, Drones and x-ray machines. You can still do that fancy EMF tomfoolery, right?"

Gabriel laughed.

"Tomfoolery, huh? Call it what you will, but yes, I can still fry circuitry."

"Good. Give me one minute to engineer and broadcast my thoughts."

Julian closed his eyes and he felt slightly dizzy as his consciousness detached from his physical body. He hovered high above the airport. At first, he saw only the outer structure. Slowly, Julian used his third eye to see past the physical. Walls became transparent and Julian began to filter out anything inorganic. For a moment, everything turned to darkness. Then, as Julian took a deep breath, each human being lit up like a firefly in the darkness. One by one he ensnared each mind into his cognitive thoughtweb. Once trapped, his projected reality became theirs. He was like a great spider, and each cognitive thread he spun was impossible to escape. It was the same thought technology that the Egyptians used to move armies with a single thought. Julian could quite literally rule the world if he so desired. Or, he could merely drive everyone in the vicinity into raving lunatics. Although both outcomes were highly unlikely, they were calculated risks nonetheless. His skill came at a cost, however. The more he disconnected from his physical body, the more he became consumed by that power.

"They're all within my reach," Julian said. "Stay behind me. Let me do the talking and let's move fast."

Gabriel waved his hand and stunned two Alpha guards in front of the airport. Before any Agents took notice, Julian sent out a thoughtwave that not only masked the Alphas, but also suggested the androids never existed in the first place.

As they approached a security checkpoint, Gabriel braced himself for the worst, but it was entirely unnecessary.

Julian took out a magic marker and wrote the word "Passport" on a sheet of paper. He then casually presented it at the checkpoint.

A stout female guard reviewed the phony credentials and nodded with approval.

"Sir, I can't help but notice your cast and crutches... Do you need a wheelchair or an escort to the terminal?" she asked.

"No, I'm fine, thanks for asking, ma'am."

"Okay... Your turn," Julian said under his breath as he passed through the x-ray machine.

Gabriel waited until Julian was cleared and then he raised his hands. First the holographic display blipped and then the sensors faded for a moment. He passed through unnoticed, but the machine began to sound an alarm for servicing.

"Security to body scan unit thirty-three, please," a synthetic voice boomed on the PA system.

Gabriel scurried towards Julian and whispered, "Close. Too damn close for comfort."

"You're fine, Gabe. I can hear their thoughts in my head and nobody saw you pass through."

They boarded the plane without incident. Unfortunately, Julian had to remain in a meditative state for the entirety of the flight.

'Sorry about this,' Gabriel said telepathically.

'It's okay. You owe me. *Big time.* I'm already thinking of ways for you to repay me.'

Gabriel fought back a laugh.

Julian turned and closed his eyes.

For most of the flight, Gabriel was silent, too. He gazed out the window and felt as light as a feather as they flew over the majestic snow-capped mountains below—free from the weight of the journey, and free from the danger that lurked back in the L.A. Megacity. With each passing moment, however, that freedom disappeared, and Gabriel's heart felt heavy again.

Just prior to landing, Julian homed in on Gabriel's thoughts.

'Remind me again why you're headed back to L.A.?' Julian asked telepathically.

'To connect with some people who can help us stop the end of the world. I'll find out more from my contact when I get to the rendezvous today.'

Julian furrowed his brow.

'I don't like it. I don't like *any* of this. I'm not an M-8 clairvoyant like you, but the whole thing smells like a one-way ticket to disaster.'

An automated pilot interrupted their dialogue, "Please fasten your seatbelts and prepare for landing."

As soon as they were safely out of the airport terminal, Julian turned and said, "This man I saw in your head...the one with the dragon tattoo...do you trust him?"

"I'm not sure, but I know I trust Akaal."

"Remind me.... Akaal is *Death*, right? As in The Grim Reaper?"

"It has a bunch of names, but, yes, it's Death."

"That doesn't make me feel any better. I mean, if Death has one function and it's hanging around you—well, that doesn't bode well, Gabe. It doesn't take a brain surgeon or a Thought Engineer to work out the math here. You're brave, and you're insanely talented, but this sounds half-baked to me."

"I know, I know… This whole thing sounds kind of insane when you put it that way. But trust me, Death has a goodness in its heart and mind. I've seen its consciousness from within, the same way you've seen my thoughts. Plus, it was a friend to the person I trusted the most in my life, Elijah. He wouldn't have led me astray."

"Okay. I guess that's good enough for me. I mean, I'm not thrilled that you're hanging out with, well *Death*, but, I suppose it's better to be friendly with something like that. Plus, with the whole Known Universe ending, I guess we're both kind of screwed, and I'd rather go out with a bang."

Gabriel laughed. Julian was being sarcastic, but there was truth in his words; this didn't make sense, it probably wouldn't end well, and, like his friend, he was the type who would go down with a fight if he had a choice.

"Anyway, Gabe, I know you need to call your contact, but I can't risk you using your implants to activate the card. Let me make the call. What's this guy's name?"

"Ambrose."

Gabriel handed Julian the small silicon calling card. Julian placed his finger over the tiny chip and it connected with his wrist-band H-V.

It beeped and then projected Ambrose's likeness.

Without any pleasantries, Ambrose asked, "Who are you?"

"Julian. We have a mutual friend."

"Why can't our *mutual friend* speak for himself?"

"The Wolves are listening. He said you could give us a rendezvous point?"

"We're meeting The Maker. Our *mutual friend* will understand."

Ambrose severed the connection without saying goodbye.

"Hmmm... I don't think he likes me. Does his cryptic response ring a bell?" Julian asked.

"In more ways than one. I think he wants me to meet him at SULACO Robotics."

"Hold on a second, Gabe. You're seeing Yantra? The guy who invented the modern android? Didn't he die over a thousand years ago?"

"Yes... Rumor has it that Yantra lives. I guess I'll find out soon enough," Gabriel said.

Julian bit his lip.

"You don't approve, do you?" Gabriel asked.

"If I said I didn't, would it matter?"

"Probably not," Gabriel replied.

"You know that place is crawling with Agents. Why on Earth would you go there, Gabe?"

"All I know is that a Rogue Synthetic named Genesis was the last one who saw the murderer, and, based on my intel, she's slated to be decommissioned at this facility tonight. We need to try to stop that."

"Fine. If you're dead set on going, then I'm coming with you. At least until Ambrose tells me to get lost."

"I'd try to talk you out of it, but I know better than to argue with a Thought Engineer."

"Good."

Julian walked over to an information booth that was operated by a human. Without paying a penny, Julian came back with two tokens.

"Whoa. I'm a little envious... That gift comes in handy."

"You have no idea," Julian said.

As the Eastbound E Train arrived, Gabriel looked at Julian and said, "Are you ready to save the world?"

"I was born ready, babe."

17

THE ALTAR OF CREATION

The doors of the Hope Street E Train opened, revealing a bustling and vibrant city below. Amidst a sea of spectacular skyscrapers and holographic advertisements, a beautiful anachronism loomed; it belonged to none other than the State Underwritten Laboratory for Cybernetic Operations (SULACO). Although exaggerated twofold in scale to appear more spectacular, the pyramid's architecture borrowed heavily from the Mayan ruins at Uxmal, Mexico, right down to an adjacent Quadrangle that housed all the corresponding Research, Software and Technology (R/S/T) facilities.

The exterior was constructed from polished, quartz-like blocks that glistened in the moonlight, while a blinding torch gleamed like a diamond at the apex. Its majesty and luminosity proved unmatched and the iconic building became synonymous with the L.A. Megacity.

Four monolithic stone stelae, or column-like monuments, stood in the great courtyard leading to the structure. Each stela was adorned with ornate bas-relief engravings commemorating four major events: (1) the founding of SULACO, (2) the construction of the pyramid, (3) the preservation of Yantra's brain and (4) the deification ceremonies that followed.

"Now I see where all the State taxes are going," Julian scoffed.

"No kidding," Gabriel replied. "They can't change a lightbulb at my office, but, apparently, they can appropriate funds for this behemoth."

As Gabriel scanned the engravings on the stone stelae, he felt a chill go down his spine.

"We have company," Gabriel whispered.

"Ambrose, I presume?" Julian said, stepping in front of Gabriel.

"I didn't mean to take you by surprise. I forget my own speed sometimes," Ambrose said. "You're Julian, right?"

"Yes. We spoke on the H-V. I have the feeling we got off on the wrong foot."

Ambrose smirked and replied, "Like you, I only seek to protect Gabriel."

"It's okay, I'm getting used to expecting the unexpected," Gabriel interjected, moving back in front of Julian. "And for what it's worth, I can protect myself, thank you both very much."

Ambrose changed the subject, "So tell me, you two, what do you think of The Mystic's Pyramid?"

"I've seen the campus from afar, but never this close. It's stunning, if a bit creepy," Gabriel replied.

"It reeks of Death," Julian said.

Ambrose nodded his head in agreement, "Indeed. Today we'll find what secrets this tomb holds."

Gabriel remembered from his Civics class that the structure served as both shrine and resting place to SULACO's Chief Engineer, a purported mystic known only as Yantra.

"Is it true that Yantra still lives?" Gabriel inquired.

Ambrose closed his eyes and turned his mind towards the interior of the pyramid. Deep below the monument, he perceived only darkness... an impenetrable darkness illuminated by six crimson eyes. The fiery orbs never blinked, never slept and slowly, but surely, drove the consciousness of Yantra to insanity.

"Aye... I found a sarcophagus and sensed echoes of a sentient presence that is at least one thousand years old. As far as whether or not it's living, well... I guess that depends on how you define existence—*life and death* in particular. As you know, Yantra found a way to keep his mind alive after his body (and spirit) passed. However, whatever dwells within the belly of this pyramid is not connected to the higher soul of Yantra."

"What aren't you telling us?" Gabriel inquired.

"He's not just mad... I fear that he's found something in his despair, or vice-versa. I saw six terrible eyes... eyes that have haunted my dreams... and I expect yours, too, young Gabriel."

Gabriel spoke the name psychically to Ambrose and Julian, 'Esurus?'

The ground rumbled and clouds covered the moon.

"Careful. Words *and* thoughts must be guarded in the presence of this particular entity and its servants. It feeds off psychic vibrations... Best to use its indirect titles, like *The Three That Became One* or *The Void Beast*. Or better yet, nothing at all."

"Duly noted," Gabriel said. "I do have one question that's been bothering me, though. You say Yantra was a mystic... If he was so all-seeing, how did this happen?"

"Free will."

"You mean he knew this would happen and did it anyway?"

"Yes. Yantra wisely destroyed all of the 'PROJECT: REDSHIFT' research after he discovered it was a failure. When he tested his so-called 'Suspended Consciousness' device on humans, their digitized minds became violent, erratic and even murderous. Yantra realized he had created monsters. The only choice was to terminate the project. He was a good man... a good man with bad ideas."

"So, how did his brain end up on ice?" Gabriel asked.

"The State was greedy. You see, Yantra was going to destroy not only the Suspended Consciousness research, but also the Oubliette prototype, which promised substantial financial potential. Just as he was about to initiate a self-destruct mechanism, the State stepped in and claimed the project for its own 'Peacekeeping' efforts. It rechristened it 'DEEP RED' and imprisoned Yantra's brain in a device of his own design."

"So The Mystic's Pyramid is a gigantic icebox... a cruel, eternal prison for AIs?" Julian asked.

"Yes," Ambrose replied. "Our journey is no longer focused on connecting with Yantra. I fear, he's lost forever and is under the control of The Shadows. It's now all about Genesis. We need her CPU for the next part of our journey. Already they've begun to dismantle her synthetic chassis. Soon, they will extricate and isolate her consciousness."

Julian looked at the heavily guarded building and then glanced doubtfully at Ambrose. Then he said, "This history lesson has been all fine and good, but, frankly, Mr. Ambrose, I don't understand why we need *this particular* Synthetic's CPU. She's as mad as Yantra, isn't she?"

"Julian, it isn't a matter of choice—or sanity, for that matter—and I don't blame you for being suspicious. I know that Akaal has been a bit cryptic about what we need to do, and you're right to want to protect your friend Gabriel. Let me clear everything up."

Ambrose turned and faced Gabriel directly. "Gabriel, before you can stop The Void Beast—the creature that is set on destroying all life in the Known Universe—you must meet with each of The Six Stars. They are the immortal protectors of the Universe. Each of the remaining Six Stars have blessings, information and gifts for you.

"So far, you've already met The First Star, Death, and Second Star, Mercy. Elsa will help you meet The Third, a being known as Charity. Unfortunately, The Fourth and Fifth Stars are in self-imposed exile. This is why we are here today. You see, a mortal like you would perish upon entering their abode, particularly if you traversed the two-dimensional space around it. It functions as a metaphysical moat that kills most organic beings.

"Thankfully, Chief Engineer Yantra inadvertently created a loophole; Genesis is capable of dreaming. In other words, her mind is a skeleton key that will allow you access to the Fifth Dimension. Of course, we will still need the help of a Dream Broker to create an interface portal for you, but we'll deal with that later."

A dozen follow-up questions buzzed in Gabriel's head, but Julian spoke first.

"You explained who everyone else was. But, *who are you*, Mr. Ambrose?"

"Think of me as a guardian to the guardians. The Sixth Star created me in The Old World to protect them and their creations."

"You failed then, didn't you?" Julian asked.

"Sadly, yes. We all did. We're in no hurry to do that again."

Ambrose pointed to the periphery. Armed Alphas stood watch at each end of The Quadrangle, while silent Aeronautic Drones and Raptorcrafts hung in the night sky like carrion.

"Julian, I need you to sweep the building and scan for any human brainwaves. Snag them into your web and cloak Gabe and I while we take care of the androids. We'll need you to stay outside while we fetch Genesis."

"I'd rather be with you, but I agree you need someone out here diverting any wandering eyes."

Before meditating, Julian turned to Ambrose and said, "Just make sure Gabe comes out alive. You may be some sort of 'extra-terrestrial guardian,' but don't underestimate me. If Gabe is harmed in any way, you'll face my wrath."

Ambrose raised an eyebrow and laughed.

"It's been centuries since someone threatened me and lived to talk about it—but, I must say, I like you, Mr. Julian. Don't worry, you have my word that no harm shall come to Gabriel. I've sworn an oath to The Six Stars to help protect Gabriel and all of The Assembly of Stars; I count you among that Assembly. Together we will ensure that Earth and, for that matter, the entire Known Universe is safe."

Seemingly satisfied with Ambrose's promise, Julian closed his eyes and began to weave a cognitive web around the pyramid. To any onlookers in the vicinity, the three of them would appear invisible.

Ambrose put his hand on Gabriel's shoulder and said, "Before we do this, I just want to make sure you know the risks. Thanks to Julian, you've been able to stay under the radar, which means your implants will work. We'll need your M-8 clearance to get into the pyramid. This will be the last time you'll ever be able to use your implants."

"I understand the risks," Gabriel said.

"Good. Follow me... this way. There's an access panel right here that leads to an underground maze of septic tubes and drainpipes."

Gabriel winced.

"Sorry, Gabe... this is the only way to avoid the Drones surrounding it. Once through, your credentials should work in the basement corridor under The Quadrangle."

"Alright... Let's do this," Gabriel said.

Ambrose pointed to the fourth stela and Gabriel understood.

They waited in the shadows until the androids made their rounds.

Gabriel snuck up behind the right-most Alpha. Although the androids were the finest fighting machines during their heyday, their occipital optic sensors were antiquated and easily thwarted.

He focused his energy on his hands and placed one atop the skull of the unit and another along the back, near the CPU, jamming EMF frequencies into the Alpha circuitry to the point of a complete meltdown.

Ambrose moved stealthily along the perimeter with such speed that he went undetected by human and android eyesight alike. Without warning, he phased into the ultraviolet light spectrum and pounced on the second Alpha. Ambrose immediately phased back and with a single bolt of lightning, he reduced it to a puddle of liquid metal and plastic.

The sweet, earthy smell of ozone now graced the air.

Ambrose stood up and wiped the liquid metal from his hands, immune to its heat and toxicity. It was only then that Gabriel noticed Ambrose was completely nude, his clothes reduced to ash amidst the cooling metal.

"It's an occupational hazard for dragons," Ambrose said with a shrug and grin. He stood tall and unashamed.

At first, Gabriel's attention was drawn to the light coursing along Ambrose's tattoos. He now understood the ink beneath his skin was derived from stardust, and it helped Ambrose channel his true etheric form, which was far more beautiful than his corporal body.

Emerald-colored light feathered Ambrose's aura and condensed along his skin in tiny, overlapping tear-shaped scales. His hands, feet and extremities glowed softly, while his heart chakra and eyes surged with radiant sparks of green energy. His nose, face and neck appeared longer and even more regal now. Finally, and most impressively, two bolts of energy emerged from his glowing crown, forming elk-sized antlers that shifted in form like lightning bolts.

"Thor?" Gabriel asked intuitively.

Ambrose closed his eyes for a moment, recalling a time that had long since slipped into the veil of twilight.

"Aye. It's a name I haven't answered to in several millennia, but yes. The Norse saw me completely, as I am before you, *as I once was*. To others I was perceived as a dragon, for they only knew my fire and wrath. Lately, believers are gone altogether, and I'm but a ghost of my former self... the stuff of dreams and faery tales."

As the Old God spoke, Gabriel noticed wings in Ambrose's subtle body. They were folded energetically behind his corporal self, rising at least a foot above his shoulders.

"You're full of surprises."

The dragon winked and laughed. His laughter rolled like thunder in the night sky.

"This is just a hint of what's possible... and you underestimate your own potential, Gabriel."

As they descended into the sewers, Ambrose replaced the manhole cover. Then, he breathed green fire around the edges, until it was securely soldered in place.

"This will buy us some time."

'Or trap us forever,' Gabriel thought to himself.

They traveled in silence for a mile or two. The light emanating from Ambrose's body illuminated the putrid tunnel ahead. As the dragon stepped into the cesspool, the river of waste evaporated, clearing the path for Gabriel. The stink and rot of the sewers was gone; sweet ozone replaced it.

A winding, two-level maze stood between them and The Quadrangle. They traveled for nearly half an hour under The Mystic's Pyramid. The path was littered with rodents and a few skeletal remains of others who'd fared worse. After trying a dozen ways through the maze, they'd reached a dead-end.

Ambrose leaned against the wall.

"Who dares trespass? Speak the word or perish."

The voice echoed through the corridor and triggered an avalanche at the other end. Gabriel and Ambrose were trapped.

"What happened?" Gabriel asked.

Ambrose pointed to something grotesque on the wall. Two disembodied lips were fused into the stone. The flesh that formed them was purple, rotten and entirely unnatural.

"Who seeks passage?" the magic mouth said with a growl.

"We do, you wretched abomination," Ambrose replied.

Laughter echoed through the corridor and the lips began to move again. They uttered a riddle:

"I stand as Truth incarnate,
Ask, but I'll never yield the way.
Yet, speak but a single word and
I'm forever reduced to clay."

Ambrose walked away from the mouth and spoke telepathically to Gabriel. 'Any ideas?'

Gabriel replied psychically as well. '*Truth incarnate* seems like an odd phrase, right? As if Truth is its essence... or its creator, perhaps? Someone uttered the word *Truth* to create it... So there must exist another word to destroy it. But what?' Gabriel asked.

'Speak but a word and I'm forever reduced to clay... That's it, Gabe! It's a golem.'

Ambrose faced the magic mouth and spoke a single word, "Met."

A low, almost imperceptible rumbling began. Soon it was so loud that Gabriel wondered if they'd triggered an earthquake or another avalanche.

After a shrill scream, the magic mouth crumbled to pieces and the enchanted wall disintegrated into a pile of dust.

Before Gabriel could ask any questions, Ambrose explained, "Your grandfather taught you well, Gabriel. Words are power. Sometimes words can bring things to life, even if they're made of an inanimate material. You see, there is an old myth in which golems can be created by inscribing a sacred power word into the forehead of a clay statue. The word is *Emet (אמת)*, which means *Truth*. To undo the magic, you remove the Hebrew letter Aleph (א). The remaining letters spell *Met (מת)*, or *Death*."

Ambrose raised his right hand and green light illuminated the chamber around him. He pointed to a cartouche with a Common Tongue translation "**Yantra Neb-Ankh**."

"The map says the door on the right leads to the Sarcophagus for Yantra," Ambrose said. "We'd be wise to avoid it, as well as all the tendrils that emanate from it."

Myriad pulsing, fiber-optic branches formed a massive trunk line that burrowed deep into the dark underbelly of The Mystic's Pyramid. From afar, the glowing mass of wires looked like some sort of synthetic spinal cord.

The dragon turned around and illuminated the smaller antechamber to the right of the sarcophagus.

"This path leads to The Quadrangle."

Though most of the symbols were worn and unintelligible, the Jargon phrase **ICE M8/R** was clear as day, symbolizing an isolated, quarantined, or otherwise M-8 restricted area.

Gabriel waved his left hand over the authentication disc. Stone began to rumble as the cement wall split in two. It revealed a small lift leading to the chamber above.

"Where are we?" Gabriel asked.

"We should be in the service lift for the R&D complex, known internally as 'The Altar of Creation.' It's the only part of The Quadrangle that has a connection to the main pyramid."

Gabriel flinched as the doors opened. If Hell existed, it might look something like this.

Hundreds of metallic endoskeletons hung from the ceiling. Some were encased in synthetic skin, but most were simply empty frames and wires, hanging upside down like carcasses in some cybernetic slaughterhouse. Early model Alphas supervised the assembly line, while several hundred robotic arms and lasers facilitated the actual fabrication.

A blast of hot air slapped Gabriel's face and squeezed his lungs shut.

"The Drones forge iron, steel and titanium in this area. Wait here, and don't cross the production line," Ambrose said. "The temperatures around The Altar are not safe for any organic life form, but the draft from the sewers should keep you cool here."

"You'll get no argument from me on that."

Ambrose shifted into the ultraviolet spectrum and moved around the perimeter of the production line until he happened upon something unusual.

An android was manacled in what looked like a medieval torture device. As strange as it may seem, it appeared to be emotionally distressed. Although the faceplate was no longer installed, Ambrose surmised it was a Genesis series, like the rest of the endoskeletons above. It had also been ceremoniously stripped of its shell, revealing a complex synthetic musculature that combined fiber optics, silicone, plastics and wires. The result was something somewhat graphic and grotesque, like an archaic illustration from an anatomy textbook. The cerebral cortex and spinal column were plugged into a mainframe. Whatever made Genesis Seven-Twelve unique was (apparently) of major interest to the State.

Her optical sensors activated and locked onto Ambrose. Without speaking, she mouthed two words: "Help me."

The production Drones froze the assembly line and a roomful of robotic eyes were now fixed on Ambrose. It appeared that the mainframe controlled all the androids—even the incomplete units overhead—like some sort of hive mind.

The robots began to speak in a tinny, homogenized chorus of mechanical voices.

"What business have you here, Earthling?"

"I seek an audience with Genesis. And I'm no Earthling, Yantra."

"So you know who we are?"

"No, I know who you *were*, but I pity the puppet you've become. I've seen the beast that pulls your strings and I implore it to release this Synthetic or face my wrath."

Terrible, mechanical laughter filled the building as the production Drones and half-finished skeletons began to swarm towards Ambrose.

The dragon wasted no time in severing Genesis's connection to the mainframe. Before he had a chance to restrain her, however, the android sprinted to the forge, plunging herself into the molten vat.

In a move that surprised Yantra's Drones, Ambrose dove into the vat as well, barely salvaging the skull of Genesis before it was destroyed. Several dozen androids jumped into the vat as well until their collective weight tipped the molten metal onto the floor.

"Run!" Ambrose screamed.

Gabriel smashed a nearby window and escaped into the courtyard.

Julian broke his meditation and ran over to Gabriel.

"Are you okay? What happened?"

"Yes, but all Hell is about to break loose. Run!"

A moment later, green flames burst through every door and window in The Altar of Creation.

From the pit of the fire, Gabriel heard Yantra's consciousness screaming. Six eyes penetrated the flames and reached towards him. *Corpus Sidera* protectively put up a light shield around Gabriel and Julian. The Shadow presence retracted in pain. For a fraction of a second, Gabriel made out the shape of a three-headed hydra in his mind's eye.

As the Research building crumbled, Ambrose emerged half-covered in molten metal alloys, holding a glowing crystal skull in his right hand. The fire had stripped it of all wires and synthetic coverings.

"Is that—?"

"Yes, Gabriel. It's what's left of Genesis," Ambrose replied.

He placed the red-hot skull on the ground and let it cool for a moment. Then, he stepped back, and with a surge of green fire, he melted the debris and liquid metal that clung to him. When the flames subsided, Ambrose pointed to a small vehicle underneath one of the palm trees nearby. Then he tossed Julian a small circular key fob.

"Here. Take my hovercar and find Elsa and Uri. I'll meet up with the four of you at the next rendezvous point."

"Where's that, exactly?" Julian asked.

"The Sedona Vortex Mines. Now, leave immediately, before the Raptors descend. I'll do my best to fend them off for a bit."

Ambrose grabbed the glowing skull and flew into the night, like a green comet.

Gabriel and Julian made a dash for the hovercar.

As they entered the vehicle, Julian paused and said, "So… one question… he was naked the whole time?"

"I almost died and you're worried that I was flirting with an extra-terrestrial?"

They both laughed.

"Point taken," Julian said, feeling a bit foolish. "Computer: set course for Deva Ink on Melrose, maximum velocity."

Through the rear-view mirror, Gabriel watched a dozen Raptor-craft and Aeronautic Drones crash into The Quadrangle.

At this point, Gabriel realized he'd officially passed the point of no return. He was destined to live as a fugitive, as was his best friend Julian. He only hoped the risk was worth the sacrifices they were both making.

18

ACROSS THE BRIDGE WHERE HOPE
IS LOST

With everyone safely in tow, Julian merged into the uppermost lane of the Skyway and headed for Sedona. For the second time in less than twenty-four hours, Julian had whisked Gabriel away from danger, and had given him a sense of freedom, however fleeting it might be.

The persistent purr of the electric engine had lulled Elsa and Uri to sleep—or something that resembled it. Gabriel, however, was reveling in the peace and quiet. He rolled down the window and let the cool desert night air blow through his hair. A thick veil of stars hung like a swarm of fireflies around the clear horizon. Not since his childhood in the Rockies had he seen stars so bright or plentiful. With no other vehicles on the uppermost Skyway lanes, the stress from his ambuscade at The Mystic's Pyramid almost melted away.

After what felt like two hours, the hovercar's AI spoke up.

"Attention: Battery at one-quarter charge. Estimated drive time remaining: one hour at present velocity."

"We'd better risk a landing," Julian said. "I don't want us to run out of juice before we get to The Way Station.

Computer: show charging stations in a twenty-mile radius."

A hologram appeared on the windscreen, and Julian tapped on the nearest location. The hover shifted into autopilot mode and Julian turned to Gabriel.

"Hey... you're a million miles away. Everything okay?"

"I'm getting there," Gabriel said.

'I'll guard the vehicle when we charge up,' Julian said telepathically. 'See if you can figure out something about Elsa and Uri for me. I'd like to know who's in the back seat.'

'Roger that. Why don't you just telepathically home into the conversation? You have my permission,' Gabriel replied.

Julian opened the pod door and hooked the hover to the charging station. All the while, he began meditating until he could hear everything in Gabriel's mind.

Gabriel pressed a button and the moon roof opened up, exposing the night sky.

Elsa, now awake, sat motionless in the back seat, her gaze fixed firmly on the firmament. Uri was still deep in meditation. Gabriel watched them in the rear-view mirror; he sensed a palpable mix of sadness and wanderlust in Elsa's emotions. She leaned forward and waited for Gabriel to ask the questions on his mind.

"The stars are amazing tonight, aren't they?" he asked, breaking the awkward silence, with transparently idle small talk.

Elsa did not reply immediately. Instead, her expressive eyes glistened in the darkness, reflecting the moon and stars above like polished silver.

"They make me miss home," she said distractedly, her sights fixed on a distant constellation.

Gabriel wasn't sure how to respond; he was fairly certain "home" wasn't L.A. In fact, if she was anything like Ambrose, he had a hunch it was some place other than Earth. Her normally expressive eyes were now larger than he remembered—still human-like, but barely so.

Elsa read his thoughts and pointed to the sky.

"There."

Gabriel looked up and saw the belt of Orion.

"Follow the belt Southeast."

Gabriel obliged and saw the brightest star in the night sky.

"Sirius?" he asked.

"Yes. There is a moon near that star system which reminds me of The Old World. I spend time there whenever I can."

He felt a warm sensation as her mood changed. It was the same energy frequency he felt around Akaal, although not as intense. As she smiled, Gabriel noticed that the stars in her eyes were not just a reflection; deep within the dark iris, they were actually moving—first one or two, then ten or twenty, then hundreds—all with a beautiful silver light that was clearly not from the firmament above. Instead of being frightened, he was curious.

She smiled and said, "You're not like most humans, Gabriel."

He laughed.

"Yeah, I think that's my problem."

"I know you have a question, so just ask," Elsa said, with a nonchalant, no-nonsense attitude.

"Well, I don't mean to be rude, but if we're going to be traveling together, both Julian and I need to know who or what the two of you are, exactly."

"You're well acquainted with The First Star, Akaal, by now?"

Gabriel nodded.

"And, with the help of my amulet, The Second Star, Mercy, helped you escape from the Aphelion Mercenaries."

"Are you one of The Seven Stars?" Gabriel inquired.

"Not exactly. I was created from the energy of The Third Star. I call him my brother, but we are twins, really, since the same essence flows through us both. To answer your question, the being beside me, Uri, is The Third Star. His gift (and name) is Charity; he can inspire kindness and light, even within the darkest being. To some he is known as Uriel, the Archangel. Today, however, worshipers are few and far between. Like Thor, whom you call Ambrose, we've *adapted*. That's why we have so many names. We don't reincarnate like mortals, but we can assume new avatars—a rebirth of sorts. But we are still all of the old aspects, as well as the new. One day you will understand."

Upon hearing his name, Uri opened his eyes.

"And my twin, Elsa, was the finest moon in all the systems— one of the last to survive before The Void Beast consumed everything. As she said, I created my twin from my energy, and she, therefore, contains my power. In Earth Mythology, we were known as Apollo and Artemis, though our true origin is of The Old World, not this one," Uri said. "You're lucky to have my sister on your side; not only is she skilled at the art of revealing hidden truths, but like Julian, she can cloak our movement. She's also an adept hunter."

"Now I understand the triptych at your store," Gabriel said. "I'm honored to be in the twin presence of Apollo-Artemis and your guardian, Thor."

"The honor is ours," Elsa replied. "We've long awaited the chance to form The Assembly of Stars—the rebel force that will thwart our Shadow brethren's plan to destroy all life.

"Tell me, how far are we from Sedona?" she asked.

"Around sixty-five minutes, based on the GPS," Gabriel said.

"Good. Fetch your friend, Julian, and let's go. This vehicle has more than enough charge to get us where we're headed. Even with the joint cloaking abilities of Julian and yours truly, we need to stay under the veil of night to remain as inconspicuous as possible."

Gabriel stepped outside the hover.

'Did you get all that?' he said psychically.

'Yes, thanks for allowing me to listen in. I like these two more than Ambrose. If I hadn't seen that *thing* reach out from the explosion at SULACO, I might have a hard time believing this.'

Julian tried his best to focus on the task at hand—driving—but he found it increasingly difficult to do so now that he understood he had two cosmic stowaways in his back seat. As he glanced at Elsa, he noticed she was watching him, too—perhaps reading his thoughts, just as he had done earlier.

Gabriel could now make out Sedona in the distance. A small tinge of doubt crawled through his belly—something Elijah would lecture him on, were he still alive. Doubt was a Shadow emotion, one that could spell complete failure for the task that lay ahead. Gabriel did his best to conceal his fear and doubt. He had perfected the act of nondisclosure, after all. He just hoped he could shake the doubt before he came face-to-face with one of The Shadows.

Julian began to fly the hovercar in the lowest Skyway lane. From this distance, Sedona's iron-rich soil was stunning, even at midnight and the moonlit Ruins looked like a Martian outpost.

The Red Gate was no less spectacular. Fused together from wreckage, the archway served a dual purpose; it housed The Hope's Pass Way Station and also served as a memorial to the disaster that struck ten years earlier. Behind The Red Gate, Interstate 179 fell into a seemingly bottomless chasm known as The Sedona Crater. The crater, and several smaller ones like it, reduced most of Sedona to a large mesa that was unreachable by highways. Due to radioactive and electromagnetic anomalies, the State deemed Sedona a no-fly zone. The Way Station provided the only terrestrial route in or out of The Ruins of Sedona.

Beneath The Red Gate, two armored Alphas scanned paperwork and provided credentials to enter Hope's Pass—a tube that connected the structure to the mesa. Tonight they were conducting random searches, however, resulting in a mile-long traffic jam.

"Damn—I'm afraid I can't help with the Alphas," Julian said. "I can hide us from humans—the ones that are queued up like us in traffic—but not the androids."

"Nor I," Elsa said. "My form of cloaking won't work with this many eyes on us."

Uri observed as roughly two dozen vehicles were processed.

"We'll be fine, I think," he said. "Fortunately, the AI programming in the Alpha neurochip is excruciatingly predictable. The search isn't random at all; the main Alpha is using a modified Fibonacci sequence (1-1-2-5-8-13-21) to select cars. They reset every time they hit twenty-one. Right now they just checked the fifth vehicle. We are lucky number seven, so we're safe."

As predicted, the Alpha guards allowed Julian to pass, but the next hovercar was stopped for inspection.

The Way Station structure was imposing and impressive all at once. Its red walls were made of the thousands of rocks that were ejected during the creation of the chasm. For miles around The Way Station, tens of hundreds of jagged rocks jutted from the desert sand like daggers. The debris field created an additional layer of security —it was nearly impossible to travel by foot.

Upon parking the hover, Julian, Gabriel and the twin celestial beings followed brightly-marked signage leading to a debriefing area for new visitors. They waited for a group to be processed before them and then entered an automated safety area that resembled a planetarium. After a ten-minute show about geography and safety, the overhead projection ceased, and a door opened.

Bright light streamed into the room as three guards—two armored Alphas and a Synthetic—entered. The Synthetic smiled disingenuously. The Alpha units were custom jobs. Gone were the ocular scanners; each android was equipped with one eye that read ultraviolet and another that scanned heat. They appeared to be examining Uri and Elsa from a distance.

The Synthetic cocked its head, seemingly listening to the binary dialogue of the Alphas. It then faced the party. "Welcome to The Way Station, humans and... *non-humans*. Place your hands on the scanners and we'll process your party. Nobody is permitted past this point without credentials."

'So you know what we have to do?' Gabriel said telepathically to the twin celestial beings.

Uri and Elsa nodded in agreement.

'Julian, get behind me for this,' Gabriel said. His voice was low, commanding and reminiscent of the night that he confronted Björn.

Julian looked in wonderment at his friend. Whatever doubt was welling earlier now seemed to be giving way to a newfound strength.

Elsa and Uri pulled out two short-range magnetic blast weapons and deactivated the Alphas.

As the units twisted and smoked on the floor, Gabriel turned to the Synthetic.

He smiled and said, "We can make this easy or hard, android. What do you prefer?"

The guard reached for a silent alarm near the guard post.

Gabriel closed his eyes, took a deep breath and pulled in energy from his surroundings. He then forcefully contracted his diaphragm, opened his hands and exhaled, releasing a volatile energetic shock-wave that short-circuited the Synthetic and caused its skin to melt off, revealing a crystalline skull and metallic spine.

Elsa exchanged a knowing glance with Uri.

Her twin brother closed his eyes and blasted the main control panel telekinetically, subsequently cancelling the silent alarm, while also bringing down the power grid for The Way Station.

"Julian? Elsa? Uri? I can't see a thing. Can you?"

"I'm behind you," Julian replied.

From that moment on, Julian clung to Gabriel like glue—showing the first signs of fear that Gabriel had seen in years. It felt good to step into the role of protector for a change.

Uri lifted his hands above his head and whispered something under his breath. A halo of light glowed over him, subsequently illuminating the corridor. Gabriel glanced over at Elsa and noticed that her entire body mirrored the light back.

She smiled, "I'm doing what a moon does best—I'm reflecting. Come on, let's go!"

Uri removed a large star sapphire memory crystal from the fried computer console and tossed it to Gabriel.

"What's this for?"

"It's your history lesson. Watch it later."

Gabriel shoved it in his coat pocket.

Uri lifted his arms above his head and, without a weapon or visible effort, blasted through the wall with his right hand—channeling some unseen energy.

"Show-off!" Julian mumbled under his breath.

The blast revealed a narrow crawlspace that ran beneath The Way Station superstructure to The Ruins of Sedona.

They quickly piled into an unoccupied service pod.

"We're in trouble," Gabriel said. "My implants will be flagged; how will we activate this?"

Uri dug into his pocket and pulled out a dismembered hand and optic nerve that he'd snatched from one of the Alphas.

"I know, I know... It's not very sexy, but it will do the job. The computer system will still register both as valid."

Uri held the metallic eye up to the retinal scanner and the pod door opened. He then tossed the smoking orb onto the ground.

The Way Station gently hummed as the backup generator powered on. The foreboding clank of metallic feet and the hiss of hydraulic joints suggested that more Alphas were already en route.

Uri quickly slammed the dismembered Alpha hand on the console. Light subsequently spread across the panel and the pod sped forward through the tube.

"Too close!" Uri said with a grimace. "Your implants are no longer of use to you or to us... in fact, they are a liability. You need to remove them before we enter the city."

Uri handed him a straight razor and an Android Repair Kit that was fastened to the inside of the pod door.

"I'm afraid this is the only way to ensure safer passage," Uri said. "We have about ten minutes until we reach ground."

Gabriel knew he was right.

He ripped the sleeves from his shirt and created makeshift gauze. Then, he grabbed a straight razor and carefully slit a precise quarter-inch opening in each of his fingertips, as well as his forehead and neck. The implants were excruciatingly small. Were it not for the magnetized tweezers in the kit, they would have been impossible to remove.

Julian's stomach felt queasy and he vomited when Gabriel began operating on himself. After the procedure was through, Julian walked over and said, "I can take away the memory of this experience... that is, if you want. God knows I wish I could erase it from my own brain."

"No, Jules. I've had enough amnesia for a lifetime, no thanks to Akaal. I know you're trying to help, but trust me, I can handle this. I was fully awake as a teenager when these damn implants were put into my body, against my will. I want to remember the day I ripped them out. This isn't pain; *this is liberation*. I earned each and every scar, teardrop and drop of blood. Don't take them away from me."

Julian hugged Gabriel and said, "You've known so much pain in your life. You're stronger than you know... stronger than I could ever be."

"We haven't much time," Uri cut in. "Put on some bandages and let's get moving."

Gabriel emptied the contents of the kit onto his lap and found a military-grade liquid field bandage. The fast-drying plastic molded to his skin, disinfecting and sealing off the incisions. It still hurt like hell, but at least it wasn't going to get infected.

The pod door opened. A Peacekeeping siren sounded in the distance.

"Gabe, are you feeling okay to walk?" Julian asked.

"Yeah, I'm good."

Gabriel gathered up the bloodied gauze and implants and tossed them into the chasm below. The gesture was cathartic; after fourteen years, he was finally free of the State's grip. It was a good feeling.

19

FENESTRAE STELLARUM

Restless windstorms and dust devils relentlessly threw debris into the midnight sky, creating a smoky, red halo around the moon. Even the clouds seemed to be painted a deep shade of crimson.

"Sister, there's blood on the moon. It's not safe for us to continue now, especially Gabe. He needs a few hours to rest and heal his wounds. Julian needs shut-eye as well."

"I know," Elsa said. "Morning, unfortunately, is still a few hours away. What do you have in mind?"

"Can you pull a Houdini?" Uri asked.

"Of course. I taught him all his best tricks."

Elsa closed her eyes and forced her subtle body outward, extending it at least ten feet in diameter. Gabriel felt dizzy as her high vibrational field enveloped the four of them.

"Go ahead, step outside my aura," she said.

Gabriel complied. Elsa, Uri and Julian remained invisible. Even more curious, whenever Gabriel placed his hand inside her auric field, it disappeared like some sort of magic trick.

"You weren't boasting, Elsa."

"Moons never do, Gabriel."

"How do you do it?"

"My brother made a reference to Houdini for a reason. I use a bit of smoke and mirrors myself. (Well, mirrors really.) I take what I see on one side and project it on the other, cloaking anything within my aura. The projection works in all directions. Ultimately, it's not unlike what Julian does, but my projection uses the visual spectrum instead of manipulating thoughtwaves. The net effect is the same; we both change how others perceive reality."

She pointed to a small plateau, devoid of debris, about a mile away.

"There... Let's rest in that spot until sunrise. No robot, human or animal will question this illusion. In fact, nothing, save another Firstborn, will be able to see us."

"How long can you maintain the illusion?" Julian asked.

"It takes an enormous amount of prana, or life force, so I can only support the projection for about four to six hours. After that, the illusion will become unstable and I'll need to meditate to clear my energy."

"How about you, Uri?" Julian asked. "Do you need rest?"

"Stars can meditate, but we do not require rest—not like humans do. I'll stand watch while you two sleep."

The star turned away and whispered something to the wind. It then raised its hands and twinkling stardust spiraled into the heavens towards a distant constellation.

"The beacon is set," Uri said. "Ambrose will know where to find us... as will an ally from afar. The Assembly of Stars will be ready by sunrise. Feel free to set up camp in the meantime."

Elsa kept her eyes on Hope's Pass, while her brother stood at her back, eyes fixed on Orion.

Gabriel took off his knapsack, rolled up his coat and made a makeshift pillow to share with Julian. As they shifted around to get comfortable, the stolen memory crystal rolled onto the Sedona soil

200 I NICHOLAS ASHBAUGH

and began to glow. Julian was already asleep, so Gabriel gently held the stone to his forehead and closed his eyes. Slowly but surely, sounds and images began to flicker in his mind.

First, he heard some sort of narration. However, like an archaic CB Radio, the voice sounded slightly distorted. This was not uncommon for psychic voice printing; it was an imperfect technology that depended equally on the skill of both the recording and receiving psychic. The more Gabriel tuned in, the clearer the imprint sounded.

This particular memory crystal was a rarity. Most of the field reports available in State Data Emporiums were purged of *inaccuracies*—information deemed inappropriate for the public—at the Propaganda Bureau. This crystal, however, contained the raw, unedited account of a State Field Agent. As such, the stream-of-consciousness narrative alternated between poetic and matter-of-fact, not unlike Gabriel's own thoughts.

"DATELINE: DECEMBER 1, EARTH YEAR TREBLE-TREBLE-NINE, NINE, DOUBLE-ZERO. I'm Special Agent Lee Ann, a Senior M-8 at SCRI Precinct Twenty-One in Sedona. This Transmission is for DEEP RED Eyes only.

"Today, at the stroke of thirteen hundred hours, three Einstein-Rosen bridges formed in Sedona. The Bureau calls them Fenestrae Stellarum, or The Starry Windows in Common Tongue. Don't let the bureaucratic names confuse you. They are stargates, wormholes, or wrinkles in time, if you wax poetic.

"Most citizens have no idea what happened; they view this as an accident. Based on my field and remote intel, the general public is dead wrong. In fact, for nearly a century, the State both owned (and operated) an atom-crasher beneath hundreds of miles of rock and sand in the Arizona desert. The official business of this Über-Massive Hadron Collider (ÜMHC) was so classified that even high-ranking officers were unaware of its existence.

However, my remote investigation revealed that its purpose was twofold: Officially, it was erected to unravel the mysteries surrounding dark matter. Unofficially, it was designed in the hopes of creating a time machine. In the end, it did something far greater and more dangerous... it created wormholes.

"The first Einstein-Rosen bridge (named Fenestra Primus) appeared in the Northeast quadrant of the particle collider. It closed moments after forming, but not before carving a seemingly bottomless crater around the city.

"The second Starry Window appeared above the Chapel of the Holy Cross. The Chapel structure was largely obliterated. Now only a few slabs of the façade still stand alongside the crucifix and steeple. For this reason, The Bureau renamed it 'The Shattered Holy Cross' (or Fenestra Sancta Cruce in State Cleric Tongue). It is a one-way portal *out* of Earth's dimension. Several probes and Drones were sent into the wormhole, but none returned. An army of Alphas and Raptors (which the State refers to as 'The Holy Guard') relentlessly patrol its perimeter.

"The third and final known stargate is called The Tower (or Fenestrae Turrim). It's situated at the peak of The Ruins of Cathedral Rock and measures in at roughly the same size as the second stargate (twenty feet in diameter). Unlike The Shattered Holy Cross, it's an incoming bridge that allows passage *to* Earth only. An army of Raptorcraft nicknamed 'The Tower Guard' surrounds it day and night."

The sapphire memory crystal abruptly cut transmission at this point, but Gabriel held onto the final image as long as he could. It shimmered in and out of view, as if it were drifting on an unseen ocean tide. In a sky filled with stars, the Fenestra Turrim looked like a subtle wrinkle through which distant galaxies and constellations would blink in and out of view.

The memory crystal flickered a few times and then went dim.

Sometime, in the early hours of morning, Gabriel drifted into a lucid dream. Within it, his attention turned back to The Shattered Holy Cross. He slipped behind the façade and stood face-to-face with the swirling light of the portal. It pulled at him with every passing second. Just as he was ready to step through, Gabriel heard a voice and the vision faded.

"Are you ready?"

20

THE DREAM BROKER

"A re you ready?" the voice asked again. "We need to go. *Now.*"

Gabriel opened his eyes. Uri's tall frame was beautifully backlit by the rising sun, almost as if a blazing nimbus emanated from his head. To Gabriel, he appeared as stately as a classic icon set in stained glass.

Pins and needles coursed over Gabriel's body as Elsa's illusionary veil dissolved into the bright white of dawn.

"Take my hand," Uri commanded.

Gabriel obliged, and as he caught his bearings, he saw two familiar faces coming into focus.

"Good to see you made it here safe and sound," Ambrose said. Then he turned to Julian and asked, "What can you see in the periphery? Is it safe for us to proceed?"

"As far as humans go, we should be safe." Julian replied. "I sense only a hundred minds scattered across the desert... the closest Agent is at least two to three klicks from our present location. I can't see into machine minds, but I'd wager that at least two armored Alphas are with that particular Agent, based on her thought patterns."

"And your cognitive web—is it set?" Ambrose asked.

"Yes. We'll be invisible to all humans in the vicinity."

"Excellent. Let's avoid the main thoroughfare and stick to side streets until we get to the Airport Mesa."

Gabriel felt a sense of sadness mixed with nostalgia as he traversed The Ruins. The city should have become a ghost town, but Sedona clearly wasn't ready for its swan song. What remained, however, bore little resemblance to the previous town. In the wake of its near-destruction, a dubious group of opportunistic energy alchemists attached themselves to the bowels of the city like barnacles. The locals called these entrepreneurs "vortex miners." Their arrival brought the ceaseless high-pitched hum of diamond drills and signaled an end of the old ways. Gone was the spiritual haven with open areas for camping, hiking and meditation. A bawdy, commercialized metropolis stood in its wake.

Several miners made a name for themselves and profited from the booming new business. However, one individual in particular— an enigmatic energy alchemist who billed himself as The Dream Broker—stood out from the pack. The Broker asserted that he could bend the boundaries between time, space and dreams. Soon, Gabriel would find out if his claims were true.

"We're nearly there," Uri said. "You can see the remains of the old airport just ahead."

The dilapidated terminal was little more than a pile of bricks and wood, with a long runway trailing off into The Sedona Crater.

Gabriel looked back at the group and noticed that Elsa was lagging a few steps behind. He watched in wonder as tiny light particles danced across her aura like sunlight on a lake. Light was quite literally attracted to Elsa; she had a magnetic aura the likes of which he'd never seen. With each step, more and more of her pranic energy recharged.

As he moved along the outer limits of a narrow but busy cul-de-sac, Gabriel felt goosebumps. The raw vortex energy from The Sedona Crater began to mingle with his subtle body, and all of his senses became heightened.

A massive obelisk stood tall, punctuating the dead-end street like an exclamation point. From a distance, it looked like an alien artifact. A persistent red haze—one that was endlessly exacerbated by the mining—severely limited visibility and obscured its height, but it was nonetheless impressive. With exception to The Red Gate, the obelisk dominated the Sedona skyline.

Gabriel walked ahead of the group and stopped ten feet shy of the object. It was completely smooth, like polished stone. If indeed it was a storefront, it was unlike any other he'd seen. It had no doors and no windows. Even more disconcerting, the structure's width and height fluctuated slightly each time he blinked his eyes.

He meditated and tried to read the energetic footprint of the obelisk. The building was rooted deep into the soil, and was surging with vortex energy. As Gabriel focused on the object, he sensed a transparent point of entry on top, and another below. A beam of light traversed both points. On the Eastern side he observed some sort of anomaly.

"Follow me," he said, motioning to Uri.

Gabriel placed his hand on the building, precisely where he sensed the anomaly. Much to his surprise, the surface was warm, and almost sponge-like. He removed his hand and the building rippled, as if it were made of liquid.

"This may sound daft, Uri, but is this building... alive?"

Uri ran his hand along the surface and noticed the rippling, too. "You're not far off, Gabe. It's part of someone's dream. So, yes, in a way it is. This is the point of access into their consciousness: it's a dreamgate."

Elsa stepped up to the obelisk and knelt down before the building. She carefully planted one hand in the soil and the other on the stone. As she exhaled, Gabriel watched the ripples coalesce around her hand until they formed an iris. The iris opened and revealed a circular door, roughly ten feet in diameter.

"You must have the magic touch?" Gabriel joked.

"Not really. You just have to ask the building nicely," she said with a grin. "You also need to know how to open the lock; it requires a connection of earth, aether and flesh."

A familiar voice interjected, *"Well done, Elsa. But, if this is indeed a dreamgate, then beware. These so-called gates are fragile at best. Think of them as blurry boundaries between the physical and psychic worlds. That being said, everything within the dream-gate can become fodder for the resulting dream or nightmare. Essentially, the dreamer's reality becomes yours—something that can be dangerous if you encounter a madman."*

Uri and Elsa knelt down and bowed. Akaal took the form of Transformation. A bright nimbus glowed above its head and light surged from its eyes as it peered into the depths of the obelisk.

"Akaal, my lord, we're blessed to see you again. Do you know The Dream Broker?" Elsa asked.

"We are... acquainted."

"You hinted at his mental state. Is he mad?"

"Madness is subjective, dear Elsa. Although it masquerades as a human, this creature is not of this world or this dimension, and it doesn't play by our rules."

"That's not very reassuring," she replied.

"Good. The last thing you should feel is comfort in its presence."

Akaal approached Julian with curiosity.

Its eyes surged with light and Julian felt it penetrate his consciousness.

He didn't budge.

"Salutations, Thought-Weaver. We are not acquainted."

"No, but I've seen your memories in my friend's mind. You're the shapeshifting god Death... Known to others as Akaal or Trans-formation. You're also The First Star from The Old World."

"I'm impressed, Julian. Gabriel chooses his friends well. Your mind works faster and reaches farther than most. For that reason, I'll need you to remain outside the dreamgate while we venture inside, maintaining a cloak of invisibility. We also need someone with a mind that can't be touched by The Broker, in case we get trapped. Can I count on you?"

"I will do whatever helps Gabriel the most, of course... but it seems like I always seem to miss the fun stuff."

"Excellent. If you sustain the thoughtweb you've set up, you'll be helping us more than you can imagine. And trust me, this journey will be many things, but I wouldn't describe it as fun."

Gabriel approached the gate and peered inside. Everything was blurry.

"I can't see a thing in there. How does this work?" Gabriel asked.

"The interior is completely psychic. You're essentially stepping into someone's mind. We can't see what it looks like until we jump inside. I know, it's not very reassuring, but you'll just have to trust me."

"What if it closes?"

"I will stand guard inside the doorway and Julian will watch the perimeter of the building."

Ambrose placed his hand on Julian's shoulder and spoke to The First Star.

"Akaal, my lord, I'd be honored to stand guard with Julian. Together we will ensure that nobody enters and, more importantly, that your presence here remains cloaked."

"Good idea. Please give the crystal skull to Gabriel for safe-keeping and I will secure passage into the dreamgate."

Akaal placed one bare foot in the dusty Sedona soil and it dug the other into the sponge-like floor of the dreamgate. Then, it gently pushed back on the circumference of the opening. Once it was grounded, the numinous being transformed into its aspect Janus with a blinding flash of light. It was the same aspect that Gabriel had encountered the night Björn attacked Elijah.

The being's posterior face looked squarely at Gabriel and said, *"You can enter now. But remember: question everything."*

Gabriel entered first, then Elsa, followed by Uri.

While moving through the dreamgate, Gabriel felt as if he were standing on the San Andreas fault. The ground shook and then thrust the three of them forward, into the center of the obelisk.

Elsa reached out her hand and pulled Gabriel up. As he looked into her eyes, he felt immediately grounded.

'Remember that you're seeing what The Broker wants you to,' she said telepathically. 'Hold on to your mind and your feet will follow.'

Against his better judgment, Gabriel looked down. He saw that there was nothing below them but a large chasm with energy surging upward. They were clearly standing on some sort of platform, but it had no shape. The walls and ceilings seemed to be, for lack of a better term, *invisible*, too. Sedona, however, was nowhere in sight. They were suspended in mid-air, and only white vortex energy surrounded them. Were it not for Akaal holding the iris open, there would be no clear exit back to Earth.

Hundreds of empty boxes lined invisible shelves on invisible walls. These alone provided some approximation for the size and width of the establishment, which was quite substantial. Gabriel felt it was easily the equivalent of a ten-story building. As he surveyed a few of the boxes, he noticed no two were alike. The box materials ranged from crystal to wood to exotic metals he'd never seen before.

"What are these?" Gabriel asked.

"Keys," Uri replied. "Each box opens a portal into a dream or nightmare. Some of the keys were created by The Broker."

"The others?" Gabriel asked.

"Hmmmm... you might say they were *borrowed*."

"I was afraid you'd say that," Gabriel replied. "Is this really the only way we can travel to The Fifth and Sixth Stars?"

"On *this* planet and in *this* dimension, yes."

"And remind me why we need to go there?"

"To get Corpus Tenebrae," Akaal said. *"Just as Corpus Sidera protects you and buoys your energy, Tenebrae can deepen the powers of The Seven Shadows. Until you find The Seventh Star, our missing sibling, the burden of protecting the book will fall on your shoulders. Only The Mortal Channel, a being we call The Starchild, is capable of wielding, and if necessary, destroying this weapon. You will succeed where your grandfather failed. Then and only then will you be The Last Steward of the Light."*

Gabriel was silent—speechless, in fact. The weight of the journey began to pull on him more than it had ever before. If he truly was some sort of chosen being, then there was no room for error, no room for fear. He must learn to become more than he believed he was.

While they were speaking, Gabriel started to feel uneasy, as if he were being watched. He turned around and noticed a man fidgeting behind the counter. The stranger had been there all along, but only now did he *allow* his presence to be seen by the group.

The man was as tall as Gabriel, but much thinner. His attire was curious; he wore a tattered silver suit and had grey hair that was perfectly slicked back. His ashen skin looked sickly, as did his pale lips. Two steel grey eyes locked onto Gabriel suspiciously. It was then that Gabriel realized The Dream Broker was a Grey.

As a child, Elijah warned Gabriel about Grå Själar, or Grey Souls. Better known simply as "Greys," they were not the aliens from science fiction, but frightening and powerful beings that walked the line between Light and Shadows. A Grey's morality was self-serving. Spirituality of any sort was rare; it owed allegiance to its ego and nothing else. The Broker fit that mold perfectly. Although he billed himself as a metaphysical locksmith, the truth of the matter is that he was a petty thief. His motives and alliances were self-serving and he was extremely cunning... the type of person who would make a good used car salesman. Gabriel knew they were going to be cheated on one level or another—it was just a matter of how much.

"Hello, Citizens. I'm The Dream Broker. I specialize in dreams and nightmares. Which do you seek?"

The man smiled, revealing grey teeth and long, sharp canines.

"Neither, Broker. We seek passage into someone else's dream," Gabriel replied.

The Dream Broker looked back at him quizzically and sniffed the air. "Who are you? What is your name?"

"I might ask the same of you," Gabriel replied, knowing it was unwise to give his true name to a stranger—especially one who dabbled in occult hijacking. Names are power, after all, and Gabriel chose to keep his under lock and key.

The Dream Broker moved closer, then sniffed again and grimaced.

"You stink of the State. Is this some sort of raid? I'm licensed to operate, you know."

"No," Gabriel replied. "I am no longer an Agent of the State; we are here on personal business. If we've somehow misrepresented or offended— "

"Enough!" The Broker interjected. "You are *strange*, and you keep even stranger company, *Dreamwalker*. Your friends travel among the stars, and you already have the skills to travel in the world of dreaming. Why are you *really* here?"

Gabriel could sense fear in the heart of the Grey. More disconcerting, he started to perceive the walls were closing in on them; the room was literally shrinking ever so slowly as The Broker lost patience. He could also sense Akaal struggling to keep the dream-gate open.

His survival instincts kicked-in and Gabriel quickly produced the crystalline skull from his knapsack. He was careful not to reveal *The Book of Stars*, however.

The room stopped shrinking and Gabriel placed the crystal skull on the counter.

"You didn't let me explain myself, Broker. The dream of which I spoke is not human in origin. It's from a Beta Synthetic named Genesis. She was nearly killed in an explosion, but we were able to save the neurocrystal that stores her consciousness. Unfortunately, the skull was melded shut by the heat of the explosion. None, save the late engineer Yantra, could repair the damage done to its data ports. But as you must surely know, this Beta is one of a kind; it can dream. So all hope is not lost—that is, if your claims are true, Broker."

The Dream Broker's eyes lit up. He was more than enticed by the offer. He flashed an authentic grin and his canines seemed longer and sharper than Gabriel remembered. As an empath, Gabriel felt The Broker's greed consuming him. Gabriel's skin was crawling, but he gave no indication of his discomfort.

"My claims are true, *Dreamwalker*. However, none have successfully opened passage to and from a constructed reality. It falls outside the realm of Spirit."

"I guess that makes us either brave or insane," Gabriel mused.

"Perhaps both," The Dream Broker replied flatly. He nervously played with a square glass sigil in his right hand and then slipped it in his pocket.

Uri walked the length of the wall and then leaned against the counter. "Tell me, Dream Broker, what is the cost for your services? I know that nothing is free."

"I charge a nominal fee for materials—one million credits for each key."

Gabriel mumbled something under his breath.

Uri gave his friend a crooked grin and whispered, "He's not done."

"You'd be wise to listen to the Firstborn Star beside you, *Dreamwalker*. Money means nothing in my circles. Isn't that right?"

The creature looked at Uri and its eyes seemed greyer and more alien than they had a few minutes earlier.

"Yes, I'm well aware of your 'fees,' Dream Broker. What else do you seek as payment?" Uri asked.

"In the heart of the Synthetic's dream, you will find a Black Box. That alone is the fare to and from its dream."

"That's it?" Gabriel bluffed.

Almost immediately, he sensed The Dream Broker poking around in his brain. He quickly chanted an ancient protection mantra in his mind. He repeated the verses at a rapid clip... so rapid, in fact, that the sound of the mantra was all that existed.

Gabriel's aura blazed with golden light and he appeared stronger and taller to The Dream Broker. Reluctantly, the ashen creature relented its psychic eavesdropping.

"You have no idea of The Black Box's worth," The Broker said. "Bring it back and your debt will be forgiven."

Gabriel knew that this was *Tenebrae*, but he dared not think the name in the presence of the Grey. He kept mantras running through his head, much to the chagrin of The Broker.

The creature turned to Uri and curtly asked, "Tell me, *Firstborn*, how many keys will you need?"

"Four total: the first one we've discussed, the second and third are to find Luminous Ones like myself, and the fourth is to return."

The Dream Broker walked over to The Wall of Keys. Much to Gabriel's disgust, the creature's arm somehow stretched unrealistically high towards the topmost shelf and then snapped back to normal.

"I'm ready to make your key, *Dreamwalker*, but I require payment in advance."

"I live off-the-grid, as you might have guessed. I assume that bank notes will suffice?" Gabriel inquired.

"It's unusual, but yes. That will be four million for your keys and one million for insurance, since I'll have to launder the old currency," The Dream Broker replied.

"Five million? What kind of establishment are you running?"

The Grey smiled.

"The kind that gladly helps a State fugitive, a Firstborn Star, a Moon, a Dragon, a Thought Engineer and The First of the Old Gods... and doesn't hassle them. Ask me again and it will be six."

Gabriel placed a stack of bank notes on the table.

"Excellent. Now, for me to cut the keys properly, I'll need personal effects from the two Stars you seek—something with their energy signature."

Uri dug into his coat pocket and produced a silken handkerchief. It contained what appeared to be a small object, no larger than the size of a marble. He carefully pulled back the silk and smiled.

"Behold, The Wheel of Truth—sigil for The Fifth Star."

As The Broker peered into the cloth, he saw a small, glowing ring that resembled a solar eclipse. Seemingly inexplicably, the O-shaped device floated a few inches above the handkerchief and then began to spin. It continued until it increased its radiance tenfold.

Its luminosity was more than The Broker could handle and he screamed in pain, "Enough! Extinguish it!"

Its light seemed to have literally caused his skin to become flush and burn.

Uri begrudgingly wrapped it in the handkerchief again and handed it to The Broker.

The Dream Broker turned to Elsa and squinted its eyes.

"I assume you hold the final sigil, my dear Moon?"

Elsa nodded and produced an intricate device made of interlocking silver geometric shapes. Like the previous sigil, it was small enough to fit in her hand, but denser than it appeared.

"Behold, Metatron's Cube, sigil to The Fourth Star."

The Broker examined the device. Thirteen interconnected silver circles created a six-pointed star within a six-pointed star. The silver structure coursed with energy and was hot to the touch.

"This will do nicely," The Broker said. I need one million additional credits to cover materials. The remaining fee is as discussed."

Gabriel didn't present an argument this time, for fear the fee would increase; he simply threw another stack of bank notes on the table.

The Dream Broker worked quickly without speaking. One by one, he carefully placed the skull, Wheel and Metatron's Cube into a single box. Then, he closed his eyes for a moment and uttered something incomprehensible.

The box started to glow dimly from within. The Broker then snapped two archaic devices on the top of the lid. The first was a rotary dial and the second was a jury-rigged RJ interface port that was crudely modified to accept modern cabling.

He handed it to Gabriel.

"Go ahead, *Dreamwalker*. Open it."

As Gabriel lifted the lid, the room was filled with blue light and a high-frequency tone. Unbeknownst to The Broker, the box contained a coded message amidst the static. Gabriel quickly replaced the lid without revealing this fact.

"I remember my grandfather telling me about these archaic devices," Gabriel said. "It's a Blue Box, right—used to hack into old analog phone systems? If so, will it even work?"

"The fact that it's antique is precisely why this will open the first gate. These frequencies haven't been monitored for at least half a billion years."

The Broker handed Gabriel a bulky device he'd only seen in history books.

"Try using the Blue Box at the condemned recharging station near The Chasm. An old trunk line was unearthed there during the last landslide. Unlike the fiber networks that feed most megacities, this one was installed eons ago by ARPANET. Unbeknownst to the State, it's still active, and it will work with an old rotary phone like this."

"Why hasn't someone shut down this security loophole?" Gabriel asked.

"Since the whole city block is sliding into The Chasm, this isn't high on the State's radar," the Grey replied.

"Technically speaking, I understand how the device interfaces with the trunk line, but how is it going to open up a portal?" Gabriel inquired.

"The Chasm surrounding you is surging with vortex energy— energy that is slowly ripping apart time and space around Sedona. The trunk line will provide necessary grounding, while the Blue Box pries open a connection to the Eleventh Dimension. Poor Genesis is the glue that holds this together... through her mind you will be able to walk in that dimension, something otherwise impossible for humans. The rest is up to you. It will work if you believe it will work. *Mind over matter*, you might say. And to that end, if her nightmares take over, there's nothing I can do to bring you back. I'm an alchemist, not God."

Uri grabbed the box and inspected it personally, taking special note of the rotary phone's delicate construction. He then raised an eyebrow and waved to the store owner.

"Broker, I'm no fool. Your devices only work one way. Where's the return key? And where are the second and third keys?"

The Dream Broker smiled and exposed its unnaturally long teeth again.

"*Firstborn*, you are wise to question me. However, you're mistaken if you think I'd send you on a one-way trip. I expect payment, after all. As far as the second and third keys, you will find those inside the dream, after you make passage."

Uri shook his head.

"That accounts for three of the four. What about the final key?"

The Broker produced a glass cube from his front pocket and handed it to Uri.

"This is my sigil; it alone is your return key. It will bring me to you, and I will bring you back here."

As he held it up to the light, Uri could see a smaller interconnected cube inside. The interlocking cubes folded and expanded simultaneously, constantly shifting, constantly moving.

Gabriel turned to Uri and flashed a knowing glance.

"I can guess what you're both thinking," The Broker said with a smirk. "Tesseracts aren't very stable. Like the Blue Box, this key can be wielded only once. After that, it will collapse on itself. Use it wisely."

'Are you sure these keys are safe to use?' Gabriel asked Uri telepathically.

'Nothing about this journey is safe, Gabriel. Let's go.'

Uri and Elsa walked through the gate and Gabriel was more than happy to follow. Everything about The Dream Broker's establishment made Gabriel feel uneasy.

Akaal waited until everyone passed through and then let go of the opening. As soon as The First Star's feet were planted on Sedona soil, the dreamgate snapped shut and the obelisk began to fade in and out of the visible spectrum.

"Did you get what you needed?" Julian asked.

"Yes. Well, sort of," Gabriel replied.

"At what cost?" Julian asked knowingly.

"We paid for two keys which we didn't get."

"Pray that was the only catch, Gabe," Akaal said. *"Your grandfather was right when he warned you about Greys. The Dream Broker owes allegiance to no one but itself. I fear crea-*

tures like that more than Shadows. At least Shadows are predictable."

"There was one other catch," Gabriel said.

"The Black Box?"

"Yes."

"I'm not concerned. I don't know why yet, but I sense that there is something working that is beyond his field of vision—beyond mine, as well. Until then, what The Broker doesn't know won't hurt him."

"But it might kill him?" Gabriel asked.

"That thing died eons ago. But yes, karma has a way of working things out. For now, let's make haste."

Gabriel wondered how much The First Star knew about the secret message. Time would tell.

Akaal wrapped a loose-fitting cloak around its body. The oversized hood concealed its posterior face, as well as most of its anterior face. The raiment flowed behind it as it walked, changing colors based on the surroundings, affording it a small degree of camouflage. Gabriel couldn't help but muse how much it now looked like The Grim Reaper.

Elsa turned to Julian and said, "We'll need you to stay here, outside the brokerage, as Akaal discussed earlier. Are you still amenable to that?"

"Yes, I have provisions for a few days."

"Good," she replied. "Will you be okay without Ambrose? The rest of The Assembly needs him."

"I should be," Julian replied.

"Fear not. Uri sent a beacon to an old friend to keep watch. Until then, may the Light stand guard, Julian!"

Akaal raised its walking staff and inscribed The Seal of The Six Stars above Julian's head, much as it did for Elijah a decade and a half earlier. The sigil glowed with a gentle, ceaseless incandescence.

"You are marked now as one of The Assembly of Stars, a friend

of The Luminous Ones and Ally of the Light. You will be safe. You have my word on that."

With this final blessing, the party took its leave.

Before walking away, Gabriel glanced over his shoulder one more time at Julian. Somehow this goodbye was harder than the others. He understood that he was coming to a point in this journey, and his life for that matter, where he could no longer rely on powerful friends and allies. If he was truly to live up to all these titles, then he had to start to embrace his own power.

Julian winked and gave him a thumbs-up.

'You've got this babe... You're stronger than you think—you always have been,' he said telepathically, echoing the final words he'd said to Gabriel at age fourteen.

For the first time in his adult life, Gabriel believed it.

21

THROUGH THE CRYSTAL SKULL

The Dream Broker was at least partly true to his word; an exposed trunk line stood exactly where he said it would be, about a mile away from the shop, on a narrow street named Nightwhisper Mews. Nearly all of the establishments on that road had already tumbled into The Sedona Crater. The exception was a decommissioned recharging station. It was proactively cordoned-off with half a dozen holographic light beacons.

"I should have known there'd be a catch," Gabriel grumbled. "The Broker neglected to tell us a Praetorian Guard and an Alpha were assigned to patrol the area.

"A *what*?" Ambrose asked.

"A Praetorian; it's a Bureau term for a rather formidable psychic warrior. From a young age, Praetorians are skilled in the deadly art of telekinetic warfare. They can manipulate objects with their minds alone and kill an opponent with a single thought. I've never met one in the flesh, and I'm in no hurry now."

"I don't blame you," Ambrose said before shifting into the ultraviolet light spectrum. "Stay with the group and let me investigate."

Ambrose traveled at faster-than-light speed until he was behind the State Agent.

The Praetorian's ears perked up and it spoke to him telepathically, 'Pray tell, who, or *what* are you?'

Ambrose moved so quickly that he was always behind the Agent's field of view.

'I'm older than anything on your little blue planet, and I don't play mind games.'

In a move that shocked Ambrose, the Praetorian mentally lifted him in the air and then threw him down, face-first. A moment later, the Agent had pinned Ambrose to the ground, painfully pulling his arms behind his back.

"You may be immortal, but you're not immune to pain," the Praetorian said with glee. Its eyes shined like quicksilver beneath a black hood. It donned no armor and carried no weapons.

Before Ambrose could call for help, something odd happened to the Agent; it smiled and pulled him to his feet.

"Julian?" Ambrose guessed.

'In the nick of time, no less," Julian replied, using the Agent's voice and mouth to speak. "Hurry. I'm not sure how long I can hold its mind. It's unlike anything that I've encountered before."

Just then, the Alpha became aware of The Assembly.

The mind-controlled Praetorian crushed the Alpha using thoughts alone. Then it returned to its post and stared directly at Gabriel.

Judging from the Praetorian's posture and gait alone, Gabriel asked "Ambrose, was that Julian's doing?"

"Yes. And I'm embarrassed to say, I would have been in a world of pain had he not stepped in."

Ambrose glanced at the heap of crushed metal and said, "Let's open the dreamgate before anyone notices Julian's handiwork."

The group carefully walked around the crushed android. As The

Broker claimed, there was an ancient trunk line hanging over the side of The Sedona Crater.

Gabriel knelt over the edge and gulped.

"Let me help," Akaal said.

The immortal held Gabriel's feet and legs securely in place, while Gabriel lay stomach-first on the ground. With great care and precision, he gently pulled a few wires from the trunk line and began twisting them into the RJ interface atop the Blue Box.

Several stones fell over the side while he was working, but Gabriel never heard them bounce off the side or reach the bottom. The fact that Death—or one of its aspects—was holding on to him somehow assuaged his worries. He would die one day; that day wasn't today, however.

"Okay, pull me up, Akaal."

Gabriel dusted himself off and then arranged the phone and Blue Box in front of him.

"Here goes nothing."

He clicked the receiver a few times. Once he heard dial tone, Gabriel used the archaic rotary to begin dialing a number. Then, he held the Blue Box against the receiver, dialed an access code and listened as the phone churned out a series of 2600Khz tones. The phone subsequently crumbled into dust, taking the cliff and all of Sedona with it. Gabriel's quick reflexes kicked-in and he grabbed the box and the skull before they slipped from his grip, as well.

The Assembly stood before a swirling iris of white light, surrounded by a sea of nothingness.

'That was easy... *too easy*,' Gabriel thought, half in disbelief.

His lungs stopped breathing and Gabriel tried to form the word "help" without avail. In the vacuous dimension he'd just entered, these words never left his lips. In fact, they never traveled from his brain to his mouth.

Gabriel's mind began to collapse.

22

COMPLETE ZERO

ou're right. We haven't passed through the dreamgate just yet. Hold fast to your consciousness, lest it slip away like quicksand.'

He heard Akaal's telepathic warning, but the words immediately lost meaning. Gabriel's mind had already begun to cave-in on itself like a crumpled sheet of loose-leaf. In the resulting Void that surrounded him, he stumbled upon six blood-red eyes. If he had the ability to scream, he surely would have. Instead, a luminous orb emerged from *The Book of Stars*, enveloping both Gabriel and his friends.

"Enough!"

Akaal's voice cut through The Void like a knife, after which The Luminous One transformed from Janus into its winged aspect, Zerachiel. It opened its myriad wings and swept the group into the mouth of the swirling dreamgate.

The portal closed almost as quickly as it opened. Moments later, The Assembly found themselves lying flat, quite literally, against a colorless slab, devoid of texture or any details.

They were in a two-dimensional space. There was no up, no

down—just left, right, front or back. Sight was binary as well; things either appeared as bright white or dark black. It was the 2-D binary moat about which Gabriel was warned. Through a bit of experimentation, The Assembly learned that they could move through the white spaces, but they were blocked when the space was black.

Incapable of carrying him, Akaal simply pushed Gabriel's flattened body through the maze for the better part of half an hour until they exited the 2-D moat. Each of their bodies quickly "expanded" back into a 3-D construct as they gathered their bearings.

Ambrose and Akaal stood up and began a telepathic dialogue.

'That was unexpected, my lord,' Ambrose said.

'And nearly disastrous.'

'Aye. Not many mortals have seen Complete Zero, much less lived to tell.'

'The Void and the Two-Dimensional Moat surrounding it are dangerous, even for Immortals, which makes it even more amazing our young Gabriel survived. Indeed, it's a testament to his character. It makes me wonder if...'

'Quiet your thoughts, your grace! He's awake.'

As Gabriel's consciousness returned, he tried to speak.

"It's okay, child. Rest for a moment."

Gabriel gazed into Akaal's glowing eyes. Gentle beams of light spilled out and warmed his face like the afternoon sun.

Gabriel's mental fog began to lift and the protective orb from *The Book of Stars* evaporated, as well.

"What just happened?" Gabriel asked.

"You gave us a scare," Akaal said.

"I mean, what was the area around the dreamgate?"

"In the old tongue: Śūnyatā. To mortals, it's known as Complete Zero or simply The Void."

"Okay, but **what** is it?"

"It may be easier to define it by what it isn't than what it is;

you'll soon see that the more you try to define it, the more difficult it becomes.

Let's start with why we came through it. Genesis's consciousness is a program; she thinks in binary code. Her mind has crashed, quite literally. Right now we're in an area of her memory banks that is turned on, albeit barely so. We just left an area that was turned off."

"So that was Nothingness?" Gabriel asked.

"Actually Complete Zero is beyond Nothingness... beyond emptiness. It's strange, but machines understand Complete Zero better than humans. In its simplest terms, if everything you know to be real or tangible is a number one in binary code, then think of Complete Zero as the corresponding zero in that code. It is the balance to Somethingness. Even the word Nothing makes it Something. Complete Zero is beyond labels."

"I understand enough to know that I should avoid it."

"Good. Complete Zero surrounds us in Genesis's dreamspace, and the flattened 2-D maze fills in the spaces between Complete Zero and where we now stand, so we must travel with care. Guard your movements and your thoughts. We are not in control of the rules here."

"One more thing," Gabriel said. "I saw... *something* in The Void."

Akaal turned, somewhat concerned.

"What did you see?"

"Eyes."

"How many?"

"Six."

"What else?"

"I heard... or maybe perceived a name, one that you've mentioned before."

"Don't speak it. Don't even think it. Bury it in your conscious-ness. A time will come when we will speak it again, but not here and

definitely not now. Names are power and we don't wish to invite **that** *presence into the dreamspace. It's too close as it is."*

Gabriel was strong enough to sit up. He squinted his tired eyes and looked around.

The walls of dreaming surrounded him. From what he could see, the surface was flat, nondescript and endlessly vast. That, perhaps, was the first oddity that revealed itself. Impossible though it may seem, Gabriel felt certain that he could walk in any direction and the floor would follow. Equally bizarre, he realized that the edges, or walls of the world constructed themselves if, and only if, he walked towards them. In essence, there was no limit to the vastness of the constructed dimension, only limits to his ability to explore or ponder it. And Nothingness only existed because Something hadn't been thought of yet. *Thoughts were creation.*

As Gabriel examined the periphery around the now-defunct dreamgate, he noticed a few anomalies. The ground and sky expressed themselves as two-dimensional planes. Three-dimensional space existed between them, and Gabriel was still a three-dimensional being, but the sky and ground were decidedly two-dimensional planes—he realized now that they'd traveled through one or both of them to get into the space they were now standing. Apparently, within Genesis's mind, two-, three- and multi-dimensional objects could co-exist within the same dimension, without fear of a paradox.

Intuitively, Gabriel felt the dreamspace lacked the concept of time, or that time itself was bent. He felt it was some sort of side effect of Genesis being in a coma.

One thing Gabriel couldn't explain is why the world lacked color. Perhaps black-and-white was more comfortable to a binary brain, or maybe it was a choice. Gabriel couldn't be certain yet.

"I can feel your questions mounting already," Akaal said. *"You are wise to try to understand the rules of this dream. Like a half-painted canvas, however, this world is very much a work-in-*

progress. Nothing exists outside of Genesis's reality and all the elements in this dream are controlled by the rules in her programming. Human dreams are often much more... well, dangerous. At least we can depend upon certain logic here. The trick, however, is figuring out that logic. "

"That doesn't make me feel much better," Gabriel said.

"It wasn't intended to," Akaal replied.

Ambrose pinched Gabriel's arm.

"Ouch! What was that for?" Gabriel asked.

"I just wanted to make sure it was you. Can't be too cautious in a dream," Ambrose said with a grin.

"Next time, just ask."

He smiled and sat next to Gabriel, content that he'd lightened the mood a bit.

"Ambrose, tell me about The Fourth and Fifth Stars."

"Expect the unexpected," he replied.

"At this point, since I'm talking to you in a monochromatic two- and three-dimensional world inside a comatose android's dream... well, let's just say, it's hard to shock me," Gabriel said with a smirk.

"Even so, The Fourth and Fifth Stars do not take on any conventional form. They are abstract entities—comprised purely of thought and energy."

Ambrose pointed to the dark sky above and continued, "You know, it may be easier if I just show you."

He took a deep breath and exhaled fire into his right palm. Soon, it transformed into a glowing pool of plasma. Ambrose then dipped his left finger into the plasma and used it to paint on the two-dimensional firmament. A fiery monochromatic trail of light followed, like the tail of a comet. He meticulously traced thirteen equally sized circles into the sky. In each circle he plotted the center point. He then traced straight lines between each point. The end result was something fantastic; it contained squares, triangles and all the

Platonic solids, with the six-pointed star being the most dominant shape.

"This is the star-being Mattara, better known to machines and men as Metatron or as its dual aspects Temperance and Bravery. It outranks almost all immortals in age, wisdom and luminosity. In fact, it shines so brightly that no creature can see it with its given eyes; its true form is perceived only in a dream, meditation or vision."

Ambrose tapped the sky and the fiery light particles faded gracefully to the ground like shooting stars and spent fireworks.

When the firmament was a clean slate again, Ambrose painted a perfectly round disc. He exhaled fire into the disc until it burned as brightly as a star. Then, he drew two rings around it, like the rings of Saturn, except they crossed over one another. Within each ring, smaller structures existed, but the two-dimensional plane was too crude for Ambrose to illustrate them properly.

"Behold The Wheel, sigil of Iophiel, The Many-Eyed One. She is the cosmic embodiment of Enlightenment. A guardian of beauty and knowledge, she sees all that ever was or will be. Only Time and Death know more than she. Much like Mercy and Metatron, she doesn't take an anthropomorphic form."

He waved his hand over the sphere and it faded into the flat sky, although its latent image still burned brightly in Gabriel's retina.

"Their chosen refuge is in the Eleventh Dimension, where spacetime bends around them, allowing omniscient access to all other dimensions. That, Gabriel, is why we are in Genesis's dream —here and only here can we open passage to their world, for it's been closed to humankind. If anyone knows the location of The Seventh Star, it is Iophiel. And if anyone can secure passage to that location, it is Metatron. Metatron has outposts at even the most remote parts of the Galaxy, manned by its Benevolent Watchers— The Machine Gods."

Gabriel paused and processed the information.

"Wait... *Eleven* dimensions?"

"Yes, there are eleven *known* dimensions. Four common dimensions exist—three spatial and one comprised of time. The seven Higher Dimensions are folded in between your Earthly planes. Higher vibrational or multidimensional beings like Akaal can enter without a problem. For those of us who aren't one of the Firstborn, travel to and from the Higher Dimensions requires astral projection, folding space via a tesseract or wormhole, or through dreamwalking, which allows us to do a little of both."

Akaal folded its wings along its back and approached Ambrose. *"We've overstayed our welcome."*

Ambrose and Gabriel looked up. The sky was quite literally falling.

23

TRAVERSING THE GOLDEN SPIRAL

"*abe, do you still have a remote Oubliette?*" Akaal asked. Gabriel dug into his coat pocket and produced a small triangular object.

"I don't have the power cell anymore, but the transceiver is still operational."

"*That's fine. I don't require an external power supply. May I?*"

The immortal held the device at arm's length and tapped forcefully. The glass exterior of the Oubliette shattered—revealing only a tiny silicon transceiver in the center. Akaal rewired the transceiver and, with the light and heat of its own hands it soldered the new connection.

"*Remove the glass skull from the Blue Box and place it in my other hand. It's time for us to jump-start Genesis.*"

Gabriel removed the glass skull from his knapsack, admiring the craftsmanship. It perfectly mimicked a human cranium, and was unsettling to hold. The crystal skull proved slippery, however, and Gabriel nearly dropped it.

"*Careful. You're holding her dream—our present reality—in your hands.*"

Gabriel literally held his breath as he handed it to The First Star.

Akaal placed the Oubliette transceiver in its left palm and the skull in its right. As it closed its eyes, the star imagined the symbol for infinity (∞) coursing through the two objects. The transceiver chirped a few times and then melted.

"It is done."

"What's done? You just broke the Oubli—"

Before Gabriel could finish, the crystal skull illuminated from within and a flash of light blinded him, followed by an audible scream that tore through the dreamspace. When his eyes adjusted, he saw a quasar surrounded by a single spiral arm, forming a perfect Fibonacci curve. He looked down and realized he was suspended in space on the outer edge of that arm, standing on particles of golden light.

"You're welcome."

"Thanks," Gabriel said absentmindedly. "Wait, I see color again. Do you see it, too?"

"Yes, things are shifting now. We are in what's left of the Eleventh Dimension. Genesis's dreamspace is around us... barely... but it isn't defining this area."

Although an enormous distance stood between Gabriel and the quasar, it nonetheless shined with the intensity of a million Earth Suns.

"The heat is unbearable!"

Akaal pointed to the middle of the quasar. Immense light radiated from a massive star-like entity in the center. There was some sort of friction at that point, causing an energy fluctuation.

*"Your mind **thinks** that it is hot, so try to allow it to be something else. In this dimension thoughts are reality. Adjust your perspective and your reality will change."*

Gabriel was not fully ready to comprehend what he'd just heard.

"Where are we?" he asked.

"We're standing on The Golden Spiral, a galactic stairwell

known as The Wheel of Galgallin. This is all part of a dimension known as The Throne."

Akaal pointed to the center of the galaxy again.

"Right there, at the center, exists Iophiel's consciousness. The light and heat you perceived, however, emanate from the numinous arms of Metatron, for it stands guard over The Golden Spiral... it is the only reason we aren't being crushed."

Akaal opened its luminous wings and spoke telepathically to Gabriel. *'We must leave now. Whatever you do, keep your eyes on me. And for the love of the Light, do not look back.'*

Gabriel could hear screams from The Void beneath and behind him. One of them called out his name.

"Who are they?"

"You mean 'what' not 'who.' They're Children of the Eight-Eyed One, or more simply, Genesis's nightmares. Bit by bit (quite literally), they're taking hold of her consciousness. That scream we just heard was Genesis losing her mind."

"So... If I turn around?"

"Don't."

Gabriel gulped. He thought of the old myth of Orpheus and Eurydice and dared not find out what might happen if he disobeyed The First Star.

"Okay, but how are we ever going to make it to the center? We're light-years away."

"Try not to think so linearly, Gabriel. Remember that this is a thought-controlled dimension and you're only as slow as you believe. Your thoughts are superluminal; let go and allow your mind to be your momentum."

Akaal unfurled its purple wings and flew across The Golden Spiral in mere seconds. Uri, Elsa and Ambrose followed suit.

'You can do it!' Akaal said telepathically from the center of the quasar. *'Perception is reality.'*

Gabriel closed his eyes. Finally, he understood he was nothing more than energy. *Anything was possible.* He imagined himself reduced to tiny particles. Then Gabriel set his sight on the center of the quasar, allowing its gravity to pull him like an enormous magnet. He traversed the galactic stairwell at faster-than-light speeds, just as Akaal promised.

As The Assembly moved into the innermost ring of The Golden Spiral, Gabriel heard something that was a welcome change from Genesis's nightmares: music.

24

A FRACTURE IN THE ELEVENTH DIMENSION

Hundreds of voices began to harmonize on a lamentation. The result was a simple, profound and powerful mantra with three repeating, overlapping verses. However, like an old phonograph, strange pops and clicks began to disrupt the music. With each repetition, the mantra grew erratic and discordant.

The voices stopped and then the process began again.

"It's a distress beacon," Ambrose said softly, answering a question Gabriel had not yet spoken aloud.

Akaal shapeshifted from Zerachiel into Transformation. Its glowing eyes peered deep into the heart of the quasar and then it spoke after a long pause.

"Yes, I feel it too. Something is wrong... terribly wrong. I feel fractures... wrinkles... cracks. Time and space are folding around us; it's not just Genesis's dream, but this dimension is... well, unstable."

"Uri and I sense it as well," Elsa said. "It's the power of The Black Box; slowly *Tenebrae* is warping this dimension. Quite simply it lacks a balancing force."

Ambrose locked eyes with Gabriel and spoke again.

"As Akaal said earlier, there are only two in The Universe capable of holding it: Metatron and *you*, Gabriel. It's time for you to embrace your duty as The Last Steward of the Light."

The words weighed heavily on Gabriel for a moment, but his mind was soon distracted. He couldn't help but marvel at the sheer beauty of the heavenly constructs all around him.

Silvery sinews of light and energy ran across the sky, forming a six-pointed star. Each point pushed the walls of the Eleventh Dimension apart, keeping them from collapsing. Iophiel existed within Metatron's avatar... a dimension within a dimension and a star within a star, much like The Sigil of The Seven Stars.

Iophiel descended from the firmament like the sun god Ra. Initially, her form was that of a brilliant disc, perfectly flat and radiant beyond description. She burned, quite literally, so brightly that the sight of her eclipsed all other light within the Eleventh Dimension.

As the disc turned, other subtle details revealed themselves. Gabriel realized Iophiel was not two-dimensional, but rather only partially visible within this dimension.

He closed his physical eyes to get a better look without the filters or lenses of his ego. It was then that Iophiel's true form revealed itself. Trillions of discs orbited an enormous ultraviolet star—the largest star Gabriel had ever seen. Each orb contained eyes... not just a single eye, but compound eyes; eyes within eyes and eyes within those eyes. Each blazed brilliantly with light and rotated quickly around the center star. Their blinding orbits created what appeared to be wheel-like structures, and trails of light followed them in a pinwheel fashion. The centermost star was, itself, a compound eye. Within the granulation of the photosphere, he detected orb-like structures... eyes that saw in every direction, dimension and time.

"She's one of the Ophanim!" Gabriel said with a gasp.

"Yes, The Fifth goes by many names, including The Wheel, The

Throne and The Many-Eyed One. Of The Four Wheels of Galgallin, she is the only one that remains," Akaal replied with a sigh.

"The others succumbed to Shadows?" Gabriel asked.

"No, they sacrificed themselves during The Battle of Adŭro on The Shadow Moon of Aurelius."

Beautiful reed-like sounds filled Gabriel's ears as Iophiel began to speak to him.

"I've been waiting for you, Starchild... Indeed, you bring me hope like I haven't felt since..."

Gabriel waited, but The Fifth Star was lost in its thoughts.

Akaal moved towards Iophiel and broke the silence.

"Salutations, dear sibling, too long have our paths been parted. Accept my apologies for the delay. I realize we barely arrived in time. How is Metatron?"

"Greetings to you as well, Akaal. Your presence warms my heart, as always. Metatron is sustaining, but that's all. I dare say speech is impossible. Between holding back the fractures in the Eleventh Dimension and containing the corrosive influence of The Black Box, not a drop of energy is left to spare."

"Have you two had any trouble keeping it out of sight?" Akaal asked.

"Fear not; it has remained safely ensconced beyond the reach of humankind and all organic life forms, for that matter. Gabriel is the first Organic we've seen since The Black Box came into our safe-keeping. Entrance here requires a complete lack of ego. Usually, children and animals are the only ones who make it here. However, with their childlike innocence and insatiable curiosity, the machines found their way to us, too. As humans became more jaded and cruel, the machines worked with us to create this safe haven, until there was a time that we might be needed again. *Until now."*

Iophiel paused and sensed questions within Gabriel's mind.

"Don't look so surprised, young Steward. Earth machines are not the first, *nor the last,* inorganic life form we've befriended. You must promise to tell us if any of our children still live on The Shadow Moon."

"Of course I will," Gabriel replied.

"*I can feel your mind drifting again,*" Akaal said. "*What is it?*"

"If I might be so bold, why was Metatron not tempted to open the tome?" Gabriel asked.

Akaal turned to Gabriel; its eyes shimmered brilliantly as it answered his question.

"*Only Two of The Seven Stars can touch The Black Box: Metatron and our missing brother, The Seventh Star. Metatron's own mathematical logic allows it to see the book in its simplest terms: a cosmic foil to Sidera. However, Metatron is incapable of carrying this burden much longer. The Fourth Star's true function is Temperance and Bravery, not transmutation. In the case of The Seventh Star, its purity of heart and intrinsic ability to maintain Hope shield it from the darkness within the tome. Also, like myself, The Seventh has the ability to transform. Thus, only our missing sibling can possess Tenebrae for all eternity.*"

"Is it safe for me, as Ambrose suggested? If so, why?"

"*Yes, you are safe... so long as you don't open it. Like your grandfather before you, you're a Steward of the Light. Stewards have powers that exceed most humans. But you... well, you're singular. You seem to possess the same essence that our lost brother did. Today we saw Corpus Sidera shield you... that has never happened with any other Steward.*"

"I'm sorry to be the bearer of bad news," Iophiel interjected, "But you've painted yourself into a corner... Each and every one of you engaged in a binding agreement with The Dream Broker. We all know he's not going to let you out alive even if you give him The Black Box. If you don't surrender *Tenebrae*, he'll simply trap you in Genesis's dream until you perish. Then he'll claim his prize."

"*Iophiel, what about sending a message through The Void... into spacetime?*" Akaal asked.

"We can travel back in time?" Gabriel asked. "Is that even possible?"

"Everything vibrates higher in this dimension," Iophiel explained. "So high, in fact, that our very presence here warps spacetime, much like the book itself... that's why you must remove it."

"I'm happy to help. But, what's the catch?" Gabriel asked.

Iophiel sighed. "If you choose to travel through time, multiple versions of you will exist—one for each message you send into The Void. Some may carry on like echoes; others may dissolve when their timethread is altered."

"If you do it correctly, none (save Akasha and you) will recall the timethreads," Akaal said.

"And if I do it incorrectly?"

"You will cease to exist, and not even I can stop that. Let's just make sure that doesn't happen."

Gabriel grimaced.

"My advice is to keep the message simple and memorable. After you've set your intention, simply look into the light of Iophiel. She will pry open the rift so that you may enter."

"Are you ready, Gabriel?" Iophiel asked.

"I am."

Gabriel set an intention on a day and time. He looked into the blinding light of The Many-Eyed One and felt warmth course through his body as her light guided him through spacetime.

25

A WORLD OF BROKEN GLASS

Much to Gabriel's surprise, traveling through the rift was easy; landing in The Mirror World was a different story altogether. The portal was several feet above the ground and Gabriel was traveling at a decent velocity. His body subsequently landed on the alien surface with a dull thud. Thankfully, nothing was broken.

'Madeleine was right; I am a little scrawny,' Gabriel thought to himself with a chuckle. It was her memory that gave him the strength to move on.

Gabriel brushed himself off and began to look around.

It took a moment for everything to set in. He was officially *inside* the enchanted Looking Glass that his grandfather gave to him on the night he died. Just as Elijah promised, it was a World Between Worlds, a space that was both vast and small; it was large enough to hold mountains and a life form like Gabriel, but it was small enough that it could fit in the palm of a human hand. It all depended if someone was on the outside looking in, or on the inside looking out.

The Mirror World was covered in smoky obsidian rock,

completely devoid of any organic life. A thick, misty atmosphere moved about the dimension, however, like the dramatic fogbanks in San Francisco.

In the distance, Gabriel saw a round circle of light.

"The Oculus Fenestra!" he said aloud. "I wish it wasn't so far away."

In the blink of an eye, Gabriel found himself in front of the swirling Oculus. He surmised that each thought brought about an absolute reaction in this dimension. Thoughts were power.

On the other side of The Looking Glass, it was precisely the time Elijah was bequeathing *The Book of Stars* to him as a seven-year-old. He called out to Elijah.

Just as he recalled, his younger self peered into The Looking Glass, moments after fastening the Tidens Svärd timepiece to his trousers.

The older Gabriel stepped very close to The Oculus Fenestra.

'I'm larger than life,' he thought.

His body grew in size until his face was as large as The Oculus, large enough to fill the entire portal.

The boy looked back curiously. It was odd to stare at a seven-year-old version of himself... but there he was.

"What... or who are you?" Young Gabriel asked, frozen in fear.

Older Gabriel took a deep breath and recited a riddle he made up on the fly:

"I'm the Man in The Looking Glass—
That's all you need know!
A shadow of a future on a path you'll forego.
Look for the Rabbit inside a Blue Box...
The key is your knowledge, so be as sly as a fox.
Zero follows eleven—
That's if you survive...
But the Grey is a trickster from which you can't hide.

So, tesser in The Void and release all fear...
Set the clock to twelve and then disappear."

The Older Gabriel stepped back from the portal and waited, unsure of what might come next. Seconds later, The Mirror World began to shake and his body slammed against one of the rocks. On the other side of the portal, the boy inadvertently dropped The Looking Glass.

He screamed.

As the mirror shattered, it took Older Gabriel and his timethread with it. The World Between Worlds was obliterated.

Light-years away, deep within the depths of The Akashic Sea, a single particle of light ignited, and burned for all eternity.

26

A RABBIT IN A BLUE BOX

Young Gabriel dutifully memorized the message from The Man in the Looking Glass. His subsequent life was otherwise identical, and all his decisions led him back to Iophiel again, with nobody aware of the original Gabriel, nor his first trip through the rift, except the Eternal being Akasha.

The problem, much as before, was that time was running out; the walls of the Eleventh Dimension began to collapse, even with Metatron holding them back.

Gabriel needed to send himself a coded message to act immediately upon meeting Iophiel or they'd never survive.

"Are you ready, Gabriel?" Iophiel asked.

Gabriel looked down at the Blue Box and said, "I am."

He took a deep breath and cracked the crystal skull in half.

The golden staircase disappeared and the immortals watched quietly (and curiously) as he shattered and then removed a homing device from the cranium of Genesis's skull. Wire by wire, he reworked it to the inside of the Blue Box, concealing it so that none save he would see it. When he was done, he'd reprogrammed the

word R-A-B-B-I-T using Morse code (.-. .- -... -... .. -), followed by
C-O-N-U-N-D-R-U-M (-.-. --- -. ..- -. -.. .-. ..- --).

Next, Gabriel dumped out the contents of the box, so it was
once again empty.

With a heavy heart, he looked into The Many-Eyed One and set
his intention for earlier that day.

Her warm starlight led him through the rift. This time, however,
Gabriel specified exactly where he wanted to land. He soon found
himself inside The Broker's dreamspace. The shop was empty and
he was carefully standing on an invisible shelf, towards the top of
the obelisk.

He laid the Blue Box on the shelf, careful not to touch the original... not just yet.

Once the modified box was in position, Gabriel slowly reached
for the original Blue Box.

His timethread dissolved, taking the box and his body with it.
This version of Gabriel was gone, lost in time. As before, a single
light particle flickered into existence in the great Akashic Sea.

27

TIDENS SVÄRD

When the third version of Gabriel stood before the blinding light of The Many-Eyed One, he not only knew what he had to do, but he also realized the sacrifices he made to get there. Unlike his predecessors, this Gabriel was intent on surviving.

Iophiel began to speak, "We have a conundrum—" but stopped short of completing her sentence.

"Yes, sister," Akaal interjected, *"I also feel Déjà-vu... something's changed in the timethreads."*

Without explanation, Gabriel broke the crystal skull.

"Sorry, Genesis... the dream stops here."

The Assembly looked at one another and nodded in agreement. They trusted Gabriel.

Metatron released the walls of the Eleventh Dimension and The Black Box fell into Gabriel's hands. He quickly placed it in his knapsack, unaffected by its influence, just as Akaal predicted.

With the fortifications released, the dimension began to crumble. Not even the mighty light of the *Corpus Sidera* could counteract the damage done by *Corpus Tenebrae*.

"We must leave now... we will see you again at the end of things," Iophiel said.

Metatron opened a tesseract of its own and Iophiel followed.

Gabriel turned around and didn't look back.

"Hurry! Follow me!" he screamed.

Uri, Akaal, Elsa, and Ambrose followed him, running from the crashing walls of the Eleventh Dimension.

"You know what exists, or more accurately, what doesn't exist in the dreamspace now that Genesis's processor is wrecked?"

"Yes. I'm prepared for Complete Zero this time," Gabriel replied. "Just trust me and I'll explain on the other end."

The edge of the dimension felt like a wall of static. Akaal opened its wings and motioned for all of the party to hop on its back. With The Assembly of Stars in tow, Akaal flew into The Void.

"Now!" Akaal commanded.

Gabriel twisted the hypercube and activated the tesseract mechanism. He threw it into the middle of The Void, if the concept "middle" indeed existed.

Almost immediately The Dream Broker appeared, although it was less human than Gabriel remembered. Its incisors were decidedly more pronounced and its skin was so grey that it almost appeared translucent.

"What is the meaning of this?" It demanded.

Even as it spoke, The Dream Broker's mind began to fade into the abyss.

Gabriel, who was fighting the same effects, grabbed his grandfather's pocket watch, broke the glass and manually changed the hour hand to twelve. Before he was completely immobilized, Gabriel released his grip on Tidens Svärd. It was now trapped in Complete Zero, freezing The Dream Broker, Gabriel and the nothingness that surrounded them into perpetual stasis.

Akaal, seemingly immune to the effects of the device, flew through the tesseract, narrowly escaping its collapse.

As time and space folded behind them, they found themselves back in Sedona in a very unstable psychic projection of what used to be The Dream Broker's establishment. One by one, each box fell onto the floor, unleashing a cataclysmic and chaotic nightmare. The Brokerage walls crumbled down, narrowly giving them time to escape into The Ruins.

Julian pried open the dreamgate until everyone escaped.

As Gabriel stepped onto the Sedona soil, he heard a series of ear-shattering explosions behind him. The obelisk was gone. All that remained of The Dream Broker's shop was an enormous crater surging with vortex energy.

"You okay?" Julian asked.

"Getting there," Gabriel replied.

"You did exceptionally well, Julian. Without you, it would have been impossible for us to return safely."

Julian bowed appreciatively towards the Old God.

Akaal turned its attention to Gabriel.

"Care to explain what just happened? How did you know to use the pocket watch? That was genius."

"You mean, Tidens Svärd? The Man in the Looking Glass told me," Gabriel said. It sounded as insane now as it did when he was seven.

"You know its true name... You weren't supposed to know about The Sword of Time until much later."

"It was a gift from my grandfather; I never knew what to do with it until the original version of me traveled through time. He figured out that we'd have to make two jumps—one to plant the idea in my mind at age seven and another to embed the beacon in the box."

The Assembly looked at him in disbelief.

"My grandfather had an old enchanted mirror in his house. On occasion, it would talk to him, and later, me—that is, until I broke it. The last thing it told me was to use an enchanted clock and tesser to Complete Zero to escape. It gave me a code phrase, one that only I knew, which I heard when we opened the Blue Box."

"Do you mean—?"

"Yes. I've been here before. Actually *we've* been here before. *Twice.*"

Uri spoke up. "I've felt a strange sense of déjà-vu the entire journey. This makes sense now."

"I weighed all the options," Gabriel said. "If we'd activated the tesseract from within the Eleventh Dimension, we'd have put The Fourth and Fifth Stars at risk. Plus, The Dream Broker would have surely found a way to steal The Black Box. If we re-entered Genesis's dreamspace, we would have been trapped forever inside a box on The Wall of Nightmares." Gabriel explained. "Ironically, The Dream Broker was right; I did find the final key from within the dream."

"Aye, but at such a cost, Gabriel," Ambrose said somberly.

"I guess you could say it was a 'matter of conscience,' as an old friend once taught me."

Akaal smiled and stared into the abyss where the brokerage once stood.

"The Dream Broker is a dangerous creature. I doubt we've seen the last of it. However, it will surely think twice before crossing paths with any of us in the future."

"I feel it was working for the same entity that corrupted Björn, Vrána and Yantra," Gabriel said.

"Indeed. We will speak of the Beast soon, before you leave for Planet Aurelius."

"Where?"

"You know it as 'The Planet Made of Snow.' It exists, and on it you'll find The Sixth Star."

Gabriel's eyes opened widely, like two blue-green sapphires.

"Before we talk of this, we must make it to the portal. You have The Cosmic Tomes stowed safely, correct?"

"Yes, both books are in my knapsack. As for the safety of the tomes, this bag is State-issued; it may not be pretty, but it will withstand fire, rain and radiation."

"Good. We'll travel to the perimeter of The Starry Window by foot. We can use Elsa's subtle body to cloak us once we arrive at the perimeter of the portal."

"As long as you huddle close, I should be able to keep us out of sight," she said.

The party walked silently towards the glittering lights and stained glass of Fenestra Sancta Cruce in the distance.

As they approached the heavily guarded perimeter, Gabriel caught something out of the corner of his eye. It shimmered for a moment and then disappeared.

"What—"

Before Gabriel could comment, Akaal motioned to its right. The shimmering being had fully materialized.

"Do not be alarmed, my child. This is an unexpected friend. It's rare that we see one of Himlens Väktare walk in the physical plane."

"A Sky Guardian?!" Gabriel asked in awe.

Akaal nodded.

A hooded being approached the party and bowed low. It spoke telepathically, using a high frequency that only Akaal and Gabriel could perceive.

"Dearest Akaal, it's good to see you. I received The Third Star's beacon and arrived as soon as I could." It bowed a second time, kissing Akaal's foot as a form of reverence.

"Rise, Rigel. Your presence is a blessing! What tidings dost thou bring from Aamĕllÿne?"

"Alas, The Shadow Moon stirs, my sovereign... and the Guardians of The Dragonfly Galaxy sleep."

"All?"

"Yes. All three... The Stone Colossus, The Sacred Heart and even The Great Tree."

"This is grave indeed. What says Aldebaran of this news?"

"After the Fall of The Darkheart Constellation, Aldebaran trekked to Bisaj Bakool. There, Antares is readying an astral host— one that almost matches The Old World in its luminance."

Rigel looked at Gabriel. Or rather, it moved its consciousness towards him. A shimmering robe flowed behind the astral being, even though the desert air was still. Upon closer inspection, Gabriel understood it was not a robe, so much as a silvery-white nebula that moved about the being. It concealed Rigel's face, feet and hands, if indeed it had any. Rigel appeared, for lack of a better word, angelic, but also a bit foreboding. Gabriel sensed a strong familial kinship with The First Star.

"Akaal, pray tell... is this the human of whom you spoke so highly? The Last Steward of the Light and mortal guardian of The Sword of Time."

"Aye."

Rigel nodded its head reverently in Gabriel's direction and then turned to Akaal.

"Speaking of the latter, what became of Tidens Svärd, my lord?" Rigel asked. "I no longer feel its presence on this planet."

"The weapon is locked in the clutches of Complete Zero, along with the greedy Dream Broker."

"I'm grateful two of our problems are at bay. It will be safe from the enemy there."

Akaal nodded.

"For now, at least."

Gabriel looked up at the stars above and then gazed at the hooded being before him.

Anticipating his question, it spoke telepathically to Gabriel alone.

'Yes. I'm *that* Rigel. I went supernova ages ago, but it will be some time before you see that event here on Earth. I'm in a bit of a *transition* right now, you see.'

Rigel lifted its cloak for a split second and bluish-white light spilled out, warming Gabriel's face. In that brief instant, it transmitted thoughts and images to Gabriel's mind, without the use of language. He now fully understood Rigel's purpose in visiting. It would act as a distraction while they made their way to the stargates.

Akaal approached and put its hand on the ethereal being.

"Careful with your light... this isn't the time or place."

It cloaked itself once more.

"Rigel, my child, thank you for answering my call."

The etheric being bowed low to everyone before it.

"The honor is mine alone, your grace. To even briefly be a part of this meeting of The Assembly of Stars is historic."

It then turned around.

"Elsa, I shall meet you and the Thought Engineer in front of Fenestrae Sancta Cruce, without my Earthly raiment."

Rigel coiled its body and nebula into a beam of light and rose into the night sky as mysteriously as it arrived.

Gabriel looked up in wonder. Far above the desert, a single star followed The Assembly as they traveled towards the stargate.

28

DOPPELGÄNGER

Julian and Elsa had volunteered to investigate the perimeter of the stargate.

Akaal sensed an anomalous presence there—something that could put the entire Assembly of Stars in danger. At Julian and Elsa's present velocity, the perceived anomaly was less than a mile away. The rest of the Assembly was safely concealed in a deserted building, awaiting their signal.

"Julian, are you the type of person that wants to know what's ahead, or do you like to be surprised?" Elsa asked.

"It all depends..."

"On what?"

"Whether or not it's good news."

Her expression was stern.

"Just show me. Whatever it is, I'd rather know."

"As you wish."

Elsa glided effortlessly across the desert sand, without her feet touching the ground. For a fraction of a second, she lifted the veil of illusion she donned in the mortal realm. In that moment, her silver skin glowed incandescently, rivaling Earth's own Moon, and she stood higher than any mountain top. Julian was now psychically linked with Elsa's avatar, Artemis. She was every bit as powerful as her brother, if not more so, for she could reveal hidden truths.

Elsa invoked **STJÄRNLJUS**, the language of The Firstborn Stars and said, "**LOOK INTO MY EYES. BEHOLD WHAT LIES AHEAD.**"

Julian obeyed. Even for a Thought Engineer, he wasn't quite prepared for what he saw.

He connected with her consciousness; it flowed deeper than any ocean and it was vaster than the furthest reaches of outer space. Within it, he saw a flash of his destiny—one where he perished.

"Gabriel may have only a handful of friends," she said, "but they are exquisitely chosen... you especially, Julian, *Engineer of Thoughts and Namesake of Jupiter*. Your love for him (and this planet) runs deep. Your soul is strong, but it is no match for the anomaly that Akaal sensed. It's a harbinger of destruction. Know this: *you will die*. Yet, I sense that your journey and your function within The Assembly of Stars will not stop there. You will return again, as something... *unknown*. What, exactly, I cannot discern... not yet. I believe that it's a choice—one that your soul will decide, when the time comes.'

"And if I don't proceed?"

"Gabriel's mission will fail, Earth will perish, and so will you."

"So the only way out is through this... anomaly."

"Yes," Elsa said, as she resumed her normal avatar, no longer a silver goddess of old.

For a moment, Julian knelt down, catching his breath and gathering his bearings.

"As I told Gabriel, I'm a fighter. I'm certainly not quitting now," he said.

Elsa pointed to the army of Drones surrounding the portal.

"Over there. Tell me what you see?"

Julian nodded and closed his eyes.

After a pregnant pause, he said, "I sense only one humanoid presence: a Dark One. She wears the body of a human but walks among Shadows... she is a body-snatcher, a doppelgänger who wears the skin of the dead. From the select memories Gabriel shared, this is Leftenant Vrána."

Julian reached out for Elsa's hand and held it tight.

"See what I see," he said.

Horrible images barraged her consciousness. They were dark, murky and filled with torment.

Elsa shuddered.

"It's far worse than I imagined," she said. "The creature who wears Vrána's skin is much more than a skinwalker; it's one of The Seven Shadows. Through her, The Shadow murdered all three men on New Year's Eve. It intends to murder Gabriel and bring eternal darkness to All Known Worlds. This is The Shadow known as Deception."

She took his hand and pulled him closer.

"Free will always exists, Julian. No human has withstood the effects of a Shadow's consciousness and lived to tell. We can seek counsel with Akaal. There may be another way."

"I may not be a Star or The Chosen One, like Gabriel, but I have gifts that the Shadows and Stars together cannot comprehend. I can turn one's thoughts against them. This is how we will win this battle; I will reflect Deception's thoughts on itself. "

Elsa acquiesced, knowing he was right.

"Would you stand by and let your twin, Uri, die if you had a chance to save him?"

"Of course not, but this is... well, it's suicide."

"No. This is sacrifice. This is my choice," Julian said. "My love for Gabriel is stronger than whatever twisted power this Shadow may yield. Evil only has power if you believe in it. And I don't believe in this *thing*."

Before he could be talked out of it, the newly invigorated

Julian closed his eyes and connected with the skinwalker. At first, it was a little like having a nightmare; his body became clammy, adrenaline poured through his veins, and his heartbeat accelerated. Then, he was one with The Shadow. Its terrible thoughts became his.

"How curious," Julian said. "I perceive something beyond darkness... beyond greed... this Shadow is afraid!"

"Afraid of what?" Elsa pressed.

"That its plot to double-cross the other Shadows will be revealed... You were right, by the way, its name is Deception, but it will forget that when I'm through with it."

Julian writhed in pain as he projected The Six Eyes of Esurus directly into Deception's mind. Then he channeled the voice of The Void Beast itself. It was the latter that spelled certain doom for both Deception and Julian.

"You would betray us?" Julian said in the voice of Esurus. "As punishment, you shall live your life in fear!"

A harrowing scream sounded in the canyon near The Shattered Holy Cross.

Deception stepped out of Vrána's skin and a terrible wind blew across the desert. It sounded like a rabbit howling in the night. At that moment, Deception transformed into The Shadow, Fear.

Elsa held her hands high above her body and whispered to the wind. Stardust spiraled upwards towards the twinkling star above them.

Rigel dispensed with its raiment and night became day; a bright gamma ray subsequently blasted away nearly two hundred Drones and Synthetics in a fraction of a second.

Corpus Sidera shielded the entire Assembly of Stars with a bubble of light. Subsequent explosions knocked-out the entire Sedona power grid.

Rigel shone brightly for a moment before catapulting itself across the Milky Way towards the far side of the Known Universe.

In a brief instant before leaving his body, Julian's spirit passed through Gabriel's mind.

Elsa pulled Julian up by his coat. His mind and body were spent. **"LOOK INTO MY EYES**," she screamed in **STJÄRNLJUS**. **"NOW!"**

Julian took one last breath and whispered to Elsa, "Tell him it was my choice... and that this is not the end of m—."

His body went limp.

"Come back!" she cried.

Her voice filled his mind. But it was too late; Julian was gone. She fell to the ground, holding his body against hers. Silver tears streamed down her cheek and landed on his face.

In the distance, Elsa heard a scream as Fear slowly lost its sanity and dove into its own shadow. It would haunt Earth no longer.

A second scream rang through the night. It belonged to Gabriel.

He ran over to Julian's body and sobbed uncontrollably.

"Why did you do this, you stupid—?"

Elsa's hand gently caressed Gabriel's cheek.

"Because he loved you. Perhaps even more than he loved himself. He believed there was no other way... and, for what it's worth, I think he was right. Though we only knew one another for a short time, Julian was many things... but stupid was not one of them."

A warm, purple light began to warm Gabriel's body. It then shifted to bright white as Death appeared.

Gabriel refused to look it in the eyes.

"You failed me once with my grandfather," he said with his back turned.

"I know your question, Gabe."

"And?"

"I can do a great many things, Gabriel, but I still cannot do that. As I said before, it would unleash a chaotic cataclysm and only bring The Shadows closer."

The angelic entity knelt down and whispered something into Julian's ear. It then kissed his cheek and the light left his body forever.

"I am no soothsayer, but I can offer you this knowledge, Gabriel. Julian's soul had already crossed over. He may not be a Firstborn, but I believe we witnessed the death and rebirth of two beings just now. Just as Deception became Fear. Julian shall return as something new, and, unless I'm mistaken, immortal."

Elsa placed her hand on Gabriel's shoulders and spoke telepathically.

'Akaal speaks the truth. I saw it, and so did Julian. He did this for Earth, the Universe, but most of all for you, Gabe.'

Gabriel turned away from The Assembly and looked towards the blazing light of the stargate. Its light and heat helped to warm his body and dry the tears streaming down his face. He gazed into the distant galaxies and quasars and sent out a message to Esurus.

'You have no idea what you've just done!' Gabriel said psychically. 'I no longer fear you. *But you should fear me.*'

29

THE ASSEMBLY OF STARS

Peacekeeping sirens wailed incessantly in the distance like a pack of angry coyotes, but there was nary an Agent in sight. Thanks to Rigel's handiwork, Sedona was still shrouded in pitch-darkness and the once-mighty Drone Army was nothing more than a heap of shrapnel. Without the aid of Raptors, it was unlikely that any State Agent would be able to reach The Shattered Holy Cross for at least a few hours.

Ambrose transformed into a dragon and flew ahead of The Assembly to survey the wreckage. Heaps of Drones and crashed Raptors lined the stargate like a rubbish pile in an archaic twenty-first century junkyard. In a single fiery breath, Ambrose vaporized the remnants of the Holy Guard into a soup of molten metal, ash and cinder.

Whilst in mid-air, the dragon flapped its enormous wings until a cool breeze ensued. The molten debris solidified into a solid sheet of glass, carbon and metal. Satisfied with its own handiwork, the dragon gently drifted towards Fenestra Sancta Cruce with the grace of a feather.

Akaal and Gabriel were the first of the Assembly to arrive at the entrance of the wormhole.

Ambrose transformed back into a humanoid aspect and spoke to Gabriel telepathically.

'Go ahead and take a look. You must be curious. Just watch your step.'

Gabriel steadied himself and approached the swirling white light. As he peered through the mouth of the stargate, he felt every chakra activate from end to end. His psychic senses were inextricably drawn to the vortex. Without giving it a second thought, he leaned in closer, squinting his eyes to see what was visible from the Earth side of the portal.

The orb-shaped stargate, much like a dreamgate, seemed to pulse and change the more he looked at it. Gabriel closed his eyes and collected his thoughts. As he emptied each distraction and focused on the stillness in his mind's eye, light emerged. At first, there was only a faint twinkle. Then, almost as if someone turned on an imaginary power switch, Gabriel was standing in front of trillions of tiny points of light—more than the eye or mind could comprehend. Each of them sparkled like polished gemstones in the darkness, in brilliant shades of blue, white, yellow and red. In the distance, he saw a very, very faint pinpoint and it called to him—quite literally.

He lost his footing and almost fell into the gate.

Ambrose pulled him away from the wormhole.

"Whoa, mate. Not so fast. You all right?"

Gabriel simply nodded—part of his brain was still stuck in the portal.

"You know this is a one-way door, my friend? It's just like those keys The Dream Broker forged."

"I understand," Gabriel replied. "In some way, I've always known I'd have to face this choice, ever since I was a kid staring through my grandfather's telescope. If I turn my back now, I'll regret it forever."

"Then get ready for the roller-coaster ride of a lifetime," Ambrose said. "You know, I envy you in a way. I spent my youth as a great comet and died my first death as ice. Then, when your world was born, I chose to become fire instead. Your Earth poet Robert Frost would have fun writing about me."

"He'd be absolutely enamored, I'm sure."

Ambrose grinned from ear-to-ear and then spoke with unusual frankness and gentleness.

"Remember that flattery will get you *everywhere* with immortals; one day it may even save your life. Human myths, religions and ceremonies have provided us with a reason to live, a function to carry out during our ceaselessly winding existence. You know, I think it was loneliness, not just hunger, that drove The Seven Shadows into their despair. If possible, show these creatures compassion when you meet them, for Love and Hope are their Achilles' heel. I believe they are not beyond saving."

Ambrose pulled Gabriel close and kissed him on the forehead. The dragon's lips warmed his skin like the afternoon sun. Had they embraced even a second longer, Gabriel was certain his skin would have burned.

"For your trip, I give you illumination."

The dragon opened its coat pocket and presented a parting gift to Gabriel. It was wrapped in an orange silken scarf that was embellished with fiery crimson runes.

Gabriel unraveled the gift and found a crystalline staff inside. An enormous 22-carat gem was set atop the scepter. Neither the crystalline base nor the crowning gemstone was of Earth origin.

"It is from Amaranth—the land of The Eternals," Ambrose said. "Its name is Eldhjärta, or Fireheart in Common Tongue. Astralis, the Light-Bringer, carved the torch from the core of a dying star and gave it to the Firstborn as a reminder of the perseverance of Light.

Since it was touched by the hands of an Eternal, it's indestructible, as well... it is older than The Old World and it will survive long after Akaal delivers the last soul to Valhalla."

The dragon handed the ancient device to Gabriel.

"I'm beyond honored, Ambrose. But, might I ask, by what mechanism is this torch activated? I see no power source, no lamp, no wick..."

"Gabe, by now you should know that all of our devices are triggered by intention. Think of things that fill you with both gratitude and love—these alone will ignite the crystal's capacity for light and heat."

Gabriel understood, and tucked it away in his knapsack.

"Guard the torch well, for light is scarce where you're headed. By some Shadow magic, the star Scintillaarė died long before her time. Her stellar remnant—a faint white dwarf—is now fading faster than it should, narrowly emitting enough light, heat or energy to sustain the integrity of the star system. Soon, it, too, will be naught but a cold diamond at the center of an even colder world. With all the inner planets consumed, and the fringe planets completely frozen, Planet Aurelius and its three remaining moons are the last bastions of life in the Scintillaarė System."

"You're quite the tour guide, Ambrose."

"Listen, I just want you to be prepared, Gabe."

"Tell me of Planet Aurelius—what has become of it?" Gabriel asked.

"Although the surface was once suffused with golden forests that shined brighter than its star, Planet Aurelius is now a dark, frozen wasteland, guarded by a single Watcher, one who survived The Thousand-Year Night."

"Is it safe for me—for a human, that is—to breathe there?"

"Yes, the remaining atmosphere is thin, and oxygen is slightly less abundant than it is here on Earth, but the air is nonetheless breathable. It's very similar to this planet's composition. The neighboring moons have similarly breathable atmospheres, even the icy Ceruleus. The exception is The Shadow Moon. To enter that decaying satellite, you'll need assistance in more ways than one."

"From whom?"

"Three Watchers wait in the darkness—each is tasked with helping you. You will find the first on Planet Aurelius. With its help, you will venture to The Sleeping Forests of The Alabaster Moon, Virídia—one of three remaining satellites. Though Virídia's forests lay slumbering in a catatonic spell, a sorceress dwells atop the highest mountain. She alone can wake them, and she alone knows what's become of the Third Watcher after The Sundering. To find him, you must secure safe passage beneath the glaciers of The Ice Moon, Ceruleus. Though water once flowed freely across the surface, the Cerulean oceans lay forever entombed beneath impenetrable blue glaciers. Its namesake, a great Titan, was one of the most powerful guardians to walk (or swim) any planet in any star system, so I hold hope that The Ice Moon hasn't become his tomb."

"And what of the other Moon?" Gabriel asked.

"Once a mighty stronghold to benevolent Machine Gods, the so-called 'Shadow Moon' now houses only a twisted Necropolis which is purportedly a home base for The Shadows. If the rumors are true, we must neutralize the beast that dwells within its walls."

"So that's my ultimate destination?"

"I'm afraid so," Ambrose replied. "Planet Aurelius is already a wasteland, but there's hope that the armies housed on the moons of Virídia and Ceruleus will be enough to turn the tide. Together you will converge on The Shadow Moon. It's there that you'll find The Seventh Star, and it's there that all of us will join you."

"Why is The Seventh Star so important?"

"In a word: balance. If we don't find The Seventh Star soon, then the binary opposites of The Luminous Ones, The Seven Shadows, will converge into a single entity and consume everything in the Known Universe. The same thing happened in The Old World.

The same thing will happen now. History repeats itself, but we can learn from our mistakes."

"And I'm the key?"

"Yes. When you face The Shadows of Hate, Fear and Despair— the ones that comprise The Void Beast, Esurus—it will create a powerful beacon that will awaken Hope from its hibernation."

Ambrose stepped back and joined The Assembly.

Gabriel moved down the procession and Elsa was waiting patiently for him.

"Close your eyes," she whispered.

He obeyed and Elsa kissed him on each eyelid. He felt his mind expand, and along with it, his capacity to see past words or surface.

Telepathically, Elsa conveyed a final blessing.

'As a moon, I give you the power of reflection. Use this gift to help others see their own potential—to light a fire within their soul where only shadow or fear exists. Open your eyes and heart, Gabriel. See yourself in me as you truly are—without artifice or prejudice.'

Gabriel opened his eyes and Uri was now standing beside his sister Elsa. He saw both of them in their true forms. Elsa was a luminous silver-winged being. In her eyes he could see his own energy reflected back, almost as if she were made of glowing liquid silver or mercury. His energy was blinding, however.

Uri stepped in front of Elsa, to block the reflection, then spoke telepathically.

'Like my twin sister, I have no talisman or tool, only a blessing and a reminder for you.'

The star placed his hands on Gabriel's heart, and muttered what sounded like a prayer. In the seconds that followed, Gabriel felt as if his heart grew as large as his physical body.

Then, Uri released his hands and said, "I give you one of the most important gifts: Charity. Love yourself and others. Emanate tolerance and forgiveness in your thoughts and actions. You've not been to a world like this before—seeing the approaching darkness will make you question the light within you. Use my sister's gift of Reflection to see your worth; use mine to help yourself and others. Remember, even the Enemy has goodness within it. Light will prevail over Darkness—and Love can awaken the Light within the Dark. You must become an agent of change. Let your actions be an extension of the Light, for that's truly what a Steward is—an instrument of Illumination."

As Akaal approached Gabriel, Uri and Elsa moved to the side, bowing before The First Star.

"Of all The Six, you're the one I will miss most," Gabriel said.

"You speak as if we won't see each other again."

Gabriel looked up at Akaal and thought, 'Will we?'

'Only once more—'

It stopped, but Gabriel understood where it was going. This was a one-way ticket.

'Why must I do this alone?' he wondered.

The star frowned and gazed into the portal. Though it did not move its mouth, he heard its thoughts.

'The Prophecy states that The Six Stars cannot defeat the darkness that befell this system. Too polar is our energy. We need someone who contains both the essence of light and dark—a human.'

'And if I fail?'

'Then, as Ambrose said, The Shadows will slowly consume all light again as they did before. Take solace in this: you shall not be alone. The Sixth Star awaits your arrival and it will help you find the remaining guardians. Trust your heart and you will recognize friend from foe. You've always had the gift to do so, Gabriel.'

Akaal reached under its shirt and unfastened a chain that was hidden from view.

"Here. Take this... it is capable of summoning The Six Stars when the time is right."

"I thought Björn destroyed— "

"This talisman is not fashioned of my remnant. Indeed, that sigil was forever destroyed the night we extinguished Björn's Shadow. However, this bauble is something equally old and powerful—it comes from The Seventh, and it contains a faint glimmer of its essence. When you find our missing sibling, it will shine brighter than any star or supernova in the galaxy. At that moment, and not a moment before, we will weep with joy at Hope's return."

The pendant resembled a lotus petal, with a perfectly smooth, circular crystal in the center. The crystal itself was no larger than a small pearl. Yet, despite its size and the delicate chain from which it hung, it felt unusually heavy. As Gabriel held it against the silver light of the moon, the polished cabochon began to twinkle with its own milky blue-white light, so faint it was almost beyond perception. He carefully fastened the chain around his neck. Once again, the light within the crystal stirred and then faded.

The Assembly of Stars fell silent. For nearly fifteen billion years, the crystal sigil had been lifeless. They realized they'd chosen their champion well, for its light was returning.

Akaal broke the silence.

"This is a gift from The Fourth and Fifth Stars."

The First Star handed him a sturdy knapsack containing a blanket, clothing, food rations, water and other camping sundries. The knapsack bore Metatron's and Iophiel's sigils. As he emptied his belongings into the bag, he realized it made use of folded space; its internal volume was at least triple that of its exterior. Conversely, everything weighed significantly less when placed into the folded space.

"This defies physics," he said.

"Yes. It's woven from the last piece of the Eleventh Dimension. It has been folded and sewn together in such a way that you'll never run out of storage. Your back will never be burdened. It was the

least Iophiel and Metatron could do for taking the burden of Tenebrae."

Gabriel looked at it in awe. He carefully emptied the contents of his old knapsack into the new one, taking special care to tuck *The Cosmic Tomes* in separate compartments. As he placed it on his back, it was indeed light as a feather, as Akaal had promised.

"And now, one last thing. Meet Himmel Sköld, The Sky Shield."

Akaal held out a flowing silver-blue raiment with an oversized hood. It shimmered in the moonlight. The immortal lovingly wrapped Gabriel in the enchanted garment. As Gabriel moved, he realized its exotic fabric exuded some sort of protective, electromagnetic field.

"This sacred raiment is a gift from Rigel, hand-spun by the Sky Guardian itself. It will shield you from space during your trip through the Einstein-Rosen bridge. This is my last gift to you, other than my blessing."

It inscribed The Seal of The Six Stars above his head. Then, Akaal stepped back, giving Gabriel space before his journey. The rest of The Assembly followed suit.

Gabriel turned around and faced the swirling stargate. Before lifting the hood of Rigel's robe, Gabriel lovingly breathed in his last breath of Earth air. He took time to appreciate the Sedona desert aroma—a fragrant mix of dust and sage. Satisfied with his last breath, he closed his eyes and jumped in.

PART V

THE MOONS OF AURELIUS

PROLOGUE

An indeterminate amount of time passed during Gabriel's long journey through the stargate. Perhaps it was hours, days or eons. From here on out, he was on his own. There existed no roadmaps and no sages that could offer advice on what he must do to succeed. Now he had only his intuition, faith and hope to lead the way. If The Seventh Star existed, he would find it. If not, he'd die trying.

30

TO A PLANET MADE OF SNOW

Dateline: Unknown; sometime after the Earth Year One Billion.
Planet: Aurelius, in the Scintillaarė Star System, within the greatest
spiral arm of the Aamĕllẏne Galaxy.

A t first, Gabriel felt a faint, cool sensation blast over his skin, as if he'd cracked open a door in the middle of winter. He marveled as a universe of tiny electrons kissed his hand and worked their way along the rest of his arms, face and hair. Every cell was stimulated. Soon, however, the wormhole started to pull at the molecules in his body... a subtle tug at first, and then an inescapable inertia as he was drawn into the gravity of the stargate. The experience started off exhilarating but soon became excruciating.

The last thing he remembered was gasping for air—drowning in a sea of space and stars as his body hurled through the wormhole with an unfathomable velocity. He now understood why the Milky Way was called Vintergatan (Winter Street) in his grandfather's native tongue. Distant, luminous stars jettisoned towards him as if he were looking straight into the face of a fantastic cosmic blizzard.

The effect was dizzying and blinding. It was also breathtakingly beautiful. The light of a hundred billion stars rushed past his face like snowflakes.

Time ceased to function within the confines of the wormhole, or at the very least, it was stretched beyond recognition.

At first, Gabriel was afraid he'd died. The Angel of Death was nowhere in sight, however, so he deduced he was having an out-of-body experience instead. While glancing down at his stomach, his suspicions were confirmed; a thin silver cord anchored his spirit and kept his subtle body from drifting too far away. From this vantage point, Gabriel watched his body being dragged through time and space, past the incandescent triple-star system of Zeta Orionis, through the great spiral arms of Andromeda and a few billion light-years past the distant, brilliant star factory z8 GND 5296. Were it not for Rigel's protective raiment, his body would have been torn to pieces.

Indeed, Gabriel had traveled farther than any human, telescope or probe had ever dared venture. Although still connected to his body, his mind simply turned off; thoughts dissolved and he'd almost forgotten that he existed.

Perhaps he drifted for a few seconds or maybe it was more like a few billion Earth Years... but eventually he regained consciousness. All Gabriel knew for certain is that the journey changed him; something within his body had shifted subtly on a subatomic level.

Gabriel felt a painful jolt of electricity when his etheric and corporal bodies slammed together, followed by a burst of sound and light as he passed through the mouth of the stargate.

The sky flickered with lightning and thunder as the portal closed behind him. It collapsed into a single star-like point of light before fading completely. Like The Fenestrae Stellarum on Earth, the terminal stargate was situated in midair. It subsequently ejected his body roughly one hundred feet above the surface of the alien planet.

Much to Gabriel's surprise, the gravity was thin, allowing his body to float like a feather. After a minute or two he safely reached the surface, landing atop a soft snowdrift—almost as if a gentle hand was guiding his descent.

Gabriel lay still for a moment in the fluffy embrace of the snow —eyes closed and body limp.

He felt a gentle nudge and heard a whisper in the dark. Its source was unclear. A nearby tree was the only visible life form.

As he looked into the branches above him, they twinkled independently of the planet's star, almost as if they were emitting their own treelight.

Thunderous noises began to sound again, this time in his head, not the environment.

The tree was some sort of sentient entity. It searched for words he would understand and then arranged the rumbling into a simple command.

'**Breathe, child.**'

Like a newborn, Gabriel took his first breath on the snowy world. The air was cold, surprisingly sweet and, although not as abundantly oxygen-rich as Earth, it was nonetheless breathable— just as Ambrose said it would be. After a few forced inhalations and exhalations, his reflexes kicked in and breathing became natural.

Once his head stopped spinning, Gabriel sat up and surveyed the surroundings. He squinted his eyes and waited for them to adjust to the faint light on Planet Aurelius.

He'd fallen under the protection of a gargantuan golden tree; it towered unfathomably high, with its upper branches reaching so tall that they somehow extended into the uppermost heights of the alien atmosphere. From his vantage point, the tree appeared to single-handedly hold the sky and the neighboring moons in place. The famed Norse Yggdrasil itself would pale in comparison.

Judging from the tree's position in relation to the stargate, Gabriel surmised that its branches grabbed hold of him and gently placed him onto the planet's surface. Tens of hundreds of small, fragrant golden flowers adorned its leafless branches—their sweet aroma reminded him of vanilla. One of them landed atop his cheek like a snowflake. It was soft as velvet and cold as ice. The tree stood as a lone sentinel and proved to be the only sign of life anywhere on the massive planet.

He sensed that the tree had been in hibernation. His arrival roused an old consciousness, one that seemed kind, wise and full of love.

After a long silence, the tree moved again. A large branch nudged Gabriel into a standing position.

He stumbled at first, and clearly needed a few moments before he could stand on his own. The tree continued to support him as he got his bearings.

A faint white dwarf star was setting in the distance; its gentle blue-white light was so soft that it barely warmed his face. In fact, it hardly even illuminated the interlocking snow dunes that lined the frozen desert of the planet. If this icy globe had ever sustained more life than the tree behind him, it had long since faded out of existence, much like its dying star.

Thanks to the planet's thin atmosphere, Gabriel was afforded a virtually unobstructed view of the alien firmament. A colorful planetary nebula enveloped the white dwarf Scintillaarė and its remaining system. Planet Aurelius was so close to the nebula that the night sky was painted brilliantly in ribbons of blue, purple and red, like a frozen aurora borealis. Interspersed between the ribbons, Gabriel counted what looked like two distant gas giants. Judging from the surface of the planet and what Gabriel could see of its three surviving moons, everything in this system was under a permanent deep freeze. A few star clusters peeked through the nebula, but they were completely alien—unlike anything he'd seen in a textbook or in his grandfather's extensive library.

He shivered and felt a momentary tinge of regret for jumping through the one-way portal; at that moment he realized just how far he'd come from home.

The tree bent its branches towards him and spoke telepathically again.

'What are you?'

Gabriel looked at it—aside from its towering height and exotic flowers, it was, well, *a tree*. There was no logical reason it should be speaking to him. There was nothing even remotely anthropomorphic about it. Yet there it stood—capable of movement and telepathic speech.

Aside from The Whispering Pine, this was the only other intelligent tree that Gabriel had stumbled upon. Perhaps, as he suspected, his psychic gift was now amplified by the journey through the Einstein-Rosen Bridge. Or perhaps things just worked differently on this side of the Universe, and this sort of thing was the norm.

'I've got nothing to lose,' he thought with a shrug.

Before speaking, Gabriel turned to the majestic tree and felt compelled to bow. His intuition told him he was in the presence of something incredibly old and unquestionably regal.

Words seemed somehow inadequate to describe its splendor, but he would later recount a few things about it. First, it was larger than anything he'd ever seen, organic or inorganic. Although he was certain it was some sort of illusion based on his perspective, the tree paradoxically appeared larger than the enormous planet it inhabited. Second, it glowed. Though the trunk and branches could be described as birch-like, they appeared to be fashioned of some sort of golden bark that emanated light... *treelight*. Although devoid of leaves, the branches were suffused with glistening blossoms. Each was graced with golden luminescent stamens that twinkled as they moved in the wind. Finally, it emanated a gentle warmth, like an enormous incandescent light bulb.

Gabriel finally answered the question.

"I'm human... a child of Planet Earth in the Milky Way Galaxy.

I came here from a star portal that opened on my home world. My name is Gabriel... who and *what* are you, might I ask?"

The tree creaked and more petals dropped onto the snow.

'This fading planet bears my given name in your Common Tongue,' it replied.

After a pause, words began to take form in Gabriel's mind.

"Of course... You must be Aurelius?" he asked.

'Yes, that was once my name... I'd almost forgotten the sound of it until you spoke it. But I'm a tree, and as is customary for all trees, I've lived long enough to have many titles.'

"Go on... I'd like to hear them."

'In days of old, my family knew me as Kāmadeva, or simply Love. My heart burned so brightly, that I was soon called Ore, The Golden One. Sometimes that love turned to passion and that passion turned to rage. Then I became Tempest, Storm-Bringer— especially when The Shadows arrived. Most Guardians in this star system still call me by that name. When this planet teemed with life, I bore the name Kairos Aurelius, the first—and as history would have it, the last—tree on this snowy planet. Others, like you, may know me solely by a number. I'm Six—The Sixth of The Seven Great Stars of Old. Like you, I'm searching for The Seventh.'

"I get the feeling you were... well... asleep. Pardon me for asking, but how long have you been in this spot?"

'Aye. I was asleep. And I've been here too long. So long that I started to forget I existed. I guess you could say I became stuck.'

"Why?"

'In a word: sorrow. Though my skills are great, I could not stop that which Akasha prophesied. A thousand years ago The Shadows came.'

Its branches pointed towards the horizon.

'With their arrival, our glorious star Scintillaarė became a red giant—*long before it should have*. In doing so, it devoured Imogen, the fourth moon of my planetary system. Much of her debris pummeled to the surface, suffocating this world with fire, smoke, ash and impenetrable gloom. I was the only Aurelian to survive The Thousand-Year Night; all my children perished. So great was my sorrow that I wept through the darkness, filling the great basin before us. As the planet cooled, the basin froze over and my tears turned to snow, creating the great snow dunes on which you stand. Here I've stayed, entombed by my own regret.'

Snow began to fall again and then ceased as the tree composed itself.

Neither Gabriel nor the tree spoke for several minutes.

An icy wind blew across the planet and Gabriel shivered as the snow dunes shifted. Aurelius picked up its telepathic conversation at this point, sensing his discomfort.

'My apologies; I've been alone too long and I'm not used to company. Where was I? Oh, yes... Despite my failure to save the planet, The Council of the Four Moons appointed me The Last Guardian of The Portal. Since that day over a millennium ago, I've stood faithful watch, waiting for The Starchild prophesied to save us all from ruin. Now that you are here, I hereby renounce all my former aspects, as well as their tendency to become stuck. I am simply *Aurelius*. I'll fight with you until Light returns to this dying system, or until my own wick is extinguished in the coming war.'

The tree began to chant three words in the magical *Alchemic Aamĕllÿne Tongue*.

'Aa-tǽl! Mĕllyr! Ẏnē!'

The High Tongue was all but lost, but its magic had not faded. As long as The Seven Stars existed, it would be the most powerful sound current of the Universe. One word alone could move mountains.

Unsurprisingly, the proclamation and the invocation of no less than three ancient words had a profound effect on Aurelius. It began to sway and move erratically while the ground beneath Gabriel rumbled, as if the tree was ripping its roots from the soil below. After the trembling stopped, the light in its luminous blossoms flickered and each and every petal fell to the ground, glistening like golden teardrops around its trunk.

Sorrow welled up in Gabriel as he empathically felt the tree let go of the past. He understood that together these three words symbolized, light, movement and abundance.

'There. It has begun. I will soon walk again with the stars, as I did in days of old.'

After a long silence, the tree stretched its branches upwards, seemingly commanding the wind to move at its will. As the wind passed by, it reverberated in a chorus of howls. The tree telepathically added words to the music. The language used was incomprehensible to Gabriel, but nonetheless familiar. At first it sounded like a lullaby, but after a few measures, Gabriel knew it to be a lamentation. By some sort of clairsentience Gabriel ascertained the song's title was *The Gloaming* or perhaps *The Twilight of the Trees*. The wind carried the fallen blossoms far away, scattering them like ashes into the distant snow dunes on the horizon. They shimmered briefly before freezing and becoming forever dim.

As he listened to the canticle, Gabriel's attention turned again to the night sky. The luminous Alabaster Moon, otherwise known as Virídia, hung directly overhead, dominating the alien firmament with its vibrancy. It earned its nickname because it blazed like a milky alabaster lamp in the sky—almost as if some unseen wick smoldered just beneath the clouds. If, indeed, any forests graced its surface, they were completely concealed under a sea of swirling clouds forming what looked like a great eye.

The Ice Moon Ceruleus loomed just to the left of Virídia. Although its orbit was closer than its alabaster sister, the icy satellite appeared less punctuated, since it only reflected light. Like Earth's moon, the Cerulean surface was tidally locked with Aurelius, always showing one face to the planet and another to the stars. Gabriel wondered what stories the two faces might tell him. Given its proximity, he could easily make out its fantastic features; deeply striated glaciers encased its blue-and-silver oceans in a marble-colored sarcophagus.

The inauspiciously named Shadow Moon hung in the distance like some sort of dark, lenticular lens. The satellite was darker than the surrounding night sky, and reflected no light back. In fact, it shouldn't have been visible, but there it hung... Perhaps it was an optical illusion, but Gabriel swore that surrounding starlight seemed to bend and eventually disappear into the distant moon, as if it were consuming it.

When his gaze drifted closer to the planet, the Aurelian ring system caught his attention. The Lost Moon, Imogen, left a beautiful vestige of her existence just outside the Aurelian atmosphere— the equivalent of a stellar rainbow. A deadly debris field of metal, ice and rock formed three exotic bands of blue, indigo and violet, circling the planet's equator.

Much like the tree behind him, Gabriel was filled with sadness. He looked down at the shifting snow dunes of Aurelius and shivered. This was a beautiful, but dying, world. He could only imagine what it looked like in its zenith.

Overcome with emotion, perhaps from the tree itself, he intuitively wrapped his arms around Aurelius's massive truck, or at least tried to—it was so wide that it would take an army of humans with hands interlocked to surround its base.

'Ambrose was right. This place is deader than dead,' Gabriel thought to himself.

'Though I appreciate your compassion, I've cried enough

for the two of us, little one. We'll have no more tears on my watch... However, your thoughts make reference of a name I've not heard in millennia. Do you mean to tell me that the immortal who walked as both fire and ice still lives?'

"Yes. The dragon Ambrose still walks the heavens, as do Six of The Seven Stars... along with a moon consort known as Elsa."

'Then all hope is not lost. We have much to discuss, but not now. Nightfall is upon us, and that's when The Shadows walk. You must protect yourself until morning.'

"What will happen?" Gabriel inquired.

'My light draws The Shadows like moths to a flame. Although I'm the only living creature on this world, there exist other spirits—echoes of the past. Many of them are fallen Shadow warriors. Some are fallen trees that cling to this world, afraid to move to the next dimension. Suffice to say these echoes have grown savage and angry in their solitude. I suppose you could say this world is haunted, much like every moon in the system.'

A branch above Gabriel pointed to a frozen sea.

'If you walk towards the setting star, in the direction of Mare Lāmentārī, The Sea of Lament, you will find an alcove, about a yard before the icy sea. It's a blessed area, a sacred vortex beneath Virídia where no Shadows may cross. Set up camp under the moon's gentle glow and we'll speak more in the morning.

May the light of The Sleeping Moon protect you.'

"You as well, Aurelius."

With that, Gabriel bade farewell to the mighty tree and headed towards the setting star, whose light was now just beneath the desolate snow dunes.

The alcove was exactly where Aurelius said it would be. It appeared to be a gnarled trunk of a once great tree, perhaps half the size of Aurelius. The charred exterior and interior suggested that it had been destroyed during the fires of The Thousand-Year Night. Gabriel shivered as the evening winds blew around him. The night here was darker than anything he'd ever seen. Though distant constellations abounded, light reflecting from the ancient woodland moon and the nebula proved the only source of significant illumination.

He pulled out Ambrose's parting gift—the enchanted staff, Fireheart—and wished for light. Nothing happened. He then recalled Ambrose's instruction to think of things that made him happy. He imagined the taste of his grandmother's freshly baked bread, the warmth of sunsets in California and the smell of autumn in Denver. As he did, the staff started to pulse with light and filled the alcove with its radiance.

Just as his body was feeling normal again, he heard a scream in the distance. Something was attacking the tree.

Before he could move, Aurelius spoke to him.

'Be still, Starchild—and be mindful of that light. Shield yourself and let me deal with this. There are Wolves in our midst.'

Gabriel kept the enchanted light of Fireheart close to him, safely hidden by his long robe. He grabbed a small satchel filled with sea salt and sprinkled it around the inside of the alcove. He then envisioned a protective circle of light, keeping out all lower vibrations.

Outside, Aurelius began to repeat a mantra in a voice that was so loud it sounded as if thunder were rolling across the surface of the planet:

'Shadow creatures...
Sovereigns of Night—
Turn back now or
Face my Light!'

A fiery vortex formed around the top of Aurelius as it channeled light from the heavens and also from within. The great tree seemed to grow in size. Then it threw out bolts of lightning as its branches ripped apart and roared like thunder. For a brief moment, Aurelius was as bright as any star in the Known Universe. Its golden light illuminated everything in the star system, save The Shadow Moon.

During that instant, Gabriel could see The Shadows flying and clawing about the mighty tree. They were devoid of color—blacker than black, if that was possible. They possessed no defining features, only great reaching claws, pulling and shredding whatever came in their paths. Like singularities, light and space bent around their bodies. Aurelius's light overpowered them and they disintegrated into the night. Not surprisingly, they left temporal disturbances in their wake, resulting in a very foul odor—a mixture of rotten eggs and sulfur.

With one last mighty flash of light, the tree sent a shockwave across the snow dunes, akin to a supernova. Any remaining Shadows let out a cry that was blood-curdling—like a chorus of banshees. The sulfur-like smell gave way to the aroma of vanilla. Then a peaceful quiet fell upon the planet. The tree's light was gone, but so were The Shadows. Only the faint alabaster glow of Viridia provided refuge from the viscous darkness.

After a long pause, the tree spoke to Gabriel.

'Rest now, child. They've left us, and morning will come soon.'

It felt less like a suggestion and more like a command. After the demonstration of the tree's power, he thought it wise to comply.

Gabriel could not sleep. He simply waited—the same way he waited when he was a kid in his grandfather's attic. He knew something big was about to happen.

31

AN UNFAMILIAR FACE

As dawn broke, Gabriel could hear the sound of something pacing about, just outside the alcove.

'Impossible!' he thought. 'The tree extinguished everything last night.'

A familiar voice assuaged his worries.

'Fear not, Starchild. Come outside. The Shadows are gone. For now, anyway.'

As he left the safety of the alcove, a sense of hope filled his body again. The sun was rising where the great tree once towered. Gnarled remains loomed on the horizon now, like a scorched scarecrow.

Something unusual stood just to the right of the charred remnant. At first glance, the creature looked a little like The Green Man, a mythic figure that he'd seen carved into the eaves of old pubs in London.

It began walking towards Gabriel. He scratched his eyes, half expecting to wake up from a dream.

'Hello, again,' it said telepathically. The very timbre of its voice hearkened to the elements; it could whisper as softly as a gentle breeze or roar like thunder. Remnants of Tempest clearly lived on, even in this incarnation of Aurelius.

The arboreal being was tall, slender and at least three times Gabriel's height—possibly taller, with skin as smooth and green as young bamboo. Its two feet were lined with over twenty root-like toes apiece, some of them opposing. They reached deep into the snow dunes, keeping it afoot no matter how hard the wind blew. Heavy golden bark covered its legs and feet, affording it warmth and protection from the elements. It possessed an unusually tall torso. The muscular stomach, chest and arms were completely devoid of leaves and were decidedly human in appearance—though not flesh, these areas seemed less like wood or bamboo, as they were more pliable. A light, feathery layer of bright green moss adorned the chest and shoulders, affording it additional protection. Four elongated arms extended from its shoulders—two on either side, each over five feet in length. Widely-spread hands reached out for several feet, ending with a dozen or so bright green finger-vines.

Although the body was humanoid, its head was decidedly alien. The forehead was long and narrow and the green skin appeared more elastic and flexible than anywhere else on its body. Two enormous eyes shined like golden lamps from under a leaf-covered brow. A six-pointed star was branded onto its forehead, adorned with a single emerald in the center. Much like the eyes, this seemed to glow from within. Although its face was long and ended in what appeared to be a chin, the creature lacked other features that a human might have. The most glaring omissions included ears, a nose and a mouth. It breathed through its skin and communicated telepathically. Seven leafless branch-like structures protruded from its head in the shape of a regal crown, extending up to a foot at the highest point. A handful of fragrant golden flowers adorned each branch. From a distance, they shined like a halo above the creature's head, illuminating everything within a quarter-mile.

The being knelt down. As it moved, its joints creaked like splintering wood.

'Let go of your fear, little one. It's still I, Aurelius, just more alive than I have been in eons.'

In relief, Gabriel threw his arms around the transformed being. This time they nearly reached around its waist.

"I've never been happier to see an unfamiliar face," he said.

The tree would have surely smiled were it capable of doing so. Instead, its crown shined.

"What happened? I thought you were dead."

'In a manner of speaking, I died several thousand years ago. You helped me see that. I'd lived too many years as a tree, I suppose—I became stubborn, stuck and unable to move forward. I'm now something different... inspired by you, no less.'

Aurelius sat down and crossed its legs, so that it was now eye-level. Gabriel peered into each orb and saw that they were indeed lamps—windows into the tree's ancient soul. After years of soaking up starlight from the heavens, the tree seemed capable of "shining" itself—or perhaps this starlight always existed from within. The light was warm and filled with love... and it felt a bit familiar.

It held out one of its finger-vines and bent it gently.

'You see, Gabriel, everything in this Universe is pliable. We are not as stuck as we may seem; only our *thinking* holds us in place. When the time comes—as it always does—we must change or step aside for those who can. Like the mighty stars above, some of us explode, some of us fade, and others are consumed by our own emotions.

You humans may walk on two feet like I do now, but many of you live your lives like trees, rooted in beliefs and fears. You've forgotten that you're forged of stardust... your thoughts have the potential to ignite and take on a life of their own, if

you'd only invest in them. There's so much wasted potential in your kind.'

The tree dimmed its eyes and its crown for a moment in contemplation.

'I'm one to talk, however. Were it not for you, I'd likely have suffered the same fate as Ceruleus. My sadness and hopelessness tethered me to this snowy world, and they weighed on me more heavily than any snow dune, glacier or mountain ever could. After countless eons of burying myself in regret, I've had enough. I choose to walk on two feet now and protect the children on Virídia... and of course you too, my dearest Starchild. Surely by now, you know how important you are? If not, you soon will.'

"Can I ask you something?"

'Of course.'

"You mentioned Ceruleus. Is that The Seventh Star?"

'No. The two Guardians above are beings known as *Ancients;* they are immortals from The Old World. Each assumed new avatars when The New World was created.'

"What is our purpose in seeing them?"

'Hopefully, they can lend support for your journey to The Shadow Moon. Like my brothers and sisters, I cannot walk its surface—not until we have awoken The Seventh Star. That's where the inhabitants of these moons come into play; they were created in The New World and, thus, can help you... that is, if they survived.'

Aurelius reached out one of its four arms and a dozen tendrils wrapped gently around Gabriel's hand.

'Come now. Take my hand and let's walk. We have precious little time to prepare for the next part of the journey.'

As the humanoid, tree, or whatever it was, stood upright, it still towered above Gabriel. Based on its transformation and seeming immortality, Gabriel understood why Aurelius belonged to the same pantheon of beings as the five Stars he'd already met.

'We need to cross the sea by nightfall. There is a Vimana there that we can use for transport. It was a gift from The Machine Gods.'

"Wait... Vimana—you mean, a vessel...a ship?"

'Yes. The star chariot will provide transport to The Sleeping Forests of Virídia.'

Gabriel looked above and then gazed at Aurelius. He felt a bizarre combination of excitement mixed with dread. Although seeing an enchanted forest sounded exciting, he felt certain that something foul lay beneath the ominous clouds.

The two walked without speaking until the dwarf star overhead had traced its way across a quarter of the sky. Gabriel motioned to Aurelius to take a break.

He stared into the tree's eyes for a moment.

'What is it?'

"Can you tell me about the Prophecy? I mean, I've heard bits and pieces, but never the whole truth."

'Aye, it's about time you knew.'

The tree planted its feet in the snow. Gabriel found a tightly packed area on one of the snow dunes and sat down next to Aurelius.

"You said you're one of The Six... are you and your siblings the oldest beings that exist?"

'We're old, but not the oldest by far. At least three older cosmic entities, The Eternals, have seen more than my family. In fact, you've met one of them already—the cosmic entity known as Akasha. At least two others exist: Astralis, the Light-Bringer and its twin Tenebris, the Creator; but I do not know how many others walk the skies.'

"*The Star Compendium* spoke of three types of immortals—

Eternals, Ancients and Firstborn. You told me a bit about Ancients, but what is the difference between all three?"

'Eternals, simply put, are those without end or beginning— they are universal constants. Though my siblings and I hold enough knowledge between us to fill all the libraries in all the Known Worlds, we know very little about The Eternals. They are the oldest, grandest and most untouchable beings that exist in the multiverse. Astralis, the Light-Bringer, is regarded as the source of all known energy in the multiverse. Tenebris, who is also the namesake for *Corpus Tenebrae*, is the embodiment of all things cloaked in the darkness of creation... seeds of thoughts yet to be, a complement to Astralis. Unlike The Shadows, the darkness surrounding Tenebris is not malicious; its energy provides space, contrast and balance to Astralis's light. And of course, you already know Akasha, the cosmic hourglass through which all time flows.'

The tree sipped in air through its skin and then continued its answer.

'The Firstborn comprise the first stars created, fourteen in all. The Firstborn subsequently created Ancients—immortal beings like Elsa and Ambrose. Although not as powerful as Firstborn, these warriors are skilled in metamorphosis, time-space manipulation and are valuable captains in the war against The Shadows. In short, both Ancients and Firstborn are immortal, but only The Fourteen Stars are Firstborn.'

"If both Firstborn and Ancients were immortal, why didn't all of the Ancients survive the transformation into The New World?"

'Facing one's fears is not an easy thing to do. Shadows are merely mirrors to our darker parts. But when we all lay in the belly of The Great Devourer, we had no way of seeing the Light. The only source of illumination was from within. Not everyone was ready for that type of a test.'

"What happened to those who didn't make it?"

'A few channeled the darkness and became Lesser Shadows. Most fought bravely, sacrificing their existence in order to neutralize the darker energy. Their brave ashes created the essence of this New World—the very same starstuff that created you, in fact. To this day, their fractured consciousness exists in all beings that were reborn in The New World.'

"How many Ancients survived?"

'They are myriad, both on the side of Light and Dark. You've met a few already. The dragon Ambrose is my dear friend. Though he's quite handsome in his present form, I knew this entity as Amrik, a fair and beautiful comet. She and I traveled the heavens together and will do so again when this war ends, in whatever form Ambrose chooses. Elsa—mightiest of the Ancient moons, created by the hands of Uri himself—is also a powerful ally. You will meet two more Ancients before your journey ends; both are Guardians of the dying moons above.'

"How did you come to be here?"

'I watched as my brothers and sisters emerged as mighty winged guardians, breathing life into worlds and igniting spiritual fires in the hearts of The Children of the Stars—the Mortals.

'After speaking with Akasha, I felt compelled to enter this star system, not only because of its beauty but also because it was under siege from darker forces. All Firstborn and Undying share one goal: to shine light where none exists. We face the darkness head-on. We never run.'

"You speak of a coming war; what brought it about?"

'What has been will be again. The weapons of darkness remain constant, even if the names change. Three Shadows, in particular, have emerged as Captains in the New War; they are Hate, Fear and Despair. As individual Shadows, they wrecked the hearts of many. When they work in concert, they're often unstoppable. It's for that reason that they've converged into a single consciousness known as Esurus, The Insatiable.'

"I sense a fourth entity. It goes by the name of Treachery, doesn't it?"

'Aye... the latter, much like Fear before it, has cast a shadow over your little blue home world. It was Treachery's dark magic that allowed Fear to become a skinwalker. Of all The Shadows, it's one of the most cunning and dangerous. You will face it once more before staring into the eyes of the beast.'

"So, what can we do?"

'Unfortunately, The Children of the Stars now face the same decision their parents did: they must either celebrate their inherent differences or risk destroying themselves in a quest for nonexistent homogeny.'

The tree's eyes now glowed brightly with golden light.

'...Which brings me to the answer of your original question —The Prophecy. Some of the Ancients claimed The Seventh was lost, or perhaps turned to the other side. But The Prophecy states otherwise: The Seventh Star chose the path of reincarnation as one of The Children of the Stars. When the time comes, it will ascend to the sky and fight with its brothers and sisters once more. So you see, little one, we're looking for someone who is mortal... a great spiritual channel like you. I guess, as is the case for all parents, the future is in the hands of our children.'

Aurelius placed several finger-vines on Gabriel's shoulders and spoke again.

'Did I ever tell you the name of our lost sibling?'

"No. But Akaal told me once. It's Hope, was it not?"

'Aye. And Hope lived up to its name.'

Gabriel could feel emotions welling within Aurelius. The ground tremored and the wind began to whirl around them.

'When we lost The Seventh Star, we also lost our brightest luminary. But for the first time since this world was seeded with life, I feel hopeful again. Surely you know by now that your arrival saved me?'

"Are you suggesting—?"

'I'm suggesting nothing. Simply stating that you helped me find an emotion... a state of being that I haven't felt in quite some time. For that, I'm honored to guide you. You are The Starchild, The Mortal Channel who can restore Hope and the balance of The Fourteen.'

The tree looked around, ensuring they were safe.

'You may not understand it quite yet, but Hope alone is enough for us to turn the tide. It's the one weapon Shadows fear the most.'

Both Gabriel and Aurelius sat speechless for several minutes. The ancient tree was the first to move; it stretched its limbs and started to walk towards the horizon. Gabriel followed quietly—his mind filled with more questions than answers, a conundrum he often experienced in the presence of a Firstborn.

32

THE SEA OF LAMENT (MARE LĀMENTĀRĪ)

As the two traversed the surface, Gabriel realized the planet was deceptively large. Minutes faded into hours and it was soon midday. Much to Gabriel's dismay, the snow dunes never seemed to end. The muted light of Scintillaarė hung overhead like a bare bulb. Gabriel was uncertain of how long an Aurelian day was, but he and the tree had been traveling for what felt like six Earth hours.

Aurelius sensed his thoughts and broke the silence.

'We are nearly there, little one.'

It pointed to an icy island in the middle of a frozen ocean. Upon it two enormous dunes rose to unseen peaks.

'We have about three of your Earth hours to get to the Vimana, but we must first journey across Mare Lāmentārī, The Sea of Lament.'

Gabriel paused as they approached the shore of the frozen sea. At first he thought it might be the reflection from the white dwarf star above, but the images rippling in the water were not reflections. They were projections. As he gazed into their depths, Gabriel saw reflections of the past playing like a movie. The sky rained fire, followed soon by inescapable darkness and sadness.

Aurelius grabbed Gabriel's hand and said, '**My tears filled this basin and so did my sadness. You mustn't look into its depths; you will be consumed by my memories. Take my hand and see this planet as it once was. This is our star Scintillaarė as I remembered her—surging with love and light. Feel her warmth.**'

A flood of memories flowed from Aurelius into Gabriel's consciousness, almost as if they were his own. The Sea of Lament was gone, and replaced by a shallow lagoon. Reflections danced along the water and Gabriel gazed upwards. Tangerine starlight from a much younger Scintillaarė gently warmed his skin. It was the *treelight* however, that truly caught his attention. Thousands of varieties of trees lined the lush lagoon and stretched all the way to the horizon. Each tree twinkled with brilliant golden or white light, making the planet's surface look more like a star cluster than a forest.

Planet Aurelius was not only rich in flora but also fauna. Tiny, fast-flying birds tended the blossoming groves. They shared some sort of symbiotic relationship with the trees and seemed to coax the light from the flowers whilst they fed. Much like the glowing nectar they consumed, the birds displayed bioluminescence of their own. The speed with which they moved made them appear like shooting stars dancing amidst the treetops.

'**These are only a few memories, but now you know why my sorrow was so great at the loss of this world.**'

Gabriel opened his eyes and looked at the frozen sea before him. Although the landscape was barren, he kept the memory close.

"Thank you for that. I'm grateful to see your world as you remember it. I now see why this was named Aurelius—it was indeed as precious as gold."

A few golden petals fell from its crown and the tree said nothing for a moment or two. Then it turned to Gabriel and spoke.

'**Jump on my shoulders and I will carry you across the sea. Keep your gaze fixed on the horizon and we'll be there in no time.**'

The tree's joints creaked as it bent low enough for Gabriel to climb onto its back.

'**Hang on!**'

Aurelius stood up and Gabriel secured himself atop the tree's right shoulder. He grabbed the branches that comprised Aurelius's crown and steadied his posture until he felt balanced.

'**Remember: don't look down and don't look back.**'

When Aurelius was certain Gabriel was safe, it started to take long strides towards the island.

Gabriel heeded the tree's warning and kept his gaze fixed on the setting star. Interlocking snow dunes sparkled like a sea of blue diamonds; their subtle peaks and valleys provided the only patterns in the white desert. The effect was mesmerizing, and soon everything blurred into a bluish-white haze.

Perhaps it was the lack of scenery, or perhaps Gabriel was simply tired from all the excitement. Either way, he was exhausted. He nodded off to sleep at some point. When he awoke, he was in the safety of Aurelius's arms.

33

TVILLING TÅRAR AND THE LOST VIMANA

'**W**elcome back,' Aurelius said. '**You had me worried for a moment or two.**'

Gabriel wiped the sand from his eyes and stared into the wispy light of Scintillaarė. Judging from the white dwarf's position in the sky, he'd been asleep for at least two hours. Dusk was near—perhaps an hour or less away, although time seemed somehow *stretched* on the planet. Gabriel felt certain that The Shadow Moon was warping time and space around them.

He looked down and nearly lost the contents of his stomach. They stood atop an enormous snowdrift... one that would rival even the highest peaks on most planets. He got the distinct feeling that this sweeping geological feature was not crafted by nature.

'**You okay?**' Aurelius asked.

"Yes. Sorry... I'm just a bit disoriented. Where are we? And how did we get so high?"

'**This is known as Tvilling Tårar in your grandfather's tongue. It's the highest point on the planet."**

"But, climbing this dune would have been... well, impossible."

'**Not if you ride upon clouds as we did. You forget that I'm**

also Tempest, Storm-Bringer. The elements are at my command.'

The tree pointed to a thick cloud deck around the peak.

"Remind me not to sleep *ever* again," Gabriel said with a smirk. "Strange things happen when I do."

'Careful what you say, Gabriel. You may get your wish.'

The tree placed one of its four hands on Gabriel's shoulder while the other three pointed below.

'The summit upon which we stand is known as Dödshära (The Dead's Keep). True to its name, this snow dune is a sacred ossuary erected by the hands of The First Star itself. Swept beneath its icy core lay the remains of all the brave warriors who gave their lives on this planet during The Thousand-Year Night. We shan't disrupt their slumber—now or ever. Our destination is over there, on the highest point, atop the sister dune named Ljushära (The Light's Keep). It houses a great artifact buried by The Machine Gods before The Fall of Adŭro. Together these two dunes are named Tvilling Tårar. In Common Tongue, you would know them as The Weeping Twins or The Twin Teardrops.'

Aurelius planted its rugged toes into the snow and they grew into the icy core like mighty roots.

'Stand back, stay behind me and, for the love of your life, hold on!'

Gabriel complied. As he hugged the right leg of Aurelius, several vines grew around his arms, legs and waist, holding him securely in place.

The immortal lifted all four hands towards the heavens and began to chant telepathically to the sky. It used the same alchemic language that brought about its own cataclysmic transformation a day earlier. Gabriel only caught one word, "Aahlyrrė," which apparently meant "reveal."

The firmament obeyed, and adjacent clouds collected around Ljushära until a vortex spun with violent, gale force winds.

As the vortex descended upon the frozen depths of The Light's Keep, Aurelius's eyes blazed like two newborn stars. The immortal focused the resulting energy into a single point of light, which subsequently melted whatever the cyclone was unable to remove.

Gabriel began to fathom the reason this immortal was known as Tempest, Storm-Bringer. If Zeus ever existed, he would have been but a candle in the wind compared to this god.

After several minutes, Aurelius's eyes returned to normal and the cyclone began to slow down.

Gabriel squinted his eyes to see what the storm had revealed. An enormous crystalline object glistered intermittently, but with all the snow and clouds, it was difficult to make out exactly what it was.

'This will help, little one.'

The tree lowered its arms and the storm system immediately dissipated to a gentle breeze.

The vines along the tree's leg released Gabriel and he cautiously stepped beside the tree to get a better look.

"My God, is that a star?" Gabriel gasped.

'Actually, that would be *Gods*, plural. It's not a star, but rather a crystalline star chariot—one that is as light as a feather but as strong as steel. This vessel is the handiwork of the benevolent Machine Gods of Adŭro.'

The enormous craft amplified and refracted surrounding light in such a way that it masked its true shape, if indeed it had one, creating what appeared to be a complex, ever-shifting multipoint star. It was ten times brighter than any other light source in the sky, most certainly brighter than Scintillaarė itself.

The tree bent down and motioned for Gabriel to hop onto its back again.

'Shall we?'

With Gabriel safely in tow, the tree jumped onto a nearby cloud and gently drifted in the direction of the starry object with the ease of a snowflake.

'**You are safe now,**' Aurelius said as it planted its feet upon the slushy remains of the Ljushära dune.

Gabriel took a deep breath and walked towards the vessel.

"How exactly does this thing fly?"

'**Hmmm. That, my friend, is what I was going to ask you.**'

Gabriel cautiously knelt down and placed his ear against the exterior of the starcraft.

The material reminded him of the dreamgate in Sedona. It felt as cool, strong and smooth as a diamond, but it rippled whenever he touched it, suggesting that it was somehow acquiescent and could be shaped by thoughts.

"I've encountered psychic devices like this before. I know it sounds crazy, but I think the Vimana is sentient, Aurelius."

'**Actually, it doesn't sound crazy at all. To use one of your figures of speech, things work differently on this side of the rabbit hole.**'

The tree motioned for Gabriel to explore.

'**It was created by the kindest and most advanced species of organic or inorganic life on this side of the Known Universe. This, like all Adŭrian creations, is sentient and magnanimous. It is safe to interact with it.**'

After mentally sweeping the perimeter of the ship, Gabriel walked to the other side and placed both hands on the surface.

The Vimana began to vibrate and emit a high pitched purr.

"GET BACK!" Gabriel screamed, "NOW!"

Aurelius complied and marveled as the star chariot rose several hundred feet above them, sending such radiance into the night sky that, for a moment all the moons were ablaze with its light, save Vōr.

'**Impressive. Very impressive. Many have tried, but none**

save the Adŭrians have been able to harness the energy of this sleeping chariot.'

Gabriel closed his eyes and reached towards the craft with his mind. The Vimana's exterior continued to shapeshift, but there was something within the core that seemed calm and constant. He could feel a sentient brain and, strangely, a heart, as well. Gabriel connected with the ship's heart and it showed him a sacred power symbol.

He opened his eyes and did his best to recreate the symbol on the ground. First, he drew a fourteen-pointed star. Then he traced a circle around it. At the center, he drew three moons and inscribed each with an alien glyph. As he traced the final glyph, the entire rune began to glow.

Aurelius turned and looked at Gabriel with surprise.

"I believe the ship called this symbol Ratha. Take my hand and together let's step onto the rune—it will provide transport to the heart of the ship," Gabriel said.

The tree obeyed and a flash of light blinded them as a star-shaped portal opened below. When they opened their eyes, they were no longer on the surface of the planet.

Aurelius remained silent for several moments, as did Gabriel. Together they stood humbly, dwarfed by the enormous interior of the spacecraft. Although the exterior was shrouded in light beams, the cockpit, at least, appeared to be tear-shaped.

"Pinch me," Gabriel said, temporarily forgetting that he needed to rethink his figures of speech.

'I don't follow.'

"What I meant to say is, *this is surreal*. I'm on a foreign planet, talking to an immortal, while standing in a psychic ship—a feat that, by the way, was achieved by channeling a magical rune that I'd never seen before. This is a lot, even for a former Psychic Investigator."

298 | NICHOLAS ASHBAUGH

'But it's only the tip of the iceberg for a Starchild,' Aurelius added.

"Anyway, I think it's safe to move," Gabriel said. "Let's have a look around."

He removed his scarf and used it to polish away some of the ice and dust that accumulated in the cockpit. The glass-like surface was covered in a series of interlocking petroglyphs and hieroglyphs—much like the engravings he'd seen on the protective medallion Elsa gave him during their first meeting.

Although it was a starcraft, the ship had no windows. The inside was created completely of a hybrid diamond-metallic material.

A series of concentric circles led to three consoles. One appeared to be for navigation, another for flight controls and the third was too difficult to decipher.

The navigator's chair looked equally outlandish. It leaned towards the ceiling and it was made of a malleable material.

Gabriel removed his gloves and sat in the navigator's seat. As he leaned back, the material closed around him like a catcher's glove.

"I think I know how this works," Gabriel said.

He closed his eyes and issued a thought to the ship. Dozens of petroglyphs illuminated on the ceiling and the control panels surrounding the cockpit.

'Can you read them?' Aurelius asked.

'They're Greek to me,' Gabriel thought... and then he realized that was it. He'd been asked that same question as a child, and whether it was fate or dumb luck, his grandfather had prepared him for this day.

For a moment, his mind wandered and he was young again, perhaps five years old at the most. Gabriel felt the cool, damp grass tickling his neck and arms as he lay on the ground. A familiar mix of dirt, honeysuckle and evergreens laced the evening air. Then he heard a voice that had almost faded from memory.

"Can you read them?" his grandfather asked.

If it was possible for a voice to glimmer, Elijah's voice somehow shined, just as it always did when he spoke about the cosmos. He was filled with life and curiosity even as an old man.

"You can read your books, but what about the stars, little one?" the old man asked.

"I don't understand, grandpa."

"The stories of the ancients are painted in twinkling lights in the heavens... you just need to know how to read them. I'll teach you about the constellations—the alphabet of the stars. You see that one?"

The old man pointed to the North Star and then traced his finger along the night sky until he reached another constellation.

"It's a constant and it can help you find other stars and groups of stars, like this one—Cassiopeia."

"Why is it called that?" Gabriel asked.

"Think of the sky as a page from history—or in the case of our ancestors, a page from a great romance or tragedy. The constellation you see is named after a vain princess. According to myth, her likeness was thrown into the heavens to teach us a lesson. More practically, these stories helped us remember the positions of the stars, and the positions of the stars tell us where we are and what season it is. Just like letters make up words, and words make up sentences, stars make up constellations and constellations tell stories. The heavens inspire us, guide us and remind us there's more to our world than this planet."

The little boy looked with awe at the old man, and smiled as he saw reflections of stars glistening on his glasses.

"You wanna know a secret?" Elijah asked.

Gabriel nodded.

"I prefer believing that there might be some truth to the myths. Who knows what gods and goddesses once walked this Earth? We've become too practical and proud. Now, in our twilight as a species, we're not unlike Cassiopeia in our belief that we're the fairest creation. The world holds more beauty and complexity than most humans would ever dare imagine."

Aurelius asked again, '**Gabriel, are you okay? Did you hear me... Can you read them?**'

The memory of Elijah on that starry night faded like a dream. Gabriel was back in the Vimana, staring into the kind, curious and ancient eyes of Aurelius.

"Sorry... I was lost in thought, but yes, I can read them."

Gabriel felt heat emanating from the pendant around his neck. He glanced down at the stellar remnant of The Seventh Star. It started to glow like a dim fire ember. He knew he was on the right track.

"The symbols are asterisms and constellations, but I'll need your help in identifying some of them. We probably need to triangulate our location."

'**Yes, of course!**' Aurelius said approvingly. '**I can pick three star systems that will triangulate the moon Virídia. Come outside and I will show you.**'

They stepped back onto the interior transportation rune. A bright light filled the cockpit and before Gabriel's eyes could adjust, he was already back on the surface of the planet with Aurelius.

The tree looked up.

'**Can you dim the ship's lights?**'

Gabriel nodded.

'**Ah, yes. Much better. Now for your crash course in alien astronomy. Look straight ahead; that cluster of stars constitutes but a few of the shining lights of Aamĕllÿne, the aging galaxy in which we reside. The ten brightest stars in this particular spiral arm form a great silver bow and arrow. At this time of year, Aamĕllÿne's Arrow always points towards the Sleeping Moon of Virídia. Can you see it?**'

"Yes, it's beautiful."

Aurelius turned and pointed to two other asterisms behind them.

'**Good. To your left is a collection of stars which resemble the hydra aspect of Esurus, the three-headed Void Shadow. A supermassive black hole dwells at the heart of this asterism, slowly consuming the centermost star—one of the brightest in our sky. For this reason, it's known as The Darkheart Star System. Finally, to your right, behold several petals emerging from Bisaj Bakool—The Lotus Petal Nebula. It's a nursery to countless baby stars.**'

The latter lived up to its name. Polychromatic gas clouds blossomed around dozens of brightly colored stars, creating the illusion of lotus petals shimmering in the night sky.

'**If you're ready, young Gabriel, then let's try this again.**'

The two stepped back onto the rune and returned to the ship.

This time, when Gabriel sat back in the navigator's seat, he began to meditate. In his mind's eye, he used his knowledge of the new constellations to triangulate their trajectory, carefully aligning Virídia to Aamĕllÿne's silver bow. The ship began to vibrate and the respective petroglyphs illuminated on the star map. He opened his eyes and the Vimana began to move towards the satellite above. He found that he merely needed to think '*faster*' or '*slower*' and '*right*' or '*left*' and the star chariot would make slight adjustments (accordingly) to the triangulated destination. Once he had control over the ship, his mind expanded further and he could see the space surrounding it. All of this was possible without opening his eyes. He flew with intuition alone.

'**The Prophecy is true,**' Aurelius thought to itself.

It closed its eyes and began to co-navigate.

Gabriel felt something stir within the ancient being, something it hadn't displayed before: a sense of surprise, followed by hope.

As the Vimana rose above the thin atmosphere, Gabriel marveled at the sheer magnitude of the planet. It easily rivaled the size of a gas giant, approximating Neptune's size. Her moons were truly worlds unto themselves, the smallest being at least twice as large as Earth.

Gabriel gazed at interlocking debris rings that hugged the planet. From space, the ring system sat vertically, not horizontally. It was then that he realized the planet was tilted on its side, likely due to one or more cataclysmic collisions during The Thousand-Year Night.

Aurelius quickly spoke up.

'Careful, Gabriel. The shards in these rings are beautiful but deadly; they're sharp enough to damage even this starcraft. Stay close to the planet until you reach the polar region and you should be safe.'

Gabriel obliged and made an arc over the pole and then up and over The Great Rings of Imogen. The next obstacle was The Ice Moon Ceruleus. He could feel its gravitational pull on the ship as he set his sights on the ancient woodland moon in the distance.

He knew there must be thrusters and activated them with his intention. This was enough to help him escape its orbit. As the Vimana swerved towards The Alabaster Moon Virídia, Gabriel caught a glimpse of something terrible atop the Cerulean surface; a great face appeared frozen amidst the glaciers. Other body parts were strewn across the moon. Gabriel's attention moved back to the face. Its glassy eyes followed him as the Vimana boomeranged into space.

Aurelius sensed Gabriel's question and answered telepathically.

'That is—*or was*, I should say—The Great Titan, Ceruleus. We will speak to him later, my friend. We must visit an oracle known as Arundhati first.'

"Why?" Gabriel asked.

'Arundhati is a powerful clairvoyant, one who may have information that can help you break into the gates of The City of the Dead.'

"I don't like the sound of that."

'Any sane being wouldn't. The Necropolis is a fortress on The Shadow Moon, a vile place that The Shadows are using as their home base. I've slumbered too long to know what's going on there now. Perhaps she has insight into what they're up to, or at least how you can sneak into The City of the Dead.'

"And if she's under their control—The Shadows, that is?"

'Well, then we'll make a run for the Ice Moon instead.'

Gabriel didn't find any of the three moons very enticing. He attempted to focus, however, on the destination-at-hand, slowing the starcraft considerably as he approached Virídia. The moon had a thick atmosphere and magnetic field, causing the instruments in the starcraft to act erratically.

Gabriel's gut told him they were entering a trap, but perhaps a necessary one. As Aurelius said, Gabriel needed help in the journey ahead. This was a calculated risk that was worth the danger.

34

THE ALABASTER MOON (VIRÍDIA)

The cloud deck surrounding The Alabaster Moon was soupy and viscous. In a normal star system, this might spell certain doom for life below. However, with the dim light of the distant white dwarf, the inverse was true; greenhouse gasses actually helped keep the moon from becoming a lifeless, frozen tundra.

Gabriel psychically swept the surface to find a safe area to land the star chariot. Although he'd used remote viewing many times at The Center, he'd never scanned the entire surface of an alien world before. Unfortunately, the magical clouds comprising The Gloaming spell were creating interference.

'**Sorry. It's almost impossible to see through a psychic storm like this, even for a Firstborn like me. Let me see if the clouds are still sentient,**' Aurelius said.

The immortal dimmed its eyes and sang to the clouds below. Much to its surprise, they responded. One by one, they moved away from the Vimana and the turbulence eased as well.

Next, Aurelius placed one of its hands across Gabriel's forehead, forming a physical and mental connection with him. Its energy helped bolster Gabriel's clairvoyance. With the tree's psychic energetic boost, Gabriel could now see the moon in all its splendor, including bioluminescent forests, enormous mountain ranges and pristine beaches.

'**We just passed over The Sea of Dreams, Mare Somnus,**' Aurelius said. '**It's safe to land along the adjacent beach on the Western coastline, just south of the large volcano.**'

Gabriel steered the ship accordingly. As promised, the beach was devoid of trees and obstructions and provided a soft landing for the chariot.

'**Well done,**' Aurelius said as it let go of Gabriel's forehead.

The two walked towards the transportation rune and, after a flash of light, they were safely on the surface of the alien moon.

The immortal rested one of its hands on Gabriel's shoulder.

'**Give your eyes a moment, friend,**' it said. '**I forgot to warn you—even in The Gloaming, The Sleeping Forests shine with great intensity.**'

When his eyes adjusted, Gabriel was in absolute awe. He now understood why the moon's given name was Virídia; underneath her alabaster façade, luminescent trees bathed the surface with a soft emerald glow.

'**This is how I remember the moon**' Aurelius mused, '**Not as alabaster, but shining with myriad shades of green treelight as far as the eye can see. Welcome to the Taiga of Arundhati.**'

The Virídian moonscape was a continuous woodland, with a few defining features. The first was a central mountain range that rose higher than the Himalayas. It traced its way longitudinally from the Northern to Southern polar regions, suggesting the land mass was made of at least two tectonic plates that now jutted up against each other. Active and inactive volcanoes were interspersed across the surface on either side of this great range. The Diamond Sea glittered to the West, accounting for less than one-quarter of the moon's surface.

The Virídian air was oxygen-rich and exponentially sweeter than Planet Aurelius. Gabriel could smell fragrances that resembled lavender, vanilla and honeysuckle with a hint of petrichor from misty, mountainous regions. Like the Aspen colonies in Colorado, each tree was connected through a complex root system. They radiated not only light but also heat—keeping the planet from succumbing to the same deep freeze that entombed its sister moon, Ceruleus. Geothermic activity from volcanoes, geysers and hot springs intensified this effect. This natural heat, coupled with the swirling clouds overhead, resulted in a tolerable greenhouse effect, mimicking the tropical regions of Earth. Gabriel shed several layers of clothing, until he was wearing only trousers and boots. He shoved everything else in his knapsack.

Although the trees were still alive, a deafening silence hung in the air. The moon was devoid of birds, grass, moss, fish or any other life that would normally exist in a biosphere. Even the wind seemed too calm.

"Something's wrong, isn't it, Aurelius? I assume there was other life here, but I see nothing now."

The tree's eyes went dim and it replied, **'Aye. Once this moon teemed with life. It... faded.'**

"*Faded?*"

'Yes. The spell wasn't strong enough to save everything. Only two life forms remain. The first is the colony of trees. Every tree on Virídia is interconnected and forms a single consciousness. Together they were stronger than The Shadows, and remain uncorrupted by the dark magic that holds them in stasis—never aging, never moving... forever glowing in the twilight of this moon.'

"And what of the second life form?" Gabriel asked.

'The Guardian was not so fortunate, little one. I wasn't sure until now. But I fear that her mind is corrupted.'

Aurelius pointed to an enormous mountain in the distance.

'What's left of her sits atop Witch's Peak. We must at least attempt to make contact with her; I owe her that much as a fellow Guardian.'

The dormant volcano loomed like a sentinel, visible from any point on the Taiga of Arundhati. Impenetrable black clouds concealed the summit.

'Upon that great vista we must seek an audience with The Eye of the Storm herself, The Colossus at Mount Augur.'

"Augur... she is a seer?"

'Yes, she *was* a powerful oracle in her youth. Now I fear the name is a bit ironic. Mount Augur is shrouded in clouds—and it is also the source of the great storm that covers this moon.'

"What happened?" Gabriel asked.

'In a moment of desperation... or perhaps just misguided compassion, Arundhati used Shadow magic to stop the moon from dying. She invoked The Gloaming, a forbidden spell that put the moon in eternal slumber. As she uttered the last words of the spell, The Guardian Arundhati was turned to stone, cursed by Time itself to watch as the world around her faded into oblivion. I fear that she's gone mad in the process. Dark magic is selfish that way; it always takes more than it gives.'

"So in effect, *she* is The Gloaming?"

Aurelius nodded.

Gabriel's thoughts returned to Elijah and their encounter with Björn years ago. Aurelius inadvertently read his thoughts.

'I see you've encountered darker magic before... I am sorry about your grandfather and his pupil. You were lucky to have Akaal at your side.

'Have hope, my dear Starchild, for I believe The Colossus can be roused, just as I was. Part of the reason for casting the spell was to save the trees on this moon. The effort was valiant, if not misguided. She is not completely lost.'

"What if—"

308 | NICHOLAS ASHBAUGH

'What if I'm wrong? Well, there are other ways to break the spell.'

"How will we get to the peak?"

'We can't make the hike to the summit in the flesh, and even if we did, we'd be consumed in sulfur, fire and steam, if not by the sorrow of Augur herself. No living thing has set foot on Witch's Peak since the forests were enchanted.'

"So what's your plan, exactly?"

'Patience, Gabe. There is a shrine in the valley near the mountain. It contains the tools necessary for our safe transit. As for my plan... I don't have one, exactly.'

'Weren't immortals supposed to be all-knowing?' Gabriel thought to himself. He imagined Aurelius heard his mental aside, but the tree did not reply.

35

THE STONE TEARS OF ARUNDHATI

G abriel looked over his shoulder at the distant green water of The Sea of Dreams. It was as still as a painting. He sighed and continued the trek towards the volcano.

It took nearly half a day to traverse the dense woodland landscape. Of course, time did not flow on this moon, at least not in the usual sense. There was no night or day, just a constant emerald twilight that painted everything—even the soil—in endless shades of green.

As they approached Mount Augur, the terrain began to shift from dense brush to rocky hills. One of these hills stood out from the rest. A deep valley scarred the top of the hill. Strange striations ran the circumference of the valley and Gabriel was now certain that they were standing at the edge of an ancient impact crater. Whether it was a meteorite or something else, Gabriel couldn't tell. Not yet.

Aurelius pointed to the center of the crater.

'There... Behold the Shrine of The Seventh Star.'

Gabriel observed that the striations terminated at an unassuming hut in the center of the valley. Aside from a large crystal on its thatched roof, the hut was unspectacular—simple, even.

'Do not judge the shrine by its appearance, Gabriel. Power comes in all sizes. Besides our dying star Scintillaarė, this little hut is the strongest energy vortex in all of the Aamĕllȳne Galaxy.'

Gabriel knew Aurelius spoke the truth; even from a distance, every hair on his body stood on end. Each blade of grass beneath him buzzed with energy—almost to the point of being overwhelming. It felt powerful and strangely familiar. The Sigil of The Seventh Star began to pulse with light and heat. They were close to something important.

Gabriel carefully followed the tree into the shrine. The moment his foot touched the interior of the modest hut, he knew that he'd stepped into another world. He dropped his jaw in wonderment.

The ostensibly modest shrine was, in fact, crafted from the remains of an alien meteorite. Its inner walls were lined with myriad sea-green crystalline structures. A series of mirrors and lenses focused the light into a pattern of asterisms on the floor. Central among them was the six-pointed star that Aurelius bore on its forehead. A particularly large clear crystal protruded from the center of the hut, forming an obelisk that rose to the height of the thatched roof.

The shrine was devoid of furniture, save for small pillows encircling the center obelisk. Aurelius sat down and Gabriel followed.

"Where are the tools?" Gabriel asked.

'This entire hut functions as a vessel. Think of it as another type of Vimana. It sails in skies of the astral plane, whereas the Vimana travels in the physical plane. Sometimes the easiest way to get where you want is to simply stand still and bring the destination to you.'

"How does it work?" Gabriel inquired.

'By physically holding the transport crystal... and through

intention, of course. Take my hands.'

Gabriel obliged.

'I must admit, it's been a few eons since I've flown one.'

"That doesn't inspire confidence."

'It wasn't meant to. Close your eyes, clear your head... and perhaps pray.'

Aurelius touched the transport crystal as its voice boomed in Gabriel's head, 'Here we go!'

Although a similar astral projection on Earth might take considerable effort, the shrine acted as a cosmic battery. Mere seconds after closing his eyes, Gabriel felt as if he were blown across the heavens like a dandelion seed in a windstorm. If the ascent was fast, the landing was equally jarring, like someone suddenly hitting the breaks after traveling at one hundred miles an hour.

He could feel his body firmly planted in the shrine, however his mind was literally thirty thousand feet above. And, mysteriously, his consciousness seemed to have the ability to affect the environment around it.

Unfortunately, the top of Augur's Peak was more dismal than he imagined. Though it should provide a gorgeous view of the forests below, it was shrouded in alabaster storm clouds that never seemed to produce rain. Not since that fateful night in his grandfather's cabin had Gabriel felt so much dread hanging in the skies.

'The Seer sleeps just ahead. Proceed with caution.'

Gabriel and Aurelius moved their astral projections along the edge of the peak.

A small island sat at the center of the caldera, surrounded by filth—both in the form of toxic water and also the skeletal remains of fish, birds and animals. Although their physical bodies were miles away, Gabriel somehow smelled the sulfur and toxic fumes gurgling from the putrid depths below. The volcano was definitely alive—but it was more than that; this was the same dark stench that had hung on Björn fourteen years earlier.

A large structure jutted out from the island. At first it appeared to be some sort of spire, but Gabriel soon realized it was Arundhati's throne.

The back was cracked and covered in thorny, leafless vines and toxic sludge. It oozed around the base and was slowly eating away at the stone.

'Stay here and don't make a sound.'

Gabriel wondered what noise could possibly rouse a stone statue, but he had learned to expect the unexpected.

Aurelius investigated and then motioned.

'Come, Gabe. It is safe.'

Gabriel moved slowly and glanced at the towering stone structure before him.

The front of the throne was unspoiled. In fact, the throne was not stone at all, but an enormous petrified Virídian conifer. Bare tree branches and roots formed the arms and legs, respectively. An ornately decorated seat was carved into the center.

If the throne was impressive, The Colossus was even more breathtaking. Were it to stand upright, the statue would tower as high as the upper atmosphere. The Guardian appeared to be just as petrified as the throne on which she sat, however.

'This is, or *was*, Arundhati, The Morning Star.'

The Colossus had six arms. The bottom two rested in a lotus prayer mudra near her heart—permanently meditating and keeping The Gloaming spell intact. With her second set of arms and hands, she clutched a great emerald staff that curved at the end—a lituus. A faint blue-white crystal spun at the innermost coil of the staff, suspended by some unseen force. Lightning occasionally flashed from the crystal, exciting the alabaster clouds in the Virídian firmament. The Seer's upper arms were permanently raised into the heavens—so high that the clouds either obscured them, or perhaps emerged from them; it was difficult to discern from below.

For a moment, Gabriel felt the ground beneath him tremble.

Against his better judgment, he peered into the statue's lifeless eyes. As her third eye opened, a slit of light cut through the clouds like a lighthouse.

By some atmospheric anomaly or storm in the clouds above, water flowed down from the other two stone eyes, gently filling the caldera one tear at a time.

His heart sank.

Moved by his intuition, Gabriel approached the statue and bowed low.

The tears turned to stone and the stones landed near Gabriel and Aurelius.

'Fool! Get back here!' Aurelius scowled.

The mountain shook again and then a voice reverberated from high above.

"Who dares awaken the Seer?"

Her staff blazed with light as did all three of the statue's eyes. Although her gaze was permanently fixed in the distance, Gabriel could feel her consciousness penetrating his crown chakra—fishing for information.

Aurelius raised its hands and for a moment the clouds, sky and lightning were at its command. Its astral projection grew to the same size as The Colossus.

'Come now... You were once the fairest star of the morning sky—a sky we once traversed as friends. Have you grown so blind that you would not recognize me?'

"Tempest?"

'Yes, it is I. Admittedly, I'm not quite myself; the same could be said of you, Arundhati.'

"That is a name I no longer use, old friend. I'm Augur, Eye of the Storm. You know that better than anyone. I paid a great price to protect your precious trees," The Colossus said.

'And for that, I owe you a debt of gratitude. But it's time to let go. You're more *Gloaming* than Augur at this point. If you

don't release the spell, it will soon entomb you, as well as your children below.'

The statue ignored the tree's request and directed her mind at Gabriel instead. Though motionless, he felt her presence next to him.

Three words sounded in his mind as she spoke telepathically: 'I know you.'

They echoed in his head again and again until he started to go mad.

Gabriel felt as if he were listening to three notes being played on some sort of cosmic piano.

Each note was piercing and resonated with such authority that he dared not ignore her. A commanding reverberation accompanied all her thoughts, so that words and sentences collided into the previous and the next one, as if they existed in a continuum—they always were there, just now making themselves known.

"ENOUGH, you witch!" he commanded.

To his surprise, Augur stopped and a small hairline fracture began to form at the base of her throne.

The Colossus spoke again.

"You wear the flesh of a mortal, but I know you. You recognize me, too, do you not?"

Somewhere deep inside, Gabriel felt he'd crossed paths with this immortal.

Augur's mind turned to Aurelius and her voice became razor-sharp.

"Are you on a suicide mission, Tempest?"

'You know why I'm here, Augur. You're a Guardian, like me. I'm fulfilling an oath—one we both swore to uphold—and I'm helping The Starchild. He seeks safe passage to The Shadow Moon. I'd hoped to take counsel with you, or perhaps have you join the young Steward and me, but I see now that is not possible.'

Augur was silent.

'I beg thee, release The Gloaming. Allow us to help you unravel the dark magic that has taken hold of your heart. Gabriel and I will then seek counsel with Ceruleus… unless you know something we do not? Speak now, old friend. The time for atonement has arrived!'

For a moment The Colossus seemed to shrink—perhaps in sadness. The waters beneath her began to boil.

"Like myself, our beloved friend is beyond repair," she replied. "His body was torn asunder, buried in remote parts of the moon above. Only the heart remains—I hear it beating, even now. But his heart stayed true to the Light, unlike mine…"

'That's it,' thought Gabriel, 'I must awaken her heart.'

He turned to the tree and said, "Lift me up."

Aurelius looked down at the human, puzzled by the request.

"Do it!" Gabriel commanded. "Hold me nearest to her heart."

Aurelius acquiesced and propped Gabriel atop its shoulders. Gabriel reached out his hands and touched the petrified statue near its heart center.

He closed his eyes and communicated with Augur, in the same manner Mercy once communicated with him—full thoughts and ideas without words. He showed Augur everything he loved in life: the sunshine on Earth, the memories of his grandfather Elijah, the taste of chocolate, the images of Planet Aurelius before The Shadows came, the scent of the Virídian trees, his love for Julian and Maddy—and his ability to forgive Death for taking them too soon. It was the latter—forgiveness—that awakened something ancient in the statue's dormant heart.

The storm relented long enough for Arundhati's spirit to break through. She gasped as she became aware of herself again. First, the uppermost hands started to tremble and fall to the bottom of the mountain. Then, a large crack worked its way from the bottom of the thrown to the crown of The Colossus.

"Aurelius, it's no use. Too long have I stayed dormant; now I'm tethered to this mountain. The atmospheric anomaly that surrounds us is a time storm. Only Akasha can help me now. I fear that I will have to pay for stealing time—either through sacrificing myself or your children below."

Aurelius knew the statue's words to be true.

Stone tears began to fall from her eyes; one by one each splashed into the putrid depths of the caldera, awakening a dark magic within the core of the volcano.

"Even as you stand here, my grasp on the storm is slipping. Look beneath you—the volcano awakens. Soon, the face of Virídia will change once more. There's nothing I can do to stop it. Hurry and forgive me for losing sight of the truth. At least I will pass from this dimension as my true self... as Arundhati."

'You need not ask for forgiveness. You saved the lives of your children—and, in the process, gave your own. That was an act of selflessness. Akasha will show compassion, as will Akaal.'

The oracle then said to Gabriel, "Know this, human: there is still hope for Ceruleus. You can awaken his heart as you did mine. Bring liberation to his last breath, dear child, just as you have to me."

The statue began to move for the first time in at least one thousand years. It knelt down and removed its third eye. Stone tears continued to fall from the other two.

"I give you Ajna, The Seer's Eye. Its powers cannot be muted or consumed, not even by the darkness of Vōr. Let this tool amplify that which you see in your heart. Use it when all Light is gone; it will work when your own eyes fail you."

The oracle paused, smiled and bowed before saying, "Shine brightly, Starchild."

With these last words, the statue split into two and crumbled irrevocably into the caldera. As the fires below consumed her body, Arundhati let out a psychic cry that shattered the heavens, quite literally. The clouds became pregnant with moisture and started to empty themselves onto the forest below.

The Alabaster spell was broken.

Aurelius and Gabriel's consciousness abruptly crashed back into their respective bodies. Much to Gabriel's surprise, a physical artifact made its way through the astral plane; he held The Seer's Eye in his hand.

A violent earthquake shook the small hut to its core, dislodging the central crystal and revealing something underneath.

The shrine subsequently filled with light and the voice of Arundhati rumbled with the shifting earth below them.

"This is my final gift, Gabriel. It will afford you safe passage on the surface of The Shadow Moon. I crafted it long before my imprisonment upon Witch's Peak, when I still upheld my promise to protect you. Now I've fulfilled my oath and can rest in peace."

He ran his hands over a finely crafted wooden box and intuitively knew the ancient symbols spelled out his name.

'Come,' Aurelius said, 'there will be time enough to examine the gift later. At the moment, we have a volcano to outrun.'

Heavy rain pelted Gabriel as he left the safety of the shrine.

'Jump onto my shoulders. We must make haste,' Aurelius commanded.

Gabriel hopped onto the tree's broad shoulders and held on tight. He watched in terror as the volcano blew its top. A low-pitched sonic shockwave ripped across the surface of the alien moon while soot and ash billowed into the valleys below.

As the deadly clouds seared across the surface, Gabriel heard something he never expected—the trees screamed in pain.

The Old God looked over its shoulders and its eyes dimmed.

"Aurelius, the trees! We must save them!"

'We already have. Like their queen, you've helped bring them rest. I will stay here until they make their transition.'

The tree raised its hands and summoned a great gust of wind

that temporarily blew the clouds back towards the volcano.

'**There. I've bought you about ten Earth minutes. Leave me now and we will reconvene on The Ice Moon. By the time you get there, I'll be waiting. Right now I have one last task... one that I must do alone.**'

Gabriel bowed his head in silent understanding.

"Where shall we meet?" he asked.

'**On a vast, frozen plateau known as The Sea of Clouds. It's adjacent to The Face of Ceruleus. Head towards the top polar region and you cannot miss it.**'

"How will you get there?"

'**I'll be hitching a ride with a mutual friend, one I haven't seen since... the beginning.**'

Before entering the Vimana, Gabriel gazed over his shoulder. An apocalyptic orange haze now encased the planet as lava and fire burned through the landscape.

Aurelius raised its arms and hands and began to sing. It projected its voice high into the heavens, reaching to the very edge of the Universe. Gabriel recognized the music. It was the same announcement that once swept through the old cabin in Denver... An announcement that summoned the eldest star in the Universe: Death.

A shooting star seared across the sky and began collecting the lost souls of Virídia.

'**Go now, Gabriel... Akaal will provide transit for me. I'll see you soon.**'

Gabriel took leave of The Woodland Moon and made his way back to the navigator's chair on the Vimana. He couldn't help but feel a sense of approaching dread and loneliness. This was Gabriel's first time in the star chariot without a companion. Somewhere deep inside he knew that this was preparation for his final voyage to The Shadow Moon.

He closed his eyes and set course for the icy Sea of Clouds.

36

THE ICE MOON (CERULEUS)

T he journey between moons proved swifter than expected, thanks to good cosmic timing; both satellites were at their perigee, bringing them closer to Planet Aurelius, as well as to one another. As Gabriel approached Ceruleus, he realized the central star and three moons were nearing a very rare event: a harmonic convergence.

Gabriel sank further into the grip of the navigator's chair and began to scan the surface with his mind.

The Cerulean moonscape was a sharp contrast to anything Gabriel had ever seen, or even dreamed of, for that matter. Gone were the interlocking snow dunes of Aurelius and the emerald treetops that graced Virídia. In their stead, razor-sharp, blue-green glaciers glistened in all directions. Although beautiful, this icy moon was fraught with peril.

Gravity was slowly tearing the satellite into pieces. Its tidally locked surface was scarred with deep crevasses that made the moon look like an enormous cracked marble. As the Vimana approached the atmosphere, Gabriel could see that many of these crevasses ran deeper and wider than the Earth's Grand Canyon.

A sparkling summit near the polar region caught Gabriel's attention. He slowed the speed of the Vimana and hovered overhead. An alien structure resembled a face, but not a human one; it was part of some sort of Titanic sea creature. He knew this was the infamous Face of Ceruleus that Aurelius mentioned, the namesake of the moon.

The Sea of Clouds was adjacent to The Great Face, just as Aurelius said.

Before exiting the Vimana, Gabriel bundled up. He wore gloves, a scarf and the same overstuffed coat he used during his first blistery night on Planet Aurelius. Then, to be safe, he donned *Himmel Sköld*, the enchanted hooded raiment from Rigel, for the lunar surface temperatures were equivalent to something one might experience in Arctic regions on Earth—manageable, but not without protection. There was no such thing as *too* much clothing on this moon.

As Gabriel stepped onto the icy surface, he took a deep breath. The air was breathable, but the oxygen level was lower than that of Planet Aurelius. He chewed on a bland State food ration that he'd stowed away in his knapsack to make sure it wasn't just low blood sugar; it wasn't. The air was just paper thin. After three or four deep breaths, his light-headedness ceased, and he looked around the majestic, lifeless sarcophagus of a moon.

Aside from the various glacial structures, there were no trees or visible land masses. This was once a completely water-based world, and now all that water was frozen. In fact, it looked as if the waves were flash-frozen in the middle of high tide. Some of them were welling, while others were cresting into each other.

Much to his horror, he saw outlines of various forms of aquatic life entombed within the ice structures around him. Though the exact features were difficult to make out beneath the striated ice, he could see that the life-forms were several times larger than the blue whales that once swam Earth's oceans in the antiquity. With his own psychic empathy, he ascertained that their death, although quick, was nonetheless painful.

The terror beneath the ice was masked by the fact that the moon itself was still breathtakingly beautiful. Like some sort of art sculpture, it was painted in seemingly endless gradients of color. Gabriel counted at least five types of blue ice swirling around him; shades of aquamarine, azure, cerulean, lapis and cobalt stretched in every direction, glittering in the faint half-light of the dead star on the horizon. Periodic masses of shamrock and seafoam green interspersed themselves between the blue swirls. Closer inspection revealed that they were comprised of kelp, algae, diatoms and plankton-like organisms.

Time also seemed to be frozen on the satellite's surface. Nothing had changed here for over a thousand years, and, without a new source of light or heat, it probably never would.

Gabriel slipped as he stood up, but a friendly twelve-fingered hand reached out to steady him.

'Careful, little one.'

He was at a loss for words, so he simply hugged Aurelius.

After a long embrace, the tree broke the silence.

'I'm glad you made it safely, Gabriel.'

"You as well. Are you okay?"

'Yes. Indeed, I'm much better than okay—I'm grateful. After all, I just freed The Children of Virídia and their Watcher. I'm ready to do the same for this moon.'

"I'm sorry we couldn't do more."

'Arundhati came through when we needed her to do so. That's all that matters! The gifts she bestowed upon you will allow for safe passage above *and below* the Shadow Moon. Our journey was therefore not in vain—far from it! It was quite productive!

'Now, we must hurry. The temperatures will plummet with Scintillaarė sets tonight.'

Aurelius pointed to a large formation, just past The Sea of Clouds.

'Behold, The Face of Ceruleus.'

"So this is The Third Watcher?"

'Not entirely—it's only his face. As Arundhati said, the great Titan's body was torn to many pieces—*too many to count*—and his children were buried beneath the ever-growing glaciers.'

"It appears that all life here perished a thousand years ago, right?"

Aurelius dimmed its eyes in contemplation.

'Unfortunately, your assumption is correct. My intuition tells me we're too late for the mortal inhabitants of this moon. Ceruleus is another story altogether. As with any Ancient, the decision to live or die exists within his consciousness.'

"Even with his body sundered?"

'Aye, the sundering did not kill the Titan, it only entrapped his body. Like Arundhati—and even me for a time—this Guardian is merely asleep. We're here to wake him up and see what insights he might share. If we're lucky, Ceruleus can bestow you with the tools, or perhaps knowledge, to defeat dark forces that dwell under the surface of Vōr, The Shadow Moon. Although he was not a Seer like Arundhati, Ceruleus was one of the wisest beings in this Star System.'

The two walked about a mile or so until they were at the base of the structure Gabriel had seen from the Vimana. If this was only a relic, then the original Titan must have been fearsome indeed; the face alone dominated the moon's skyline, looming taller than any other geological feature. It was—without doubt or exaggeration—the most beautiful and alien thing Gabriel had ever encountered. At first glance, it was vaguely reptilian in form, or perhaps a distant relative to a dragon. But, as Gabriel gave it more thought, he realized this may be the grandfather of all of the aforementioned.

Unlike its progeny, this creature was more aquatic in nature—a king of water, not fire.

Its face rose higher than the highest peak on Mars, roughly fourteen miles above the rest of the glaciers. It was frozen in mid-scream... its three eyes closed in agony. The eyes were arranged in a perfect triangle above its elongated nose. Beautifully elaborate tendrils fell from the nose, jaw and crown in an almost lion-like mane. The frozen scales that adorned them sparkled like blue sapphires in the icy half-light of Scintillaarė.

"He... It... Whatever this is... is just beautiful."

'I agree; Ceruleus was beautiful in mind, body and spirit. I just hope this icy tomb hasn't driven the kindness from his heart.'

Gabriel stepped closer to the face and laid his hands on its neck. Although covered in several feet of ice, he connected with the energy signature of the creature. As he closed his eyes he could see the last days of the moon and the final breath that its namesake took. He watched in terror as The Shadows moved in on Scintillaarė, forcing it into an early demise. Red fire filled the lunar sky, followed by a cataclysmic explosion of the sister moon Imogen. As rock and fire filled the sky, Gabriel felt something else... something familiar, descend into the waters of the moon. As The Void Beast touched the water, the planet froze solid and Gabriel heard cries of terror as the inhabitants of the moon perished.

He opened his eyes and looked at Aurelius.

"The Void Beast itself is responsible for The Sundering?"

'Yes... I'm sorry you had to see that.'

"The Void Beast literally ripped Ceruleus into pieces?"

'Aye. And it scattered them across the freezing moon. Ceruleus's talons lay beneath the polar region; its body lay along the ocean floor. Its heart, however...'

"...is straight ahead? I hear it... I feel it. Don't you?"

'Yes.'

Gabriel glanced at a deep fissure that lay beside The Great Face. At regular intervals he heard tectonic pounding that was amplified by the chasm itself. It portended doom.

"How do we get down there?"

Aurelius looked at the foothills of The Great Face and pointed to three cracks along the neck.

'The gill slits. They lead to a series of interlocking tunnels that should bring us to The Sacred Heart.'

Aurelius's eyes glowed as bright as fire.

'However, tread lightly. The tunnels are icy and some corridors lead into the soupy undercurrents of The Sea of Clouds. Although the surface is ice, there are some parts of this moon—deep in the dark shadows—that survived The Sundering. They are worse for it.'

Gabriel shivered. He knew that the same ghosts that nearly killed Aurelius also lived beneath the ice. He followed Aurelius silently and carefully.

Light from the immortal's crown chakra brilliantly illuminated the ice-covered tunnels as they descended into The Great Face.

37

AN AUDIENCE WITH THE SACRED HEART

G abriel was afraid the tunnels below The Great Face would be unsightly, since they were literally walking through parts of an immortal being. He couldn't be further from the truth; both the iridescent outer scales and inner membranes glistened in a beautiful shade of seafoam green.

A reverberating *lub-dub-lub-dub* sound shook the ice and made traveling the icy gill, throat and esophageal passages rather dangerous.

'I know a shortcut,' Aurelius said.

A major artery had burst open eons ago, and the crack was wide enough for both of them to enter with little struggle.

After a small slide through the aorta, both Aurelius and Gabriel found their way to the main chamber.

The heartbeat reminded Gabriel of tribal drums: rhythmic, animalistic and capable of drowning out all thoughts.

It was impossible to ascertain if they were in the left or right atrium or whether this Titan had more than two chambers.

Before they could discuss the matter, The Sacred Heart spoke telepathically.

'Tempest? Is it you? It warms my heart to have you back here.'

'It warms mine as well. I only wish I'd come sooner.'

'Your presence can only mean one thing: the end is near?'

The heartbeat began to slow slightly, then Ceruleus spoke again. 'Is this the prophesied Starchild?'

'Aye, and he seeks passage to The Shadow Moon... to Vōr.'

At that moment Gabriel could feel a chill pass through the entire moon. The ground within Ceruleus's Atrium shook as thoughts formed and then reverberated in Gabriel's mind.

'Ah, yes... Vōr. Three simple letters, but how foul that word is. We called The Shadow Moon Adŭro in days of old. I wish you could have seen it then. The city sparkled like a distant diamond. That is, until Esurus defiled its beauty.

'The Machine Gods—have they fallen, Tempest?'

The tree nodded.

The heart paused and then rhythmically started to speak again, each sentence punctuated with a low-pitched thud as it finished a thought.

'These Shadow words have fallen into disuse for a reason; as you know, thoughts are power, and words are manifestations of that power. Akaal wisely taught you these truths once, no? I sense The First Star's presence among your thoughts.'

"Yes, Akaal and I are old friends; this was one of the first lessons it taught me." Gabriel replied. "May I ask a question that has been bothering me for some time now?"

'Of course,' the heart replied with a thud.

"Is The Shadow Moon alive?"

Aurelius placed its hand on Gabriel's back and answered for Ceruleus.

'All of the celestial bodies in this system are sentient to some degree, but Vōr is the most awake, and the most tortured. It works symbiotically with Esurus—channeling and responding to its each and every wish.'

The heart took a few beats and spoke again.

'Aye, but there may be hope. If we can sever the connection, it may be key to weakening Esurus's hold. I sense a lightness within the moon. It is held captive and seeks liberation.'

'You may be right, old friend,' Aurelius replied. **'But we must prepare ourselves for the grimmer possibility that the moon and its inhabitants can't be turned.'**

'I sense another question in your thoughts, Gabriel,' Ceruleus said. 'You seek strategy on how to defeat The Great Ruiner, right?'

"Yes... I would be honored to receive the gift of insight from you," Gabriel said.

Ceruleus's consciousness reached in Gabriel's mind and searched for the right words.

'You want to know how you'll recognize Esurus. You are wise to ask. Like your friend Akaal, The Great Beast shapeshifts at will. Sometimes it's a hydra, sometimes it's an elemental, but it's never what you expect. Far from menacing, it's frighteningly seductive and its intelligence should not be underestimated. It is an amalgam of three Lesser Shadows. It once had three main faces—Hunger, Doubt and Fear—but it now appears mostly as six eyes shrouded in darkness. Even now, its power grows. It's only a matter of time before their brethren—Want, Ignorance, Treachery, and Stagnancy —find them. They are presently planning a sort of beacon within the singularity of The Darkheart Star System to call the other Shadows home. I believe they've hidden a terrible weapon there, one they will use to extinguish all Light (and life for that matter) in the Known Universe. To stop—or at least delay—this outcome, you must venture to the gates of The Necropolis, near Mare Esurus.'

"The Sea of Hunger?"

'Yes—it's the site of The Last Stand of Aduro, the exact spot where the war was lost and the moon fell to The Shadows. The name is an oxymoron, as no sea exists—only a crater from a massive impact.'

"Like an asteroid?"

'Aye, but it was a psychic weapon known as Brahmāstra—much like the device your grandfather yielded years ago, but on a more cosmic scale. The energy channeled by the device stripped the moon of its atmosphere and emptied the waters of Mare Esurus into space, where they were lost forever.'

"So nothing is left?"

'Only the skeletal remains of The Machine Gods. The Shadows known as Hate, Fear and Despair erected a Necropolis with the twisted remains of Adŭro and dwell there today. It is here, in the depths of The City of the Dead, that you will find The Great Beast.'

"How do I defeat it?" Gabriel asked, knowing the answer before he finished uttering the phrase.

'You cannot defeat Esurus outright, but you *can* outsmart it,' Ceruleus replied. 'We seek time, not revenge.'

The heart beat several times, and then continued.

'In your knapsack you have two books; one is imbued with light, the other with darkness. Esurus will tempt you to use the latter and renounce *The Book of Stars*. You must do the unexpected— embrace both, though it will not come without sacrifice. I've seen your demise, Starchild. A great fire will tear this world to pieces. But a phoenix shall rise. The Seventh Star will return.'

The remnant of The Seventh began to pulse with light, illuminating the interior of The Sacred Heart. In this moment, Gabriel realized what none of them were able to say. He was The Seventh Star.

'I must object to this, Ceruleus. He was never meant to—'

"I'll do it," Gabriel said. The words fell out of his mouth, without hesitation. It was something he'd been ready to say and do since he was seven years old.

'Are you sure? There's no turning back if this is your choice?'

"I know what this entails, Aurelius," Gabriel replied. "The only way to win is by displaying three things Esurus does not have—selflessness, bravery and hope."

As Gabriel uttered the word *hope*, The Sigil of The Seventh Star glowed even brighter. He held it up for Aurelius.

"The Sigil does not lie. This is the only way."

Aurelius's eyes went dim.

'You will not be alone when the moment comes, dear brother,' the tree said as it embraced Gabriel with all four of its arms.

"I know. From the minute I met Akaal, to the moment you broke my fall, Aurelius, I've been preparing for this task. This was always a one-way trip. But I don't fear what is on the other side anymore."

The Sacred Heart began to tremble and beat erratically.

'For the first time since my sundering, neither do I,' the heart said. 'It was my honor to see you both... here at the end of things.'

With its task complete, The Sacred Heart beat one last time, sending tremors through the core of The Ice Moon.

'This moon is now truly dead. Like its namesake, it will fade away. Akaal will soon be here to claim Ceruleus's soul. I will travel on the wings of Death as I did before. Together, we will gather all of The Six Stars. Look for our heavenly lights when you're on the surface of Vōr.'

Before Gabriel could reply, the tree added, **'You must leave. *Now!* Run to the surface quickly. I cannot die, but *you* still can.'**

Aurelius ripped two branches from its crown and handed them to Gabriel.

'Shine brightly, brother. Long have I dreamed of your return!' Aurelius said as The Sacred Heart began to collapse.

The sharp wooden spikes allowed Gabriel to steady himself as he climbed along the icy passages. They also provided illumination.

Gabriel heard the walls of the fortress cave-in as the heart withered and died.

He ran to the surface and narrowly made it to the Vimana before the ice surrounding The Sea of Clouds began to splinter.

From the safety of the Star Chariot, he watched as the final vestiges of Ceruleus were forever consumed beneath the icy surface.

38

THE SHADOW MOON (VŌR)

Armed with the newfound understanding that his task wasn't to find The Seventh Star, but rather *to transform into that celestial being*, Gabriel couldn't help but feel a bit overwhelmed. However, the timing was cosmically perfect; everything had prepared him for this moment. After losing his grandfather, his best friend and his lover, he realized that he had to find strength from within. Star or no Star, the fate of the Universe was in his hands. He must at least try to succeed, or all his friends' sacrifices, not to mention his own, would be in vain.

As he drifted like a derelict asteroid towards The Shadow Moon, Gabriel's mind began to wander far away from the dying star system. A childhood memory flickered into his mind. He was seven again, back on Earth, straining his eyes to see the details on Earth's Moon. It was then that he first felt a burgeoning wanderlust that would make his life as a human a difficult one. Even as a kid, he felt trapped in his own skin. Like the dark side of the Earth's Moon, there was a dormant part of Gabriel that was waiting to see the light of day. Vōr seemed an unusual destination to find that light, but he was growing more comfortable with facing the unexpected.

He snapped back when the Vimana started to shake. The instrument panel flashed with dozens of incomprehensible warnings.

Esurus's grip had begun to pull the chariot towards the dead moon.

Gabriel tried to regain control of the Vimana, but the more he struggled, the more the ship trembled and veered off course.

'I could use some help on this one,' Gabriel thought.

Somewhere in the depths of time and space, Elijah's familiar voice reached out and answered.

"Now isn't the time to fight—let The Shadows make the first move."

Gabriel pulled back from the controls and let the moon steer the ship. The warning lights faded and the Vimana safely entered the orbit of Vōr.

Due in part to its distance from the other moons, Gabriel had underestimated its size. Almost immediately, the gravity of the moon started to claw and tug at the Vimana. Also, much to his surprise, a thin atmosphere still existed—likely not enough to trap gasses, but enough to create some turbulence.

Although it was a large moon—large enough to be considered a planetoid—something didn't add up. Its gravity was enormous. As the ship approached the limits of its upper atmosphere, Gabriel noticed behavior that mimicked a singularity more than a satellite. First, it bent all visible light... and apparently thoughts. This created anomalies, like the ability to see the back of the ship as he gazed forward. The size of the moon, also, was unclear. It seemed to be ever-changing—growing, perhaps—as he gazed at it with his mind's eye. The gravity of the moon continued to pull not only on the ship, but at Gabriel's mind, until soon he could think of nothing else. He sensed its hunger... and he could smell the stench of death.

Gabriel gasped as the Vimana entered the lower atmosphere of Vōr. From the present trajectory, it appeared as if The Shadow Moon actually *consumed* light. With Planet Aurelius and its three moons in a rare harmonic convergence, the white dwarf Scintil-laarė's light was completely eclipsed. As a result, the surface of The Shadow Moon was darker, more barren than a deserted stretch of the Nevada highway, making Gabriel wonder if this was the darkest place in all of outer space.

Although it took an immense amount of mental focus, a few peculiar details started to materialize amidst the shadowy debris. Strange, twisted metallic frames jutted up from the surface like skeletons—perhaps ribcages. Many of these metal skeletons spanned the distance of an Earth skyscraper—it was difficult to tell from the Vimana, but he was certain they were enormous. These twisted carcasses almost certainly belonged to the legendary Machine Gods. Right now Gabriel was in no hurry to investigate. The first order of business was finding a suitable landing area.

A massive, black fortress loomed on the horizon, just behind a large impact crater—Mare Esurus, The Sea of Hunger. Were it not for the faint stars twinkling behind it, the citadel would be completely invisible. Three gnarled spires reached towards the sky; the center-most curled into the heavens like a snake, while the right and left towers ended in sharp, giant pointed claws. Much like the iron skeletons that were stacked against them, all the structures around the citadel were gnarled and misshapen. This befouled city was surely the fabled Necropolis.

The crater comprising Mare Esurus appeared to be both free of debris and structurally stable, so Gabriel landed in the center. He powered down the starship, but kept the auxiliary lights active. The ship's light faintly illuminated the perimeter of the barrier surrounding The Necropolis. From what he could perceive, The Barbican was in complete disarray. A few rods jutted up in obtuse angles, while the rest of the structure had melted in an ancient fire.

'The Machines put up one hell of a last stand,' Gabriel thought to himself.

He unfastened the arm, leg and head harnesses of the Vimana

and opened his eyes. He imagined that he'd never get used to flying psychically... shifting from astral to ocular sight proved tricky at best. As he stood up, his legs felt like jelly; it took several minutes for him to regain balance. Given what was awaiting him, he was happy to procrastinate while his Eustachian tubes adjusted.

Before leaving the safety of the ship, Gabriel prepared for the journey ahead. He carefully unpacked the enchanted torch, Fireheart. Knowing that its light might attract unwanted attention, Gabriel covered the end with several inches of burlap. The staff now looked like a giant matchstick, but he knew it would do the trick.

Next, Gabriel stripped down to his boxer briefs and carefully unwrapped Arundhati's parting gift: a Virídian spacesuit. The ornate suit consisted of eight parts. He began with the helmet. It proved to be the most alien and elaborate part of the suit. Although he couldn't be certain, it appeared to be made from the head carapace of an enormous insect. The iridescent green shell was as smooth as glass and as hard as a rock. Two enormous compound eyes protruded from either side of the helmet. Each eye was comprised of two parts: a sturdy, clear and retractable outer membrane and a complex honeycomb structure underneath. The latter contained thousands of photoreceptors, which glistened like a sea of black diamonds.

The technology lining the inside of the mask was a bit of a mystery to Gabriel. The compound eyes connected to a tube in the underside—presumably some sort of nerve or ocular transmission membrane. A sticky, sap-like substance lined the back of the membrane—the same material that lined the bottom of the mask. By Gabriel's estimate, this would sit dead center on his forehead, near his third eye. The rest of the carapace was hollowed out, but not devoid of organic matter. A colony of harmless single-celled lichen organisms, perhaps fungus or bacteria, lined the interior.

They consumed exhaled carbon dioxide and produced oxygen and other breathable gasses as a byproduct.

He placed the helmet over his head and exhaled, activating the colony. The sap-like seal immediately affixed to his skin, forming a firm, resealable bond around his neck. Once the seal was in place, he inhaled. The symbiotic colony had already transformed the carbon dioxide into oxygen. The now-breathable air was laced with scents of pine, sap and the sweet Virídian soil. Each exhale fed the colony; by the time he needed to inhale, they'd already converted the carbon dioxide into a breathable mix of nitrogen, oxygen and other Earth-like gasses.

The inside of the helmet was completely dark. He waited patiently as the optic membrane connected with his forehead. Once the sap-like seal was formed on his third eye, Gabriel closed his eyes and simply believed the photoreceptors on the helmet would work, similar to his navigation of the Vimana. At first he only saw flickers of light. Then, slowly, his third eye opened and he could see the room coming into focus. The compound lenses were enormous; both wrapped around the back of the helmet, essentially doubling Gabriel's field of view. Although the honeycombs created a slight pixelation of everything, the tradeoff was substantial: they afforded an enhanced sensitivity to light—particularly ultraviolet—and an ability to perceive thermal fluctuations. With the helmet securely in place, he fastened the lotus-petal Sigil of The Seventh Star around his neck once more.

The next two pieces—a pair of form-fitting trousers and a skin-tight shirt—both sealed off at the feet, waist and neck in a similar fashion as the helmet. Judging from the somewhat rough texture and construction, Gabriel guessed that they were crafted from some combination of caterpillar silk, reeds and Virídian pine bark.

Both the shirt and trousers were snug but sturdy. Arundhati had crafted a "second skin" that locked on top of the aforementioned material. Similar in function to medieval chain mail, the armor contained hundreds of overlapping dime-sized Cerulean seashells that sparkled like sapphires. Their elegance and featherweight mass belied their strength; they were as strong as steel.

The next three items—a pair of boots, a pair of gloves, and a cuirass—were fashioned out of the same carapace as the helm. They were lined with dried moss, which provided a soft thermal cushion. A small concave area sat in the middle of the breastplate, creating something that looked like an empty eye socket. It was the exact size of Ajna. He snapped The Seer's Eye into the slot and it was a perfect fit. Upon its installation, ornate glyphs radiated outward from the center stone like a spiral galaxy, forming some sort of a protection symbol. It remained dim, but Gabriel intuitively knew that this device could conjure light and could also reveal that which was hidden.

The final component of the suit proved the most unusual. Hundreds of tiny flower petals were sewn together to create a hooded cape. Each petal was pliable and would take on the color of its surroundings, providing excellent camouflage. As Gabriel fastened the cape in place and raised the hood to cover all but a sliver of his face, it also heightened his vibration—each petal functioned as a tiny battery, boosting every chakra and every cell in his body. The higher his vibration, the less vulnerable he was to Shadow magic.

Gabriel fancied that he looked like something out of an Egyptian myth—some half-human, half-insect god. Elijah's speeches about Ancient Astronauts were starting to sound undeniably plausible right about now. Thinking of his grandfather helped to buoy his spirits. This memory alone effortlessly ignited Fireheart with a gentle glow.

He stood upon the transportation rune and took a deep breath as he descended into the darkness below.

39

THE SEA OF HUNGER (MARE ESURUS)

The moon vibrated with a very low, but faintly audible, frequency, as if a chorus of voices was singing together helplessly in despair. The surface was also filled with a sense of dread and sadness, much like The Sea of Lament on Planet Aurelius. But there was something else, something familiar; underneath the lamentation lurked a primordial presence Gabriel hadn't sensed since he'd peered into Akasha's mirror as a boy. The only word he could use to describe it was *hunger*. As this word formed in his head, the atmosphere became heavy.

Esurus now knew Gabriel was near.

The light from his torch glistened on the surface of the impact crater. Based on the texture and morphology of the rocks around him, he deduced that they were a mix of glass, tektites and obsidian. The size and heat of the explosion that originally generated these formations must have been formidable.

Gabriel held his torch to the gate and psychically increased its light. His resulting gasp was audible, even through the thick carapace.

The partially destroyed Barbican was comprised of metallic,

femur-like skeletal structures from The Machine Gods. The fortress behind it was also crafted from similar remains, like some sort of catacomb turned inside out. Tens of hundreds of metallic endoskeletons and exoskeletons were piled on top of one another to create a structure that would dwarf even the largest Earth skyscraper. Gabriel winced when he noticed that some of the interspersed metallic skulls had melted together in mid-scream, their terror forever on display on this godforsaken moon. He also perceived a psychic echo within Mare Esurus—a sort of mantra that initiated the destructive explosion.

'Could all of this have really been done by a psychic weapon?' Gabriel wondered. The question was rhetorical; he knew the answer was *yes*.

Ceruleus's description of The Brahmāstra gelled with an old manuscript in Elijah's library. According to the artifact, the device was invoked not by explosives, but by channeling energy, through the means of intense meditation. If this doomsday weapon existed, perhaps it could explain the utter annihilation wrought upon Vōr, for the destruction here was far worse than any nuclear bomb or other weapon of mass destruction humans were capable of crafting. Given the fact that he just psychically navigated a Vimana, this seemed completely plausible.

A large chasm lay just beyond the Mare Esurus crater and The Barbican. Some sort of violent explosion or aftershock had gutted the courtyard surrounding the fortress as well, creating a moat of darkness. The Necropolis appeared to be rising from a bottomless pit, with only a single point of entry—a narrow stone bridge. Just past the bridge lay a gate that was too far away to clearly see from his present distance, even with the enhanced night vision of the carapace.

Gabriel slowly walked around the twisted femurs in The Barbican and inched towards the bridge. Movement over The Shadow Moon was surprisingly harder than he imagined. For a planet with a nearly nonexistent atmosphere and minimal gravity, he should have felt weightless. Instead, each step was laborious, almost as if something was intentionally weighing him down or pushing him away, making his journey harder than it needed to be.

The bridge was surprisingly sturdy and appeared to be some sort of natural rock formation. It lacked a railing, however, and Gabriel moved slowly along the center. One false move would equal certain death. As he tiptoed across the mile-long bridge, the rumbling vibrations below became louder and louder. For a moment, he thought he heard them speak his name in an eerie, drawn-out baritone. The chorus grew more pronounced and, with each recitation, Gabriel was certain that millions of voices were calling to him.

"Gaaaaaaabrieeeeeel."

Gabriel now stood approximately twenty feet from the gate. He held his torch high and looked at the dark expanse above him.

'Where the hell am I?' he thought.

The sentient moon seemed to whisper a response.

'Nil-Aedis, The Hollow Temple.'

He intuited this to be the name of all three structures comprising The City of the Dead—including The Barbican, The Necropolis itself and the bridge between the two structures.

The citadel contained dozens of medium-sized turrets created from the bowels and skeletal remains of The Machine Gods, but three towers loomed above the twisted turrets—the same ones he viewed from the navigator's chair in the Vimana. From this distance, Gabriel was now certain that they were comprised of a different source material, something that was more organic than the metallic exoskeletons.

The center-most tower housed the entry to the citadel. He could hear its name whispered in his mind. This was Tamas-Mukha, The Mouth of Darkness. The main entrance below it was crafted from a large skull whose interlocking fangs sealed the entrance, like deadly stalagmites and stalactites. The winding turret above the skull was a great skeletal tail that coiled upwards, creating a makeshift spiral stairwell. A small thatched watchtower sat at its terminal point. Gabriel surmised that the right and left turrets were part of the same creature, likely the remains of its arms and legs. If that was the case, then the structures that scraped the night sky were quite literally claws.

Two colossus-sized Sentinels stood rigidly beside the clawed towers on either side of Tamas-Mukha. Though the details of their bodies remained cloaked amidst the shadows, two large ibis-like heads sat atop The Sentinels' broad, humanoid shoulders. Each Sentinel balanced a scythe between its hands so that the bases formed an "x" and the blades pointed in the direction of their beaks, which themselves looked like scythes. Scattered skulls were piled around them. Although they appeared to be motionless, Gabriel was certain they were watching his every move.

'Who seeks entrance into The City of the Dead?' Much like the thoughts he had earlier, he recognized that this came from the moon itself, not from an actual being.

As he stared into the dark abyss above, Gabriel slowly made out the twisted silhouette of a watchtower.

Gabriel answered back in his head.

'Tell me who or *what* you are and perhaps I'll answer your question.'

Gabriel saw two red searchlights appear in the darkness, which were accompanied by a low vibration. The lights scanned the surface until they shined on him. Much like the telepathic being Mercy, this creature used light to transmit information.

'I'm The Gatekeeper; I serve as the eyes and ears of our Master. What business have *you* here? Answer truthfully, or face the wrath of The Sentinels.'

Words formed in Gabriel's mind. He issued them psychically to The Gatekeeper, even though he, himself, didn't fully comprehend the full weight of his proclamation until much later.

'I know who you are, *Gatekeeper*... and I'm quite certain you know me. I'm The Seventh Star. I seek audience with your so-called Master.'

The Gatekeeper laughed and replied, 'You are no *Star*. You may be fooling yourself, but not me.'

The Sentinels stirred and Gabriel heard the sound of wings as The Gatekeeper descended. Instead of coming directly to him, it perched upon one of the upward facing fangs of the main gate. Though cloaked in shadows, he perceived enough details to know it was some sort of undead entity—with featherless, bat-like wings. Its enormous red eyes were uncomfortably large—evolved perhaps, to pick up movement in the pitch black. They glowed like red lanterns; he now understood they were the searchlights. A thin, nictitating inner eyelid slid down involuntarily when the creature looked at Gabriel's torch. Its ears were equally as large, pointed high and wide above its head. With the exception of the eyes and ears, the rest of the creature was quite literally skin and bones. The nose and mouth—if they once had existed—were now absent or atrophied beyond recognition.

The Sentinels moved closer to the front gate and held their scythes tightly, ready for a command.

The Gatekeeper opened its eyes wider and the light intensified as it transmitted a warning.

'You call yourself Prophet, but you're blinded by your faith. You understand that nothing can come out of an audience with Esurus but death?'

'Perhaps, but that's my decision to make.'

It closed its eyes halfway, so only narrow slits of red light shined on Gabriel's face.

'Why should I let you pass, *Prophet*?'

'Because I have Sentinels of my own, Gatekeeper.'

Gabriel pointed towards the sky. The Alabaster Moon, now free of its clouds, glowed brightly with volcanic activity. Just beyond it a host of light glimmered in the sky.

'Look to your East... The Six Stars are approaching, and they bring a great army of Light with them.'

The Gatekeeper and its Sentinels gazed into the sky. Then, Gabriel heard a low rumble from the dark chasm below as Esurus saw what they saw: the stars were physically moving closer, just as Aurelius had promised.

The Sentinels hastily returned to their posts, but now kept their eyes fixed on the stars. They were clearly puppets of The Beast within The Necropolis.

The Gatekeeper flew back to its post as well and the red searchlights shined back onto Gabriel.

'You may enter The City of the Dead, human. But mark my words: you will not leave this moon alive.'

Gabriel knew this was true, but fear no longer motivated his decisions. With the weight of the world on his back, he felt certain that it was now more important than ever that he complete what he set out to do.

'Oh, and one other thing. Leave your torch behind. Light is not welcome within The Necropolis.'

Gabriel begrudgingly obliged, leaving the now-extinguished Fireheart near the entrance.

The Sentinels silently knelt down and operated a pulley mechanism that opened the skull and the metallic portcullis underneath it.

As Gabriel stepped through the mouth, he heard the snap of ivory as the jaw closed behind him.

Darkness enveloped Gabriel.

40

THE CITY OF THE DEAD

A lthough Gabriel had experienced the darkness of the woods growing up, nothing compared to the complete absence of light in the interior of The Necropolis. The compound eyes in his helmet were rendered all but useless inside the gloomy fortress. The mask was not without purpose, however. As Gabriel inhaled its sweet lichen-based air, his memory returned to his brief time on The Alabaster Moon; it was this memory that triggered Ajna.

He placed his hands over The Seer's Eye and conjured memories of Virídia's sleeping forests. One by one he called upon each tree, and said a prayer to Arundhati. As he did, ribbons of emerald and sea foam green light bathed the interior of the fortress. One of those ribbons penetrated his heart chakra. He now saw not with his eyes, or the compound eyes on the carapace, but symbiotically through his heart and Ajna. It provided a near-omniscient view of the surroundings, with a slightly fish-eyed effect.

The Seer's Eye confirmed his fears; the fortress was, in fact, the hollowed-out and petrified remains of what appeared to be a serpentine creature. Perhaps it was one of the Titan-like sea creatures that had dwelled beneath the waters of Ceruleus. Or perhaps it was something else—far older and far less noble. Its body was dissected, twisted and rearranged to suit the architect's design—and what a terrible design it proved to be.

Two winding passageways stood on either side of a large spiral stairwell. A dais sat in the center of the room. Dark, inverted asterisms—the same ones that lined the cover of *Corpus Tenebrae*—decorated its surface. The symbols glowed a putrid green, just long enough for Gabriel to read them.

HOPE HAS NO PLACE IN THE SEAT OF DARKNESS; ONLY THOSE WHO LEARN TO HATE, SUBMIT TO FEAR, AND EMBRACE THE DEPTHS OF THEIR OWN DESPAIR CAN DEMAND AN AUDIENCE WITH THE NAMELESS ONE.

As the symbols faded, the dais descended and Gabriel understood that he would have to deal with whatever dwelt within the Two Temples first.

The entry to the left was closed off.

He turned to his right and realized this was the only way.

An inscription appeared in the keystone above the entryway:

FEAR IS THE GREAT EQUALIZER.

Ironically, this statement gave Gabriel hope, for it reminded him of Akaal's words of encouragement the night his grandfather faced Björn. Only by facing fear could Gabriel succeed at the task-at-hand. He took a deep breath and walked down the corridor.

41

THE TEMPLE OF FEAR

The misshapen walls of the Temple of Fear sent an involuntary shiver through Gabriel's body; hollowed-out turrets rose to vast, dark heights above him, while rusting shrapnel and shattered metallic skeletons lined the damp floor beneath him. The walls dripped with a gooey, black sludge that seemed to swallow up all sounds. This alone would have given Gabriel reason enough to pause, but it was the questions in his head that got the better of him.

'Who or what was lying in wait? And where was it dwelling?' he wondered.

Gabriel felt a mounting sense of paranoia and took a deep breath.

He closed his eyes and activated Ajna. Ribbons of green light coursed through The Hall of Fear. It was vast and empty, save for something at the far side.

Gabriel used The Seer's Eye again to scry into the depths of a hidden vestibule at the end of The Great Hall of Fear. An enormous black mass stirred and writhed in pain as Ajna bathed it in light.

At first, it seemed as though there was a great altar in the antechamber ahead. However, as everything came into focus in Gabriel's mind, he realized it was not an altar at all, but The Face of Fear itself. Some sort of hooded raiment shrouded The Shadow Lord's head and descended down into unseen depths. Like Rigel, Fear had no form. The raiment seemed to somehow help contain its energy. Unlike the resplendence in Rigel's raiment, however, the tattered suit that cloaked Fear somehow warped and destroyed everything in its wake. There was no light beneath it, only darkness. With every move, Fear carved away more and more of the fossilized interior, creating a cavernous vacuum in all directions. Gabriel wondered how long it would take for The Face of Fear to completely consume its own temple.

'I remember you!' Gabriel thought to himself. This was The Shadow that possessed Leftenant Vrána—and ultimately killed Julian!

A trembling vibration coursed through the vast emptiness of the antechamber as The Shadow Lord spoke. Each word sounded like a low, rolling thunder.

"We sense that you remember us, Prophet?"

"My grandfather told me about you when I was a child. Du heter Rädsla... You're The Shadow Lord who was once known as Deception, but who became Fear the day you murdered Julian."

"Yes, we were once known as Deception, until your precious Julian twisted our mind around."

'We?' Gabriel thought, 'I knew something else that used plural pronouns and was fascinated with its own power.'

The creature read his thoughts.

"Yes, we." Its voice boomed through the Temple. "We are One of Three. And you have met us in many forms."

The hooded Face of Fear floated away from its antechamber and rushed towards him, its raiment destroying shrapnel and debris in its wake. Only now did Gabriel fathom the enormity of The Shadow Lord. By his estimate, its face alone was the width of the Vimana.

He turned for a moment and felt the power within Rädsla begin to swell and grow.

"Yes, let the fear course through you and destroy your resolve! Run if you'd like, we don't care."

Gabriel turned and found himself quite literally face to face with Fear, which now hovered above him.

A vapor-like cloud emerged from within its cape and Gabriel saw the twisted face of Björn, larger than life. The apparition bore no resemblance to Björn's brilliant Great Bear avatar. It was the undead lich that had taken his life.

Gabriel saw through the illusion and stood tall. The Shadow Lord snarled.

"When we were still Deception we took over the weak human known as Björn. He served us as well as our brother Treachery. With him as our puppet, we nearly destroyed both you and your grandfather. But he tricked us—*betrayed* us," it shrieked in disgust.

Gabriel continued to hold his ground and The Shadow Lord's face morphed into that of The Dream Broker.

"We nearly thwarted you in the Sedona Ruins when we bribed a Grey, whom you call The Dream Broker, to double-cross you. But you wielded a weapon that we haven't seen since The Old World. We were cheated of our victory. But we did get even when we killed your precious Julian, didn't we?" it said.

Gabriel's annoyance turned to anger at the mention of his deceased love again.

Fear's final face, however, chilled Gabriel's blood. It was not a monster, not a denizen from his past, but Gabriel's own likeness.

"Even now, you feel the inevitability of your own failure, you sense your downfall. Don't deny it. You will die alone, on a dead moon in a dead star system, without anyone to mourn or even know about your passing. Your fall will be terrible and grand... and with it, eternal darkness shall cloak the land. Nothingness will finally prevail and our hunger shall finally end."

The Face pushed him into a corner and Gabriel fell backwards. He hit his head on the Temple floor, blacking out for a moment.

The creature laughed and resumed its normal form, as a Shadow cloaked in shadows.

Then, it taunted him, "This is The Great Prophet that has come to undo *us*?"

After the concussive jolt to his system, Gabriel was lost in his thoughts. For a moment, he saw a kernel of truth in Fear's words. He *would* die without having friends or family around him. In fact, everyone he loved had already passed. His grandfather, his best friend and his lover all died to save him. Even Eternal beings like Arundhati and Ceruleus ceased to exist after meeting him. Aurelius itself transformed into a new creature. This was not a coincidence.

Elijah once observed that Akaal always brought Death and Destruction in its wake. Gabriel understood now that he, too, was an agent of change. It was in this moment that Gabriel began to truly understand he *was* The Prophesied One. In this instant, his strength returned and his fear began to dissolve.

The Shadow Lord grew in size and spoke again.

"Join us now, Prophet... or die here, alone."

Gabriel tried to speak, but his throat was dry. He got back up on his feet and looked straight into The Face of Fear.

He closed his eyes and an arc of light formed over his crown chakra. He projected his voice psychically through his third eye and throat chakras, using **STJÄRNLJUS**, the elevated **Divine Tongue**, just as he did when he was a child.

"**I WILL *NEVER* JOIN YOU.**"

Fear did something unexpected... it retreated a few feet in disbelief.

"You ask me to join you so I may become one of your many faces? I think not. Your illusions grow tiresome, Rädsla."

Two red eyes began to glow from within Fear's raiment.

Gabriel realized this was his chance, and somewhere from

within the depths of his belly, he found more bravery and intellect.

"You know, for one of The Seven Shadows, I'm disappointed. Intimidation is one of the weakest weapons," Gabriel said.

"Are *you* calling *us* weak?" it screamed.

The Shadow Lord was now unnerved and Gabriel used this to his advantage.

"I RELEASE YOUR GRIP ON ME, RÄDSLA. I RELEASE YOU FROM MY MIND, FROM MY BODY AND FROM MY SPIRIT. BUT MOST OF ALL, I RELEASE MY FEAR. I'M FREE OF YOU, SHADOW LORD. YOU FEED OFF THOSE AROUND YOU AND I CHOOSE TO STARVE YOU. BE GONE!"

He held up his right hand and channeled light, just as he did in the old cabin.

"Lumini Veritatis!"

The Shadow Lord shrieked and retreated into the back of the antechamber.

Gabriel followed and quickly invoked **STJÄRNLJUS** once more. ***"YOUR WORDS ARE TRANSPARENT, RÄDSLA, WEARER OF FALSE FACES. I SEE THROUGH YOU."*** His words reduced The Shadow Lord into mist.

He'd passed the first test, but Fear was not dead. He heard its screams echoing through the Necropolis as it rejoined its two brothers and reformed Esurus. After the cowardly Shadow retreated, the walls tumbled down in The Great Hall, trapping Gabriel in the small vestibule.

Once he caught his breath, Gabriel scryed the periphery using The Seer's Eye. A monochromatic marble mosaic graced the opposite wall. In the mosaic, a strange astronaut stood before a wishing well. One hand pointed to the stars above, which were falling towards him. Another hand pointed to the well. In the reflective waters Gabriel spied a face that was familiar... his own.

He reached his right hand towards the mosaic and touched it.

His third chakra came to life and he could see brilliant asterisms floating in the air above it, translating to the following message:

HATRED IS A THIRST
THAT CAN NEVER BE KEPT AT BAY,
LOVE IT NOW,
OR FOREVER TRAPPED YOU SHALL STAY.

As he meditated, Gabriel saw the brilliant light currents of The Akashic Sea. He gazed through the waters until two figures began to take shape. From beneath the sea, Gabriel saw both Death and his younger self looking down at him. He was looking through Time... and both his younger and older selves received a symbolic message in a bottle.

Gabriel had come full circle.

Akaal's voice reached through the psychic connection between the past and present and reassured him:

"Remember, never fear the dark, for the dark is afraid of you. Hope will live again, and I will see you soon, brother. Until then, stay strong and remember who you are. Remember..."

Death's voice faded and the room began to shake. Somewhere, deep beneath the The Shadow Moon, Esurus screamed in terror. The terrible sound created a seismic shake within The Temple of Fear, which ultimately destroyed the mosaic. As it crumbled, it revealed a hidden entrance into The Temple of Hate.

At first, Gabriel thought this was too easy. But he realized that, just as The Gatekeeper had warned him, nobody left this moon alive. Each step he took was a step closer to his death. If his fate was sealed, he had nothing to fear, and no one to blame but himself. He breathed slowly and found courage nestled deep within his heart. He moved one foot, then the other. He was on his way to meet his destiny. Finally, he was embracing his duties as The Last Steward of the Light.

42

THE TEMPLE OF HATE

The entrance was far narrower than it looked, so Gabriel exhaled and sucked in his stomach. With a bit of effort, he squeezed through the narrow passageway.

His first step in The Temple was almost his last; the room was narrowly bigger than the dark waters it housed.

Five words were scrawled along the walls in dark asterisms, written by one of The Seven Shadows:

BEWARE THE WELL OF REPUGNANCE.

The execrated liquid within the well appeared as black as oil.

As he gazed into its waters, it reflected painful memories he'd long since buried. He watched as bullies beat him up in the school-yard. Every word stung just as hard now as it did then. He felt the hatred within the children around him... it stung him like a swarm of bees. The Well of Repugnance showed other terrible things that Earthlings did to one another, acts of rape, murder and neglect. He watched as children cried, the homeless starved and his best friend and his lover were murdered long before their time.

Gabriel shed a single tear, not of sadness but compassion. The Well of Repugnance recoiled and seemed to tremble.

"Of all The Shadows, I have the most compassion for you," Gabriel said. "For you've never been shown tenderness, kindness or empathy. Let me be the first to do so."

The water in the rancid well began to retract even more.

"You show me the world through a twisted lens," he continued.

He knelt before the pool and spoke telepathically to the water beneath him.

'I send you love, where you had only emptiness. Feel the light course within me… allow my love to transform your emptiness into light.'

Gabriel placed his hands into the pool and activated his heart chakra. Images of love spread through his heart and his hands. He transmitted memories of Elijah, Akaal and Aurelius, each of whom were equal parts father figure to Gabriel. He shared his first kiss with Julian, the joy he felt when he first met Maddy, how he'd taken time to hug several of the Quaking Aspens near the cabin and how a simple smile could change someone's day.

Upon touching the pool, the water turned from black to liquid light. For a moment, he could feel something he didn't expect from a Shadow—joy and surprise. Then, almost immediately, it revolted and sent an explosion that emptied The Well of Repugnance and caused the turret above to collapse.

In this moment, The Sigil of the Seventh Star began to glow brightly.

As Gabriel held on to the amulet, he sent out a psychic S.O.S. to The Six Stars.

They answered immediately.

The foundation of The Necropolis began to rumble.

Gabriel watched in a combination of horror and wonder as the entire fortress was torn from its foundations, raised into the firmament and subsequently shattered into dust. All that remained of the great Necropolis was a pile of rubble and a large hole about a yard away from him—one that had been hidden from view until now.

A familiar face greeted him as the dust settled. A resplendent arc of golden light surrounded it.

"Aurelius?"

'Yes... and I brought some friends as well. Look up.'

The alien sky was filled with movement. The stars traced their way across the firmament like comets, or perhaps cosmic teardrops, leaving brilliant trails of light in their wake. Something amazing was happening.

'Don't be alarmed, Gabriel,' a familiar voice said psychically. 'This is the celestial host that Aldebaran and Antares are gathering for you. The Sky Guardians are waking up the stars in the neighboring star systems. Too long have they slumbered.'

"Is that you, Ambrose?" Gabriel asked.

'Yes, look up!'

Gabriel squinted his eyes and smiled as a green ball of light streamed across the sky. It was none other than Ambrose, now appearing as a dragon. Elsa sat upon its back, pulling on two silver reigns.

The dragon flew close to Gabriel and Elsa spoke telepathically.

'I know you are afraid, but you mustn't be. I don't know if Akaal told you this, but you are an energy alchemist, Gabriel. Do not run from darkness—expose it and transform it as you did with Hate. In its presence you must shine your inner light. It will either retreat or transform with you.'

Elsa's wide eyes twinkled in the darkness and in their reflection he could see six bright stars behind him.

Gabriel watched in wonder as the six beings joined hands and became light. They rose like the Pleiades into the sky.

'We are all here, waiting for you,' she said. 'This is a task you must face alone. You are stronger than you know—as strong as any

354 | NICHOLAS ASHBAUGH

of us, if not more so. That is why you are The Prophesied One. Surely, you know that by now?'

Before he could reply, The Six Stars were high above, waiting and watching patiently.

Amidst a pile of dust, debris and dirt, Gabriel peered into an enormous hole in the ground. A twisting stairwell descended into the darkness. Like the rest of The City of the Dead, it was created from the remains of something once living—in this case, a spine from the same beast that formed The Towers of Hate and Fear.

A warning was scrawled in blood around the entrance:

DESPAIR IS NEVER-ENDING,
A ROOM WITHOUT LIGHT, A CELL WITHOUT A DOOR;
FEED IT, AND IT ONLY WANTS MORE.
THERE IS ONLY ONE WAY OUT, ONE WAY TO COPE;
BRING FORTH WHAT IT FEARS MOST—
RESTORE HOPE.

As Gabriel took his first step down The Ladder of Despair, his heart sank.

He'd overcome Fear and Hate, but Despair was stronger than its siblings. He found it difficult to move, difficult to breathe. His thoughts became crowded and he questioned the courage that welled within his heart only moments earlier.

Despair was beginning to take residence in his thoughts.

In **Mörkvilja**, The Dark Tongue, it whispered lies into his ears. It spoke in riddles and rhymes.

"You are but a pawn
for those who claim to be of the Light.
There is no difference between The Stars
and The Shadows in the Night.
Your fall will be grand,

and your heart will be mine—
One that I shall slowly devour
until The Stars cease to shine."

Gabriel paused for a moment and conjured up a spell Elijah taught him. He called upon a mighty sword and whispered "Jai Te Gang" aloud.

With one hand on the ladder, he closed his eyes and searched the darkness. In one swift movement, he severed the tongue of Despair and it was silenced.

He called the sword back and absorbed it into his aura, just as his grandfather had taught him.

Gabriel may have appeared to be brave, but his heart was wavering. Tongue or no tongue, Despair's words were poison. He knew it. Despair knew it.

The Shadow silently waited for Gabriel's next move.

He slowly climbed down the ladder, not knowing what awaited him below.

THE LADDER OF DESPAIR

With each step down the ladder, the previous rung broke in two, falling to some unseen depth. This process repeated as he climbed down the twenty-one rungs. If Gabriel had any doubts before about the nature of this journey, they were now laid to rest; there was no turning back.

The surface of the ladder felt cold and clammy. Every cell in his body wanted to let go or get as far away from it as possible. It pulled him into a deep, dark, emotional abyss—as if he was once again in Complete Zero.

Within minutes, Gabriel felt his grip on sanity loosen. The vision of the star-filled sky he'd just witnessed faded like a dream or hallucination. By the twentieth rung, he found himself in complete darkness and sorrow. When he wavered, the last rung broke and he fell into the belly of the beast below.

He heard a crack as The Seer's Eye broke into pieces, blinding Gabriel. Soon, he lost consciousness, as well.

Akaal's familiar voice whispered to him in the darkness.

'Help is coming, little one.'

But it was too late. Gabriel had already blacked out.

THE HALL OF ILLUSIONS

A lthough his body slammed against the floor, Gabriel's mind felt as if it were still free-falling into an endless abyss.

"You're stronger than you think," a familiar voice called into the darkness. It was as warm and rich as Gabriel remembered, but now it had a new resonance—an ageless quality to it.

"Julian? It can't be—"

Gabriel's third eye activated and an etheric light-being materialized in Gabriel's mind. It was composed of trillions of tiny points of light, like a swarm of fireflies moving en masse. Slowly, the light coalesced into something that resembled the silhouette of his deceased lover. The energy was concealed beneath a silver robe.

"Never doubt yourself—or me. I'm a Thought Engineer, after all," the etheric being replied. "*Anything* is possible."

"Julian, what happened? *What* are you?"

"I'm not sure exactly. The last thing I remember was that I was literally inside the mind and essence of Rädsla, The Shadow of Fear. I found a light within the darkness of Rädsla's essence, and that light helped me transcend my own death. *There is still good within The Shadows, Gabriel.* They fear this light, Rädsla more so than the others. As for your question, I think I'm like Rigel—in a state of cosmic chrysalis. But as for what I'll become, your guess is as good as mine."

Julian's light began to fade.

"Know this: it takes great energy for me to be here, so I must be brief. The Watchkeeper was right; this can only end one way. But you can still take Esurus by surprise. Use the essence of both books; then and only then can you succeed.

"One last thing—in this Hall of Illusions, hold fast to this truth: I love you. Our love transcended my death. It will transcend yours as well. I'll see you on the other side."

The points of light that formed Julian slowly faded into the darkness, but Gabriel felt heartened. Indeed, anything was possible.

He sat up and slowly felt his arms and legs to inspect for damage.

The landing was quick but painful. The Virídian spacesuit absorbed most of the impact. He was especially grateful for the carapace, which showed nary a scratch or crack, despite hitting what felt like solid rock. Unfortunately, the helmet itself was damaged in the fall. The breathing apparatus and the sap-lined seal remained intact, but both of the compound eyes shattered. The Seer's Eye also splintered into dozens of shards, rendering him blind in the darkness. Gabriel had only his own intuition to light the path. He pocketed a single shard of Ajna, with the hope he could rekindle its flame if needed.

He waited several moments before moving. With his eyes closed, Gabriel focused on the surrounding contents of the room. Slowly, with great concentration, it came into focus. Like each of the preceding chambers, The Hall of Illusions owed its structure to the petrified remains of some unnamed, Titanic creature; judging from the bowed rib-like columns that held up the cathedral ceilings, Gabriel now stood in the belly of the beast. Despite its grotesque origins, the gilded hall sparkled in his mind's eye as if Midas himself had kissed it. Polished gold leaf lined the interior of the enormous chamber, covering every surface. Golden, bat-winged gargoyles stood watch atop the pillars, each with ruby eyes, like The Gatekeeper. Lastly, and most disturbing to Gabriel, a fresco of The Old World lined the ceiling. In a series of fourteen stations, it detailed The Fall of The Old World, from glorious light to eternal night. The final station, which should rightly show the explosion of dark and light matter that formed The New World, was curiously missing from the fresco, desecrated by myriad claw marks.

The Hall's great splendor was amplified by another ostentatious feature: towering mirrors. The mirrors stood along each of the fourteen pillars, reaching from floor to ceiling. No two mirrors were alike; each bowed inwards, mimicking the curvature of the pillars. This imperfect construction afforded each mirror a unique power of distortion. The subsequent effect was dizzying. The size of the room seemed to shrink, grow or change form depending on the looking glass into which he gazed.

As he walked through the sinister gallery, chills ran down his spine. Gabriel looked into the third mirror on his left and perceived a new structure, one previously invisible: a throne.

Some dark magic had corrupted a majestic Aurelian tree—perhaps the only in existence besides Aurelius itself. Instead of growing right-side up, its golden branches reached down into a dark, tar-covered pit, while its roots twisted and grasped upwards in the shape of a large claw.

Gabriel took a single shard of Ajna and held it towards the throne. Though weakened, it nonetheless glowed softly, reminding Gabriel of the ever-cooling light of Scintillaarė.

In this gentle light, Gabriel could see three pairs of compound eyes, six in all. Had he not known better, he'd assume each was comprised of a perfectly cut ruby. Curiously, they did not reflect any light. Two eyes looked slightly larger than the rest. Their arrangement reminded Gabriel of an arachnid's face. Though it once had three heads and three bodies, everything appeared to be morphing into one terrible *thing* now.

A bat-like creature—the Shadow that called itself Treachery— flew around the head of The Six-Eyed One, guarding its Master.

Esurus sat regally upon its twisted wooden throne. It appeared to have multiple sets of limbs. Only a few were visible, but Gabriel guessed it had at least as many arms and legs as it did eyes, each covered with hexagonal scales, as sharp as knives and as smooth as obsidian. He strained to make out the shape of its body, but soon realized this was futile. Esurus could take on any shape, but it preferred none at all. Like the thirteenth station in the fresco above, Hunger had no form. It was only defined by the light and matter around it—by that which it destroyed. It lacked the imagination or desire to create.

Gabriel had always been able to see auras; most of them resembled one of the colors in the visible spectrum—red, orange, yellow, green, blue, indigo, violet—or pure silver or white, for ascended beings. This creature contained no aura, not even a shadow or grey one. If anything, it seemed to consume all that which surrounded it, light and shadows alike.

"We knooooooow who you are."

At that moment Gabriel felt an ancient connection to the beast before him. This thought was disgusting to him.

"I know you too..." He said involuntarily.

"We've been waaaaaaiting for you for longer than you know, Gaaaabrieeeeeeel."

"You think I'm afraid of you, but you're wrong, Esurus. We're all energy; you're simply polarized."

"We could say the same of you."

"Perhaps you're right, but not for long."

This retort upset the beast.

Esurus spoke in a chorus of three voices. Normally, they

harmonized and sounded melodic, but now the rhythm broke and the individual voices began to stand out. The first voice sounded cunning, the second sweet, and the third sounded reptilian. The latter took particular joy in holding certain vowels in a sort of whispery growl. This creepy effect drove chills down Gabriel's spine.

"We know the sacrifices you made to get here and weeeeee want to help eeeeeeease your pain," the reptilian Third Voice replied.

"I can't imagine how you could do that, Esurus."

At this point The First Voice spoke for The Three. He knew, even before it spoke, that this was The Shadow of Fear.

"Hand *us* *Tenebrae* and *we* will help you!" it said, invoking **Mörkvilja**.

Even as Esurus said this, Gabriel saw a tentacle inching towards the hand in which he held The Cosmic Tome, *Corpus Tenebrae*.

"YOU'VE SLUMBERED TOO LONG IN THE HALL OF ILLUSIONS, WRAITH-LORD... I SEE PAST YOUR THIN VEILS OF DECEPTION AND I DISSOLVE THEM. BEHOLD: THE FLAME OF TRUTH," Gabriel replied, invoking **STJÄRNLJUS**.

He placed *Sidera* in his right hand and it served as a torch in the darkness. The pages burned with the words of each Steward before him.

He then lifted *Tenebrae* in his left hand. The darkness of creation swirled around it in ribbons of black.

Unlike the beast before him, *The Cosmic Tomes* held no power over his mind or heart. He'd transcended past their vibrations.

The crystal upon his neck began to blaze with light, as well.

Esurus retracted its tentacles in fear.

"No huuuuuuman can wield the power of both books!" it shrieked in anger.

"I'm no human; I haven't been since I stepped foot on Aurelian soil. True ascension requires making peace with the darker and lighter parts. I've spent a lifetime doing that. Ironically that's what you fear most, isn't it?"

"YOU'LL DIE!" it screamed, avoiding his question.

"I already have. *So have you.* Death approaches... I can feel it in my bones. It's no worry to me, for we are old friends."

He then added in **STJÄRNLJUS, "HATE, FEAR AND DESPAIR: YOUR DOMINION ENDS... HERE AND NOW. BEHOLD AS I TRANSFORM OUR COMBINED DARKNESS AND LIGHT INTO SOMETHING...** *MORE.***"**

All six of Esurus's eyes grew wide in horror as Gabriel slammed the two books into each other. The last thing Gabriel saw as a human was the look of surprise in Esurus's eyes. After eons of wallowing in fear, pain and selfishness, it couldn't perceive how or why anything, human or not, would sacrifice itself for the good of others.

The creature shrieked in pain as the light from the books illuminated the cavernous expanse of the catacombs. The six eyes evaporated and three separate shadows fled into the cosmos.

Glyphs, images and music from *The Cosmic Tomes* shone brilliantly on the walls, morphing and becoming something altogether new. Shadow and Light became one and were stronger for the union. A new energy emerged that was neither dark nor light— something that was no longer defined by the absence of the other. The words and pages of the two books flew around Gabriel in a vortex. He held his hands up high and the energy traveled through his veins. Gabriel felt every atom in his body tremble and rearrange. The very skin upon his bones burned like fire as light spewed from every pore.

His eyes grew in size, until they were as large and as deep as a galaxy. For a moment, they were.

He inhaled, then exhaled.

Gabriel knew that his life had ended.

THE WEEPING STARS OF AAMĔLLẎNE

D eath appeared exactly as it had years earlier; its pale, luminous body shimmered in and out of focus, casting multicolored shadows in its wake as it moved. Only two details differed from the first time they met. The first was Death's size; it was now larger than a planet, indeed perhaps larger than a star system. Two wings reached high into the heavens, two reached to the ends of the horizon and two reached forward, surrounding Gabriel in radiant purple light.

"So this is how it ends?" Gabriel asked rhetorically.

"In a manner of speaking, yes. It's more of a portal than a full-stop, at least from my perspective."

Gabriel heard the words of the immortal, but they didn't completely compute.

"Have you learned nothing from Akasha? Your present incarnation was but one epoch in the infinite aeon of your being; it was a single facet of your soul. You think of dying as some sort of end. Your physical death is the ultimate Vimana... a vehicle to transport you to the next state of being. As Transformation, I am a catalyst and loving guide, not a reaper."

"I started to die the minute I stepped through the portal, didn't I?"

"We had no way of knowing what effect it would have on you; after all, you were the first of your kind to use it."

"That's a 'yes' in my book. If you knew it was dangerous for a human to use it, why didn't you stop me?"

"It may have been dangerous for humans, but as you declared to Esurus, you were never completely human."

Death pointed to the amulet around Gabriel's neck. As Gabriel glanced down, The Sigil of The Seventh Star now shined brighter than ever—like a mighty spotlight, almost blinding him in the process—revealing a truth that Gabriel intuitively understood all along, but was only now starting to accept.

"You actually started your transformation the very night I met you at age seven, not when you passed through the portal. You see, your battle with Esurus only proved what I always knew in my heart; you contained the essence of our missing brother. You, Gabriel, made the choice to end this life and start the next. Not me. Contrary to common belief, I come only when souls call me.

You called for me from the telescope as a child and I answered. You called out to all Six of us then, and we wept at your loneliness, as we weep now. Can't you feel the truth in my words?"

The being's eyes welled with light and, one by one, beads of pure energy streamed down its face, twinkling as they became stardust.

"If that's true, then I've let you down, as well as the memory of your lost brother. I failed in destroying Esurus."

Death moved towards him, reducing its size so it could look Gabriel straight in the eyes.

"Destruction was never the plan, Gabriel. You most definitely did not fail. If anything, you surpassed our expectations.

Hope is rather contagious—like the source of a river, it starts with a trickle and then, through the force of its own momentum, it gushes downstream. You've planted a seed of change in the belly of the beast, just as you did billions of years ago. In doing so, you've succeeded, where we failed. You brought balance to The Darkness. The war is far from lost; we won the most important battle—one that will have a domino effect that not even the wisest sage could've foreseen.

All I need from you is an answer and your real journey will begin."

The star waited patiently, for the question was already planted in Gabriel's head. It was one his grandfather heard... the one he himself knew as a child. It was the same question he heard when he met each of The Six.

Three words echoed in his mind once more: *'Are you ready?'*

Just like his monumental step through the portal, Gabriel understood there was no turning back. Without the ability to stop it, a single word fell from his lips and sealed his destiny.

"Yes."

"Very well. Take my hand."

Gabriel's head was swimming with questions, yet all fear was gone. Like a reflex that was beyond his control, he reached for the star's hand.

Nothing happened.

"Sorry. I couldn't resist. The touch of Death is not deadly."

Gabriel laughed, first nervously, but then emphatically. He felt the energy change within him from sadness to joy... and then from joy to hope. He realized his last sound as a human would be laughter and laughed again... this was not how he pictured the end of things.

It was in that moment of ease that Death pulled him close and planted a kiss on his lips.

'My kiss, however, that's another thing altogether,' Death said telepathically.

Lightning coursed through his body, followed by thunder the

likes of which he hadn't heard since he was a child in Colorado. A subsequent series of shockwaves blasted through the rocky remains of Mare Esurus as Gabriel transformed from *whatever he was* into *whatever he was meant to be.*

As Death stepped back, the physical vessel that was Gabriel ceased to exist. His light, his consciousness and his life force compressed into a point so small that it was beyond comprehension or measurement. For a moment—a fraction of a fraction of a second —Gabriel felt as if he may be crushed under the realization of his true identity as The Seventh Star.

The exact opposite happened. As his memories returned, Gabriel's life force sprang forth, euphorically filling the sky with more light than a trillion, trillion Earth Suns.

In the surge of light, everything within the Aaměllÿne Galaxy was transformed; billions of dying stars went supernova and new stars sprang forth. During the shockwaves, Death appeared briefly as the archetypal skeleton Gabriel had seen in countless books and movies. By the time the blasts faded, it had transformed into a bodiless, resplendent star—so beautiful, in fact, that Gabriel felt small in its presence.

He now understood why Death preferred the moniker Transformation. He also understood that he shared much in common with Transformation. Hope was merely another agent of change... a different way to spark metamorphosis.

Gabriel felt as if he was falling through the sky, but his body stood still; his soul was no longer tethered to time or space. As he got his bearings, he realized he was no longer alone.

The Six Stars—Transformation, Mercy, Uri, Aurelius, Metatron and Iophiel—now took on the appearance of their highest ascended frequency, which was light. Each stood in a formation, which, if the points were connected, formed the six-pointed sigil of their family. Gabriel now stood in the center instead of Transformation, assuming his new role as Sovereign of The Seven.

Ambrose and Elsa appeared in their corporal forms outside the formation.

First, Ambrose projected himself behind Gabriel. He lovingly placed a robe around Gabriel and spoke.

"This is a gift from Rigel; it's fashioned from the stellar debris left behind during its supernova. It grants you the ability to walk between dimensions."

Gabriel looked down at the flowing robe. It was light as a feather and rendered his body translucent. He realized now that his thoughts could transport him anywhere in the Known and Unknown Universe.

Ambrose bowed and resumed his station outside The Seven Stars.

Elsa astrally projected herself in front of Gabriel. She kissed him on the forehead and placed an etheric seven-pointed crown on his head.

"I gift you the Crown of Iset."

The crown fused with his seventh chakra and seven spikes of light rose from his head into the cosmos. Much like Transformation's aspect Shiva, Gabriel's third eye also began to burn with the intensity of a distant star. He could now see across time and space.

As Elsa lovingly straightened a few unruly tresses of hair, Gabriel was inexorably drawn into her eyes; they were larger and more reflective than he recalled. Gone were the galaxies of stars in their pupils; in their place he saw mirrors upon mirrors, all reflecting aspects of who he had been, who he was now, and even a few glimpses of what he might become. Unlike The Great Hall of Illusions, these mirrors showed truth.

"See yourself now as I do, as I always have."

Elsa reflected back something that wasn't entirely human—or, perhaps more accurately, a being that was *much more than* human.

Gabriel recognized the general shape of his face and body, but he quickly realized all corporal matter, namely flesh and bones, were obliterated during his ascension. All that remained was pure, malleable energy... Elijah would have called it *thoughtmatter;* something that existed merely because he believed it existed. In this ascended form, Gabriel's eyes were comprised of pure starlight that shifted between shades of sea foam green and turquoise. Jets of blue-white light exploded from his shoulders, reaching outward like beads of energy from the Sun's corona. Slowly, they coalesced and formed three sets of enormous wings, reaching taller than Yggdrasil. The stellar remnant that once hung around his neck had now symbiotically fused with his heart chakra and pulsed with blue-green light.

Elsa pulled her projection back into her body and Transformation spoke to Gabriel.

"I once told you that we were old friends, but you know now that this was a half-truth... I followed light from distant quasars and listened to the dying gasps of white dwarves at the edge of the Universe... all in the hopes of finding your whereabouts.

"When I first set eyes on you, I recognized a spark of something I'd lost—and for the first time, Hope entered my heart again.

"Today, Hope is restored, not only for The Luminous Ones, but for all The Children of the Stars.

"Look up."

Artifacts from the *Tenebrae* and *Sidera* orbited around his head, like a halo. Each page glowed with light.

"Now, reach out your hands and allow the pieces to fall as they may."

The contents fell one by one into his open hands, until they were whole again. At this moment, a forgotten truth existed—one that could not be bound by paper, ink or stardust. The volume, like The Akashic Sea, was more than a mere object or container; it was a space, as well... a space anyone could access through an open mind and open heart.

"The combined essences of Light and Dark have forged a

balance in the pages of this volume, one that is bound to you. Contained within the tome are the secrets of The Fifth Dimension— one that transcends polarity, where Stars and Shadows walk as one. This is our future, Gabriel—in a world where dreams, time and space converge—it is here where we can turn the tide.

"Read the title aloud, for it's also your new name and aspect."

Though his memory was still returning, Gabriel was now able to discern the symbols: SAMANVAYA.

Gabriel translated the name into Common Tongue.

"Harmony."

As he uttered the word he could feel the cosmic dust around him coalesce. The word echoed until it ignited a newborn star out of the ruins of the Scintillaarė system.

"Thoughts are power. Words are manifestations of that power..."

"...And the rest is magic, I suppose?" Gabriel said with a smirk.

It was at this point that Gabriel truly understood that his old consciousness was merely a single expression of his whole. He simultaneously embodied Hope, The Lost Star; Gabriel, the ascended light being; and the newly christened cosmic aspect named Harmony. As the latter, with a marriage of divergent elements in one being, Gabriel accomplished something that neither Shadows nor Stars had been able to do in The New World. He was indeed Harmony personified. But the transformation was not complete; he still had to face his Twin Flame.

Gabriel looked at the newborn star and then spoke to his family.

"We've been chasing Mercury."

'**How so?**' Aurelius asked.

Gabriel looked at the tree and smiled.

"We've spent our lifetimes dashing in pursuit of shadows of our former selves. I'm reminded of the god Mercury, whose speed none could match. For billions of years we've futilely chased after a mercurial vapor trail that was of our own making. We're chasing ourselves, don't you see? We have to stop running."

Gabriel's third eye turned towards The Darkheart Star System and the sky rumbled.

"The Shadows will come to us this time, but we have much work to do. They know our collective potential and will not be fooled twice. I feel a new schism forming as we speak."

"Yes, Despair is gone. But something worse replaced it," Transformation declared.

'Aye. It is *evolving* to counter Harmony,' Aurelius said solemnly.

"And like both myself and Transformation, it is an agent of change. My destiny is to join with it... I see that now."

The sky rumbled as billions of ancient stars went black.

"Chaos is born," Gabriel proclaimed with a sigh.

Following his proclamation, The Darkheart Star System disappeared forever, consumed by the newly transformed Shadow.

"And so the next phase of our journey begins—a time when each of us must meet our Shadow pair and become a combined essence of higher and lower frequencies. And more importantly, a time where we must awaken the Light within all The Children of the Stars."

"Are there alternatives?" Metatron asked.

Iophiel, who'd been quiet previously, now stirred.

"No alternative exists. Esurus has disbanded, but, if we do not act, The Seven Shadows will coalesce until they form a singular entity—The Great Devourer. We must stop the war once and for all by balancing out our binary pairs before they join again."

Iophiel transformed into The Wheel and then spoke again after a brief pause.

"I've gazed into the future. As immortals, we can fight this war forever... and most likely will. It is our Children, however, that can and *will* turn the tide."

She then shifted into her stellar aspect.

Gabriel closed all three of his glowing eyes and replied, "Although my memories are just now returning, I see the truth in your thoughts, sister. We need to rally support among all The Children of the Stars, from all the worlds, and work together. Our essence is no longer contained wholly in our aspects. If our ashes created this world, then we must work with our children to help them ascend and meet the challenge ahead. They are part of us, after all."

Gabriel's third eye opened wide and its resplendence eclipsed his avatar for a moment. When it faded, Gabriel had fully transformed into The Seventh Star, Harmony.

The Sigil of The Seven was now incarnate.

The Seven Stars, along with their consorts Elsa and Ambrose, rose into the gas clouds surrounding the newly formed Hope Nebula and watched as stars sprang into existence around them.

'**Where to?**' Aurelius asked.

The newborn Sovereign replied, "To Bisaj Bakool, the last unsullied world. There we will take counsel with Aldebaran, Antares and Rigel to survey the army they've assembled."

Gabriel embraced his new and old aspects; he was Hope and Harmony. He was the Prophesied Starchild, an Earthling who learned how to face and liberate the Shadows of Fear, Hate and Despair from his own life, and ultimately the Universe, as well.

If thoughts were power, then he couldn't wait to expand his horizons, to dream the unthinkable, for the only borders that existed were the limits of his imagination.

Death was only the beginning.

He closed his eyes and drank in his first real breath as an immortal.

The Universe came rushing in.

PART VI

APPENDIX A: GLOSSARY OF NOTEWORTHY LIFEFORMS, LOCATIONS AND TECHNOLOGY IN THE KNOWN UNIVERSE

A

amĕllÿne's Arrow: This bow-and-arrow shaped constellation was comprised of ten brilliant silver stars. It existed in one of the longest spiral arms of the Aamĕllÿne Galaxy and was often used as a marker during interstellar navigation.

Aamĕllÿne Galaxy (a.k.a. The Dancing Sea of Light, The Dragonfly Galaxy, or simply Dragonfly): The galaxy in which the Scintillaarė, Darkheart and Bisaj Bakool Star Systems existed. It was one of the oldest galaxies in all of the Known Universe.

Alchemic etymology of the compound word Aamĕllÿne:
The vowel **Aa** was derived from the sacred phrase **Aa-tǽl**, which meant *to spark* or *kindle*. It was the first word uttered by Astralis during the creation of The Old World.

- **Aa:** To radiate, glow or emblazon.
- **Mĕll:** The root of a verb mĕllÿr, which meant "to move or to dance freely."
- **Ẏnē:** In sky-based dimensions, ÿnē was used to describe orbs of light or collections of clouds, but in aqueous worlds like Ceruleus, ÿnē also referred to bodies of water.

Adŭro, The Machine World: Prior to its fall—and eventual transformation into The Ghost Moon, Vōr—the fourth moon of Aurelius was known as Adŭro. In the *Alchemic Aamĕllÿne Tongue*, its name translated to "jewel." Not surprisingly, The Machine World was unparalleled in its beauty, technology and architectural splendor. It was universally regarded as the "glittering gem" of The Scintillaarė Star System. • **See also:** *Vōr* and *The Ghost Moon.*

Agents & Agencies: After The Great Wars, the State erected six peacekeeping agencies, with eight types of highly trained (and feared) Agents. See below for the breakdown and class descriptions.

THE STATE OMNIPARTY AGENCY BREAKDOWN					
Agency Name	Common Tongue	Jargon Tetragram	Agent Type(s)	Function	Language Variant
State Center for Remote Investigations	The Center	SCRI	M-Agent (Jacks) and AI Sentients*	Intel	Common Tongue
The Bureau of Propaganda	The Bureau	TRUE	Propagators	Press	Protocol and Cleric
Central Hospital for Citizen Wellbeing / Sanctuary	Sanctuary, Central Hospital	SANC	Medics (Wolves)	Corrections	All: Cleric, Protocol, and Common Tongue
The Corps of Peace Enforcement	The Corps	PAXX	Enforcers, The Praetorian Guard and AI Alphas	Peacekeeping	Common Tongue
The Eradication Division	The Division	NULL	Erasers and AI Mercenaries**	PR/Damage Control	Common Tongue
OMNI Committee for Obedience	OMNI	OMNI	The Eye	Internal Affairs	Unknown

*Sentients (AIs) functioned as Agents but were denied the title. See #8 below for more details.

**Mercenaries (AIs) were not officially acknowledged by the State, but they existed as henchman who would work to make things go away.

Note: Beta Synthetics were manufactured by the State but not employed in any official function. Instead, they were assigned tasks as "worker bees" to fill jobs that humans did not want.

Alphabetical listing of the eight types of Agents:

- **Enforcers:** Human cyborgs tasked with locating and impounding unlicensed Synthetics. Enforcers were androgynous and outfitted with extensive implant technology to "sniff out plastic." Ironically, most of them ended up nearly as plastic and mechanized as the androids they so rigorously pursued.
- **Erasers:** State Agents responsible for making people, facts and crimes disappear. • **See also:** *Deletion.*

- The **Eye:** The title was singular and assigned to a very elusive—possibly even extra-terrestrial—agent known as Prime Investigator Oculum. Although The Eye's official function was "internal affairs," it would be more accurate to call The Eye a spy. Oculum conducted unannounced psychic "sweeps" to monitor any behavior that deviated from what the State desired, irrespective of whether any laws or regulations had been broken. • **See also:** *OMNI Committee of Obedience* and *Oculum.*
- **M-Class Psychic:** Under the historic State Directive Treble-Five-Delta, every metaphysically gifted human being (read: psychic) was subjected to mandatory testing, microchipping (via implants) and was subsequently drafted into State employment. Their abilities were placed on a scale of M-1 through M-8. See below.

The M-Class Ratings, from M-1 through M-8:
   The numerical value after the letter "M" prefix indicated the number of skills an Agent had in their arsenal. An M-3, for instance, would have at least three metaphysical skills, such as clairvoyance, clairaudience and, perhaps, telekinesis. Some agents never achieved M-8 status, instead choosing to focus on one skill. Others, like Gabriel, actually exhibited skills far beyond the State system of classification.

M-8s (a.k.a. Metas, Remote Agents, Remotes or Jacks): These Agents mastered all eight basic levels of psychic abilities, including:

1. Psychometry—reading information from objects.
2. Telepathy—reading and broadcasting thoughts.

3. **Telekinesis**—manipulating objects with thought alone.
4. **Clairvoyance**—seeing the past, present and future.
5. **Clairsentience**—often called empathy. The ability to feel and know others' emotions, pain and physical or emotional feelings.
6. **Clairaudience**—the ability to hear spirits.
7. **Clairalience & Clairgustance**—to smell or taste things in a precognitive vision.
8. **Claircognizance**—simply knowing a fact, without having any training or way of knowing something.

Note: Some M-8s, like Gabriel, exceeded these documented abilities, and could manipulate EMF, space or even time around them.
On the street, the public used a derogatory term *"Jack"* to refer to an M-8, shortened from the portmanteau Mindjacker.
The term also could be used as a verb: *The M-8 jacked the info from his subconscious.*
Remote was a term used internally *(e.g., SCRI threw a Remote on the case).*

- **Medics (a.k.a. Wolves):** State interrogators who worked at Sanctuaries like The Hospital for Citizen Wellbeing. Their purpose was, quite simply, to hunt or recruit for the State.
- **Praetorians:** An elite squad of powerful psychics capable of brute force and object manipulation through the use of telekinesis. They used no weapon, save the

power of their minds. As such, Praetorians were feared by all intelligent forms of life, organic and otherwise.

- **Propagators:** State "reporters" responsible for spreading propaganda. Other agents jokingly referred to their activity as "cooking," since the truth was often obscured or missing altogether.
- **Artificial Intelligence (AIs):** Although sentient programs and androids were myriad, only two classes of AI were cleared to work for the State: (1) armored Alphas that kept the peace and (2) the bodiless Sentients, who projected their holographic likenesses with the help of Oubliettes. Dangerous Mercenary-class Aphelion 600s served as henchmen, but their existence was systematically denied by the State. Humanoid Beta Synthetics were mostly assigned manual labor jobs. • **See also:** *Alphas, Aphelion 600s, Beta Synthetics, Drones, Oubliette* and *Sentients.*

Note: Although AIs were crafted by humankind, and many of them served in an official State function, they were universally denied the official title "Agent." The State's reasoning was one of caution; the AI allegiance was a tentative one, and the State viewed their involvement with a skeptical eye.

Ajna (a.k.a. The Seer's Eye): A round stone bauble infused with mystical, protective and clairvoyant properties. It was once the third eye of Arundhati, The Stone Colossus who guarded Augur's Peak on the Aurelian moon Virídia. • **See also:** *Arundhati* and *The Moons of Aurelius.*

Akaal (a.k.a. The First Star, Death, Transformation, Zerachiel, Janus, The One that Stands at the Nexus of Ends and

Beginnings): The oldest (and truest) name of The First Star, Transformation. When repeated in mantras or put to music, the word "Akaal" contained great power for healing and spiritual ascension. • **For full description, see:** *The Seven Stars* > *The First Star* • **See also:** *Death, Transformation* and *Zerachiel*.

Akasha (a.k.a. **Aeon, Time, The Akashic Sea, The Sea of Time, The Sands of Time, The Great Record-Keeper and Seer of All Things):** Akasha functioned as the fabric which held together all events past, present and future. Although Akaal affectionately called it "sister," Akasha was a genderless time-space entity with infinite reach, knowledge and size. It usually expressed itself as a boundless sea when communicating with Immortals and Eternals. The Sea of Time functioned as a mirror or lens through which all things past, present and future could be seen. Akasha sometimes appeared as an endless desert, through which each grain of sand represented a moment (or memory) in time. Though it rarely assumed corporal form, Akasha could appear as three sisters, representing past, present and future. It was one of three known Eternals. • **See also:** *Eternals*.

Alchemic Aamĕllÿne Tongue **(a.k.a. High Aamĕllÿne):** In this ancient, magical language, words were power. Each syllable, each vibration could alter the fabric of space and time. Aurelius was one of the few immortals who dared to yield its power, and the consequences were life-altering. • **See also:** *Alchemic Aamĕllÿne Tongue: Vowel Sounds and Pronunciation*.

Aldebaran, The Sky Guardian: A brave and intelligent warrior, Aldebaran was a member of an elite regiment known as Himlens Väktare, The Sky Guardians. Together with Rigel, this immortal guarded the ancient weapon, Tidens Svärd. **See also:** *Himlens Väktare, Rigel*, and *Tidens Svärd*.

Alpha Series Androids (a.k.a. **Alphas, Drones and X-Series):** Commonly called Alphas or, more colloquially, Drones, these metallic armored androids were developed by the State and manufactured by SULACO Robotics. Replacement parts continued to be widely manufactured several millennia after the Alphas were originally created. Despite their age, Alphas remained the primary means by which the State maintained peace, a role attributed to their nearly indestructible nature. The X-Series were the most plentiful and the most heavily armored of the Alpha Drones.

Differences between Alphas and Beta Synthetics:

- **Skin**—Alphas were completely metallic and nearly indestructible, whereas Beta Synthetics were more prone to overheating, melting and malfunctioning—due in part to their heavy silicone and plastic outer skin.
- **Intelligence**—Alphas were self-aware, but did not have the IQ inherent to Beta Synthetics. Also, the archaic Alpha programming omitted emotions and placed an emphasis on cunning and obedience.
- **Weapons**—Only Alphas were armored; after the complete failure of the Aphelion 600s, Beta Synthetics were designed to be pacifists. Some of the Alpha Series standard weapons included a short-range blast gun, dangerous ocular lasers and an electrically charged chassis.
- **See also:** *Beta Synthetics, Aphelion 600 Series* and *Genesis 700 Series.*

The **Altar of Creation:** Part of the SULACO R/S/T Quadrangle. It housed secretive R&D efforts, as well as all robotic operations and production. • **See also:** *SULACO.*

Amaranth: The home world or dimension of The Eternals.

Amaranthine **(a.k.a. The Language of Creation):** The musical, native language of The Fourteen Stars, passed on to them by Astralis, the Light-Bringer. Much like their musical thoughts, the language was melodic and magical. The *Amaranthine* alphabet was equally majestic; the highly glyph-like letters were derived from ancient constellations (asterisms) from Amaranth, the home of The Eternals. Much like the *Alchemic Aamĕllÿne Tongue* that Aurelius spoke, a single word could create, destroy or alter reality.

Ambrose (a.k.a. Amrik, The One Who Walked as Fire and Ice, The Emerald Dragon and Thor): In The Old World, Ambrose —then known by its female aspect, Amrik—expressed itself as a bright icy comet, orbiting around many of The Seven as a courier and messenger. It was the last being to be consumed by The Great Devourer. When The New World formed, the comet was reborn as Ambrose, a fiery being capable of igniting hope and courage in the hearts of the living. Some perceived it as a dragon, while the more spiritually attuned realized it was something far older and more regal, often attributing it God-like status, particularly in Nordic cultures. Like all Immortals and Ancients, it had the ability to appear as any gender. In The New World, it mostly appeared as a humanoid male.

Ancients: A catch-all phrase that included any Immortal that wasn't one of The Firstborn. • **See also:** *Eternals, Firstborn* and *Immortals.*

Antares: A mighty warrior and one-time wielder of Tidens Svärd, The Sword of Time. • **See also:** *Himlens Väktare.*

Aphelion 600 Series - **(a.k.a. Aphelion 600s, Aphelions, A600, 600s, Beta Aphelions, Six Hundreds, Series 600, 6x, A6 Series and Mercenaries):** Unlike the partially organic Genesis series, the Aphelions were primarily silicon and metal androids. Although they provided a major improvement over the Alphas and the archaic Series 100-500 Beta Synthetics, the Aphelions were far from perfect. On a purely visual level, their crude plastic skin and unnerving eyes made them unsettling to look at. It was their erratic AI, however, that led to a full recall. A fatal programming flaw rendered the entire series devoid of morality. Years after a full recall, several 600s unofficially resurfaced in a Mercenary capacity, carrying out the State's dirty work. • **See also:** *Agents & Agencies > Artificial Intelligence (AIs).*

Arundhati (a.k.a. **The Colossus, The Colossus at Mount Augur, Augur, The Morning Star, The Oracle, The Seer, The Eye of the Storm, The Gloaming, The Sorceress and The Witch**): One of The Three Guardians of Aurelius, Arundhati lost her true form in The Aurelian Shadow Wars. She was transformed into a mighty Colossus atop the highest point of Virídia. In her uncorrupted form, her beauty was unparalleled and her clairvoyance was comparable with that of Iophiel or Akasha; as Augur, her vision was greatly diminished.

The **Assembly of Stars:** The formal name for the fellowship that guided Gabriel in his journey. The Assembly comprised The First, Second, Third, Fourth, Fifth and Six Stars. Additional members included Julian, the enigmatic Rigel (of the Himlens Väktare) and the Ancients Elsa, Ambrose, Arundhati and Ceruleus.

Astralis, the Light-Bringer (a.k.a. **The First Steward of the Light**): One of the three known Eternals. True to its title, it was the bringer of all light, energy and creation in the Known Universe. Additionally, it forged the volume known as *Corpus Sidera* and was therefore known as The First Steward of the Light. • **See also:** *Eternals.*

Augur (a.k.a. **The Eye of the Storm, The Seer, The Stone Oracle, The Gloaming**): A lesser avatar of Arundhati, infamous for placing Virídia under an endless spell which manifested itself as a storm called The Gloaming. • **For full description, see:** *Arundhati.*

Aurelius: The name Aurelius could be applied to both The Sixth Star and also the planet on which it lived. The epithet "Planet" was typically used to disambiguate. See below for information on both meanings.

1. **Aurelius, the Firstborn (a.k.a. Aurelius, The Golden One, Guardian of the Three Moons, Tempest, Storm-Bringer, Kāmadeva, Love, The Last Guardian of the Portal, The Sixth Star and Kairos Aurelius):** Its name translated to The Golden One. As one of The Seven Stars, its known avatars included a star, a dragon, a guardian tree, and a humanoid-tree hybrid that used telepathy for communication. Aurelius's powers included shapeshifting, telekinesis, telepathy and atmospheric manipulation, among other things. Its ability to conjure storms at whim—often out of anger—resulted in the nickname Tempest, in some star systems. • **For full description, see:** *The Seven Stars > The Sixth Star.*

2. **Planet Aurelius:** The last remaining rocky planet in The Scintillaarė Star System. It was once covered with brilliant, sentient trees that illuminated its surface with treelight that rivaled its own star. Unfortunately, during The Thousand-Year Night, this radiant forest was destroyed by The Shadows, transforming the planet into a barren ice world, buried in massive, shifting snow dunes. Only one lifeform, an immortal guardian remained. It stood guard beneath the portal, awaiting The Prophesied One. • **See also:** *The Aurelian Shadow Wars* and *The Thousand Year Night.*

The **Aurelian Shadow Wars:** A two-thousand-year battle with The Shadows that started with the premature death of Scintillaarė and the subsequent "Thousand-Year Night," during which all life was extinguished on Planet Aurelius. The most notable battles during The Great War included: The Sundering of Ceruleus, The Destruction of Imogen, The Fall of The Machine Gods and The Gloaming of Virídia.

Avatar (a.k.a. Aspect): In short, an expression or projection of an Immortal soul—often into the form of a body or other physical matter so it could walk in the Known Universe and communicate with sentient mortal life. All Immortal beings had the capacity to project themselves in a body of their own choosing. "Death" to immortals was a temporary thing. They would soon emerge in a new avatar. Unlike reincarnation, their memories remained intact. The creation of the new aspect did not necessarily destroy the old one, unless the immortal chose to shed its old identity. Some immortals could switch between multiple avatars if it served their function—particularly Transformation.

Beta Aphelion Series • See *Aphelion 600 Series.*
Beta Genesis Series • See *Genesis 700 Series.*
Beta Synthetics (a.k.a. simply as **Betas or Synthetics):** Second-generation SULACO androids which included the Aphelion 600 and Genesis 700 models, respectively. Unlike their Alpha counterparts, Betas were capable of "simple, human-like emotions" and significantly more complicated thoughts than Alphas, due to their crystal-based CPU. • **See also:** *Alpha Series Androids, Beta Synthetics, Aphelion 600 Series, Genesis 700 Series* and *SULACO.*

Bisaj Bakool (a.k.a. The Lotus Petal Nebula and The Last Unsullied World): A colorful and gaseous constellation that resided in one of the great spiral arms of The Aamĕllÿne Galaxy. The polychromatic nebula was burgeoning with baby stars and contained something within it capable of holding back The Shadows.

Brahmāstra: A psychic doomsday weapon that was responsible for the desecration of Adŭro. It transformed the once-burgeoning Machine World into the lifeless shell known as Vōr, The Shadow Moon. • **See also:** *Vōr* and *The Shadow Moon.*

The **Bureau of Propaganda:** A State-run broadcast facility that managed all forms of official State communication. Its Agents were called Propagators. They altered (or "cooked") information to suit the State's needs. Following its establishment, other forms of reporting were deemed unpatriotic and were removed. • **For full description, see:** *Agents > Propagators.* • **See also:** *Agents & Agencies.*

C azador: A powerful "hunter-seeker" cyborg that specialized in reconnaissance, molecular manipulation and teleportation. Cazador was stationed at Central Hospital, but it also worked in the field to track down metacriminals. Its teleportation and telekinesis skills were unmatched by any Agent. • See also: *Agents & Agencies* and *Central Hospital for Citizen Wellbeing.*

Central Hospital for Citizen Wellbeing (a.k.a. Central Hospital, The Loup and Monocle, SANCTUM CIVITAS and Sanctuary): Outwardly branded as a Central Hospital for Citizen Wellbeing, this "Sanctuary" was widely regarded to be a prison by any "patient." In addition to being nearly impossible to escape, the facility was rumored to have the capability to wipe memories and recondition (brainwash) citizens. Its Medics (a.k.a. Wolves) hunted, detained, intimidated and interrogated so-called criminals. The secondary (and perhaps most important) purpose was to recruit future Enforcers, Erasers, M-Class Psychics, Propagators and Medics. Central Hospital contained two notable structures: (1) **The Monocle**, a dome-shaped entrance and (2) **The Loup**, an inescapable subterranean maze.

Ceruleus: This name may refer to either the Titan Ceruleus or the moon on which it resided. See below.

- **The Great Titan, Ceruleus (a.k.a. The Ancient, The Guardian, The Sacred Heart):** A benevolent immortal that held the key to defeating Esurus. Its natural form was serpentine. During The Thousand-Year Night, its body was sundered by Shadows and strewn across the glaciers of Ceruleus. Though the rest of the Titan, namely The Great Face, was frozen solid in stasis, The

Sacred Heart of Ceruleus survived the Sundering. Ceruleus was rumored to be the progenitor of the entire Titan (and possibly dragon) race.

- **The Ice Moon, Ceruleus:** Once a water world of sparkling seas, the moon evolved into a frozen wasteland that entombed its namesake, an ancient Titan and guardian. The epithet and sometimes standalone name, "Ice Moon," was often used to differentiate it from the Titan.

Chief Engineer Yantra: During his life, Yantra was a brilliant State scientist in charge of innovation at SULACO. He was credited with inventing the Alpha and Beta Synthetic lines, as well as creating the Oubliette communication terminal. Genesis was his magnum opus. Prior to his death, the State preserved Yantra's consciousness—against his will—storing it somewhere deep within the confines of The Mystic's Pyramid. • **See also:** *Yantra's Pyramid* and *SULACO*.

The **Children of the Stars:** The Seven Stars used this term to define all sentient life in The New World, since it was created from the ashes of The Firstborn.

The **Collective (a.k.a. The Hive):** An evolved, viral, hive-like intelligence that grew from the seeds of the world's networked computers. The Hive frowned upon individuality. However, several anomalies, so-called "forks" in the digital code, known as Sentients, evolved nonetheless. The vast majority of these Sentients voluntarily split from The Hive and functioned in service roles within the State (proving their allegiance by living within a firewall known as an Oubliette). Others, the true Rogues, owed allegiance to neither The Collective nor the State. • **See also:** *Oubliette*.

The **Colossus at Mount Augur (a.k.a. Augur, Arundhati and The Seer):** An enormous colossus guardian that stands watch atop the tallest point in Virídia. Once an oracle with great vision,

Augur's clairvoyance was later obscured by a great storm on The Alabaster Moon—one of her own making. Known as The Gloaming, the storm was the source of the enchantment for The Sleeping Forests. • **See also:** *Arundhati, Augur* and *The Gloaming.*

Complete Zero • **See:** *The Void.*

The **Conservatory** • **See:** *Youth Conservatory*

The **Corps of Peace Enforcement** (a.k.a. **PAXX and The Corps**): Home of two of the most feared agents—the Enforcers and Praetorian Guard—The Corps' main job was "peacekeeping." It did this with aplomb, and with force, whenever necessary. • **For complete description, see:** *Agents & Agencies.*

Corpus Sidera (a.k.a. *Sidera, The Star Compendium, The Book of Stars* and *The Body of Light*): This book contained sacred knowledge and magic passed on by Astralis, the Light-Bringer. It was protected by a long line of guardians, known as Stewards of the Light. Gabriel and Elijah were the last of this esteemed lineage. Both *Corpus Sidera* and *Corpus Tenebrae* were indestructible. • **See also:** *Corpus Tenebrae, Cosmic Tomes* and *Stewards of the Light.*

Corpus Tenebrae (a.k.a. **The Black Box,** *The Shadow Compendium,* ***The Body of Darkness,*** **Pandora** and *Tenebrae*): Originally written by The Eternal Tenebris, the book was supposed to be a complement to *Sidera,* not its opposite. Esurus, however, corrupted the book's essence during The Thousand-Year Night, after which it became the antithesis to *Sidera.* It quickly grew into something dark, sinister and dangerous. Unlike *Sidera,* this book had no guardians, only servants; any mortal or immortal who touched the book became entranced and subject to its magic. Two known exceptions existed: The Seventh Star and Metatron. No other entity, save Tenebris itself, could touch it unscathed.

The Cosmic Tomes (a.k.a. *The Compendia, The Corpora* and **The Two Books**): The history of The Stars and Shadows were contained in two books, *Corpus Sidera* and *Corpus Tenebrae,* respectively. Together, they were known as *The Cosmic Tomes.*

The **Council of the Four Moons:** A governing body that formed prior to the devastating war known as The Thousand-Year Night. The Council governed Planet Aurelius and its four moons, Ceruleus, Virídia, Adŭro and Imogen. Per its name, it consisted of a representative from each moon prior to their sundering, slumber, corruption and destruction, respectively. • **See also:** *The Moons of Aurelius* and *Thousand-Year Night* and *The Three Guardians of Aurelius.*

Cypher District (formerly: Hollywood): This was a popular meeting place for metacriminals, social outcasts and anyone who sought refuge from the State's prying eyes.

Dark Watch of The Necropolis, The • See: *The Necropolis Shadow Sentinels*

The **Darkheart Star System**: A hydra-shaped constellation that resembled The Void Beast Esurus. It received its nickname because of a supermassive black hole that was slowly consuming the brightest, center-most star of the constellation.

The **Darkness (a.k.a. The Great Devourer):** A collective Shadow entity in The Old World, comprised of all Seven Shadows. It was also known as "The Great Devourer," as its appetite was insatiable.

Death (a.k.a. Transformation, Akaal, Zerachiel, Janus, The First Star, The One that Stands at the Nexus of Ends and Beginnings): Death—or more accurately, Transformation—was an aspect of The First Star, one of The Fourteen original Firstborn. This resplendent being could be in many places at once. • **For complete description, see:** *The Seven Stars > The First Star* • **See also:** *Akaal, Transformation, Zerachiel* and *The Fourteen Stars.*

Deletion: A Bureau term for a State-ordered assassination.

Digital Detective Constables (DDCs): DDCs were bodiless, State-employed Sentients (self-aware AIs) who'd agreed to exist in a secured firewall known as an Oubliette, while also abjuring their ties to The Hive-like program which grew from the ashes of the internet, known as The Collective. Once relegated to Oubliettes, all DDCs were partnered with other Agents, like the powerful M-8s. However, they were not afforded full "Agent" status. Gabriel's partner, Johan, was one of the more notable DDCs. • **See also:** *Agents & Agencies, Oubliette, Sentients,* and *The Collective.*

Digital State Peacekeepers (a.k.a. DSPs): Sentients charged with manning Confessionals. They interfaced with the PAXX database and processed confessions and new crimes. • **See also:** *Agents & Agencies* and *Sentients.*

Directive Treble-Five-Delta (a.k.a. 555-D): Under this monumental State mandate, all metaphysically gifted human beings were tested, tagged and drafted into State employment. Their abilities were rated M-1 through M-8. Those who refused were considered Rogues, and could be taken to Sanctuary. • **See also:** *Agents & Agencies, Rogue* and *Sanctuary.*

Dödshära (a.k.a. The Dead's Keep): One of the two "Weeping Twins," this ossuary was the second-highest peak on Planet Aurelius. It housed the fallen warriors from The Thousand-Year Night. Its sister, Ljushära, or The Light's Keep, was taller and wider. • **See also:** *Tvilling Tårar* for a full description of both.

The **Dragonfly Galaxy:** A Common Tongue name for the distant spiral galaxy named Aamĕllÿne. • **For full description, see:** *Aamĕllÿne.*

The **Dream Broker (a.k.a. The Broker, The Grey, The Grey Soul, and Grå Själar):** While there were many energy alchemists that were capable of manipulating the Sedona vortex energy, The Dream Broker was singular; through some unknown means, he was capable of hacking into the sacred dreamspace of any organic or inorganic being capable of dreaming. Described as one of The Grey Souls, or Grå Själar, he served only his own interests. • **See also:** *Grå Själar.*

Dreamgate: an energetic bridge wherein a physical entity could enter a metaphysical plane, namely a dream. The only being capable of opening a dreamgate on the planet Earth was The Dream Broker. • **See also:** *The Dream Broker.*

E, The: The Trans-Californian Electromagnetic Train—or simply, The E—was an ultra-fast train that stretched the entire distance of the massive California megacity that included all of the coastal cities from San Francisco to San Diego. The latter two cities were absorbed into the Greater L.A. Metropolitan Area.

Eldhjärta (a.k.a. Fireheart): This exotic staff was carved from the core of a dying Amaranthine star by Astralis, the Light-Bringer. Some of Astralis's energy was infused into the device, rendering it absolutely indestructible.

Elsa: This powerful, singular Ancient was created out of the very same luminous material as The Third Star—by the hands of The Third Star itself, no less—making her more powerful than any Moon in The Old or New World. In her first incarnation, Elsa was a silvery metallic moon which had the gift then, as she does now, of reflecting any soul's true self. In her second incarnation, Elsa was often worshipped as a demigoddess or goddess—namely, Artemis. Uri considered her his twin sister, and the two were rarely seen apart. In fact, she often amplified his power.

Enforcer: A highly modified human cyborg tasked with seeking out unlicensed androids. • **For complete description, see:** *Agents & Agencies > Enforcer.*

Erasers • **See:** *Agents & Agencies.*

Esurus (a.k.a. The Ruiner, The Void Beast, The Void Shadow, The Three Shadows, The Hunger, The Great Shadow King, The Three That Became One, The Six Eyes): A six-eyed Shadow beast purported to reside on the dark side of Vōr, The Ghost Moon. Esurus was the amalgam of Hate, Fear and Despair. Its singular goal was to reunite with the other Shadows to reform The Great Devourer (from The Old World) and consume all matter

—dark and light—in the Known Universe. • **See also:** *The Great Devourer*.

Eternals: Those without end or beginning—i.e., Universal constants. Also known as Untouchables or The Infinites, these beings existed before the Known Universe took form, and would exist long after. Old, wise and trans-dimensional, their essence touched all that lived, even more so than the Fourteen. They rarely spoke with immortals and interacted even less frequently with humans or other life forms. Their home world is known as Amaranth, but its location remains a mystery.

- **Akasha (a.k.a. Time)** was the oldest and most well-known Eternal; all things existed within the threads of her consciousness.
- **Astralis, the Light-Bringer** was regarded as the source of all known energy in the Universe. It was also "The First Steward of the Light," the author of *Corpus Sidera*.
- **Tenebris, the Creator**, the namesake for *Corpus Tenebrae*, was the embodiment of darkness, space and possibilities—a complement to Astralis.
- Note: There were many others, but they remained safely anonymous, preferring not to meddle in human affairs.
  • **See also:** *Immortals, Firstborn* and *Ancients*.

F.A.T.E.: State Jargon for **F**acility for **A**dvanced **T**hought **E**xperiments, F.A.T.E. was a privately funded hospital and research facility operated by Julian, one of the only known Thought Engineers. It was located in an annex of Denver's Metropolitan Clinic (The Met) and specialized in helping gifted youth. • **See also:** *Julian* and *Thought Engineer.*

The **Fenestrae Stellarum (a.k.a. The Starry Windows, The Sedona Stargates or simply The Fenestrae):** These three Einstein-Rosen bridges formed from an atom-collider accident. Only the second and third stabilized. **Note on disambiguation:** Terms like wormhole, stargate, gate, bridge, and Einstein-Rosen bridge could be used interchangeably to describe the The Fenestrae Stellarum.

The three stargates included:

1. **Fenestra Primus (The First Window):** The temporary bridge that formed before the second and third bridge. It was unstable and disappeared almost immediately after forming.
2. **Fenestra Sancta Cruce (Window of The Shattered Holy Cross):** This wormhole existed behind the Chapel of the Holy Cross. Like The Tower, The Shattered Holy Cross was a one-way bridge. It provided transit from Earth to another dimension. Several Drones were sent through, but none survived the journey. It was heavily protected by armed Alphas known as the Holy Guard.
3. **Fenestra Turrim (The Tower Window):** This stargate sat on the remains of Cathedral Rock and intermittently phased in and out of view. It appeared to be a one-way

portal to Earth. The Alphas protecting this stargate were known as The Tower Guard.

The **Firstborn** • See: *The Fourteen Stars*

FORTY BELOW: A notoriously dangerous prison cell within the lower levels of Central Hospital.

The **Fourteen Stars (a.k.a. The Fourteen and The Firstborn):** During their earliest days, the mightiest Immortals existed as uncorrupted, radiant beings beyond comprehension. Their closest and crudest approximation in the human mind would be that of a star. These Fourteen Stars seeded The First Known Universe (a.k.a. The Old World) with their essence. During this dance of creation, there came a polarizing moment in The Old World when each of The Fourteen made a conscious choice to follow the Light or Dark, creating two groups: The Seven Stars and The Seven Shadows. Their energy—which was part of an unknown divine source— permeated all living things. Only Eternals were older. • **See also:** *The Seven Stars* and *The Seven Shadows*

Genesis (a.k.a. 712, Genesis Seven-Twelve and Seven-Twelve):** Although there were numerous 700s in production, "Genesis" was the only with anomalous emotional "glitches" and a sense of individuality. Each series (600, 700, etc.) was normally produced in runs of one billion. Genesis was the first successful android in her production run (after eleven failures) and was considered the progenitor of her series. For this reason, the State recalled all Genesis units for research and repro-gramming after Genesis Seven-Twelve malfunctioned. • **See also:** *Alpha Series Androids, Beta Synthetics, Aphelion 600 Series* and *Genesis 700 Series.*

Genesis 700 Series (a.k.a. Genesis units, A7, A700, 700s, Beta Genesis units, Seven Hundreds, Series 700, 7x, A7 Series): Genesis units were a marvel of technology, providing a near-perfect marriage of organic and synthetic matter (namely in having a more natural, albeit still synthetic, skin). The 700s proved to be the most human-like androids SULACO ever produced. • **For information on Genesis Seven-Twelve, a unit that called herself "Genesis,"** see: *Genesis.* • See also: *Alpha Series Androids, Beta Synthetics* and *Aphelion 600 Series.*

The **Ghost Moon:** The third remaining satellite of Planet Aure-lius, its surface lacked an atmosphere. It was also home to The Shadow Beast Esurus. Although a great benevolent machine race once walked its surface, they were wiped out of existence in The Battle of Adŭro. Their melted remains were used to fashion the twisted walls and spires of the dark Necropolis.

The **Gloaming (a.k.a. The Twilight of the Trees):** The name of a spell whose shadow magic put the forests on Virídia into an endless slumber. In latter days, The Gloaming was synonymous with the sorceress Arundhati as she became consumed with the dark spell, as well—becoming the personification of its essence. It was this spell, coupled with the radiant light from the trees themselves, that produced the alabaster appearance of Virídia from afar.

Grå Själar (a.k.a. Grey Souls): Elijah described extremely intelligent and egocentric entities as **Grå Själar**. These beings owed allegiance to no one but themselves and were perhaps the most dangerous form of life in the Known Universe, since they would double-cross anyone. • **See also:** *The Dream Broker.*

Gråvarg (a.k.a. The Deputy and The Grey Wolf or Greywolf): An independent State operative known only as Greywolf, or Gråvarg, in his native tongue. Though formally part of The Division of Eradication, he was a double, or possibly triple agent. This high-ranking Deputy oversaw all Medics within Central Hospital. His exact function within the State remained intentionally obfuscated. By his own admission, he owed allegiance to no one.

The Great Devourer: A great singularity comprised of all Seven Shadows. • **See also:** *The Darkness.*

Grey • **See:** *Grå Själar.*

Greywolf (a.k.a. The Grey Wolf) • **See:** *Gråvarg.*

Gudsrösten (a.k.a. God's Voice, The Gods' Voice and The Divine Tongue): When one employed this technique of communication, it was as if God itself were speaking through the mortal or immortal instrument. It took great skill and power. It could either motivate or dominate weaker minds. Note: when written in Common Tongue, **Gudsrösten** is always written in bold text, without any underlining.

- **Mörkvilja** (The Dark Tongue) was the lesser form of The Divine Tongue. It allowed for complete domination and manipulation of a weaker mind. Note: when written in Common Tongue, it was denoted by **bold, underlined lower-case letters.**
- **STJÄRNLJUS** (Light of the Stars/Starlight) was the

most elevated form. It was invoked for peaceful means, such as mediations, benedictions or de-escalating altercations. As a result of its magnanimous energy, **STJÄRNLJUS** always defeated **Mörkvilja** and cancelled its effect. Note: when written in Common Tongue, it was denoted by **BOLD, UNDERLINED CAPITAL LETTERS.**

H **-V:** Short for Holo-Vox, a hologram and voice communication device used for two-way video chats. Terminal, mobile and wrist versions existed. Although H-Vs replaced V-Terminals for most applications, the V-Terminals existed in security panels, some older offices and for nostalgic or personal preference.

Himlens Väktare (a.k.a. The Sky Guardians and Heaven's Guard): Aldebaran, Antares and Rigel served as the highest ranking generals and guardians in the Known Universe, fighting on the side of The Seven Stars. They alone guarded Tidens Svärd (The Sword of Time) until it was passed along to Elijah. • **See also:** Tidens Svärd

***Himmel Sköld* (a.k.a. The Sky Shield):** A hooded raiment hand-crafted by Rigel after its own supernova. The raiment's exotic composition exuded some sort of protective electromagnetic field.

The Hope's Pass Way Station: An outpost within The Red Gate that controlled all ingoing and outgoing traffic into The Ruins of Sedona. • **See also:** *Ruins of Sedona* and *The Red Gate.*

Hovervehicles, including Hovercabs and Hovercars (a.k.a. Hovers): All hovervehicles utilized a hybrid engine capable of terrestrial and airborne movement. The term "hovercab" referred exclusively to public transportation. "Hover" or "hovercar" could be used for any private vehicle that utilizes the same technology.

I **mmortals:** Simply put, those with a fixed beginning, but no conceivable end, unless self-imposed. Though they were incapable of death, they regularly made use of metamorphosis, and each had at least one alternate aspect or avatar. Throughout their existence, many immortals existed as stars, moons, dragons or even singularities, in the case of Shadows. Only The Eternals had lived longer. Among the immortals, there existed two classes: The Firstborn—The Fourteen original stars, and Ancients—all those who came after. • **See also:** *Ancients, Avatar, Eternals* and *The Firstborn.*

Imogen: (a.k.a. The Lost Moon of Aurelius and The Rings of Imogen): This satellite fell during The Thousand-Year Night when Scintillaarė expanded into a Red Giant. Its destruction was not absolute; its debris resulted in a beautiful ring system around Planet Aurelius.

Jargon: The language (visually) resembled Braille; its alphabet, numbers and symbols were mapped to a fixed grid and were represented by dots that were either turned on or off—essentially a compressed form of binary code. Although confusing to someone unfamiliar with the symbols, humans, Sentients and all SULACO-branded robotic machines learned Jargon as a second language. Whenever possible, the language made use of Tetragrams (four-letter combinations). The nefarious goal of Jargon was to "compress" thoughts, as well—in effect, to reduce the intelligence of the masses.

Julian (a.k.a. Friend of The Luminous Ones and Ally of the Light): Julian was a powerful and talented Thought Engineer. He was able to manipulate people's perception of reality. • **See also:** *Thought Engineer.*

Kairos Aurelius: Kairos was the first and most tempestuous of Aurelius's incarnations—a holdover from its days as a star. As its later title *Tempest* implies, the being was more passionate in its past—one of the strongest and most feared of the Immortals. It adopted the mononym Aurelius shortly after it transformed from a tree to an ambulatory being. Under this incarnation and name, Aurelius was a gentler presence— perhaps humbled by the events leading to the destruction of all life on its home planet. • **See also:** *Aurelius* and *The Sixth Star*.

Last Great War, The (a.k.a. The War That Ended All Others): After centuries of fighting, a devastating Earthly war took place, one that ended all others. Chief among its weapons were human-engineered Artificial Intelligence (AIs). Notable examples include: Alphas, Beta Synthetics and Sentients— the latter of which were the most dangerous, since they inhabited no body and could infiltrate any digital device, save implants. In an effort to survive, humans evolved into a more sentient species themselves, with an increased focus on Metaphysics. This effort led to the formation of the State OmniParty, which viewed itself as a sort of peaceful dictatorship. Peace, of course, was a subjective word. • **See also:** *Agents & Agencies, Alphas, Beta Synthetics,* and *Sentients.*

The **Last Guardian of The Portal**: A name for the mighty, sentient tree that guarded the entrance above Planet Aurelius. • **See also:** *Aurelius* and *The Sixth Star.*

The **Last Stand of Adŭro**: A historic battle at Mare Esurus (Sea of Hunger) during which The Machine Gods lost control of the moon. Though the exact details remained a mystery, this much was certain: The Shadows used an ancient weapon known as Brahmāstra —one that systematically destroyed all life on its surface and stripped the moon of both water and its atmosphere. After this battle, Adŭro transformed into Vōr, The Ghost Moon.

Ljushära (a.k.a. **The Light's Keep**): One of the two "Weeping Twins," this towering snow dune was the tallest point on Planet Aurelius. It was notable because it concealed an Adŭrian Vimana. • **For complete description, see:** *Tvilling Tårar.* • **See also:** *Vimana.*

The **Los Angeles Megacity** (LAMC): This coastal megacity reached from San Francisco to San Diego and contained the Historical City of Los Angeles (a.k.a. Olde Towne), as well as all the smaller towns in between.

The **Lotus Petal Nebula** (**a.k.a. Bisaj Bakool and The Last Unsullied World**): A colorful and gaseous constellation that resided in one of the great spiral arms of The Aamĕllÿne Galaxy. • **For full description, see:** *Bisaj Bakool.*

The **Luminous Ones:** Resplendent and numinous beings from The First World who maintained their light throughout the wars with The Shadows. Included in this pantheon were The Six Stars, The Seventh Star and all members of The Assembly of Stars. • **See also:** *The Assembly of Stars, The Seventh Star* and *The Six Stars.*

The **Loup and Monocle:** Two structures that made up Sanctuary—namely a subterranean maze and an above-ground forcefield. They were intentionally devised to allow entry, but not exit. • **For full description, see:** *Central Hospital for Citizen Wellbeing.*

M **-8s:** Powerful psychic investigators who mastered eight levels of psychic abilities. • **For full description, see:** *Agents & Agencies > M-Class Psychic > M-8.*

M-Status: A State-mandated identification program for all natural-born psychics. The number following the letter M described the magnitude of their ability. • **For full description, see:** *Agents & Agencies > M-Class Psychic > M-8.*

The **Machine Gods of Adŭro** (a.k.a. **The Benevolent Watchers, Benevolent Machines, The Kind Machines, or simply The Machine Gods**): These extinct beings played some role in the defense of Aurelius and its moons. In doing so, they lost their life and home world to The Shadows.

Memory Crystal • **See:** *Star Sapphire Memory Crystal*

Meta: A slang term for psychic, particularly an M-Class Psychic. • **See also:** *Agents & Agencies > M-Class Psychic.*

Metacrimes and Metacriminals: Knowingly concealing one's M-Status—or the M-Status of others—constituted a Metacrime. All metacriminals were immediately subject to "holding" and "treatment" at Central Hospital.

The **Moons of Aurelius** (**Lunarum Aurelii**): Planet Aurelius had four satellites. **They were:**

1. **The Lost Moon Imogen (a.k.a. The Rings of Imogen):** Though little was known of the moon, her vestige remained as a beautiful ring system encircling Planet Aurelius.

2. **"The Ice Moon" Ceruleus:** Tidally fixed and covered in striated glaciers, this moon was home of the sundered

Titan and Guardian, Ceruleus. • **For full description, see:** *Ceruleus.*

3. **"The Alabaster Moon" Virídia (a.k.a. The Woodland Moon):** The forest on this moon was placed under a spell known as The Gloaming and were cursed by a never-ending storm that obscured the sky. Home of The Colossus at Mount Augur, the remnant of The Guardian Arundhati. • **For full description, see:** *Virídia.*

4. **"The Ghost Moon" Vōr (a.k.a. The Shadow Moon):** Once a glittering city, the moon was destroyed by The Shadows and became home to their twisted city, The Necropolis. Esurus dwelled within the heart of the moon. • **For full description, see:** *Vōr.* • **See also:** *The Necropolis.*

The Mortal Channel (a.k.a. The Starchild): The Prophecy stated a powerful, psychically gifted "mortal channel" would one day discover The Seventh Star. This so-called "Starchild" was destined to reunite The Lost Star with the remaining Luminous Ones. • **See also:** *The Prophecy.*

Mount Augur (a.k.a. Caldera of Mount Augur, Witch's Peak and Augur's Peak): An extinct volcano and the highest point on Virídia. A holy shrine sat at its base and a powerful vortex emanated from its peak. Physical bodies could not enter the dangerous Caldera; only through meditation could one reach its peak and command an audience with The Seer.

The Mystic's Pyramid (a.k.a. Yantra's Pyramid): A massive structure on the SULACO Robotics campus, named after Yantra. • **For full description, see:** Yantra's Pyramid.

Necropolis, The (a.k.a. The Machine Necropolis, The City of the Dead, and Nil-Aedis): A mysterious structure erected by The Shadows and constructed from the remains of The Machine Gods. It exists on the desecrated Machine home world known as Vōr, The Ghost Moon. In the old tongue, The Necropolis was also known as Nil-Aedis, The Hollow Temple.

Defining features, in order of proximity to the Vimana:

- **The Sea of Hunger (a.k.a. Mare Esurus):** an impact crater in front of The Necropolis.
- **The Barbican:** Ruins of the old Adŭrian city gate.
- **The Bridge:** A delicate structure that perilously reached from Mare Esurus to Tamas-Mukha, providing the only passage in and out of The Necropolis.
- **The Watchtower:** A lookout manned by The Gatekeeper, an undead creature that psychically controlled two Colossus-sized, ibis-headed Sentinels, known as "The Dark Watch of The Necropolis."
- **Shadow Sentinels (a.k.a. The Sentinels and The Dark Watch of The Necropolis):** Two ancient guards who stood watch over The City of the Dead. Their size equaled that of a Titan or Colossus. They were denizens of the Dark Star, Treachery.
- **Tamas-Mukha (a.k.a. The Mouth of Darkness):** Tamas-Mukha was fashioned from the petrified remains of a wretched creature. The Mouth of Darkness housed not only the entrance to The Necropolis, but also The Watchtower, which sat atop a coiled staircase.
- **The Two Temples (The Temple of Hate and Temple of

Fear, respectively): Two claw-shaped spires guarded by ibis-headed Shadow Sentinels. From time to time, these two chambers were inhabited by their namesakes, The Shadows known as Hate and Fear.

- **The Ladder of Despair:** A spiral staircase that spins from The Watchtower to The Hall of Illusions. All those who descend lose hope.
- **The Hall of Illusions:** Esurus's lair. As with all of The Necropolis, this was fashioned out of the petrified remains of an unnamed beast.

Non-existence in mortals: A cataclysmic "breaking point" during which the nucleus of a soul could splinter irrevocably. The splintered soul energy eventually re-emerged as something entirely new—often combining with other splintered or recycled souls. This was not reincarnation, but a complete re-imagining of the energy, without the baggage or benefit of karmic memory or advancement. This mechanism only occurred in mortals. Immortal souls had the capacity to re-emerge as a new avatar. • **See also:** *Avatar*.

Obligation of Truth, The: For "the protection of the State," all Citizens charged with any type of crime—large or small—were immediately assumed guilty and had to comply with State investigations until proven innocent. The official speech that Agents issued during arrests or interrogations was:

"You are charged with [said crime or offense]. You do not have the right to stand trial. The burden of proof is on you and, as such, you have an obligation to speak when questioned. It will incontrovertibly harm your defense if you do not mention when questioned something that aids this investigation. You will be subject to further inquiries by an Agent upon booking. Anything you say, think or do will be given in evidence to the State. Do you understand your obligations and the charges as explained?"

Oculum (a.k.a. The Eye and Prime Investigator): As the sole ranking Agent on The Committee for Obedience, Prime Investigator Oculum was responsible for all Internal Affairs investigations. This Agent's function involved psychically "sweeping" and reporting on any (and all) suspicious activities at SCRI, The Division, The Bureau and Sanctuary. Few, if any, humans saw Oculum in the flesh, prompting rumors about its true origin and/or species. • **See also:** *Agents & Agencies* and *OMNI*.

The **Oculus Fenestra:** A compact dimension (a World Between Worlds) that fit in the palm of a human hand.

The **Old World**: A resplendent world, originally filled with only radiant beings. It was destroyed by The Seven Shadows. With the aid of The Seventh Star, this was reversed and The Seven Stars and

Seven Shadows seeded The New World with their combined essences.

Olde Towne (a.k.a. LA, L.A., Olde L.A., Olde Los Angeles, Historical Los Angeles and Historical L.A.): Simply put, the former boundaries of Los Angeles before it consumed the cities surrounding it.

OMNI Committee of Obedience (a.k.a. OMNI): Despite being called a committee, OMNI consisted of only one member—the mysterious and much-feared Prime Investigator Oculum, The Eye. Its function was technically Internal Affairs. But, more accurately, The Eye spied on all major State agencies and reported back to high-ranking, morally questionable officials within the State OmniParty. • **See also:** *Oculum.*

OmniParty: After The Great War, the State OmniParty (more commonly, "the State") emerged as the controlling entity for all the people on Planet Earth. The State oversaw the propaganda, the justice system, all political matters, medical care, education and every major function of civilized society. • **See also:** *the State.*

Oubliette: A SULACO-crafted firewall that afforded a Sentient the ability to walk and talk in the physical world. It also helped the State separate cooperative programs from Rogue AIs. **Note:** Oubliettes were used as a weapon to counter the otherwise uncontrollable Hive intelligence known as The Collective. • **See also:** *The Collective.*

P **EV (a.k.a. Peace Escort Vehicle):** These armored maglev vehicles provided unmanned transit for Peace Officers and criminals alike.

Plastic (a.k.a. Plastic Jobs): Derogatory term for Synthetics. • **See also:** *Synthetics.*

Praetorians: An elite squad of State Agents who were capable of telekinesis. They were feared by all intelligent life. • **For complete description, see:** *Agents & Agencies.*

PROJECT: REDSHIFT (a.k.a. DEEP RED): A rumored top-secret division of the State concerned with developing advanced robotics, androids, cybernetic life and sentient intelligence. It later expanded its focus to include time travel.

Propagators: State Agents tasked with reporting—and often fabricating—news and information for the masses. • **For complete description, see:** *Agents & Agencies.*

The **Prophecy of the Seventh Star (a.k.a. The Prophecy):** A prediction that The Seventh Star, Hope, was not lost, but rather waiting to re-emerge; one day, it would return with the assistance of a mortal channel known as "The Starchild" or "Prophesied One." Its reappearance would hearken the dawn of the first intergalactic war of The New World—*A Clash of Stars and Shadows.*

The **Prophesied One (a.k.a. The Starchild):** A mortal channel through which The Seventh Star (Hope) would find its way back to The New World.

Raptorcraft (a.k.a. **Raptors**): State-owned hovercraft used to secure dangerous crime scenes. Raptors ranged in size; the largest units were able to deploy smaller unmanned police probes and Drones. They derived their name from their silent, predatory nature and their bird-like appearance in the sky.

Ratha (a.k.a. **Transportation Rune**): An enchanted power symbol that, once inscribed, creates a portal which allows access to the Vimana.

The **Red Gate**: A façade to The Hope's Pass Way Station. It also stood as a memorial for the ÜMHC disaster. • **See also**: *Hope's Pass Way Station.*

Rigel, the Sky Guardian: One of two guardians of the ancient weapon Tidens Svärd. Little was known of Rigel's origin, except that it somehow shared a familial kinship with Akaal (Zerachiel). • **See also**: *Himlens Väktare* and *Aldebaran.*

Rogues: Any organic or inorganic life that rejected State rule—essentially a rebel.

The **R/S/T Quadrangle**: A structure that housed all robotic research and production for the SULACO company. • **See also**: *SULACO* and *The Altar of Creation.*

The **Ruins of Sedona**: After the Über-Massive Hadron Collider (ÜMHC) imploded, Sedona was cataclysmically reshaped and placed under State control. All visitors passed through a checkpoint known as The Red Gate, and were processed through The Hope's Pass Way Station. The two biggest points of interest on the mesa were The Dream Broker and The Fenestrae Stellarum. • **For expanded descriptions of each, see:** *The Red Gate, The Hope's Pass Way Station, The Dream Broker* and *The Fenestrae Stellarum.*

Sacred Heart of Ceruleus, The: The only living remnant of the mighty Titan, Ceruleus after The Shadows tore it asunder and froze the aqueous moon on which it lived. • For full description, see: *The Great Titan, Ceruleus* and *The Sundering of Ceruleus.*

San Angeleno Megacity (a.k.a. SAMC): The SAMC is a district within the larger Los Angeles Megacity. It consists of everything south of Long Beach. • See *Los Angeles Megacity.*

San Angeleno Peninsula: A fractured land mass that contains what remains of Long Beach, San Diego (and everything in between) after The Great Wars and earthquakes over the millennia leading to the year One Billion. The Peninsula is a district within the LAMC. • See: *Los Angeles Megacity.*

Scintillaarė: Once a beautiful yellow star, this white dwarf remnant met an untimely demise in The Aurelian Shadow Wars and became a fading white glimmer of its former self. The stellar remnant resided in the largest spiral arm of the ancient Aamĕllȳne Galaxy. Of all its planets, Aurelius was the most famous. It was also the only rocky planet to survive its red dwarf phase.

SCRI (a.k.a. State Center for Remote Investigations): The State intelligence agency responsible for intel gathering. Its revolutionary use of M-8s, Synthetics and Sentients rendered other intelligence agencies obsolete.

The Seal of The Six Stars: This sacred symbol consisted of two parts, a six-pointed star with a point inside, representing the Seventh Star. This glyph warded off Shadows and Shadow magic.

The Seas of Aurelius (a.k.a. Maria Aurelii): Each object in the Aurelian system, including the planet itself, contained a topographical feature called Mare (Sea). They included:

- **Sea of Lament (Mare Lāmentārī):** A frozen sea on Planet Aurelius, comprised completely of frozen tears.
- **The Sea of Dreams (Mare Somnus):** A glittering sea upon The Woodland Moon Virídia.
- **Sea of Clouds (Mare Cirrus):** A frozen plateau on the Moon Ceruleus. It was named after the wispy patterns in the ice, which appeared cloud-like from afar.
- **The Sea of Hunger (Mare Esurus):** An impact crater outside The Necropolis. This was also the site of The Last Stand of Adŭro—the battle where the Machines lost control of the moon and it became Vōr. Whatever occurred in this battle not only emptied the sea, but also destroyed the atmosphere, leaving Vōr a desolate satellite devoid of life.

The Seer's Eye: Another name for the third eye of Arundhati, The Stone Colossus. • **For full description, see:** *Ajna.*

Sentients: Bodiless, self-aware computer programs that interacted with humans through a device called an Oubliette.

The Seven Shadows (a.k.a. Shadows, Cosmic Devourers and Dark Stars): The binary pairs, or twin flames of The Seven Stars. These "corrupted" pairs brought about the destruction of The Old World and continued to wreak havoc and chaos in The New World. Three of the greatest merged to form The Void Beast Esurus.

The Seven Shadows included:

- **Hate:** The left head (and hand) of Esurus. Its Twin Star was Love.
- **Despair:** The heart and center-most head of Esurus, Despair was the strongest of the three shadows comprising the entity. Its Twin Star was Hope.
- **Fear (a.k.a. Rädsla, Whisperer of Lies; The Dark**

Liege; Hrókr; and *formerly* **Doubt and Deception**):
The right head (and hand) of Esurus. It was once Doubt, and later Deception before choosing Fear as its identity. It could sometimes take the form of a raven, but it usually worked as a shapeless puppet-master, manipulating (or even possessing) weaker beings to do its work. It was often associated with crows, ravens and other birds of prey. Its sigil was two armed ibises with interlocking scythes, which represented The Dark Watch of The Necropolis. Its Twin Star was Bravery.

- **Want (whose other aspects include Greed or Desire):** Its Twin Star was Charity.
- **Ignorance:** Its Twin Star was Enlightenment.
- **Treachery:** Its Twin Star was Justice.
- **Stagnancy:** Its Twin Star was Transformation.

The **Seven Stars (a.k.a. The Seven):** Of the original Fourteen, the ones aligned with Light, countering the energy in The Shadows. Their primary function in The New World was to find The Shadows and end the constant waves of destruction that they left in their wake. Few of The Seven Stars took human form. Gender-based pronouns were difficult (if not impossible) to apply to The Seven—they transcended human classifications, and had the ability to project themselves through the aid of multiple avatars. Most were revered as angels or gods.

The Seven Stars included:

- **The First Star:** Of The Seven, this entity was the least attached to any of its avatars, and as such, it was often referred to as "the shapeshifter." It often shifted in and out of focus and it had the ability to be in multiple dimensions at once. Its avatars included:

Transformation, Death; Akaal, the Undying; Archangel
Zerachiel; Destruction; Shiva; Osiris; Janus; various
unnamed human, half-human, half bird forms; a golden
phoenix; an iridescent blue bird and sometimes a
shooting star. The Shadow pair to Transformation was
Stagnancy.

- **The Second Star (a.k.a. Mercy, Justice, Retribution
  and The Triple Deity):** A telepathic, bodiless entity that
  identified itself primarily as Mercy, though at times it
  was Justice and Retribution. Like Metatron and Iophiel,
  this being did not present itself in humanoid form and
  rarely used spoken language. The Second Star usually
  transferred its thoughts in entire ideas or visions to other
  sentient beings. The Shadow pair to this triple deity was
  Treachery.
- **The Third Star (a.k.a. Charity, Uriel and Apollo):**
  Uri, also known as Uriel, was the most "human" of all
  the stars, and usually appeared almost exclusively in
  humanoid form; it often expressed itself as male. Its
  most distinguishing features were elaborate winged
  tattoos that were enchanted and infused with power. Its
  true name was Charity and its Shadow pair was Want. It
  was the only star that had a twin sibling (Elsa), though
  she was born after The Fourteen and created by The
  Third Star itself. Therefore, Elsa was classified as an
  Ancient.
- **The Fourth Star: (a.k.a. Metatron, Mattara, Måtta,
  The Scribe and The Cube):** The Fourth Star, Metatron,
  was a completely thought-based construct. It often
  expressed itself through geometric solids, cubes and
  through numbers. It once created a brilliant extension of
  itself in the form of inorganic life on the moon Adŭro. It
  alone was the heart and mind behind The Machine Gods

and it was revered by all inorganic life. As the only Star capable of holding the *Corpus Tenebrae* without becoming corrupted, it demonstrated profound Temperance and Bravery, revealing its dual aspects. Its Shadow pair was Fear.

- **The Fifth Star: (a.k.a. The Many-Eyed One, The Wheel, The Wheel of Galgallin, The Throne, The Golden Spiral and The Golden Stairwell):** The trans-dimensional Iophiel, which often presented itself as a wheel of pure light, was the most clairvoyant of all the stars. Its vision was trumped only by Time (Akasha). The Fifth Star presents itself as a fiery wheel, a spiral staircase, an orb of eyes or a dimension of endless windows. Its true name was Enlightenment and its Shadow equivalent was Ignorance. It was often referred to as the Trinity of Iophiel, referring to The Golden Spiral (a galactic-shaped bridge encasing the star), The Throne (a dimension in which it resides) and The Wheel (a physical aspect). Though neither male nor female, it was referred to as "sister" due to its maternal energy. It exuded a healing energy to all those in its auric field.

- **The Sixth Star: (a.k.a. Aurelius, the Golden One, Tempest, Kairos and The Storm-Bringer):** Although it was the youngest of The Six Stars, it was wiser than its years and the most paternal/maternal of the stars. It existed as many forms through the ages, including a star, a tree and a thunderbird. Its true name was Love and its Shadow pair was Hate.

The Sixth Star's Titles (Chronologically):
—Kāmadeva (Love)
—The Sixth Star
—Ore, The Golden One

—Kairos, First Tree of Aurelius (a.k.a. Kairos
   Aurelius)
—Tempest, Storm-Bringer (a.k.a. Tempest Aurelius
   or simply Tempest)
—Aurelius, Guardian of the Three Moons
—Aurelius (no titles)

* **The Seventh Star (a.k.a. The Lost Star, Hope):** Its
essence evanesced when The New World began and it
was lost to stars and men. A prophecy stated that it was
waiting to be reborn and would emerge again as one of
The Children of the Stars. The Prophecy claimed its
arrival would coincide with the banishment of Esurus.
Its name remained largely unspoken by The Six, though
Aurelius later revealed that it was once called Hope and
it would, one day, return as Harmony.

The **Shadow Moon:** Another name for The Ghost Moon. • **For
complete description, see:** *Vōr, The Ghost Moon.* • **See also:**
*Adŭro, Last Stand of Adŭro, The Moons of Aurelius > Mare Esurus
(The Sea of Hunger).*

The **Sigil of The Seven Stars:** The sacred emblem of The Six
Stars was a six-pointed star with a central point, symbolizing their
missing sibling, The Seventh Star. The center point also symbolized
every living being's ability to channel the light of The Luminous
Ones.

The **Six Eyes of Esurus:** Although it once took the form of a
hydra, during the time of The Last Steward, Esurus often appeared
simply as six all-seeing eyes. The eyes belonged to The Three That
Became One; they included Hate, Despair and Fear. • **For complete
description, see:** *Esurus.*

The **Six Stars (a.k.a. The Six):** In The Old World, when The
Seventh Star defeated The Void Beast, its essence disappeared and

The Prophecy was born. The Luminous Ones were henceforth known as The Six Stars—together they searched time and space for The Seventh Star, Hope, aspiring once again to bring balance to the Universe. • **For complete description, see:** *The Seven Stars* • **See also:** *The Prophesied One* and *The Prophecy.*

Skyway: Premium airspace on Earth set aside for hover travel only. Usage of this space required a premium authentication (and an autopiloted hovervehicle), but it guaranteed speedy and safe travel. • **See also:** *Hovervehicles.*

The **Snow Dunes of Aurelius:** Like the Sea of Lament, the snow dunes were comprised of the tears of their namesake, The Sixth Star, Aurelius. • **See also:** *Sea of Lament* and *Planet Aurelius.*

The **Stacks:** A secret dimension where Gabriel stored books and other artifacts. It was contained (literally stacked) between the atoms of the door to his wardrobe in Elijah's old cabin.

Star Chariot (a.k.a. Vimana): A psychically navigated vehicle. • **For full description, see:** *Vimana.*

Star Sapphire Memory Crystal: These polished gemstones were capable of storing data, memories and other metaphysical energy. They were primarily used by M-8 psychics in SCRI.

The **Starchild:** a mortal channel through which The Seventh Star (Hope) would find its way back to The New World. • **See also:** *The Prophecy.*

The **State (a.k.a. the State OmniParty):** An omnipresent—and some would argue *omniscient*—governing body for Earth. With the help of its M-Class agents, it saw and knew all there was to know. Through its more frightening Mercenary and Praetorian Agents, it removed all obstacles in its path. **Punctuation note:** By decree of The Bureau, "the" was intentionally set in lower-case whenever the article appeared before the word "State," unless it began a sentence, or appeared after a period in a sentence. This was a somewhat futile effort to make the State appear less imposing and controlling than it truly was. • **See also:** *Agents & Agencies* and *Omniparty.*

State Tongues and Dialects: The Bureau of Propaganda oversaw four official dialects on Earth. These included:

- **State Common Tongue (a.k.a. Common Tongue or State Common, SCT and SC):** Per State law, Common Tongue was the mandatory standardized language for all citizens on Earth. The State engineered it to be compressed and simple, to help eliminate rebellious thoughts, while also maximizing productivity across the planet.
- **State Protocol (a.k.a. Protocol and SP)** was the antithesis of SC; this language was filled with superfluous, complicated and abstruse words. Only elite State Agents or select members of The State Intelligentsia were afforded an opportunity to master it.
- **State Cleric (a.k.a. Cleric and CT)** was an efficient and scientific tongue predominately used by the State Intelligentsia Officials (SIO), including but not limited to doctors, mathematicians, scientists and all State Agents.
- **Jargon** was an ultra-compressed language that closely resembled binary machine code. It used as many Tetragram acronyms as possible. The nefarious goal was to suppress free thought. • **See also:** *Jargon.*

The **Stewards of the Light:** A sworn guardian of *Corpus Sidera.* Each Steward willingly and knowingly imparted his, her or its essence and wisdom within the tome. As such, all Stewards remained connected to the wisdom, light and strength of their successors. Elijah was the Seven-Thousand-and-Tenth Steward to hold the title since The New World came into existence. Through the ancient Ritual of Stewardship, he passed guardianship on to his grandson, Gabriel. **Note:** Not all stewards were human. The First

Steward (and the original author of *Corpus Sidera*) was an Eternal known as Astralis, the Light-Bringer. The only other Stewards called out by rank or name were Elijah, The Second-to-Last Steward, and Gabriel, The Last Steward of the Light.

SULACO (a.k.a. SULACO Robotics/Software/Technology, SULACO Robotics, SULACO R/S/T and SULACO): A State owned-and-operated supplier of all androids on Earth. Its jargon acronym stands for **S**tate **U**nderwritten **La**boratory for **C**ybernetic **O**perations. The company's prize models included Alpha- and Beta-class Synthetic androids and the Oubliette System for interfacing with Sentients.

Originally, the company devised several Marine and Aeronautic Drones for military purposes, and later became a leader in AI technologies, too. Though land Drones and Synthetics constituted their main focus, they manufactured robots and androids of all sizes and functions, some of which were classified and unknown to even M-8 and Bureau Agents.

SULACO Robotics was managed by a top-secret State agency that operated under various code names including REDSHIFT and DEEP RED. The aforementioned projects were the handiwork of Chief Engineer Yantra, an influential and controversial engineer. Though few met him while he was alive, almost all scientists knew of his work. He extended his own life through the use of cybernetics, and lived to the age of three hundred. Upon his death, his consciousness was passed into code, creating a Sentient.

The headquarters for SULACO closely matched (some claim replicated) portions of the Mesoamerican pyramid of Uxmal, for reasons unknown or unstated to the public.

The **Sundering of Ceruleus:** (a.k.a. **The Sundering**): A historic battle on the Cerulean Moon during which the chief guardian was torn to pieces and buried amidst the glaciers. • **See also:** *Ceruleus.*

Śūnyatā • **See:** *The Void*

Synthetics (a.k.a. **Beta Synthetics**): A second-generation SULACO Robotics-crafted android capable of complex thoughts and simple human emotions. Though other models were purported to be in development, the term "Synthetic" only applied to the Aphelion 600 and Genesis 700 Series. • **See also:** *Aphelion 600s and Genesis 700 Series.*

Taiga of Arundhati, The: An enormous continent on Virídia, The Woodland Moon. The topography of the taiga was noted for its sentient and bioluminescent forests, beautiful geothermic formations, enormous mountain ranges and pristine beaches.

Tempest, Storm Bringer: One of Aurelius's many titles. • **For full description, see:** *The Sixth Star*. • **See also:** *Aurelius*.

Tenebris, the Creator: The embodiment of darkness, space and possibilities. A complement to Astralis, the Light-Bringer. • **For full definition, see:** *Eternals*.

Thought Engineer: Gabriel's lifelong friend, Julian, was the most famously documented Thought Engineer. Others existed, but their propensity to elude authorities and simply disappear into thin air kept them proverbially off-the-radar. Julian was able to weave a cognitive web between several organic brains, projecting his reality onto the minds of those ensnared. Julian originally opened F.A.T.E. to further his studies and help the next generation of psychically gifted children and young adults to hone their gifts. • **See also:** *F.A.T.E.*

The **Thousand-Year Night:** A dark period of war on Planet Aurelius. The war began when The Shadows corrupted Scintillaaré. The dying star subsequently destroyed The Lost Moon, Imogen, which hurled enormous debris towards the planet's surface. This destroyed the golden forests on Planet Aurelius. The darkness persisted for at least a millennium, during which time The Shadows wrought havoc on the surface.

The **Three Guardians of Aurelius:** Ancient beings tasked with guarding the dying Planet Aurelius and its three remaining moons. • See also: *Aurelius, Arundhati* and *Ceruleus*.

The **Three That Became One:** This name referred to the three strongest Shadows during the time of The Last Steward. The Three Shadows included: Hate, Despair and Fear. • **See also:** *Esurus.*

Throne: The dimension inhabited by Iophiel. • **See also:** *The Fifth Star,* and *Iophiel.*

Tidens Svärd (a.k.a. The Sword of Time): Tidens Svärd was forged by Akasha and wielded in an ancient cosmic battle. Its properties were deadly enough that it was placed in the safekeeping of two Sky Guardians, Rigel and Aldebaran. • **See also:** *Himlens Väktare.*

Titan: A serpentine Elemental species. They were among the largest lifeforms to walk, swim or fly across The New World and were as old as (if not older than) dragons. According to legend, the progenitor was none other than The Great Titan, Ceruleus. • **See also:** *Ceruleus*

Transformation (a.k.a. Death, Akaal, Zerachiel, Janus, The First Star and The One that Stands at the Nexus of Ends and Beginnings): Transformation was the true function and preferred moniker for The First Star. Its true name was Akaal, a word that, when uttered, was quite powerful. It was therefore invoked primarily by celestial beings (namely The Luminous Ones, Ancients and Eternals). See *The First Star* for a complete history and description. • **For full description, see:** *The First Star.* See also: *Akaal, Death, Transformation* and *Zerachiel.*

Tvilling Tårar (a.k.a. The Weeping Twins and The Two Teardrops): These two dunes reached as high as mountains on Planet Aurelius.

- **Dödshära,** The Dead's Keep, was the smaller of the two. Forged by The First Star itself, this mighty ossuary was a frozen catacomb for the fallen warriors of The Thousand-Year Night.

- **Ljushära,** The Light's Keep, was the tallest peak. It served as a hiding place for an ancient artifact left by The Machine Gods when Adŭro fell into The Shadows.

The **Twilight of the Trees** • **See:** *The Gloaming.*

—V—

V-Terminal (a.k.a. Vox-Terminal and Voice-Operated-Terminal): As the predecessor to the H-V, V-Terminals were two-way voice-operated telecomm devices. The most common variants included security panels and small wireless boxes. • **See also:** *H-V.*

Vimana (a.k.a. The Star Chariot): A sentient, acquiescent and psychically navigated craft left behind by the benevolent and mysterious Machine Gods. Its most common shape was that of a multi-point star.

Virídia (a.k.a. The Alabaster Moon, The Sleeping Moon and The Woodland Moon): Virídia was home to The Sleeping Forests and was guarded by The Great Colossus Arundhati, a seer and sorceress of unparalleled power. It was named after the lush, luminescent forests that slumbered indefinitely under an enchantment spell known as The Gloaming. • **See also:** *Arundhati* and *The Moons of Aurelius > Virídia* and *The Gloaming.*

The Void (a.k.a. Śūnyatā and Complete Zero): The opposite of somethingness; it was the nothingness that remained when everything faded away. No living thing could exist in The Void for long. Even immortals faced certain peril traveling along its boundaries. The only beings who could temporarily resist its effects were: Eternals, Esurus and multidimensional beings like Death. It was not to be confused with the creative energy of the Eternal being named Tenebris, as it worked with potential energy, whereas The Void prohibited any and all possibilities.

Vōr, The Ghost Moon (a.k.a. The Shadow Moon, or Adŭro before its desecration): Formerly a glittering mechanized megopolis known as Adŭro, the Guardians rechristened the moon "Vōr" after its desecration by The Shadows. It was more commonly known as The Ghost Moon or Shadow Moon; this was an effort to avert invoking the dark word "Vōr," as it subsequently grabbed the attention of The Shadows, chiefly Esurus, with whom the moon shares a symbiotic relationship. • **See also:** *The Moons of Aurelius* and *Adŭro*.

Vortex Mining: The licensed or unlicensed act of harnessing the raw energy from an exposed vortex for the use of energy alchemy. This included, but was not limited to: healing, clairvoyance and, more nefariously, the various services offered by Dream Brokers (e.g., selling dreams, nightmares and passage into others' dreams).

Wall of Nightmares, The: An area within The Dream Broker's dreamspace that contained keys to the most heinous and frightening dreams ever imagined.

The **Wheels of Galgallin:** Four all-seeing celestial beings that stood as guardians to Earth, Water, Wind and Fire, as well as the Four Dimensions of Spacetime. Of them, only the fiery Iophiel survived. • **See also:** *Iophiel* and *The Fifth Star.*

Yantra (a.k.a. **Chief Engineer Yantra and The Father of Synthetics**): This Chief Engineer at SULACO Robotics was credited as the father of all Synthetic life on Earth. • For complete description, see: *Chief Engineer Yantra*.

Yantra's Pyramid (a.k.a. **The Mystic's Pyramid**): The Common Tongue name for SULACO headquarters, which was adjacent to the R/S/T Quadrangle. The quartz pyramid loomed above the city of Los Angeles, and contained magical qualities unknown to the public. • **See also:** *Chief Engineer Yantra, The Altar of Creation* and *SULACO*.

Youth Conservatory (a.k.a. **The Conservatory**): A halfway house for underage metacriminals. At age fourteen, these young metacriminals were put before a State judge in a confessional to face sentencing.

Zerachiel (a.k.a. The First Star, Akaal, Death, Transformation, Janus, The One that Stands at the Nexus of Ends and Beginnings): Zerachiel was a shapeshifting, humanoid aspect of The First Star—one of the Firstborn. • **For full description, see:** *The First Star.* • **See also:** *Akaal, Firstborn, The Seven Stars* and *Transformation.*

PART VII

APPENDIX B: THE ALCHEMIC AAMĔLLẎNE TONGUE: VOWEL SOUNDS AND PRONUNCIATION

THE ALCHEMIC AAMĔLLẎNE TONGUE:
VOWEL SOUNDS AND PRONUNCIATION

This is a partial guide to pronouncing unique vowel sounds in the transliterated Alchemic Aamĕllẏne alphabet. In this language, words (quite literally) were power. Each spoken phoneme could result in either beautiful or cataclysmic transformations, as evidenced by The Sixth Star, Aurelius.

In addition to A, E, I, O and U in Common Tongue, nine other vowel sounds exist in the Alchemic Aamĕllẏne Tongue, including Æ, Aa, Ë, Ė, Ē, Í, Ia, Io, and Ō. See below for examples and proper pronunciation. Unless otherwise noted, consonants were identical to those found in Earth's Common Tongue.

Vowel	Stress	Notes on Pronunciation	Examples in the Alchemic Aamĕllÿne Tongue	Examples in Common Tongue
ǽ	Always stressed	The sound "eh." The E is short but stressed.	Aa-tǽl (AH-TELL, equally stressed)	fair, aware, hair, err
aa	Always stressed	Short A sound, extended as in "awe"	Aamĕllÿne, Scintillaaré, Aa-tǽl	awning, awe, drawn, ah-ha
ĕ	Always unstressed	The sound "uh" or the schwa (ə) sound	Aamĕllÿne	understand, fun
é	Stressed if first (or only vowel), otherwise unstressed as in Scintillaaré	Long A	Scintillaaré	fray, pay, sleigh
ē	Always stressed	Long E	Ÿnē (EYE-NEE), equal stressing)	bee
í	Always stressed	Short I	Virídia	fit, spit
ia	Stressed if first or only vowel. Unstressed when following other vowels.	The I takes a "Y" sound, followed by a short A. (YA)		yacht, the name
io	Stressed if first or only vowel; unstressed when following other vowels.	The I takes either a J or Y followed by a long A. (JO or YO)	Iophiel (YO-fee-ehl or JO-fee-ehl)	Joseph, joke, yes
ō	Stressed	Long, extended O. Modifies some consonants, such as R or T. The consonant R is rolled when preceded by the stressed ō. When a T follows, it takes on the sound "th" as in the English moth.	Vōr	door
ŭ	Stressed	ew or ewyr	Adŭro	dew, too, you
ÿ	Stressed, unless it appears at the end of a word, in which case it's unstressed.	Long I	Aamĕllÿne	find, mind, eye

PRONUNCIATION GUIDE FOR SELECT PROPER NAMES

- Aa-tǽl: AH-TELL
- Aamĕllẏne: AH-muh-line
- Adŭro: ah-DEWYR-oh
- Akasha: əh-KAH-sha
- Arundhati: err-un-DAH-thee
- Aurelius: oh-RAY-lee-us
- Ceruleus: suh-ROOL-ee-us
- Gråvarg: grow-VAHR-ee
- Kairos: KEH-russ
- Scintillaarė: sin-ti-LAR-ay
- Virídia: Veer-RID-ee-yah

PART VIII

APPENDIX C: BUREAU GUIDELINES FOR LANGUAGE COMPRESSION

BUREAU GUIDELINES FOR LANGUAGE COMPRESSION

The Bureau of Propaganda prided itself on being a "beacon of efficiency, clarity and compression." The State Common Tongue constituted its shining achievement. However, dates proved problematic. In an effort to deal with increasingly long dates in the centuries leading to the Earth Year One Billion, the State standardized date and time. As with all syntax and language compression, The Bureau developed and enforced these revisions.

It took inspiration from scientific notation and adapted it to a more speakable form. The use of Double and Treble would be used, whenever possible, to eliminate repetitive leading digits.

Dashing: Dashes connected digits that were doubled or trebled. Remaining digits were also dashed, but separated by commas and said as individual numbers. E.g., 321 would be three-two-one, not three hundred twenty-one. (**See:** Compression.)

Stacking: If needed, doubles and trebles could be stacked (e.g., Double-Double and Treble-Treble-Treble). The Bureau attempted using other n-tuple groupings like Quad, Quin, Sex, etc., but they proved tedious. Having only two stacking terms required less thought, and this enhanced efficiency. When used in conjunction with Earth Year, the Treble or Double was capitalized, as were subsequent numbers.

Compression: Words like hundred and thousand were compressed (read: omitted) whenever possible in Common Tongue, as they were deemed superfluous.

Jargon Compression: In Jargon, the numbers were compressed even further. The Double and Treble system proved very easy to convert: D9 for Double-Nine, T9 for Treble-Nine and so on.

Examples of Dates and Their Subsequent Compression:

- **New Year's Eve 999,999,999:** Instead of having to say *nine hundred ninety-nine million, nine hundred ninety-nine thousand, nine hundred ninety-nine*; State Common Tongue reduced it to Treble-Treble-Treble-Nine. (Jargon: TTT9)
- **Gabriel's year of birth, 999,999,978** reduced to Treble-Treble-Nine, Nine-Seven-Eight. (Jargon: TT9978)
- **Gabriel's 14th birthday, in the year 999,999,993** reduced to Treble-Treble-Nine, Double-Nine, Three. (Jargon: TT9D93)
- **The "1B" Shift: Effective on Earth Year One Billion, all numbers would move towards Jargon notation.**
- **Examples:**
- **1,000,000,000 = 1B**
- **1,000,000,001 = 1B1**
- **1,000,000,114 = 1BD14**

Time: The 24-hour time system, a.k.a. Military Time—later known as State Time Reckoning (STR)—constituted the only State-sanctioned method to record and speak time. It was clear, compressed, and, although it included the word "hundred," it eliminated the otherwise confusing AM/PM notations.

ACKNOWLEDGMENTS

I'd like to express heartfelt gratitude to the ever-present hand of Spirit—especially my guides, the archangels, and the ascended masters. Thanks for inspiring me, pushing me, and showing me the way. You've helped me to become a clear channel.

To my closest friends and family, you're my real-life Assembly of Stars and I love you.

Lee Ann, thanks for being a steadfast friend, mentor and cheerleader. As a beta reader, your insights and constructive criticism proved invaluable to the success of the novel! As a friend, you gave me courage to release this to the world. Thanks for your love and support.

Christy, thanks for your honest feedback as a beta reader and, more importantly, for being an amazing friend throughout this process.

Martina, tack så mycket! Thanks for double-checking my Swedish.

Dena, thanks for our chats about spirituality and for confirming that my Golem and Hebrew sections were accurate.

Melissa, thanks for your patience and legal expertise.

John and Art, thanks for the constructive feedback during my early drafts.

M.K., thanks for the life raft at the eleventh hour!

Au'Rana, Patrick, Peter and Séamus, thanks for showing me the possibilities.

Thanks to IngramSpark, Amazon, Apple, Barnes & Noble, Google and Kobo for giving indie authors new ways to distribute their work.

Mom, thanks for the wishes in the fountain, and for being my number one champion every step of the way.

Apollo, thanks for your unconditional love.

To my YouTube followers, thanks for taking this journey with me.

To those who said "no" to my idea, thanks for convincing me that I needed to do this on my own.

To anybody out there who doesn't fit in, for whatever reason, know that you are valued and loved. Like Gabriel, find your inner Light and let it shine brightly. In the realm of Spirit, there is only energy, and all the Earthly labels quickly fade. One day we will rediscover that truth.

Finally, and most importantly, to you, the reader—I leave you with three tenets:

Magic is simply a new truth waiting to be discovered.
Hope is never truly lost.
Practicality is entirely overrated.

ABOUT THE AUTHOR

Nicholas Ashbaugh is a popular YouTuber and a psychic intuitive with a worldwide audience. Throughout all facets of his work, he aims to raise the collective consciousness and start intelligent conversations about spirituality.

Nicholas spent a decade-and-a-half working for several Hollywood studios. That technical acumen, plus a love for all things Sci-Fi, helped color the dystopian and post-apocalyptic landscape of *The Luminous Ones.*

In 2009, Nicholas underwent a spiritual and psychic awakening that inspired him to start writing this novel. Due to a restricted writing schedule—comprised of nights and weekends only—it would take five years before he finished the first draft.

He quit his corporate job in 2015. Free from a nine-to-five job, Nicholas set his sights on growing his YouTube channel. He launched a successful coaching business and continued to edit his manuscript in his free time.

In 2020, he founded his own publishing company and decided to distribute the novel himself.

He presently lives in Southern California with his dog Apollo.

Scan QR code for author website, or visit NicholasAshbaugh.com

Follow Nicholas on major social media platforms @NicholasAshbaugh

- amazon.com/author/nicholasashbaugh
- goodreads.com/NicholasAshbaugh
- youtube.com/NicholasAshbaugh
- instagram.com/NicholasAshbaugh
- facebook.com/NicholasAshbaugh
- twitter.com/NAshbaugh
- patreon.com/NicholasAshbaugh
- pinterest.com/NicholasAshbaugh
- linkedin.com/in/NicholasAshbaugh

CPSIA information can be obtained
at www.ICGtesting.com
Printed in the USA
LVHW091546150621
690284LV00001B/5